T0162486

SPANISH SURRENDER

RACHEL SPANGLER

SPANISH SURRENDER
© 2019 BY RACHEL SPANGLER

THIS TRADE PAPERBACK ORIGINAL IS PUBLISHED BY
BRISK PRESS, WAPPINGERS FALLS, NY, 12590

SUBSTANTIVE EDIT BY: LYNDA SANDOVAL
COPY EDIT BY: JONATHAN CROWLEY
COVER DESIGN BY: TREEHOUSE STUDIO
AUTHOR PHOTO BY: WILLIAM BANKS
BOOK LAYOUT AND TYPESETTING BY: KELLY SMITH

FIRST PRINTING: JUNE 2019

THIS IS A WORK OF FICTION. NAMES, CHARACTERS, PLACES, AND IN-
CIDENTS ARE THE PRODUCT OF THE AUTHOR'S IMAGINATION OR ARE
USED FICTITIOUSLY. ANY RESEMBLANCE TO ACTUAL PERSONS, LIVING
OR DEAD, BUSINESS ESTABLISHMENTS, EVENTS, OR LOCALES IS EN-
TIRELY COINCIDENTAL.

THIS BOOK, OR PARTS THEREOF, MAY NOT BE REPRODUCED IN ANY
FORM WITHOUT PERMISSION FROM THE AUTHOR OR THE PUBLISHER.

ISBN-13: 978-0-9987907-9-4

This one is for DREAMers

And, for Susie,
because while the first trip to Spain
was for me,
this one was all your fault.

Author's Note on Use of Italics

My previous romance novel, *Full English*, was born out of my time spent living in England and the love affair I had with that country during my time there. It might be easy to claim a similar impetus for this project, as during our time abroad, we spent just over a month in Spain. Alas, that would be too simplistic a story behind a very complex motivation. I will not go into all of my reasons here and will largely let this story speak for itself, other than to make this note on a very deliberate stylistic choice I made in the novel that follows.

It is traditional in English-language publications to italicize foreign words and phrases. I haven't done enough research into why or how this practice originated, but I do know it denotes a clear line of "difference" some readers likely find helpful. However, English has always been a language that builds on and borrows from others, and that is truer in our increasingly global society than it has been in any recent epoch. As I wrote *Spanish Surrender*, featuring an American traveling in Spain accompanied by someone with a much more complex background, I had to ask myself questions about what constitutes "foreign." For instance, words like "taco" or "salsa" have Spanish origins but are common enough not to require italicization. What about words like "fiesta" or "siesta" or "tapas?" Every middle-class, middle-aged American I spoke to understood their meaning without explanation, and yet no one felt they were exactly English words. It was generally agreed that italicization wouldn't be wrong, though neither would it be necessary for comprehension. In the end, it came down to style, and when in doubt I chose not to italicize.

I ran into a similar issue with names. We don't, in general, italicize foreign sounding names of people. In a purported melting pot culture like America, how could we even begin to decide whose names are foreign enough to warrant such a mark of difference? And yet in some cases we do just that with the names of places. Not places like Barcelona or Madrid, but what about Larios or La Alhambra? Perhaps my choice not to italicize these was more political, a refusal to see the places I love as somehow existing separately or as wildly divergent than places like Broadway or the Ozarks are to me or in relation to each other. More than that, names are names. Your name is the same wherever you go. My name is the same no matter what country I happen to live in. I do not become Raquel when I cross the border. I am a firm believer in the power of chosen names, and I am a steadfast believer that names themselves have power. I would never dare to tell someone what their name should be, and I worry that to do so with places would be equally insensitive. The Alhambra has been the Alhambra for centuries. There is no translation that captures its essence, and I refuse to suggest it might have some English translation I should alert you to in italics.

I understand there are times these choices might be disconcerting for some readers. I hope that if you are one of them, you will humor me, and perhaps even see those moments as a chance to add a little bit of international flare to your vocabulary.

Chapter 1

Simone sighed dramatically and tapped the tips of her high heeled shoes against the terra-cotta tile of the hotel lobby floor. The lone woman working the registration counter had been on the phone for six minutes and forty-three seconds. Simone checked her watch again, mentally preparing her strongly worded complaint to this woman's supervisor. The clerk turned to Simone, giving her a little smile and shrug before laughing at something the person on the phone said and turning away once more. Simone's jaw tightened, but she didn't blow her top. Her temper simmered, slow and exacting, liquid nitrogen in place of fire.

"*Perdoname, señora,*" someone said behind her, but Simone didn't turn around until the person added in unexpected English, "Excuse me, ma'am."

"Yes?" Simone spun on her three-inch spike of a heel, hoping for a manager, but the sight of a short, unassuming woman caught her off guard. She couldn't be more than mid-twenties, with a broad, easy smile that didn't seem consistent with management material.

The woman scanned her up and down before giving her a knowing smile. "I'm sorry, *señorita.*"

Simone was vaguely aware that the title made some sort of comment on her age, or her marital status, but she got enough of those speculations in English that she wasn't going to indulge them in Spanish, too. "Can I help you?"

"May I buy you a cup of tea?"

Simone was exhausted from her red-eye flight from Milan, but she examined the woman more closely. Her chestnut hair wisped deliberately across her forehead, and her bright blue polo shirt that read 'Corazones Española Tours' made her cornflower eyes stand out against her golden tan. Even without having slept in twenty-four hours, Simone recognized a tempting little dish when she saw one. Had she been on the vacation she was supposed to be on, she would've accepted. However, the vacation had turned business trip, and she hadn't gotten where she had by mixing business with pleasure.

"Thank you, but I need to get checked in, and if that doesn't happen in"—she glanced at her watch again—"the next thirty seconds, heads will roll."

"Spain has seen a few beheadings over the years," the woman said, not seeming the least bit intimidated, "but it seems a shame to get blood on those fancy shoes."

Simone arched an eyebrow but didn't budge.

"Fine," the woman said with a grin, "would you like some company while you wait?"

"I really don't think that's—"

"I'm Ren, by the way." She extended her hand.

Simone accepted with a quick firm shake, her frustration slipping despite her effort to maintain it. "Ren, you are persistent."

"You really have no idea, *Americana*."

"Simone. I'd love to chat, but I don't have the time."

"I doubt that."

"Which part?"

"Both," Ren said, her grin disarming despite the comment. "But we can focus on the latter, because I've been in this hotel every two weeks for the last two years, and I can tell you with authority, no one's getting into any of the rooms until at least noon."

"We'll see about that," Simone said, causing Ren to laugh softly.

She didn't appreciate the humor. Drawing herself up to her

full height and folding her arms across her chest, she fixed Ren with a steely glare, but the smaller woman continued conversationally.

"The clerk doesn't speak English, and I take it you don't speak Spanish?"

"I speak with a Visa platinum card."

"Ah, so this your first time in this part of Spain?"

"I'm an experienced traveler."

"Good. So, tell me this, experienced traveler, what do you notice about that sign?" Ren pointed to a white sheet of paper in a wooden frame that said, "Wait your turn."

"It's shoddily made."

Ren laughed outright this time. "What about the fact that you can read it?"

Simone read the sign again, then contrasted it quickly with the other signs in the hotel lobby. This was the only one in English, and it was written only in English, with no Spanish counterpart.

"You, Ms. Impatient *Americana*, are that sign's audience," Ren said, "and you're not the first of your kind to be in this predicament, so you have two choices: continue to stand here fuming, only to be summarily told there's no room available yet, or have a nice, soothing cup of tea with me while my wife finishes up in our room. Then I'll ask the clerk, in Spanish, to give it to you."

Impatient American? Simone's anger at Ren's presumptuousness warred with her practical side, which recognized a useful partnership when she saw one. She glanced once more at the clerk, who was still chatting happily on the phone with little sign of wrapping up, and decided that, despite the well-timed mention of a wife, Ren was clearly the more enticing option for getting what she wanted right now.

Loreto opened one eye enough to see that the clock read nine. She mentally reviewed her schedule. It was a free day for her current tour group, so she didn't have any responsibility to the students until dinnertime. She should be entitled to sleep off whatever it was she did last night, so why was her boss yelling at her from the other side of her hotel room door?

"Loreto, open the door, *por favor.*"

Lina didn't sound like she was here for a fun chat, and Loreto tried a little harder to remember the fuzzy parts of the previous night as an arm snaked over her shoulder and slid down her chest. The details came back to her. She rolled onto her back, allowing herself to look at the owner of the hand, who was now drawing circles around her nipple. *La Señora* Markus. Loreto smiled. She always loved finding out one of those deliciously studious teacher types by day turned into a hellcat by night.

La Señora bit Loreto hard on the shoulder and sucked her skin. Apparently, she could be a hellcat during the day, too.

"Loreto, if you don't open this door right now, I'm going to get the housekeeper to open it for me," Lina called, her voice holding both annoyance and amusement.

"*Mierda.*" Loreto groaned and disengaged herself from *La Señora* Markus's lovely mouth. "I'm coming."

"That's what I was afraid of," Lina said dryly, and Loreto laughed. She loved her boss's dry sense of humor, and if she was wielding it so early in the morning, odds were good Loreto wasn't in that much trouble.

She pulled on a pair of boxer shorts but left her chest bare and opened the door. Lina stood in the hall with three of the girls from their current tour group. "*Buenos dias, chicas.*"

All three students immediately turned bright shades of red and averted their eyes, while Lina took the chance to give Loreto a warning glare, then shook her head.

"Loreto, the ladies are worried because they can't find their teacher. She usually meets them for breakfast and then spends some time on the phone with her husband back in London, but she wasn't in the restaurant, and her husband has been calling for her."

"Her husband, you say?" Loreto rubbed the bite marks on her shoulder.

"She went out with you last night," one of the girls cut in. "Do you know where she is?"

Lina shook her head almost imperceptibly, and the little lie rolled naturally off Loreto's tongue. "After dinner I suggested she take in the sunrise on the beach and then maybe walk through the markets back up through the old town. I'm sure she'll return within the hour."

"See, girls, I told you Loreto had likely played tour guide to *La Señora* Markus," Lina offered soothingly. "She's always eager to introduce people to the finer experiences Spain has to offer."

"Well if you see her, tell her we're going shopping in Larios this morning," the same girl said, her tone infinitely more relaxed.

"If I see her, I'll let her know," Loreto said, and the girls hurried off, but Lina stayed put. "Yes, boss?"

"What do I have to say to make you understand we have a responsibility to the people on our tours?"

"A responsibility to introduce them to the finer experiences Spain has to offer?"

Lina rolled her eyes. "We've talked about this, Loreto."

"No, we talked about not sleeping with the students, you never said anything about the teachers."

"Then put on your pants and come downstairs so I can clarify the company policy."

"Right now?" Loreto whined. "I have plans."

"Your *plans* have to call her husband back."

Loreto's stomach tightened just a bit. "Oh yeah."

Lina tapped lightly on the large hickey on Loreto's shoulder. "And wear a shirt with sleeves."

Ren set a small kettle of tea on the table between them. The hotel's restaurant was more of a café or collection of tables on a patio off a small kitchen. Simone had no idea why her boss's secretary had booked her in a place like this. Something about a film festival, and last minute. The excuse hardly seemed acceptable.

"What brings you to *España?*" Ren asked, pouring the tea through a small mesh sieve and into a baby blue mug.

"Work."

"*Trabajo,*" Ren said, then added, "just in case you wanted to pick up a little Spanish."

"I'd rather pick up a good translator. Are you interested? I'd be willing to pay well above the going rate."

"I'm a tour guide, not an interpreter."

"I could use a guide, too. I have an important meeting this time next week, and I need to pick up some conversation topics between now and then that make me seem in tune with Spanish culture. If you want the job, I'll gladly compensate your employer for your time."

Ren's smile faded. "Make you *seem* in tune with Spanish culture, not actually help you get in tune with it?"

Before Simone had the chance to dismiss that idea, a sexy, young woman with long, dark hair and olive skin sidled up next to Ren and placed a sweet kiss on her cheek. "I'm so sorry to interrupt, but Loreto is on her way down."

Ren snorted softly. "Down on who?"

"*La Senora* Markus, but then down here for a talking-to before we head home."

"This day just keeps on getting better." Ren sounded tired for the first time, but she regained her smile quickly enough. "Lina, this is Simone, *una Americana* with money to burn and in need of a tour guide to help her fake an affinity for Spain."

"*Hola* Simone. Forgive my wife. Spain has softened her edges, but she hasn't lost all her American bluntness yet." Lina ran her fingers through Ren's hair and gave it a loving tousle.

Simone sipped her tea. "I can respect bluntness as long as it's paired with efficiency."

"*Excellente,*" Ren said with a mischievous grin. "Then I'll go tell Marcela to turn over our room so you can get some rest. After the siesta we'll meet back here, and I'll introduce you to your guide."

"Introduce me? I made the offer to you, or maybe to your employer."

Lina slipped an arm more possessively around Ren's shoulder. "Her employer isn't willing to share her."

"*Corezones Española* is your company?" Simone asked coolly, refusing to show the hint of disappointment that pricked her chest.

"It's *our* company," Lina corrected, exuding pride, "and between school trips and family holidays, this is our busiest time, but if Ren thinks we can spare one of our guides, I'll trust she has a good reason."

"I'm certain her reason is better than good," Simone said. "It's platinum."

Lina bit her lip as if trying not to smile. "Be careful. The last time I underestimated her, I ended up wearing this." She pointed to a gold band on her left ring finger.

"Thankfully, that's not something I have to worry about." Simone stood. "Now if you'll be so kind as to show me to my room, I'll freshen up and meet you back here at one o'clock?"

"Three o'clock," both women said in unison.

Simone sighed. She was used to setting the schedule. Why was everyone in this country so contrary?

Loreto checked her coal-black hair in a mirror she passed on her way down the hotel's wrought-iron staircase. Not that she minded looking disheveled. If anything, she preferred it. Women like *La Senora* Markus seemed to prefer it, too. The fact that her white T-shirt and cargo shorts weren't exactly business attire didn't bother her either. Lina and Ren had always been lax about stuff like that, though judging by the stern look on their faces when they saw her, that may be about to change.

Loreto was not what anyone would call a morning person, so she bypassed the table in the café and ordered a café cortado, a strong, black coffee with just a kiss of milk, before joining them and laying her arm, palm up, across the table. "Okay, here's my wrist, boss. Go ahead and give it a little slap."

Lina shook her head. "We've been through this before."

7

"Not exactly this. You said no university students, and I listened. *La Señora* Markus is a teacher, and she crawled into my lap, not the other way around."

Lina showed no sign she found this logic any more compelling than she had earlier, so Loreto changed tactics. "And wasn't Ren one of your clients? Can you honestly say if she'd showed up in your room wearing nothing but a bath towel, you'd have just said, 'Sorry, my boss wouldn't like that?'"

"*Sí.*"

"It's the truth," Ren said wistfully. "It took me days before she even let me kiss her."

"You're not helping, *amor*," Lina said, but the bite drained from her tone, leaving her sounding more tired than angry. "And we aren't talking about us. We're talking about a habit that's getting out of hand."

Loreto sighed, finding the topic as tedious as Lina now seemed to. "You can't tell me not to sleep with a grown woman on my own time. It's my business."

"No, it's my business. Your meeting a woman and taking her back to your place is not the same thing as one of my guides taking one of my guests back to one of the rooms I've paid for, leaving my underaged guests unattended overnight . . ."

Loreto slumped in her chair resignedly. Lina obviously had a speech prepared, and Loreto had sat through worse. Ultimately, she'd learned she didn't have to win every argument. She didn't even have to engage them if she didn't care to, and she didn't care about much. Besides, a stern talking-to was a small price to pay to keep a job as good as this one. Still, she wondered how long this was going to take. Lina seemed to be on quite a roll.

". . . but it's not only bad for our business. I'm starting to worry about you, too. I know you've been through a lot, and it's probably hard to have faith in people, but you've moved past irreverent and into self-destructive. Are you even listening?"

"*Sí*, you're irreverent and self-destructive."

Ren set her forehead down on the table with a thud. "Uh-oh."

Lina threw up her hands. "Clearly, nothing I can say is going to change anything."

"It's good we realize we can't change each other. No use going on about it."

"No, we're done *talking*. You've forced me to take action. You're relieved of your next tour."

Loreto sat up straight. "What? You're firing me?"

"Not firing, just a leave of absence."

"I don't have an apartment, or income. What about my papers? *Dios mio.*" Loreto turned to her other boss. "Ren, help."

"Why do people always think you're the nice one?" Lina asked.

"Sorry, Loreto. This was my idea," Ren acknowledged. "You've worked nonstop for three months. You need a break. Or maybe you need a new challenge to pull yourself out of this rut you're in."

"Living ten days without a paycheck will be a challenge all right. What am I supposed to do? Lay on the beach? Go to the clubs? No offense, but that's not exactly the way to get me away from women."

"We thought of that. Obviously, we care about you."

Loreto snorted.

"We don't want anything to jeopardize your status," Ren continued, "and the choice is yours. You can mope around if you need a break, but there's another option."

"Why do I have the feeling I won't like this other option?"

"It's a private tour."

"I didn't think you did private tours."

"You don't work for us for the next ten days," Ren explained. "The client doesn't seem very interested in playing *tourista*, so you'll likely do a lot of driving and translation, maybe offer context and cultural insight, but I wouldn't be surprised if she expects you to carry her bags while you're at it."

Loreto started to understand. "So, the tour's not the challenge, the client is?"

"Nicely put," Ren confirmed. "An *Americana* on business for some important meeting next week. She's willing to pay heavily for what I can only assume will be a very long seven days."

"She wants a pack mule?"

"Pretty much, so if you want to sleep in hostels for the length of your suspension, no one would blame you, but personally, I think the job will be good for you."

"Lina, you think working for this woman is what I need to do my penance?"

"No, I think one of you is likely to arrive at our next meeting in a box," Lina deadpanned, "but if it's you, just remember you dug your own grave."

"Ouch." Loreto had enough experience to know Americans with money could be a high-maintenance breed, and she had a particularly low tolerance for them. "So, it's a test?"

"Consider it a contest," Ren offered cheerfully. "You versus the naysayers."

Loreto rolled her eyes. Nothing about this sounded promising, but she did have a competitive streak, and virtually no cash. Ten days of no plans and no money didn't exactly appeal to her either. "Fine. I'm in."

Ren grinned and Lina sighed again.

"When do I meet this woman?"

"Two-thirty," they both said in unison and then laughed, Loreto assumed at one of their inside jokes. Then Ren added, "Go get some sleep."

"Thanks," she mumbled and headed up the stairs. If this client was as bad as they were making her out to be, she'd need all the rest she could get.

Simone woke up to the familiar ring of her cell phone. It was two o'clock in the afternoon, which meant it was morning in New York, though she was too foggy to figure out what time. She'd had four hours of sleep, which was more than enough to function, but not enough to thrive.

"Hello," she said, instantly sounding professional even if she didn't feel it yet.

"I take it you're on the ground," Henry Alston said without introduction. He was used to being instantly recognized.

"Yes, sir. I arrived in Málaga this morning. I'm checked into the hotel your secretary suggested, and I have a meeting with a potential guide in an hour."

"Good girl. I know I don't have to tell you to do your homework on *Liberdad*. I want this fish mounted on my wall by this time next week."

Simone grimaced, both at being called "girl" and at her senior vice president's absurd fishing metaphor. They were talking about a small publishing company, not a large-mouth bass. "Have I ever let you down?"

"Never," he laughed, "which is why I wrecked your first vacation in over a year, but you know I'll make it up to you."

He'd make it up to her bank account, which to him was the same as making it up to her, and generally it was. "Of course. I had a chance to glance at the specs on the flight from Milan, and it looks like an insanely generous offer, given their limited assets."

"Asset. They only have one, Juanes Cánovas. He's a fucking god with a pen, and American women are going to think he's sex on a stick, but Liberdad Press has everything from translation rights and movie rights to right of first refusal on future works."

"No one has everything. There's no way their lawyers can stack up to ours. Why not poach him?"

"Already tried. He's got some misguided loyalty to that little mom-and-pop shop in Málaga. They've fed him some line about his artistic integrity being compromised. He says they are quintessentially Spanish, whatever the hell that means. They're all afraid we're going to Americanize Juanes and sex him up."

"Are we?"

"Of course."

"If they won't sell him, what makes you think they'll sell the company?"

11

"Two reasons. One, we're going to make sure the owners never have to work again, and two, I sent you, and you never let me down."

"Both very good points."

"Wine them, dine them, hell, tattoo a Spanish flag on your ass. I don't care how you do it, but get the contract on my desk without giving me any more headaches."

Simone realized her window for asking questions had ended. "I'll be in touch."

She ended the call and got out of bed, mentally making a list of what she needed to do to get going on this project. Powering on her laptop, she perched it on the bathroom counter while she hopped in the shower. There wasn't time to luxuriate under the warm water. In a matter of minutes, she was drying her long, blond hair with one hand while she Googled "ebooks on Spain" with the other. She picked out one on history and one on the country's economic development, as well as a guidebook to southern Spain. She had them downloaded by the time she slipped into a pair of gray linen slacks and a white Oxford shirt, a move she regretted the moment she stepped onto the hotel patio.

It had to be one hundred degrees outside, and the humidity made her hair seem to double in both volume and weight. She stopped to pull an ink pen from her leather business satchel, and winding her long locks into a bun, she stuck the pen through the center to hold it up off her neck.

"Nice," someone said in a suggestive tone. Simone turned to see a rakish boy laying on his stomach on a lounge chair by the pool. He wore ratty shorts and beat up sandals. His dark hair was a mess, cascading over dark aviator glasses as he propped his chin atop his folded arms.

"You wish."

The boy shrugged and resumed his nap while Simone headed inside to find a table in the lobby. Was there anything in this country that wouldn't annoy her? The café was closed, and there was no one working the front desk. The entire place was empty and quiet in the middle of the day. What kind of establishment was this?

She took the seat that put her back to the wall, giving her a view of both the front door and the entrance to the patio. She was in control of this meeting, and she wanted to situate herself as such. She pulled out her iPad and checked the time. While the meeting wasn't scheduled until three, anyone who wasn't at least five minutes early was late. It was 2:40, and her tour guide was now on the clock.

She was tapping her toe like a ticking clock ten minutes later when Ren and Lina pushed through the front door to the lobby.

"*Hola*, Simone," Lina said, her smile more welcoming than earlier. "I hope you got some rest."

"I did, but I'd really like a bottle of water, and I can't get any service in this hotel. It's like no one works here."

"It's siesta time. No one works from one to three in the afternoon."

Ren had said the words clearly enough, but they made so little sense she might as well have spoken Spanish. "Siesta? Surely that's not a serious thing."

"I know it's probably a little jarring, but we do things differently in Southern Spain."

"I don't care where we are. You can't shut a business down for two hours in the middle of the day. You can't run a company like that."

"And yet this city has thrived exactly like that for centuries. You'll find billion-dollar homes less than three miles from here, and Michelin-starred restaurants, and upscale boutiques to rival New York or Milan. They're all doing just fine. Spain sets her own tempo. It's best to go with it."

"It's best to do what you're paid to do. I'm being paid to work, and my guide will be expected to do the same. I hope that won't be a problem."

Ren sighed. "You can negotiate your terms with Loreto when she gets here."

"I thought I'd be contracting her services through you."

"No," Lina said quickly. "We don't do individual tours. Loreto's completely free to accept or deny any terms she sees fit. We're merely offering an introduction."

"Why?" Simone eyed her suspiciously.

"Why what?"

"Why offer an introduction? Why give up your room early? Why provide one of your guides to a stranger if you aren't going to accept payment?"

Ren shrugged. "Spanish hospitality."

Simone didn't buy that. No one did something for nothing, and she was about to say so when the door from the patio opened and the boy from the pool came strolling in, only upright and facing forward. Without the sunglasses, he was most definitely a she, and a very good looking she at that.

Her baggy shorts now hung off of the feminine curve of her hips, showing a tantalizing glimpse of tanned midriff, and her plain white T-shirt barely concealed her pert breasts. The style was grungier than Simone usually went for, but despite her disheveled appearance, the woman exuded a confidence anyone would find appealing. Most alluring, though, were her eyes. Deep brown irises swirled so dark, then almost melted into her pupils.

"Good afternoon, Loreto." Ren rose to meet the newcomer. "This is Simone. Simone, meet your guide, Loreto Molina."

"My guide?" Simone was caught off guard, a feeling she detested. This woman may be a fine candidate for eye candy, but she didn't appear to have an ounce of professionalism. Shouldn't tour guides look like, well, she didn't know, closer to zoo docents or the retirees who sat on stools in art galleries, rather than some sort of sexy skateboard model or a Latina boi band front man?

"*Hola, Señorita.*" Loreto extended her hand, and Simone accepted it, sneaking a peek at her watch in the process. It was two minutes until three, so technically she wasn't late.

"I don't speak Spanish."

"That's not a problem. I'm a native English speaker," Loreto replied with little more than a wisp of an accent, proving she couldn't be discredited on the basis of a language barrier.

"How long have you been a guide?" Simone asked, as they took a seat.

"This is my third season working for Lina and Ren. Before that, I spent a few years traveling through the country on my own."

"We can vouch for the fact that Loreto is one of our most knowledgeable guides. She consistently gets very high satisfaction ratings from our clients."

Loreto's grin flashed something more smug, and Lina gave an almost-imperceptible shake of her head. The move may have gone unnoticed by someone who didn't watch for tells, but Simone wasn't one of them.

"If she's one of your best guides, why are you willing to part with her?"

All three of the women exchanged another quick look before Ren stepped in diplomatically once more. "She just finished with a group from England this morning. She's got the next week off, and we thought she might be a good fit for you."

"But if you want to shop around, feel free," Loreto added quickly. "It's only peak travel time, school holidays, and film festival week on short notice."

Simone's jaw tightened at the challenge in Loreto's voice, but again, she only chose battles she expected to win, and she didn't have enough information on viable alternatives to dismiss this woman's points. She'd had plenty of practice swallowing her resistance over the years, but it still tasted bitter as she tried to hedge her bets. "I'm on a tight time frame. I'm willing to give you a trial on your employer's recommendation."

Loreto nodded, as if she were neither impressed nor offended by the tepid offer.

"We can come to terms on a price per day, but I reserve the right to terminate the agreement with payment made only for services rendered. Does that make sense?"

Loreto shrugged. "I don't work, I don't get paid. I piss you off, I don't get paid. You find a better offer, I don't get paid."

Simone fought the urge to defend herself against an accusation of unfairness that hadn't actually been spoken. The harsh summary of terms wasn't exactly false, so much as blunt.

Lina shook her head. "That's very one-sided. There should be some sort of neutral metric put in place for the possibility—"

"Nah." Loreto cut her off. "I'm good. She wants me gone, I'll go."

"Reto," Lina said, dropping her voice. "Make sure it goes both ways."

Simone smiled slightly as she realized what Lina was suggesting. "She's right. Some people find my standards too high. If that turns out to be true of you, you also have the right to terminate the agreement at the end of any day without financial obligation."

Loreto seemed to ponder the offer, lowering her chin and closing her eyes so that her full, dark lashes rested on smooth skin for a second, then opening them, she said, "No commitment. I like that."

Simone pursed her lips as the feeling the comment should have inspired in her butted up against the ones it actually did. "So, we have a deal?"

Loreto nodded once more, this time resolutely. "Deal."

They sat staring at each other for a long, heavy moment before Ren broke the silence by pushing back from the table. "All right then, we'll leave you two to hash out the details."

Lina didn't jump up so quickly, instead looking from one to the other. Her eyes narrowed as she seemed to inspect each of them, but whatever thoughts spun in her head were silenced before they reached her lips as Ren laid a hand on her shoulder.

"All right," Lina said and rose. "You're right."

Simone shook her head slowly, not understanding who or what the comment referred to.

"It's not you," Loreto whispered conspiratorially. "They just do that sometimes."

"Do what?"

"Have conversations no one else can hear."

"We do," Ren said, without a hint of chagrin, "and now we've decided to leave you to your own devices."

Simone found the choice of words a bit odd, but everything about this country had been odd so far. She thanked them both and tried not to examine the minute twist of wistfulness in her stomach as she watched them walk away hand in hand.

Chapter Two

As the door closed behind Ren and Lina, Loreto sat back and watched the American gather herself. She'd clearly done this sort of thing before. Most tourists were hesitant and nervous in a new country, around new people, and their sense of frustration or anxiety mixed with their entitlement in all sorts of unappealing ways. This woman carried plenty of entitlement, but she also oozed confidence. From her rod-straight back and the level set of her shoulders to the subtle lift of her angular chin, Loreto suspected a bit of middle-class overcompensation. The way she'd shot off the terms of their agreement in contractual language spoke not only of a familiarity with corporate lingo, but also a desire to make certain she sounded like she belonged in those circles. There was an insecurity to her hypercompetence, and Loreto quietly tucked that knowledge away for later as Simone turned to face her once more.

Those electric blue eyes landed on Loreto as if searching for something, and not in a tender, endearing way. The scrutinizing gaze left her feeling like a cadet under inspection or a patient on an operating table. Loreto fought the urge to shift away from their probing, knowing that to shrink now would be seen as surrender, but surrender to what, she wasn't quite sure. Still, she felt it a small victory when Simone spoke first.

"We should come to terms about expectations."

"I expect there will be a lot of them."

Simone smiled fleetingly. "You're not wrong."

"Then do you mind if we discuss them over tapas? I haven't eaten yet today."

Simone pursed her lips, then laid a hand across her flat stomach. "I don't usually like to do business while I eat, but now that you mention it—"

"You can't remember when you ate last, can you?" Loreto saw the answer in the frown and used the lack of a negative response as a positive. "I know a place close by that'll serve us tapas early."

She pushed back from the table and rose, stretching the tension from her core by arching so far back her T-shirt rose halfway up her abs. When she straightened, she noticed Simone's electric gaze had shifted to the exposed skin. So, Little Miss Uptight wasn't as straight as she was buttoned up, and she wasn't just hungry in the conventional sense. Another tidbit to file away for later.

"I don't really like spicy," Simone said.

She snorted softly at the juxtaposition of the comment and her previous thoughts. "We'll find something you can handle."

Rising from her chair to stand a good two or three inches taller than Loreto, Simone said, "It's not a matter of what I can handle, so much as what I prefer."

"We'll get to that, too," Loreto said, feeling steadier as they moved toward the door and out into the streets of Málaga. This was as close to home turf as she'd ever had. She strode at a leisurely pace as the afternoon sun baked the concrete beneath her feet. The path she cut through ancient streets wasn't any straighter than she or Simone, but at least it was all downhill, and Simone's business-oriented footwear didn't seem to slow her down across the uneven pavement or around the winding turns. The heat, on the other hand, might've given her some pause as she ran a thumb across the beads of sweat dotting her forehead. Then again, maybe she'd been trying to smooth out the worry lines starting to form there the farther they went into the *barrio*.

The hotel was in a picturesque, little neighborhood just north of the old city core, but as Loreto turned down another white-washed row closer in resemblance to an alley than an American street, she wondered whether Simone began to suspect she'd been kidnapped. No doubt she'd heard horror stories about women who looked like her being lured into white slavery by unsavory characters who looked a lot like Loreto. Maybe Loreto could've eased her concerns by chatting a little bit. She would have with her students or travel moms, but Simone didn't fit into either category, and Loreto suspected she wouldn't be easily distracted by details about their short distance from the birthplace of Picasso. Instead, she simply said, "We're almost there."

"Where is 'there,' exactly?"

Loreto smiled. "Plaza de la Merced."

"Which is . . . what?"

"A plaza."

"Right," Simone said curtly, as asphalt gave way to gray tile beneath their feet. "And there's a restaurant in there?"

"Well, there's an obelisk and a statue of Picasso. Actually, there are a lot of statues there sometimes, but only one is permanent. It's of Pablo. The rest of them are just people who've painted themselves up and stand real still."

"Why?"

"I think they'd say it's performance art, but likely they're in it for the spare change tourists throw at them," Loreto redirected cheekily.

Simone rolled her eyes. "Why are we going to a plaza when I asked you for business conversation and you offered tapas?"

"We can do both near the plaza. I know a great tapas bar and—"

"Bar?" Simone came up short. "It's not even five o'clock. If you think I'm going to spend the next week day-drinking with you, we've had a vast misunderstanding."

Loreto laughed, which was apparently the wrong response, as Simone folded her arms across her chest and tapped the toes of her fancy shoes against the tile.

"Tapas bars serve tapas," Loreto explained, unable to keep a little tremor of laughter completely out of her voice. "They also serve alcohol, of course, but if, what did you call it, day-drinking?"

Simone nodded.

"I like that, but if day-drinking isn't your thing, then we'll add it to the first line of this contract we're supposed to be hammering out."

"I'd rather just go to a restaurant," Simone sighed, "preferably a nice one, with air conditioning."

"You've got trust issues, don't you?"

Simone's face flamed from pink to red. "Excuse me?"

"It's okay. I do, too." Loreto forged on as she started walking again. "It might be the only thing we have in common."

"I don't think—"

"Good, that's a good plan. Don't think."

Simone jogged to catch up. "Have you lost your mind?"

"Gleefully."

"I think we've made a mistake."

"I've made many in my lifetime," Loreto admitted in a serious voice, but she couldn't manage to suppress a grin as she turned another corner.

"This isn't going to work," Simone snapped as Loreto came to an abrupt stop in front of an ornate, wooden door.

"Isn't it?" she placed a palm flat on the door and gave a gentle push. It swung wide, and the first thing to hit her was the blast of cool air. The second sensation sent a different kind of warmth through her, the soothing spread of satisfaction.

Simone's eyes widened in confusion, then quickly narrowed as she inspected the room before her. Dark wood floors gave way to warm orange stucco on the walls and a ceiling rimmed in azure tiles. The furnishings were modern with a Spanish flare, sleek lines and lush curves from the high back chairs in carved oak to the sleek, glass tabletops. The mismatch probably wasn't as posh as Simone was used to in New York or Los Angeles or whatever American metropolis she'd migrated to from the suburbs, but there was no mistaking the restaurant for a dive bar.

"Something does smell amazing," Simone said softly, as if she didn't quite like that fact.

"It's the food," Loreto said, "and every item on the extensive menu tastes better than it smells."

Simone's stomach growled.

"Why didn't you just tell me where we were going?"

"I did. I said, 'I know a tapas bar.'"

"You might have undersold it a bit."

"Be honest. If I'd said I was taking you to a place you'd like, then walked you through all of those back alleys, would you've been any less nervous?"

Simone pressed her lips into a thin line.

Loreto didn't force her to answer. She simply nodded toward the cool interior of the restaurant. "Either way, we're here. All better now?"

Simone hesitated for just a moment, her eyes meeting Loreto's once more, but without the same challenge they'd held moments earlier. Then, without a word, she turned and walked inside.

Loreto's heart gave one extra thump against her ribcage as she followed at a more leisurely pace.

"*Hola,*" an older woman called from behind the bar.

"*Buenas tardes,*" she answered as she watched Simone take a seat and scan the menu from top to bottom, then flip it over.

"Do you have any dietary issues or strong dislikes?" Loreto asked.

"Spicy," Simone said, "but I don't know what—"

Loreto turned her back on her, effectively cutting her off. If she waited for Simone to have another hissy fit about not understanding the menu, they'd never eat. Instead, she turned back to their hostess, bartender, and waitress to place an expansive order in Spanish.

"Excuse me?" Simone asked, as Loreto joined her. "I didn't understand any of that."

"You're excused," Loreto said flatly. "It's expected. You know the old joke, right?"

"I get the feeling I don't."

"What do you call someone who speaks three languages?"

"Trilingual," Simone said quickly.

"And what do you call someone who speaks two languages?"

"Bilingual," she said a little slower, as if expecting a set up.

"And what do you call someone who speaks only one language?"

Simone pressed her lips tightly again.

"An American!" Loreto chuckled at her own punchline.

"I took French in high school and college."

"Shocking," Loreto deadpanned.

"What did you order?" Simone asked curtly.

"I got us a wide variety of tapas and *pintxos*. Some hot, some cold, seafood, pork, and vegetarian. You don't have to eat anything you don't like. They are all small plates made to share."

"I don't generally share food off my plate."

"One of these days you're going to surprise me," Loreto said, "but that moment hasn't come yet, so why not assert yourself by talking contract terms until the food arrives?"

Simone opened her mouth like she might object, then seemed to think better of it. "Actually, yes, let's do, because as you may have noticed, I'm not an easy person to work for."

"Continue."

"I work nonconventional hours if needed, and I'd expect you to be on call—"

"Twenty-four seven. Got it."

"I'd rather not drive in unfamiliar areas where I don't speak the language."

"You need a driver. I can get a car."

Simone raised her eyebrows. "You can get a car?"

"From the company, not like from stealing."

Simone sighed. "I'm going to forget your mind went there."

Loreto didn't point out that Simone's mind had obviously gone there, too. "And you need a translator, which I can also do."

"And we already agreed I'd pay you at the end of each day."

"In cash," Loreto added.

"No, that wasn't what we agreed to."

"We only agreed to *when* I'd get paid, not *how*. You said we could hash out the details, and I'd prefer we hash it out in cash."

"I'd prefer we have a paper trail for me to invoice."

"I can provide you with an invoice and receipt." She fished an iPhone from her pocket. "We're not living in the Stone Age here."

"I'd feel more comfortable using checks."

Loreto leaned forward and met Simone's eyes. She'd rolled over without blinking on every other point, but she needed to stick on something, and it might as well be this. "You need a day laborer who drives, navigates, translates, and stays within arm's reach around the clock for an admittedly high-maintenance employer, all on short notice, and you're going to balk over the idea of invoiced and receipted cash?"

Simone sighed. "I understand how unreasonable that probably sounds to you. I'm not unaware of how I come off, but I generally get what I want because I don't really care what other people think of me."

Loreto snorted. "Something else we have in common. Look at us hitting it right off."

"So you'll take a check, then?"

Loreto shook her head slowly. God, this woman was entitled and pushy and uptight, but those eyes, and those legs. The constant complaining would be exhausting, but God, there was something maddeningly sexy about a woman who didn't roll over for anyone. Still, there was no shortage of entitled blondes in Southern Spain this time of year. Maybe it was time to pull the plug on this one before the hot water got deep.

Still, the challenge in those eyes hadn't released her yet. As good as it might feel to leave this woman stranded right here, caving now would also feel like a bit of a defeat. She hated feeling trapped, and she was about to say as much when a plate of food dropped between them.

Both women sat back, blinking and breaking the stare-off. The waitress set another plate between them, then another, and another. The aroma of still-sizzling meat and freshly baked bread overwhelmed Loreto's senses, but she wasn't nearly as hungry as Simone had seemed earlier.

As the woman across from her reached out for a thick slice of bread slathered with tapenade and red pesto, Loreto held up a hand.

"Wait. No eating until we're done with the business."

Simone swallowed a little squeak that sounded close to a whimper but managed to nod.

"You clearly dropped everything to get to Spain in a hurry, and there's obviously something important on the line for you, business-wise. Sorry, I don't know what kind of business you're in?"

Simone stiffened. "I'm in publishing."

"You buying or selling?"

"I don't see how that's relevant to you."

Loreto shrugged. "Probably not, but it seems relevant to you."

"It's an acquisition."

"So buying, which means there's likely a lot of money at stake, right?"

"I'm not at liberty to expound on the details."

"Fine, I don't particularly care about them," Loreto said honestly. She didn't care about any part of Simone that didn't affect her directly, though as Simone sat back and crossed one long leg over the other, Loreto could admit that something about the woman did affect her. And while she was truth-telling to herself, she should probably also acknowledge that she wouldn't mind affecting her in a few non-business like ways as well.

Lina's warnings about not sleeping with clients flashed red through her memory, but then again, she wasn't working for Lina this week. If she accepted these terms, she'd be working for Simone, which meant that anything that happened between them wouldn't be between a client and guide so much as between a boss and subordinate. She gritted her teeth. She didn't much care to think of Simone as a superior or herself as subordinate to a woman like her.

"My point," Loreto continued, "is that if you're willing to let me walk over something like the method of payment on a deal that likely comes with a lot more zeros than I'll ever see from this deal, maybe it's best to just go our separate ways."

The corner of Simone's mouth quirked up as if she might get some perverse pleasure from calling that bluff, either way it ended, like she might just enjoy watching her go as much as she'd like watching her walk back to the table. Most of all, she'd probably enjoy the way Loreto's heart beat a little faster at the thought of having to make that choice. Damned if she did, damned if she didn't. Again.

The idea was enough to throw a bit of ice water into the lap of her libido. She didn't want to play someone else's game, and she damn sure wouldn't play one she couldn't win.

Placing both hands on the end of the table, she pushed back, the legs of her chair scraping their way across the floor. "You've been charming, really, but I think it's better to call this off right now."

"You're probably right," Simone admitted. "We don't seem well-suited to each other."

"Fire and flood," Loreto agreed. "No hard feelings."

"No feelings whatsoever."

Loreto nodded and rose. "Enjoy your meal and your travels."

With a slow exhale and a steadfast refusal to look back, she took two steps toward the door, but before she got a chance to take a third, slender fingers caught her around the wrist.

She glanced down, first at the hand, pale and elegant and strong, then up at the woman who held her.

Simone turned over the palm, producing a felt-tip pen from the pocket of her khakis, and scribbled a number across it. Then she said, "In case you change your mind."

Confused, Loreto squinted at the digits scrawled across her lifeline. No matter how many times she read what Simone had written, it didn't add up to a phone number, but it was too long to be a room number. Glancing at those electric blue eyes once more, she raised her brows in an unspoken question.

"Per day," Simone said.

Returning her focus to her own palm once more, the digits finally connected with her brain. The numbers weren't any invitation. They were a price.

A literal price on her skin, for her time, her experience, her attention, her labor. It wasn't the first time anyone had made a claim on those things, but it was the first time anyone had made such a staggeringly high offer.

Her heart seized in her chest as she did the math, and her pride shrank as the total butted up against what she'd usually make in three months of tours. A little twinge of disgust tried to assert itself at thoughts of what she could do with all that money. She could buy the types of things she'd spent years trying to convince herself didn't even exist.

There was still a huge part of herself *that* would love to tell this woman no, to see her response to that two-letter word she probably wasn't used to hearing, to wipe the ink off her hand, maybe on Simone's starched, white shirt, or simply to walk away without giving her the satisfaction of any acknowledgement.

Instead, she eased slowly back into the chair and said, "I guess we can eat now."

The clock on the dresser said 6:30, but her body disagreed emphatically, without giving a clear answer to the question of what time it was. She'd been in Málaga less than twenty-four hours and in Milan less than forty-eight hours before that. The week before, she'd been at her New York apartment for a few days, followed by a short conference in Chicago. None of those stays had been long enough to fully unpack, much less acclimate, and the longer she stared at the hairline cracks in the off-white ceiling, the less she thought a construct like time zones really mattered.

Her eyes were open, the sun had risen, she had plenty of work and work-related items on her to-do list. She might as well get moving.

And coffee. She definitely needed coffee.

The business attire options left in her carry-on didn't leave many choices. Pushing aside the bikini and the translucent coverup she'd hoped to wear today, she pulled out a neatly folded pair of brown linen slacks and a white linen shirt. Dressing quickly, she pinned her hair up off her shoulders and snagged a sleek, black leather satchel off the dresser on her way out the door.

The lobby was unsurprisingly quiet. Given the fact nothing in the hotel had functioned well before noon yesterday, she didn't have high hopes for quality service or caffeine at this hour, either, but she did manage to find one young woman working at the front desk.

"*Buenas dias, Señora.*"

"*Hola,*" Simone managed with a slight smile, homing in on the woman's name tag. "Marta, do you speak English?"

The girl returned the smile nervously. "Little English."

"Promising," she muttered. "Where can I get some coffee?"

Marta nodded slowly, then her mouth twisted into something that didn't quite reach a grimace as she processed the request. Her eyes brightened as if the lightbulb in her brain had switched on. "Coffee is . . . closed."

"Closed?"

"Yes," Marta said emphatically.

"What time does coffee open?"

"Breakfasting open at eight," Marta said, sounding quite proud of herself, then for emphasis, she pointed at the sad excuse for a café where Simone had sat with Ren the day before.

"The restaurant opens at eight?"

"For breakfasting."

"I don't need breakfasting," Simone said tersely, "only coffee, or caffeine. Actually, do you have tea or pills or, I don't know, an IV where you can mainline it right into my veins?"

Marta blinked several times, her nervous smile returning. She opened her mouth as if she might respond, then closed it and shook her head.

Simone sighed. Of course, she'd pushed too hard, for too much. Lowering her expectations, she tried again. "I need coffee."

"Coffee," Marta repeated.

"Yes. I need it . . . now."

Marta nodded sympathetically.

She didn't need sympathy, she needed a solution. There was always a solution. Usually it involved a little determination and a well-worded bit of persuasion or a well-timed payment, but she needed someone to understand her long enough to get to the payment part.

"Not at eight."

Another nod.

"Please." She practically squeaked out the word. "Any coffee, but now."

Marta looked over her shoulder at an open door. "Bad coffee?"

"Any coffee. All the coffee," Simone bargained. "Do you have coffee?"

Marta's smile turned almost conspiratorial.

"I'll pay you." She fished a handful of euros from her satchel, but Marta shook her head and ducked through the door.

Simone waited, impatiently drumming her fingers on her leg. She was aware she was twitching like an addict jonesing for a fix, but the coffee was only the first layer. She needed a win. She needed to feel some modicum of control. This country had been more disorienting than all of her jet lag combined. Nothing here followed the laws of physics, and by "physics" she meant "business," because in her world, the two were equally fixed.

Marta emerged, holding a large mug with the hotel's logo on it. It wasn't steaming, but the way she cradled it in her hands gently suggested warmth, and Simone nearly whimpered in anticipation.

Marta placed the mug on the counter, and Simone slapped her money down in exchange.

"No," Marta said, causing Simone to freeze, her fingertips already curling around her salvation.

"No?"

"No monies," Marta said. "Bad coffee, for liberty."

"For liberty?" Simone couldn't handle any more confusion.

29

"Free? Do you mean the coffee is free? Oh for crying out loud, take the money."

Marta's expression went blank again.

"For you, Marta. The money is for you. For thank you."

Marta's smile brightened more than Simone had yet seen on her. "You are welcome."

Simone sighed heavily. Of course she knew those words. Niceties would prevail in a place like this. Fine. Whatever. She lifted the mug to her mouth and sipped, unconcerned with how well the descriptor, bad coffee, fit the sludge coating her throat. It might not have been terrible four hours ago, but now all she could say for the stuff was it was viscous and caffeinated. She downed the whole thing, warmth spreading through her esophagus and into her stomach, and she envisioned that warmth lighting up everything it touched with the energy she craved.

"Thank you," she muttered, more to the coffee this time than the person who'd delivered it, but Marta answered anyway.

"You are welcome, *Señora.*" Then she pressed one finger on the euros between them and slid them back across the counter to Simone.

Her shoulders fell as she took the money back. "Okay. Fine. Free bad coffee."

With a little wave she turned and wandered back up the stairs. Why the hell didn't anyone want to be paid? Not Ren, not Lina, not Marta. It didn't make sense. She'd been to plenty of places where she didn't speak the local language, but she'd thought cash was a sort of universal way of communicating, only these Spaniards didn't seem to agree.

Well, maybe that wasn't completely true. Loreto had seemed pretty keen to be paid in cash last night.

Loreto.

Why hadn't Simone thought of her sooner? She had access to a car. She'd agreed to be on call. Surely she could also be expected to produce basic human needs like coffee. And she respected the natural order of service and payment. Her dark eyes had practically glazed over when she'd read that number on her palm last night. Simone shivered a little at the memory.

She'd made the move almost flippantly, but what she'd seen in Loreto's eyes was anything but glib. She'd watched countless people process innumerable offers over the years, but none of them had flashed through the type of emotions she'd seen in Loreto. The depth of them had almost frightened her. She'd seen none of the contained or calculated greed or ambition she'd grown used to. Loreto's reaction had delved deeper and encompassed something broader than that, a hunger maybe, but not the polite kind. It was more like famine.

She shivered away the thought. Not only was it melodramatic, but also it didn't make sense. Loreto didn't strike her as a person who lacked for anything she really wanted. She carried herself like someone used to being in control, at least of her own sphere. The tension between them at dinner last night had been palpable enough to suggest Loreto was used to working on her own terms almost as much as Simone.

Almost.

Still, she'd done her job. She'd ordered an array of dishes and eaten civilly. She made conversation when needed by explaining the food, and she walked Simone back to the hotel at an efficiently early hour. The way she rebounded after their initial disagreement spoke to an admirable amount of control.

Simone liked control. She liked knowing what she needed and where to get it. She liked being the boss. It was time to get back to all those things by wrestling this day onto the right track. That thought, and the early effects of the caffeine seeping into her system, gave her the impetus to walk past her own room and down the hallway to rap on Loreto's door.

Loreto was awake and reading when she heard the knock on her door. Glancing at the time stamp atop her Kindle, she managed a faint smile. Almost 7:00. She'd have expected the American to come calling an hour ago. Maybe this wouldn't be as bad as she feared.

31

She swung her feet off the balcony railing and padded across the room, casting a glance at the still-unmade bed. She briefly considered leaving her shirt across the rumpled comforter and greeting Simone the same way she had Lina the day before. It might throw the woman out of focus for long enough to get a barb or two in, but somehow the thought of Simone seeing her naked in the morning light made the hair on Loreto's arms stand on end.

She grabbed the shirt and pulled it roughly over her head as another knock came.

"Coming," Loreto called in English. No self-respecting Spaniard would knock at this hour. In the second before she unhooked the latch, she impulsively snagged her sunglasses from the dresser and put them on. Maybe she wasn't ready to face those electric blue eyes so early, or perhaps she worried she'd give away too much if she looked at Simone before she'd properly fortified herself, but she didn't have time to examine her motives too carefully. No sooner had she cracked open the hotel room door than the American pushed right on through.

"Good morning, Loreto. Sorry to wake you."

She hadn't woken her, and she wasn't sorry, but Loreto let the intro stand.

"Hello, *Rubia*."

Simone arched an eyebrow, then glanced from Loreto's wrinkled shirt to the rumpled bed. "It's Simone, actually. I hope you do better at remembering your girlfriends' names than you do your employer's."

Loreto shrugged. She didn't feel the need to explain to Blondie that she'd been given a nickname, or that she had, in fact, on rare occasion, forgotten the names of women she'd slept with.

"Also, I really don't care what you do with your personal time, but if you feel the need to wear sunglasses indoors shortly after sunrise, I do worry the hangover might alter your responsiveness."

The way her heart rate accelerated at the third misconception in two minutes suggested her auto responses were working quite well, but Loreto barely had time to wonder if there was some tree-falling-in-a-forest equivalent for assholes going uncorrected before Simone launched into her desires for the day.

"If you don't mind, I'd like to get started with our orientation of Spain, perhaps a quick tour of the area, and a chance to acquire some more business-appropriate clothing for the next week." She ticked through her list as she paced over to the open balcony and back.

"All doable."

"But first I'd like to find a place that serves a healthy breakfast paired with strong coffee, and I'm told that doesn't exist in this establishment until at least eight o'clock."

"Correct," Loreto confirmed, her own stomach rumbling. The remnants of last night's tapas had long since burned out of her system, but she'd been too tense to eat a proper dinner before bed. "We'll have to go into Málaga."

Simone stopped pacing. "I thought we were in Málaga."

"We are, but Málaga has a lot of different neighborhoods, and the one you're looking for is the old city."

Simone glanced pointedly out the window. "I'm not sure I want a neighborhood older than this."

And there they'd reached the end of Loreto's willingness to abide ignorant assumptions. "Trust me, Rubia. I know what you want. It's Calle Larios."

Simone pursed her lips but seemed to forcibly hold back an argument. Loreto took that as progress and stepped more fully into the void left by Simone's silence.

Within half an hour, she parked the company car she'd borrowed near the harbor.

Simone had been studiously quiet as they'd wound their way through crooked streets toward the Port of Málaga. The first glimpses of the Mediterranean hadn't sparked much more than a passing acknowledgement, but as they turned onto a busier thoroughfare, Simone's eyes wandered more, her head on a swivel between the large cruise ships docked to their left and the increasingly gentrified city on their right.

Tall palm trees lined the sidewalks along their route, interspersed with large banyans, their trunks, branches, and raised roots meeting in gnarled knots.

"Was that a parrot in that orange tree?" Simone finally asked.

"Probably," Loreto said, as she searched for a parking space. Normally she would've walked or taken the bus. Only tourists drove in Old Town, which was mostly designated as a pedestrian area. Thankfully, even most of the Brits and Germans who flocked to the *Costa Del Sol* this time of year had the good sense not to start their days this early. With only a few turns and minimal backtracking, she located an empty spot just a block from the base of Calle Larios, near a massive, modern hotel.

Killing the engine, she stole a glance at Simone, whose eyes lit up as she surveyed the impressive property with its crisply uniformed valets standing sentry out front.

"It's fully booked this week," Loreto said as she climbed out of the blue Peugeot. Then, without waiting for Simone to catch up, she strolled toward the center of Old Town.

At the first glimpse of Calle Larios, Simone fell in beside her. "What is this place?" she asked, a new reverence in her voice.

Loreto felt a flash of satisfaction in having been right about what Simone wanted, tempered with the annoyance at having been right about what Simone wanted. Still, she slowed her stride enough to take in the walkway large enough to almost constitute a plaza or promenade. Marble tiles made up the area that might have been called a street, but it was abundantly clear few cars were ever allowed to scuff the surface running between pristine storefronts. And while she suspected the labels didn't quite rival Rodeo Drive or the Champs-Élysées, Simone would have her pick of several international brands of clothing, fragrances, and jewelry. Overhead, archways were strung with sheer fabric so well-heeled patrons could walk between stores shaded from the inconvenience of the sun freckling their alabaster skin.

"Be still my heart. Do I see a Swarovski?"

Loreto shrugged, and Simone sighed dreamily, no doubt thinking of all the shiny things she might buy.

"Is this Spanish heaven?"

"This is Calle Larios." Loreto tried to keep the resignation out of her voice. "It's the main line of the city for people like you."

That comment broke through some of Simone's reverence. "People like me?"

Loreto didn't take the bait. "By noon this part of the city will be completely overrun. The film festival brings throngs of people to the area."

"That's fine, I want to see it all. I want to experience real Spanish culture."

"You most certainly do not," Loreto said with an eyeroll, but as Simone placed both hands on her hips and lifted her chin as though bracing for another holier-than-thou lecture, Loreto cut her off. "Can we save that particular argument for after breakfast?"

Simone pinched the bridge of her nose, as if trying to staunch a headache. "Fine, truce until we're fully fed and caffeinated. Where do we make those things happen?"

"These shops won't be open for at least another hour, but a few places two blocks up and over serve breakfast this time of day."

"Lead the way."

Loreto noted Simone's willingness to follow. She supposed her easy compliance in the moment should be considered a vote of confidence, a reward for not screwing up the first task of the day. As they emerged from a narrow off-shoot into a small square, she suspected she'd scored another point when Simone saw the Starbucks.

"Oh, thank you, Jesus."

"It's 'Loreto' actually. I hope you do better at remembering your girlfriends' names than you do your tour guides."

Simone smiled. "Touché, and yes, thank you, Loreto. Shall we?"

"You go ahead," Loreto said. "I'm not a big coffee drinker, and you won't need a translator in there."

Simone once again pressed her lips tightly together, as if choosing her battles took great restraint.

"Go ahead." Loreto nudged her. "I'm going to duck into a place across the plaza, and we'll meet at one of those tables to draw up the battle plans."

Simone relented, and Loreto made a mental note that her need for caffeine could be used as either a carrot or a stick, tucking it away for future negotiations.

She used her few minutes of peace and quiet to breathe for the first time in an hour. She'd had students and teachers test her cool many times over the last few years but rarely this early in the day. Maybe Simone was right in her desire to fortify herself. With that thought in mind, Loreto stepped up to a window on the alleyway side of a nearby building.

Standing under a small, red awning, she breathed in the mingled scent of hot oil and frying bread, with just a hint of salt in the air from the nearby sea. A middle-aged woman in a white apron took her order and shut the window again. Nearby, two busboys kicked a ball of wadded up brown paper between the tables, narrating their game like announcers at the World Cup until an old man scolded them from inside. They picked up brooms to resume the work he'd demanded of them. Across the way, she heard the metallic rattle of storefronts being unshuttered, and in the distance, the bells of the city's central cathedral chimed the hour.

Loreto had always scorned the tourists who never left Larios to see anything farther away than the beach, but she couldn't blame them for being charmed with this area. The Romans, the Moors, and the Christian kings had all sought to make this place their home, so she supposed the foreigners who flocked here now were no worse off in their tastes. Maybe if she'd come from some gray, English suburb or one of the millions of map dots of the American Midwest, she would've seen Larios as a paradise unto itself as well.

But she hadn't, and she didn't. She also didn't harbor any illusions about belonging here any more than she belonged in any of those other places. So when the woman behind the window shoved her order through, she accepted the gifts of this moment and moved along.

※ ※ ※

Flush from another, albeit much easier, attempt to meet her most basic needs, Simone wandered out of the Starbucks and into the sun-streaked square. She shouldn't have doubted Loreto's assertion that she wouldn't need a translator. For all her tour guide's laissez-faire attitude and demeanor, she did seem exceptionally good at reading various situations. Simone valued competency in others as much as she did in herself, and she had no problem admitting Loreto had been spot on both last night at dinner and this morning. Calle Larios exceeded her every expectation on the utility front, and with a latte in one hand and a fruit and granola yogurt parfait in the other, she was also more prone to appreciate the beauty of the area. Several streets too small for cars converged in an open space dotted with palm trees and patio umbrellas. Pigeons watched from wrought-iron balconies, and elaborate, azure-and-emerald tile work encircled windows with sheer drapes wafting in the early-morning breeze.

In the middle of the picturesque scene sat Loreto. Everything about her posture exuded the unhurried aura of this place. She'd taken a seat in the shade of an awning, but as she leaned back in the chair, she'd kicked her legs out into the sun, crossing them at the ankles and folding her arms behind her upturned head. Perhaps she'd found something pleasant to admire in the palm fronds overhead, or maybe she'd closed her eyes in a moment of serenity. Simone couldn't be sure, as Loreto had yet to remove her reflective aviator-style sunglasses. Were her eyes bloodshot from a late night or too much reverie the night before? She'd assumed so earlier, but as the day went on, she'd begun to suspect Loreto might be protecting something more so than hiding.

Neither option particularly mattered to Simone, but she did find herself wondering what she might see in those eyes as Loreto turned to look at her and asked, "Did you find what you were searching for?"

The question, or the way she'd worded it, struck Simone as more pointed than she cared to answer, so instead she raised her yogurt a little higher in acknowledgement and joined Loreto at the table.

She'd barely sat down before the aroma of something hot, rich, and sweet hit her nostrils. There between them sat a pile of cinnamon-sugar coated goodness encircling a steaming cup of molten chocolate.

"*Churros con chocolate.*" Loreto answered the unspoken question. "Want some?"

Suddenly her yogurt didn't hold the same appeal. "Maybe after breakfast."

"You wanted Spanish culture?" Loreto asked.

"Of course."

"In Spain, *churros con chocolate is* breakfast. The same way the French eat chocolate croissants and Americans eat fruit loops, the Spanish believe in starting their day with a dose of carbs sprinkled with sugar. But because the Spanish are superior in every way, they go a step further and dip their sugar carbs in chocolate."

"Well played, Spain." Simone nodded her approval. "I won't quite concur on 'superior in every way,' but you're certainly winning breakfast. However, can I also assume the inevitable sugar crash also contributes to the national nap time?"

Loreto laughed, and Simone found herself relaxing at the first easy exchange they'd had since, well, ever.

"I've never thought about the sugar crash, but I guess it could be a factor. Mostly, though, the siesta comes as a product of the heat and the late hours we keep. The brutal mid-afternoon sun makes productivity challenging through that part of the day, so we seek shade and rest when we need to, then simply tack on those hours to the end of the day. Shops will stay open until around eight, and dinner is served nearer to ten."

"At night?" Simone asked, unable to believe that math.

Loreto laughed again. "Which, in turn, is why we sleep later in the mornings."

"So the whole country isn't just sleeping all the time?"

"No. I mean, we may sleep more than you, but also at different times. You can judge the locals for sleeping in this morning, but in turn, they will judge you for calling it a night when they are still feeding their families dinner."

Simone got the point. She could see the logic without particularly caring though. She'd spent half of her life bowing to other people's schedules, and now that she'd achieved what she had, she didn't mind making other people bow to hers. Call it the natural order of paying your dues. When the Spanish ruled the world, she'd respect their authority and eat dinner at ten. Until then, she had too much on her plate to bank on nap time.

"I'm glad you brought up work time." Simone forged on between bites of her yogurt, trying not to imagine how much more satisfying Loreto's churros would taste. "I've got six more days to get in tune with Spanish culture."

"What does that mean to you?"

"To be honest, the concept is a little vague at this point. I only know I've got to make a pitch that shows not only financial commitment, but also Spanish sensibility."

Loreto grimaced.

"What?"

"No offense, but maybe you should try a bigger financial commitment, because you're going to have a hard time pretending you have anything approximating a Spanish sensibility."

Simone's jaw twitched. "That's what I hired you for."

"You hired me to be a guide, driver, translator, and general lackey. You never said anything about miracle worker."

"I don't think teaching a little Spanish culture should qualify as a miracle for any credible tour guide."

"You're using the words 'culture' and 'sensibility' interchangeably, and they're not." Loreto flipped her sunglasses atop her coal black hair and met Simone's eyes for the first time all morning. "I can certainly teach you the history of Spain. I can explain how the world's great religions all put down roots on this very land. I can tell you about the resilience and warmth of the people who have survived them and managed to flourish. I can tell you about the food and wine and music and art that thrive in this climate, and what their abundance means for the psyche of a people predisposed to generosity. In fact, I can explain all of these things in detail, but I can't make you appreciate them, and I sure as hell can't help you internalize them."

The flash of passion and animation in the otherwise sedate woman caught Simone off guard. So did the intensity of Loreto's gaze, as her irises swirled from dark to darker. She felt a rare wave of excitement crest in her chest, only to crash back into the much more familiar sensation of being challenged. The muscles in her shoulders tightened in response. "I'll internalize whatever I need to internalize to make this deal. You can judge me or underestimate me along the way if you want. You wouldn't be the first, and you won't be the last, but I'm not paying for your opinion. I'm very good at what I do."

"So am I," Loreto said, "and your opinion of my skills or knowledge has about as much relevance to me as mine does to you, but if you want to get your money's worth, you've got some decisions to make."

"Decision-making isn't something I shy away from. In fact, I'd like to share a few of them with you right now."

"Shocking."

Simone ignored Loreto's sarcasm. "I'd like to transfer to a hotel in this part of town."

"I'm sure you would."

"I'd like for you to make that happen."

Loreto laughed and pulled her phone from her pocket. "Let me get on that."

Simone folded her arms across her chest while Loreto tapped the screen a few times before sliding the phone across the table to her. "Why don't you go ahead and scroll through the myriad of options."

Simone clenched her jaw and ran her finger down the screen, revealing one sold out listing after another.

"We could look into home rentals," Loreto offered.

"Yes!" Simone agreed.

"Just kidding," Loreto laughed. "They're booked solid, too."

40

"There has to be a way."

"Look, *Rubia*," Loreto said patronizingly, "let's for a second pretend you're right, and you find a vacant room no one in all of Europe has been able to locate for the last six months, and you get yourself a nice flat overlooking the Plaza de la Constitutión. You won't sleep, for days."

"I don't know about—"

"I do know. That Spanish schedule you turned your nose up at a few minutes ago will be reveled in and flaunted, loudly, every night from now through Friday. These squares will be filled with Brits and Americans and Germans with lights and cameras and sound systems."

"I'm sure there are noise ordinances."

"There aren't. Wes Anderson is going to debut a new action film at eleven Thursday night, followed by a party, and then an after-party. It'll be fancy and loud, and probably entertaining, but it will not be Spanish. No local that doesn't have to work will stay within a five-mile radius of this event. Which brings me back to my original point. You have a decision to make. Do you really want to move hell and earth to get to a place that won't do a damn thing to help you achieve your stated goal of soaking up whatever sliver of Spanish sensibility you're capable of internalizing, or do you want to do the job you're so fond of telling me is so important?"

If Simone's jaw had been tight before, now she could practically feel the individual tendons begin to fray under the strain of her tension. She hated being wrong almost as much as she hated to lose. Almost.

Loreto sat back. "You're the boss, another thing you seem real invested in reminding me. You set the tone. I'll follow your lead in this relationship. I'll play whatever role you assign me. I can be an adversary, an employee, or a partner, but I can't work without direction, and you'll find me considerably more useful if you don't fight me every step along the way."

The tension slipped from Simone's jaw with each sentence of Loreto's pronouncement. Reluctantly, she found herself relaxing.

41

How could she not? Loreto offered such a unique mix of challenge and support. She refused to be a doormat, but neither was she a combatant. The blend of self-assuredness and pliancy made for a good mix in business. Simone liked to think she could employ both when the situation called for them, and she'd be unfair not to recognize the usefulness of both traits in a guide.

"Fine."

Loreto raised her eyebrows. "Fine?"

"You make some good points."

"I do?"

Simone rolled her eyes. "Don't backtrack now. If this event that's filling every hotel in a five-mile radius is truly an international event, it stands to reason it's not uniquely Spanish and, therefore, doesn't fit the purpose of my trip."

Loreto's eyebrows remained elevated, though the question in her expression slowly shifted to suspicion. "But?"

"No 'but,'" Simone said, a hint of humor replacing some of the defensiveness in her voice. "I want to succeed. You playing the role of a yes-man won't help me do so. I can recognize a legitimate point when I see one, so I want you to feel comfortable voicing them when you see the need."

"You do?"

"I can't promise I'll take every suggestion, but I do promise to consider them," Simone said earnestly. "You may not believe me, and that's fine, but I'm not a bad person, and I'm not unreasonable. I'm driven and competent, and I'm used to being the hardest working person in the room."

"I don't doubt that," Loreto said quickly.

"Women, particularly young women, have a hard time being taken seriously. I've spent fifteen years proving I can be as cutthroat as my male counterparts. I've made enemies. I've made mistakes. I've made hard choices. I've made sacrifices most people wouldn't, but I'm finally nearing the point in my career where I see them all pay off. If I have to play the bad guy or the hard-ass to finish the job, I won't lose sleep over that."

Loreto shrugged. "I'm not sure you have to play any roles this week, not for me. I've got no investment here. I get paid whether you make the deal or not."

Simone couldn't remember the last time she worked with someone who wasn't judging her with something to gain. The people above her were always testing her to see if she could move up or, worse, take their job, and the people beneath her gunned for her position or, worse, just wanted to knock her down a peg. Loreto might get some sort of pleasure in tripping her up, but she didn't seem like the kind to mastermind subterfuge for enjoyment's sake, and she had no vested interest in Simone's job. In fact, she'd made it clear she couldn't care less about what Simone did, other than pay her, of course.

Her shoulders suddenly felt lighter than they had in weeks, maybe months. "You've made some more good points."

Loreto snorted. "What? That I'll do whatever you want? That's a thought that hadn't occurred to you?"

"Not fully. I'm used to having to use a strong hand with subordinates."

"Maybe that's because you only think of them as subordinates, but again, not my problem. I have experience making tours to fit my clients' needs, but it's up to my clients to make the most of the experiences I provide. If they don't, it's no skin off my nose."

Simone nodded. "Fair enough. I know a thing or two about seizing opportunities. Make your pitch."

"My pitch?"

"Tell me about the tour you'd arrange to provide a crash course in Spain."

"Well . . ." Loreto's brow furrowed momentarily, but then she sat up a little straighter. "This acquisition you need to make, I take it the company or person or whatever you're after is in Málaga?"

"Yes."

"Then you don't need to cover all of Spain, which is good, because you can't in a week. What you need is a crash course in Andalucía."

"Andalucía?"

"Spain is broken into regions, and the official boundaries have shifted over the ages, but Southern Spain is a beast unto itself. The differences between where we are and, say, Barcelona, can't be measured in mere miles. We've got different priorities, different food, different schedules, even different languages. There, lesson one complete. You're here for Andalucía."

"Andalucía." She said the word more confidently now. She liked the way it filled her mouth like the bouquet of a fine wine. "Sell me on the details of that tour."

"First, we shop. Here. Now," Loreto said. "Then we get the hell outta Dodge."

Simone frowned. Even though she saw the wisdom in making the move, she didn't like being shown a glimpse of civilization only to have to head back into what she assumed was the wilderness.

"Don't worry," Loreto said kindly. "We'll make a full circle. You'll get your Larios life at a time when it's more suited to you. In the interim, I'll make sure you see a few jewels to rival anything they sell two streets over."

Simone had her doubts as she remembered the alleyways they'd walked the night before. "The main thing is that there's a missing piece in this deal. The ownership has clearly been presented with other offers, and they've turned them down. All I've got to work from is a vague clue about something in their make-up that's tied to Spain or, if you're right, Andalucía."

"And you want to solve the mystery," Loreto concluded. "My suggestion would be to start by casting a wide net. I can plan you a loop through the region. A different city each day, where we hit the things that make them unique, and not just the tourist attractions, but their food, their music, their people, and hopefully their essence. If you see something or sense something worth examining deeper, I'll roll with you, but otherwise you let me set the route, the daily itineraries, and the overall pace."

Simone had been buying what Loreto was selling right up until that last point. "I need to reserve the right to veto at any time."

"Of course you do."

It wasn't an argument, just a statement of fact, but Simone realized she'd played right into the image Loreto must have of her. Oh well, not everything could be free, easy, and egalitarian. They'd mostly agreed on a plan of action. That would be enough for now. She was restless and ready for action. "Okay, let's assume that plan for now, with the understanding that it's a work in progress, and we can reconceive as needed."

Loreto smiled. "Work every day, reevaluate every night. Sounds perfect for our one-day-at-a-time method of doing business."

Simone tilted her head to the side. "Are you making another commentary on my personality or sincerely agreeing to remain flexible?"

Loreto flipped down her sunglasses and rose from the table. "Why choose between the two? Let's just say that trust issues and commitment issues are two things I find appealing in women."

Simone opened her mouth, then closed it again, not sure how to respond, but before she had the chance to collect her thoughts, Loreto strolled off, leaving her to catch up yet again.

"It's not Michigan Avenue or Times Square," Simone said, as she exited another clothing store.

"Thank God," Loreto mumbled.

"But it manages to pack a good bit into a small area."

Loreto accepted another designer label shopping bag to add to the four others hanging off her arm. They'd been shopping only an hour, but Simone had covered an impressive amount of ground. They'd purchased several business casual outfits, two pairs of shoes, a sun hat, and a pair of cheap sunglasses. The last item amused Loreto more than she let on. Still, the dresses were the highlight of their march through the shopping district. Three of them covered enough skin to be professional but showed enough to make Loreto hope she'd be around long enough to enjoy the view of Simone wearing them.

Simone obviously had money to spend and a taste for luxury,

but she didn't overpay just to prove she could. She wasn't a fool, either. She knew what things were worth, and while she paid insane amounts for things Loreto would've never dreamed of, she also pointed out several items with exorbitant markups. Loreto had seen plenty of tourists get fleeced on this street, but Simone wasn't among them.

Simone always walked a step ahead, either on purpose or out of excitement, but as she stopped in front of a men's clothing store, Loreto nearly bumped into her.

Simone turned and stared at her expectantly.

"What?"

"Shall we?"

Loreto examined the polo and khaki clad mannequins in the window. "Doesn't seem like your style, but whatever floats your very expensive boat."

"Not *my* boat," Simone said, a playful gleam in her eye Loreto hadn't seen before. "Yours."

"Oh no."

"Oh yes." Simone's grin had turned mischievous, as if her enjoyment had peaked at the thought of torturing Loreto. "I have expensive tastes."

"To each their own, but—"

"But nothing. Where I go, you go, for the next week anyway, and I expect to go to several places not suited to the clothes I assume fill your current wardrobe."

Loreto shifted from one foot to the other. "I have khakis."

"How many pockets do they have?"

"A lot!"

Simone laughed. "Wrong answer."

"I don't see how one can ever have too many pockets."

"Which is precisely why I'm going to help you choose one or two options to diversify your fashion portfolio."

"Which is your fancy way of saying you'll dress me up like a butch Barbie."

Simone laughed as she headed into the store, calling over her shoulder, "Come along, Ken. I don't like to be kept waiting."

She wanted to strangle this woman. Instead she glanced down at the numbers still clearly visible on her palm, gritted her teeth, and went inside.

In the ten seconds it had taken her to make up her mind, Simone had already zoomed in on a rack of slacks. She had a pair of black ones in her hand, running her fingers down the crease and eyeballing them in relation to Loreto. "These should fit."

She snorted. "Really. Just like that, you know my size?"

"I'm good at assessing fit, physically, interpersonally, and businesswise. I've got a well-honed gift."

Loreto rolled her eyes.

"You don't have to believe, yet," Simone said casually. "Try these on."

Loreto had already resigned herself to playing dress up, so she didn't argue. Maybe if she complied quickly, they'd get out of there quickly, so she approached the first salesperson she saw and asked for a fitting room.

The exchange happened quickly and efficiently, but Simone had more questions of her own.

"Ask her if they sell shoes, also suits, or maybe just blazers, and also ask her about belts."

Loreto nodded and opened her mouth, but Simone cut her off again. "And while you're at it, can you ask her if they do alterations on the spot?"

"Shoes, suits, blazers, and uh . . . actually, you know what?" Loreto turned to the woman. "*Lo siento, hablas ingles?*"

"Of course," the salesclerk answered.

"Great, then you can answer the rich lady's questions."

She didn't wait for either of them to argue. Snatching the slacks from Simone, she made a break for the fitting room.

She could hear Simone talking to the other woman as she retreated. Loreto could clearly pick out her voice even from halfway across the room. She wasn't loud so much as commanding. "Would you please fetch me that vest," or "I'd appreciate seeing some different colors of this style." Simone didn't make outright demands. She always phrased her wishes as requests, but her tone, or maybe the confident way she addressed people, left little room for question. She carried herself with the efficiency of someone used to having her needs met.

Not that she ever really approached impoliteness. She didn't talk down to anyone, either. She clearly had high demands of the people around her, and sometimes they failed to live up to them, but Loreto had yet to hear her treat any of them like morons. It was more as if she simply expected everyone to be competent. Loreto didn't really share her expectations. She tended to find people interesting, amusing even, but she knew better than to expect too much or get too attached.

She entered the fitting room and closed the door behind her. She didn't like feeling exposed, and she found the solitude inside refreshing after the sensory barrage of both Larios and Simone. The solace was gloriously short-lived, though. She'd barely stripped down to her boxer briefs when Simone tossed a pair of khakis so they hung over the door. "These are next."

Loreto closed her eyes and took a deep, calming breath, then she yanked the slacks on roughly, or as roughly as possible given the smoothness of the silky inner lining. Damn, they were comfortable, and that sort of pissed her off. The last set of dress clothes, or rather church clothes, she'd owned had been stiff and scratchy, probably because they'd come off the rack at a thrift store outside of Punta Gorda, Florida. It had never occurred to her that rich people's clothes didn't just look better, they felt better, too. All this time she'd convinced herself she'd chosen comfort over style, but of course, people with money got both.

She shook her head and ground her teeth again, but this time for a different reason. She no longer needed to steel herself against the annoyance of Simone's attempt to dress her. Resentment still pricked at her skin, but now the balm wasn't in the resistance but in the surrender. She would let her buy these pants and every other pair she wanted to over the next few days. The same went for food and wine and accommodations. Why shouldn't she? Why should she insist on principles or pride when they'd never even bought her a pair of silky slacks? Simone would not be impressed, and even if she were, Loreto didn't care. She was in this for the money, and so was Simone. At least they were both honest about that.

She decided in that instant that Simone could flash her cash wherever she damn well pleased if this was the sort of thing Loreto had been missing out on. It might be her only shot to experience luxury a woman like Simone took for granted. Besides, Loreto had too many real-life lessons etched onto her skin and her psyche to worry about getting attached to the types of things money could buy. It was exactly those life lessons that had taught her comfort never came to stay, and she might as well enjoy it when she could.

"Do those fit you?" Simone called through the door.

"They sure do," Loreto called, then with a nod to her own reflection in the mirror, she added, "Did you say something about a blazer?"

Chapter Three

Simone had been surprised by how quickly Loreto acquiesced to her inclusion in the shopping trip. She'd seen the initial resistance on her face as they'd stood in the doorway, followed by a sort of grudging resignation. She'd actually felt a twinge of sadness at winning so easily, but it had been eclipsed by the prospect of seeing Loreto's classic form dressed in clothes tailored to show it off.

Perhaps she should've been a little more careful with what she wished for, because as Loreto stood in front of a triplane mirror, dressed in khakis and a sky-blue dress shirt open at the collar and cuffed at the sleeves, Simone wondered if she hadn't made a mistake. She'd matched the size and the style right, but she hadn't expected two and two to make ten. And physically, aesthetically, Loreto was a ten. The lighter colors only made the contrast of her brown complexion even more pronounced, as if the sun had ordained her palette specifically for this color scheme. Simone hadn't been blind to her good looks before, but now Loreto had gone from sexy beach bum to absolute eye candy. For the first time since their formal introductions, Simone considered making an exception to her rule about mixing business with pleasure.

"Do you approve, Miss?" The salesclerk asked, clearly pointing the question at Simone instead of Loreto. She shook off the disconcerting feeling she'd forgotten she was supposed to be in charge and nodded.

"Yes, that'll do. Also the black slacks, the same shirt in white, the white and gray polos. Do you have a black suit coat in the same size as the navy blazer we chose?"

"Yes," the clerk said excitedly, "do you want her to try it on?"

"That won't be necessary." Simone didn't want the image of Loreto dressed in full, formal black just yet. "Just snip the tags off and have them hung properly in a garment bag. I'll meet you at the counter in a moment."

"Yes, Miss." The woman retreated, and Simone turned back to Loreto once more. Her smile had returned, but now the expression appeared more pointed than the easy grin she'd worn earlier in the morning, and it wasn't directed at her reflection so much as at Simone.

"What?"

"Nothing."

"You don't like the new clothes?"

"They're fine."

"They suit you," Simone said, knowing the statement was both unnecessary and an understatement.

Loreto shrugged. "They fit me. They suit you."

"Do you resent that?"

Loreto sauntered back to the fitting room. "Yes."

Before Simone could formulate a response, much less voice it, Loreto shut the door behind her, effectively stopping any chance for conversation unless she wanted to shout, which she didn't. She didn't even know what she would've said. She wasn't used to that kind of candor stated with so little animus. She blew out a deep breath and made a mental note not to ask Loreto any more questions unless she was certain she wanted an honest answer.

She went back to what she knew by pulling out her credit card and paying for the clothes. By the time Loreto joined her and added the other two items to the bag, Simone felt steadier for completing the simple transaction. She wanted something,

51

someone provided it without comment, she paid fairly for the goods and services. This was how life should work, and she felt an unreasonable amount of relief at the fact that Spain wasn't completely immune to the draw of basic transactions.

"Anywhere else you want to stop?" Loreto asked as they stepped back onto the marble street of Larios and the heat of the sun hit them, even under the man-made shade strung above their path.

She glanced at her watch to see midday approaching. "Can I assume it's only going to get hotter for the next few hours?"

Loreto laughed in a way that made it clear how silly she found the question.

"Then no," Simone said dryly. "I suppose we should go back to the hotel and prepare for your beloved siesta."

"I have a better idea," Loreto said. "I know a place where it's much cooler."

"I'm listening."

"Are you ready to hit the road?"

Simone scanned her surroundings, the beautiful buildings, the five-star accommodations, the luxury stores where the world worked the way it should. Then she turned back to Loreto, who'd changed from debonair captain to grungy cabin boi, at least in outward appearance. She forced herself to remember that she'd agreed to follow her lead, regardless of how she dressed in any given moment. Still, she didn't have Loreto's easy ability to relinquish control or stifle her inherent resistance to the unknown. And yet, they'd made an agreement, and Loreto had lived up to her end of the bargain despite her own reticence and resentment.

"Okay," Simone said with a sigh. "Let's go."

Loreto didn't have to be told twice. She immediately began walking in the direction of where they'd parked the car, but she did manage to grin over her shoulder at Simone and say, "It'll get easier to let go the more you do."

Simone forced a smile, but she didn't bother saying she didn't plan on practicing that skill enough to perfect it.

"You're not really a stop-and-smell-the-flowers sort of person," Loreto said matter-of-factly.

Simone didn't argue. "Your point?"

Loreto nodded out the window at neat rows of squat trees. "They're olive groves. Tourists tend to enjoy the way they smell. Sort of like freshly pressed olive oil warmed by the sun."

"Oh?" Simone didn't sound convinced. "What about locals? Are they impressed with them?"

"To be clear, you're asking me if you can somehow use the olive trees as leverage in your business talks?"

"Basically."

"Probably not specifically."

"I eat olive oil," Simone offered. "Does that help?"

"Probably not specifically."

"Do you have anything specific that would probably help me?"

Loreto shrugged. "It's hard to be specific with you being so vague."

Simone sighed. "I know. I'm generally more prepared for meetings than this. I wasn't on this account from the beginning, though. I only got pulled in after previous negotiations went south."

"Because you're a fixer?"

"Actually, yes, or sometimes I'm called a closer. Or at least I have been for the last five years."

"What did you do before that?"

"Everything."

"Again with the specifics."

Simone stared out the window as they wound their way along the highway between two olive groves on a steady incline toward the hazy blue sky. "It's a long story."

"It's a long drive to Granada."

"Why does it matter to you?" Simone asked seriously.

"It doesn't."

Simone rested her head back and closed her eyes, as if the comment somehow freed her.

She was beautiful. The realization hit Loreto with so much force she couldn't even pretend to deny the truth of it. All the lines of worry and stress faded, leaving Simone's pale skin smooth, and the slight uplift of her chin showcased the elegant curve of her throat. Loreto stifled the urge to trace the line of her neck with her fingers only by reminding herself that if she didn't keep her eyes on the road, she'd drive off a cliff and kill them both instantly. At least then she'd be free from the temptation of wealthy blondes with entitlement issues, but surely there had to be better options on the table.

"I started in the secretarial pool at Summit Publishing during college, just interning for credit hours," Simone said, unexpectedly.

Loreto tried not to show her surprise. She'd only been trying to make conversation, but if Simone wanted to talk about herself, she knew enough not to interrupt.

"I did well enough to be kept on after graduation. Then I did well enough filling in for people during their vacations that I got assigned a more stable secretarial position in submissions."

"In submission?" Loreto asked cheekily.

"Manuscript submissions," Simone said flatly. "Don't get ideas."

"I have no ideas you don't pay me to have."

Simone shook her head, but the corners of her mouth curled up. "Anyway, I distinguished myself as a department secretary, and I ingratiated myself to the right people, so they started offering me chances to proofread their reports."

"They offered you the chance to do more work for them? Generous," Loreto snarked. She shifted the Peugeot into a lower gear as the incline of the highway grew steeper.

"It gave me the chance to learn the lingo, the format, the types of books they wanted to sign, so when the time finally came for someone to pass one of those submissions across my desk, I knew exactly what I needed to do."

"And let me guess, you excelled at that task, too?"

"I did," Simone confirmed, without a hint of bravado, "so they gave me more manuscripts to review, and I took them all. I spent years wading through a slush pile of the most self-indulgent, navel-gazing, atrocious grammar, pathetic prose, and nonexistent plots. I never once turned down an assignment, not when plagued with the flu or exhaustion or a boss who liked to stand too close and put his meaty hands on my waist as he told me I should give some masochistic drivel another look.

The hint of venom in Simone's voice at the end told her the last one bothered her more than all the others.

"And I never once lowered my standards."

"So they promoted you again."

Simone laughed without humor. "You'd think so, but there were a hundred other people just like me in the pool. I saw them move up for any number of reasons, their last names, the school they went to, the clubs they frequented, the sheer luck of having a gem land in their laps. But I couldn't count on any of those things, so I got an MBA in an accelerated program on nights and weekends. And I learned to golf. I invested in the wardrobe and manicures, and I started sharking top agents."

"Sharking?"

"You know how when there's no parking spaces to be had at the mall or the grocery store, and you get tired having to drive up and down the aisle hoping to have one magically appear, so you wait for someone to exit the store and you drive behind them very slowly until they get to their car, then as soon as they back up, you dart in?"

"No."

"Well, most people do, and it's called sharking."

"So you followed agents to the grocery store?" Loreto asked. The road began to double back on itself as it neared a high plain with a panoramic vista of the rugged terrain.

"Never the store, but the golf course, the wine bars and gyms and yoga classes. I inserted myself into their spheres and made sure they thought I'd always been there. It took a year of working a sort of social second-shift, but I started to see dividends. Before long, they opened up to me over drinks or on the fairways. I learned about their client lists. And then I'd casually offer to take a look at something for them, you know, before they'd formally submit them, like a favor."

"A favor that suited you more than them."

"I always made it worthwhile for them."

"Magnanimous," Loreto mused.

"It's smart business. It meant the next time they found themselves in the same boat, they'd call me. Before long, my bosses couldn't ignore my influence any longer. When top clients ask specifically for me to see a submission or to attend a contract meeting, you don't tell them no."

"So they stopped telling you no, too."

"Exactly. My career took off. I applied the same techniques to every new position, from acquisition editor all the way up to associate vice-president."

"Which is where you sit now?"

"For now."

"I take it you've got another promotion in your crosshairs?" Loreto asked, finding the story almost as dramatic as their surroundings.

"Senior VP."

"Sounds impressive."

"It is," Simone practically purred. "The position would come with a corner office and a view of the New York city skyline, an insane salary, and more power and market influence than most people could even comprehend. I'd have final say on every book published by one of the biggest, most influential publishers in the English-speaking world. All before my fortieth birthday."

"I'm sure you'll enjoy the view from the top."

Simone sighed. "I can only imagine."

Loreto took her eyes off the road to steal another quick glance at Simone. She had her blue eyes open, but they were hazy and unfocused, as if trying to picture what that famous skyline would look like from the fiftieth floor of some ivory tower.

Loreto turned her focus back to the horizon as the green valley gave way to the majestic peaks of the Sierra Nevada mountains, rising proud and rugged against the azure sky. They stood taller, longer, and stronger than any high-rise in the world, but in that moment, she knew for certain Simone couldn't even see them.

"You weren't lying when you promised cooler temperatures," Simone said as she got out of the car. How high up are we?"

"Only about two thousand feet higher in elevation than where we started."

"I knew we were going up," Simone said, "but the mountains surprised me. I always thought of Spain as being flat."

"Ah yes, the old Henry Higgins rain-and-plains misconception."

A quick laugh escaped Simone before she had a chance to ponder the unexpected Broadway allusion and how out of place it felt given her understanding of Loreto. Maybe she'd merely been caught off guard, or perhaps the temperature in the low seventies had improved her mood. Or perhaps, more surprisingly, the moments spent opening up to Loreto about how far she'd come had actually eased some of the tension knotting both her back and her emotions. She always kept her focus sharply on what lay ahead, but taking the time to reflect on what she'd accomplished gave her a renewed sense of confidence that she had what it would take to make the next jump up the ladder.

"And where are we now?"

"Granada." Loreto said the word as if it held a hint of drama. "Tomorrow we'll walk in the footsteps of kings and caliphs. Tonight, we'll eat and sleep like them."

"Now you're speaking my language." Simone used her hand to shield her eyes from the afternoon sun so she could inspect the property before them. "Even if you do seem to have chosen another rustic accommodation."

The building before them looked positively ancient, with tannish-orange stucco walls rising to various heights ranging from humble abode to look-out towers. The wooden, arched windows and tiled roofs reminded Simone of the old Spanish mission buildings she'd seen around Southern California. The walkways around the property were inlaid with white and black rocks to form elaborate, swirling patterns. Everything appeared tidy and well-kept but not exactly modern.

"Have faith," Loreto said as she pushed through a heavily studded wooden door, then clasped a wrought iron ring to hold it open for Simone.

What she found inside raised her opinion significantly. Overhead lights reflected off polished, wooden floors leading to a mahogany reception desk. A man stood behind it in a full suit. He smiled broadly and ran a hand over his already slicked-back hair. "*Bienvenidos*, welcome."

"*Gracias*," Loreto answered just as Simone said, "Thank you."

He looked from one of them to the other, his smile still plastered across his face. "English or *Español?*"

"English," Simone answered quickly. She might be paying Loreto to translate, but she always preferred to be in the know, which often translated to being in control.

Loreto shrugged. "Sure. I called and made a reservation earlier under Corazones Española Tours."

"You did? When?" Simone asked as the man behind the desk began to tap several keys on his computer.

"While you were packing up your purchases back in Málaga." She nodded approvingly.

"Ah yes, Lina's people," the man finally said. "We saved you two of our best rooms and secured your tickets to La Alhambra for tomorrow."

"Early entry?" Loreto asked.

"Very." The man grimaced. "I can move to later."

"No, thank you. The *Americana* will be awake in plenty of time."

The man gave her a sympathetic look Simone didn't understand. Actually, there were a few things she didn't understand about the interaction, but she caught enough of the gist to gather Loreto had made some advanced arrangements and had possibly leveraged some sort of clout to do so. Simone tucked the information away for later, appreciating the confirmation that Loreto wasn't flying completely by the seat of her pants.

The man scanned two key cards and slid them across the desk to Loreto, who once again reverted to Spanish to express her thanks before leading Simone down a long corridor flooded by light from the high, arched windows. They turned a few times, leading her to wonder how big this property was and if she needed to leave breadcrumbs to find her way back, but when they reached another door, Loreto pushed through to reveal a lush courtyard.

Simone paused to take in the sight, so unexpected in the otherwise brown and orange pallet of the property. Balconies rose four stories high in the surrounding walls, each one draped in rich, green vines laced with flowers in yellow, blue, and red. Brilliant mosaics lined the lower walls in cerulean and white depictions of dancing women and pastoral scenes. In the middle of it all, a porcelain fountain gurgled as water spilled from a smooth sphere into an ornate basin, then fell over the sides into wide, running channels in the stone floor. The canals spread out in the cardinal directions before joining large rectangular reflecting pools along the perimeters of the square. There was something deeply soothing to the geometry of it all. The space managed to somehow be both free and well-ordered.

Loreto stood, watching Simone examine her surroundings, but she made no comment, which saved Simone from having to reply. She didn't want to speak yet. She was still working hard to maintain her initial judgment, though the courtyard made the task more difficult.

With a nod she conveyed her desire to move on, and Loreto led them to the other side.

They entered another building and climbed a set of wide, wooden stairs, passing a single-piece chandelier reminiscent of a Middle Eastern lantern casting its light through cutouts in the shape of suns, diamonds, and crescent moons. Finally, they turned down an upper hallway lined with much smaller windows set deeply in the thick walls, giving an air of seclusion.

59

"I think this one should be mine," Loreto said, stopping in front of a smooth door. "You should take the one on the corner."

She didn't know why the difference mattered, but she'd momentarily lost her will to question. Instead she accepted the key card with a simple, "Thank you."

When she opened the door to her own room, she regretted not being more effusive. The size of the space fell short of cavernous, but compared to the city hotels she frequented in Chicago, LA, and Toronto, it felt huge. The bed alone had more square feet than her entire first apartment in New York City. High ceilings with exposed wooden beams only amplified the sense of openness. The windows were smaller and shuttered, but a series of small, circle-cut latticework allowed bits of light to dance across the thick blue and white area rug in the middle of the room.

The hotel hadn't initially met her expectations of what luxury should look like. There was no slick stainless steel or glass, no nickel or leather accents, and yet the surroundings still managed to exude a refined sense of comfort and elegance. It was as if the surroundings didn't have to work at being impressive. They simply existed, secure in the assuredness that they were. She found the combination and their contrast to everything she was used to disconcertingly appealing.

"Well done, Loreto," she finally whispered.

"Dios, have mercy," Loreto muttered.

Simone was wearing one of the dresses she'd bought this morning. How had the saleswoman described it? Scoop-neck, halter top, or something like that? The terms didn't matter as much as the way it showed off her creamy shoulders. The skirt was cut in a way that made girls twirl when they were young. While she suspected Simone had grown too serious to do so, the dress showed plenty of her legs even when standing still, and the rich color only amplified the smooth expanse of skin. Deep, rich, royal blue. Blue like the sky as the sun sank low over the terrace. Blue like the Mediterranean. Blue like her eyes.

Loreto fought the urge to stand and pull out a chair as she approached. So not her style, and so not their relationship, but something unnervingly chivalrous thumped through her chest.

"Good evening," Simone said.

"*Buenas tardes*," Loreto answered, still in a bit of a haze.

Simone tipped her head to the side. "I thought *tardes* was afternoon?"

"Yes," Loreto confirmed, "the afternoon lasts longer in Andalucía, sometimes all the way until dark, regardless of what the clock says."

"Another one of those Spanish liberties with time, I presume?"

She nodded and watched Simone settle into the chair opposite her, crossing one impressively long leg over the other, letting her eyes wander over the expansive vista before them.

The slate terrace overlooked a steep drop into a vegetation-laden valley, followed by an almost equally-steep climb back up a nearby mountain basking golden brown in the sun's rays. Little white houses specked the rugged landscape, but only sparsely, and the thin vines threading through the beams of the trellises overhead made them feel more a part of it all than mere onlookers.

"Not a bad view for dinner," Simone offered with her usual reserved praise.

"The food's not bad, either, but they won't serve dinner until at least nine o'clock." Loreto took the liberty of pouring them each a glass of ice water from the pitcher on the table.

Simone sighed but refrained from another tirade about Spanish eating schedules. "Tapas then?"

"Of course. And they've got a much more upscale take on the genre here. I suspect they'll meet your high standards."

Simone raised her eyebrow over the rim of her glass as she sipped her water, a playful challenge Loreto willingly accepted as she once again took charge of placing their entire order in Spanish.

"I also chose a glass of locally grown red wine," she explained to Simone when their waiter departed.

"I didn't request that."

"Consider it part of your cultural studies program."

"You're pushing the definition a bit."

"You're paying me to take you out of your comfort zone, not that drinking a single glass of wine with dinner should constitute much of a stretch." Loreto relaxed back into the contour of her chair, enjoying the subtle sparring. "Surely your male counterparts have a glass of scotch at the club. I've seen enough episodes of *Mad Men* to know these things."

Simone smiled slightly. "Then I assume you've also seen enough episodes of *Mad Men* to know there's a double standard for men and women. Drinking at work helps one group while being frowned upon for others, but honestly I prefer to stay fully in control of myself while on the job."

"Shocking."

She rolled her eyes. "I don't expect you to share the sentiment, which is probably why we should talk about the schedule for tomorrow before you begin your libations for tonight."

"Or you could trust me and the day to take you where you need to go."

"You diagnosed me with trust issues, remember? Now indulge them by giving me a rough outline of the itinerary."

"I'm not sure there's an itinerary so much as a starting point," Loreto admitted, "and possibly an ending place if we continue along our expected path, but there's no guarantee we won't find a more alluring detour."

"Are you being serious or toying with me because you know how much uncertainty makes me uncomfortable?"

"Why does everything have to be either/or with you? I can do both. However, I will say I've booked us early entry to La Alhambra."

"I heard that at check-in, and I saw the word "Alhambra" on the signs as we came through some gates on the way to the hotel, but I don't know what it means."

"It's a name. It means 'the Red One' in Arabic, because the red dirt of the mountains in this area gave all the building stones their color."

"But what is it?"

"This." Loreto gestured to everything around them. "La Alhambra is a palace and a fortress, a large complex that houses a collection of royal residences, gardens, galleries, and military outposts. We're actually staying inside its outer boundaries."

Simone glanced around again, noticing the reddish-brown hotel walls behind them. "The hotel was part of the palace complex?"

"A monastery originally, built at a time when the Catholic kings had a lot to prove in this part of the world."

"Catholics with inferiority issues?"

"You have no idea."

"Tell me."

"I will," Loreto promised, "probably repeatedly, but that's part of your lessons. A big one for this region, but we're not talking business over food. Remember?"

"I see no food," Simone said quickly.

Loreto nodded toward the doors from the building to the terrace just as their waiter reappeared, balancing four plates along his arms. "Saved by the dinner bell."

Simone shook her head. "The tapas bell."

Thankfully she didn't seem too terribly bothered by the interruption as she began to inspect the dishes set between them.

"This one looks like cheese, with jelly?"

"Yes, all local."

"And this one is some sort of meat with tomatoes."

"Iberian ham, a carefully cured Spanish delicacy."

"And this?"

"A red pesto made from sundried tomatoes, freshly pressed olive oil, and a fragrant blend of smoky Spanish seasoning," Loreto explained. "It goes well with the sesame-baked bread sticks."

"And this one has"—Simone stopped and raised her eyes—"tentacles?"

Loreto laughed. "*Pulpo.*"

"Excuse me."

"It doesn't have tentacles, it *is* a tentacle. From an octopus."

"It still has the suction cups on it," Simone stated flatly.

"That's how we eat it. Also, it's often served at room temperature, but this one has clearly been broiled with olive oil, fine Spanish paprika, and sprinkled with . . ." Loreto leaned forward, cut off an end piece, and popped it into her mouth before groaning in pleasure. "Almonds."

Then she pushed the plate a little closer to Simone. "Come on, you don't strike me as the kind of woman with a weak constitution."

"Don't goad me. It's beneath you."

"No, it's beneath you," Loreto replied, "but I stand by the statement, because I wasn't goading, only stating an observation."

Simone sighed. "Fine."

She used a knife and fork to select a piece only slightly smaller than the one Loreto had chosen, and without so much as a grimace, she slipped it into her mouth. She chewed slowly, tilting her chin first to one side and then the other. Finally, after a long, heavy minute, she swallowed and nodded. "Not bad."

"Not bad?"

"I expected something slimier," she admitted, "and maybe chewier. I don't know. But the texture isn't much different from lobster."

"And the flavor?"

"Magnificent, actually. The smokiness of the spice blends well with the smoothness of the olive oil, and the toasted almond bits add another layer of both taste and texture, so the whole thing doesn't get monotonous."

Loreto grinned. "I make few promises, but I can guarantee nothing on my watch will be monotonous."

Simone stared at her, eyes so intensely probing Loreto had to physically fight the urge to drop her sunglasses back into their protective positioning, but just when she didn't think she could take the scrutiny anymore, Simone lowered her gaze. "Then what do you suggest I try next?"

Loreto blinked a few times, having a hard time processing the question and its infinite possible answers until Simone gestured toward the food.

"Which dish should you try next?" She blew out a heavy breath. "Any of them. They're all good."

This time Simone didn't so much as wrinkle her nose at Loreto's pronouncement, and they had a few moments of blissfully contented silence to enjoy their meal and let Loreto gather her composure before Simone came at her from another angle.

"So, tell me your story."

Her shoulders tensed immediately, but she kept her voice neutral. "You'll have to be more specific."

"The same vein I shared in the car." Simone made a rolling motion with her hand. "School, career, how did you end up as a tour guide?"

Loreto relaxed only a little. At least she hadn't asked about her upbringing. "My story's not as long or as involved as yours."

"Because you're younger?"

Loreto smiled. "I wouldn't dare to presume such a thing."

"When did you graduate?"

"I didn't," Loreto said flatly. "No college for me. I worked odd jobs around America before coming to Spain in my mid-twenties."

"Why Spain?"

She shrugged. "I already spoke the language, mostly, or something close enough to it that I could get by. It felt far enough away to be different, and, you know, stuff like that."

Simone furrowed her brow, but she'd just taken a bite of bread and pesto, so Loreto used the mandatory chewing time required by good table manners to shift the subject in a way that stifled the usual line of questions.

"I spent half a decade drifting. I hadn't initially expected to stay so long. I'd expected to wander my way through Europe, but Spain seemed to suit me. People were nice enough without being too intrusive. Seasonal work was easy to find, and I never ran out of things to explore. Every time I reached the Pyrenees in the north, I'd hear about something farther south, and I'd head back that way again."

"For five years?"

Loreto laughed. "You'd be surprised how fast five years goes by when you're enjoying yourself."

"I don't think I've ever had five years of full-on fun."

Loreto didn't find that surprising, but she didn't feel the need to say so this time. "It's not too late."

Now it was Simone's turn to shift in her chair and change directions. "Somewhere along the line you became a tour guide though?"

"I did. Ren and Lina found me a few years ago in Bilbao." Some more of the tension slipped from her shoulders at the memory. "They'd gotten lost one Friday evening down in El Arenal and asked me for directions to the Guggenheim. I told them I could show them the way but they'd be better off to save the museum for the next morning and take in the *pintxo* culture that night."

"What happened?"

Loreto laughed. "Lina shook her head no at the same time Ren agreed."

"Relationships."

"No kidding, right? I sort of stood there awkwardly until Ren said, 'Wait, your accent, are you an American?'"

"I told them it was complicated, and apparently that was the magic word. They both burst out laughing. The next thing I knew, they were buying my drinks and food and telling me about their new tour company, and the next morning I was hired for a job I hadn't applied for."

Simone's eyes widened. "So they have a habit of picking up strays? Glad to know it wasn't just me."

"No, totally them. They saw something in me that first night, and they pounced. I kept waiting for the other shoe to drop. I kept testing their patience and boundaries, looking for the weak spot."

"Did you find it?"

Loreto snagged the last piece of Iberian ham and dropped a dollop of red pesto right in the middle. "Probably, but they keep trying to take care of me, so maybe I should just be

66

grateful. I guess I just have a hard time accepting or believing or . . . I don't know. But being a tour guide makes more sense for me than anything else I've ever done. At least it fits my nomadic tendencies."

"Are you just a wanderer at heart?"

Loreto frowned. "No. I'm not that sentimental. Moving around was always a learned, or maybe a necessary, behavior for me, but it's ingrained there now. Might as well get paid."

Simone's eyes narrowed as if she'd just seen something small and shiny in Loreto's gaze. "Necessary how?"

"Just, you know, life happens." She stumbled over the non-answer, her skin prickling under Simone's scrutiny, and finally looked down at the food on the table between them. "Hey, do you want the last bite of the *pulpo,* or should I?"

Simone blinked a few times, probably trying to process the abrupt change of topic. "No, I mean, you can have it, but—"

"Thanks," Loreto said quickly, then added, "Why don't you go ahead and have the cheese and jam. Which one do you like better?"

"Um." She scanned the few remaining choices before pointing to a lighter piece of cheese.

"That's a manchego, a sharper sheep cheese, and the topping is made from the type of oranges we saw growing all over Málaga. They're too bitter for eating, but they make for a good marmalade. Why am I not surprised you went for the mix with the most bite?"

Simone scoffed. "I didn't know my food choices could be used as a personality inventory."

"Then consider that another cultural lesson. In Spain, food tells you much more about a person than their job or what kind of car they drive. Will there be eating at this business meeting of yours?"

"Not impossible," Simone admitted. "Wining and dining clients is one of my fortes."

"Then maybe we should break our no-business-over-food rule just long enough to teach you to order a few basics in Spanish."

With that they were back on more even footing. Loreto made another mental note about the ability to distract Simone with the combination of food and work. She tucked the information away for later, but with it she stored the reminder not to let herself get into another situation where she might need to use it. Simone was not her friend. She was an employer. A sexy, hot, maddeningly stubborn, cutthroat, ladder-climbing executive who openly admitted to using personal contacts to manipulate people into business deals. In other words, she was exactly the type of person who could wreck everything Loreto worked so hard to tell herself she didn't need.

She was still trying to remind herself of those facts as they wound their way through the corridors of the hotel and up the grand wooden staircase that danced with artificial starlight. Somehow it got harder to remember the words to her newly adopted mantra with Simone's hips swaying as she climbed each step just ahead of her, that blue dress swishing across her thighs right at Loreto's eye level as she went.

Her head told her she was being silly to even look at something she definitely shouldn't touch. Nothing good could come of that sort of temptation, but all of the blood seemed to be leaving her brain for points farther south.

Mercifully she reached the door to her room before her libido subdued all her good sense. "Good night."

Simone kept right on walking, but when she reached her own door, she stopped and called playfully, "Oh, Loreto."

"Yes?"

"I'm not quite finished for tonight."

She sagged against the door. "No?"

Simone laughed. "Honestly, I'm a little surprised you're not more eager. I got the sense earlier you were biting your tongue and biding your time for this last stop on our little tour."

Loreto's heart hammered in her chest.

"Don't make me do this in the hall like some sort of illicit transaction."

Her face flamed at the choice of words. She should run. She

should tell her where to take her damn transactions. She should tell her to put her money and her sexy ass back on a plane tomorrow morning because she didn't belong here. Then again, as Loreto looked at the walls, the floors, the windows, anywhere but that dress, she remembered she didn't belong here either.

And then her feet moved of their own accord one step at a time, each one as fleeting and temporary as what she felt for the woman whose room she stepped into. She watched, entranced, as Simone walked purposefully over to the bed, reached up, and unclipped her long, blond hair, shaking the shimmery strands loose across her bare shoulders, then quickly swiped something into her hand. She turned to smile at Loreto once more.

Closing the distance between them, she pressed close enough for Loreto to catch the scent of what she could only assume was some very expensive perfume before she took Loreto's hand in her own.

"Thank you for today," she said softly. Then she abruptly withdrew.

Loreto gritted her teeth at the spinning sense of disorientation, but as she slowly shook the lust-tinged haze from her vision, she realized she was holding something she hadn't been a moment earlier. She glanced down at her palm to see a piece of paper. That's all she could process at first, until the numbers came into focus.

The realization hit her like a wrecking ball of emotions. Disappointment, relief, embarrassment, greed, and hunger, along with the realization that she hadn't been propositioned. She'd been paid.

"Good night," she managed, her voice only slightly lower than usual as she backed out the door.

Closing it behind her, she ran her hand along the rough stucco wall, both to keep herself upright, and to feel something physical grate across her skin. Only when she got to her own room and crashed with a heavy thud onto her too-big bed did she allow herself to exhale.

She'd come too close, misunderstood too much, left herself too open. And it wasn't like she hadn't had warnings. She'd spent much of the evening reminding herself not to go there with this woman. She had every logical reason to keep her distance, both physically and emotionally, and yet the minute Simone beckoned, Loreto had answered like a well-trained puppy.

Staring up at the exposed beams, she was forced to admit the problem wasn't that she failed to see how dangerous a woman like Simone could be, it was that Loreto liked to live dangerously.

Chapter Four

"A reasonable breakfast at a reasonable time makes all the difference to a day," Simone said as they exited the hotel and headed down another decoratively tiled path. "Don't you think?"

"I wouldn't know," Loreto grumbled. "I didn't get either."

Simone laughed. "The sun's been up for almost an hour."

"The sun and I don't generally keep the same schedule." Loreto flipped her shades into place.

"And it's not ungodly hot," Simone observed aloud.

Loreto grunted her agreement. She'd been surlier than the day before, though she'd clearly been awake when Simone had knocked on her door. She'd already dressed in the same style of cargo khaki shorts she'd worn every day since they met, but she'd traded her work polo for the gray one Simone had purchased on Calle Larios the day before. It fit more snugly than the others, showcasing the little swell of muscle in her biceps and the subtly feminine taper of her waist. Simone approved of the improvement more than an employer probably should, but at least she refrained from saying so as they shared a morning meal of coffee, yogurt, and healthy, whole-grain cereals that Loreto groused only meant the hotel catered too much to wealthy Europeans on summer holiday.

Simone argued upscale hotels didn't usually stay open because of locals wanting a staycation, but she suffered a twinge of disappointment when Loreto gave her a grudging nod of agreement.

So Loreto wasn't a morning person. She could understand that, at least hypothetically. It even made her wonder if her assessment about Loreto's hangover the previous morning had been unfounded. Then again, maybe she was hungover now, too. She could have gone back to the terrace and had more of that Spanish red wine she'd insisted meant so much to the culture. She would have been within her rights to do so, but for some reason the thought of her sitting at their table, drinking alone under the stars, made Simone's stomach tighten.

She'd rather make peace with the fact that her guide wasn't a morning person. She'd even consider allowing them to start their day a little later tomorrow, but they were up now, and with the meal over, they were on company time. She preferred company time. "This Alhambra we're seeing. Should I have a crash course before we arrive?"

Loreto nodded reluctantly. "Probably, but there's no arriving. Technically we're already here."

"Right, because you mentioned the hotel used to be this place's monastery when it was built."

"Not when it was built," Loreto corrected. "It was added after the fortress was conquered."

"When the Catholics took it back?"

"There was no taking it *back*. The Catholics hadn't owned it before then, despite what the church would like you to believe." Loreto straightened her shoulders and adopted a more professional tone. "At that point there was no Spain as we know it, only a group of regional kingdoms. Some of them were Visigoth, some Roman, some barely more than tribal alliances. They considered themselves Aragon, or Castilian, or Andalusian."

"Andalusian, like the people I'll be pitching to."

"Roughly the same concept, but much less cohesive. The Andalusian identity would be tested and redefined and tested again over the ensuing centuries, starting in roughly 711, when invaders from Northern Africa ventured across the straights of Gibraltar." Loreto grew more animated as she talked.

"What did they do?" Simone asked, momentarily caught up in the story.

Loreto's smile spread for the first time all morning as she pushed open an outer door in a stone wall and revealed a massive botanical garden. "This."

Trees bloomed with vibrant, red flowers. Immaculately trimmed hedges crisscrossed to produce maze-like patterns. Trellises strung with leafy vines cast intricate laces of sun and shadow into sunken, shimmering pools. If the courtyard and terraces inside the hotel had been surprising, these were awe-inspiring.

All around the gardens, massive buildings rose brown, red, orange, and Loreto wove a purposeful path in and out between them all as she continued with her tale.

"The Muslim Moors were doing advanced algebra and geometry when most of Europe had fallen head-first into the Dark Ages. They built magnificent structures many stories taller than most people of the time thought possible from such simple designs." She led her between two buildings that very much fit those descriptions. "And they brought advanced concepts of irrigation, which, I get, doesn't sound exciting, but remember those jams you ate last night? None of the fruit needed to make them could've been grown in this part of the world until the Moors arrived."

"And these gardens," Simone mused, understanding for the first time that such lush landscaping shouldn't naturally exist in a mountainous region.

"These gardens are nothing compared to the ones above us at the *Generalife*." She said the word with a thick Spanish accent she didn't generally carry while speaking English, like "Hen-ah-rah-leaf-ay."

Simone shook her head, unwilling to even try to replicate the word.

"It's another smaller place in La Alhambra, where the Caliph and his immediate family would go to get away from the fortress."

"They had to build another palace to get away from their palace?"

"Just up the hill from the first palace, like it seriously looks down into the main palace." Loreto snorted. "Rich people aren't so different across time and cultures."

Simone didn't know if she'd go that far, but she didn't want to get off track. "So the Moors revolutionized the region?"

"You cannot overstate their influence in this part of the world. They reigned for nearly eight hundred years."

Simone's steps faltered. "Eight hundred?"

"From roughly 700 to almost 1500 AD."

Simone did the math quickly in her head. "The time from the beginning of their reign to the end is longer than the time between 1500 and now."

Loreto's smile grew to full force for the first time all morning. "Well done, *Rubia*. If we're judging culture by time in office, the Moors still beat them all, the Romans, the Catholics, the Fascists, the modern monarchs, and the socialists."

"That's quite a laundry list of ruling ideologies," Simone said, a little overwhelmed by them all. She'd always had a mild interest in empires, a fact she doubted Loreto would find surprising.

"And no matter what some people would like you to believe, the Moors might've stormed the country by force, but it didn't take many generations for the people to embrace them fully," Loreto said as they stepped into another, more open courtyard, with a much more expansive view of the mountains above and valleys below. "But I'm getting ahead of myself, because I didn't bring you here at ass o'clock in the morning to lecture you."

She hadn't minded the lecture, but she didn't say so. She had a feeling Loreto was working up to something, and the anticipation built in her chest in ways it hadn't since she'd arrived in this country. She felt like she stood on the precipice of something big, something exciting, something important, and when Loreto handed over two paper tickets to a man standing by a huge, ornate wood and brass door, he swung one side open and in clear English said, "Welcome to the Nasrid Palaces."

Simone stepped into another world.

As her eyes adjusted to the dimmer light, her breath caught. She stared up in awe at a long chamber, a gilded relic of another time, another civilization.

"The Moors were scientists and philosophers and architects, but they were also artists," Loreto said, her voice lower and carrying a bit of wonder. "See the plaster work?"

How could she not? The ceilings were covered in it, so were arches and doorways, sometimes even cascading low enough to touch. Delicate scrolls and swirls spun outward with the looping scrawl of Arabic script running around the room. She could barely focus on the details because there were simply so many of them, but as she walked slowly along the masterpiece, she took note of vines, flowers, stars and moons, and crests, some as big as her head, some no bigger than her smallest fingernail.

"How could anyone possibly carve all of these details? They cover everything. The sheer volume of this room . . ."

Loreto chuckled. "Not just this room, the whole palace, but they didn't carve it. It's not engraved. It's all molded. While the rest of Europe was chiseling things out of rocks, the Nasrid perfected a technique of molding plaster in ways that could be connected, strung together, built upon, and even painted."

Simone wandered through one of the ornate arches to another room and noticed several of the minuscule details still held hints of blue in their grooves and ridges. "I see the paint."

"And that's original, with no air conditioner, no moisture control. Hell, there weren't even window shades or doors on some of these rooms. Think about how often you have to paint your apartment or office, and yet that plaster and paint has lasted nearly eight hundred years."

Simone felt oddly humbled by the idea. Or maybe she merely picked up some of the awe in Loreto's voice. Something about this place inspired reverence, but Loreto amplified it in surprising ways. Simone found it hard to reconcile the sloppy, grumbling, laissez-faire woman who'd grunted through breakfast and who'd lost years wandering aimlessly around Spain with the poised and knowledgeable guide currently exuding appreciation for history, innovation, and elaborate craftsmanship.

"They made similar advancements in tilework," Loreto said, oblivious to the fact that Simone's appreciation had shifted from the walls to the woman describing them. "Here, look at this space."

Simone followed her into another room, or rather, another set of high walls, though they didn't have a roof. Overhead, the morning sun didn't have enough height to shine down on them, but the light still radiated in, reflected in the polished colors of tile mosaic encasing doorways in the opposite walls. The vibrant yellows, blues, and greens would have been pretty even if they'd been installed yesterday, but they were made even more impressive by the hundreds of years of exposure they'd weathered. Above them, more plasterwork of flowing Arabic letters extended several stories high.

"The Moors were the most advanced mathematicians on the planet in their day, using algebra in their architecture and geometry in their art," Loreto explained as she pointed out advanced concepts in several of the patterns they passed.

Again, Simone felt herself as impressed with the teacher as she did the subject. Loreto knew so much more than anyone would suspect from looking at her, or even sharing a few conversations. Sure, plenty of tour guides could probably relay dates of invasions and the names of rulers or wars, but Loreto went deeper. She clearly had more than a passing knowledge of history, art, and architecture. She understood the concepts behind why a place like this was special, why it worked, why it survived.

Simone didn't know what to make of the revelation. She'd grown so used to people constantly overstating their knowledge. They did so to posture for power, money, dates, proximity to pretty things. Why would Loreto want to conceal her genuine expertise when it could offer her many more opportunities?

They passed through another set of low arches and down a narrow hallway, Loreto tracing some of the Arabic script lightly with her fingers as they went. Then glancing over her shoulder, she asked, "Remember how I told you about the Moorish techniques of irrigation?"

Simone nodded.

"Well, here they're flaunting it." Loreto turned another corner, and they stepped into yet another courtyard much bigger than the first. Long and narrow, and lined entirely in white marble, it was much more open to the sun, with only the two shorter ends of the rectangle covered under high, arched columns. Above them was a row of windows, and then another level lined with beautiful balconies, before rising into another set of ornate arches. In the ground, running from one side of the courtyard to the other, a sunken pool shimmered with pale-blue water so still and clear it might have been covered in glass.

"The emirs who built this palace knew something the rest of the world didn't, and they're using spaces like this to remind you of it every chance they get."

Loreto stood on the slightly raised patio, surveying the length of the courtyard, hands on her hips, chin lifted, her coal-black hair wispy over her dark eyes. If not for the style of her clothes, Simone could have easily pictured her as one of the emirs she described. There was a confidence and ease to her demeanor that fit this space.

"Water would've flown freely in and out of the little grooves in the floor to keep this pool full exactly to its rim."

"Which would've had a cooling effect on the whole space?"

"Very much so. They used gravity to angle the water down from higher in the mountains. It would be impeccably clear and cool even at the height of the day. Actually, there's no past tense there. It's the same water today. The irrigation channels are another thing that's stood the test of time. The thing we're missing in today's picture is the silk."

Simone's eyebrows raised. "Go on."

Loreto laughed. "I thought that might get your attention."

Simone didn't say Loreto had held her attention all morning, she merely nodded for her to continue.

"At the height of Moorish rule in Granada, the city was known for producing some of the world's finest silks, both in texture and in color. Picture all these walls and rafters draped in luxurious, shimmering reds and blues and greens. And all along the outer edges of the reflecting pool, mats would've lined the floors, piled high with feather pillows. In the corner, someone plays a sitar or gently drums a lazy rhythm. You and I enter, dressed in silks of our own, bright, loose, airy, the cool, smooth comfort of it barely brushing our skin."

Simone's heart rate picked up, as if echoing the drumbeats in the scene Loreto described.

"We wander, barefoot, across the warm, stone floor until we find the perfect spot near the middle, then we sink onto a giant silk pillow, big enough to recline fully." Loreto enacted this part of her prose, dropping slowly, gracefully to the white marble floor and easing onto her side, propped up on her elbows in a semi-recumbent position. "And only when you settle onto your side to gaze into the cooling waters do you see their full magic." Loreto stared up at Simone expectantly.

For a moment she froze, a series of unbusinesslike images flashing through her mind. Thankfully, Loreto must have mis-understood her expression, because she shook her head. "What's the matter, *Rubia*? Afraid to get your clothes dirty?"

She glanced down at her lightly colored linen slacks. She hadn't given them a single thought when Loreto dropped to the floor, and she couldn't manage much concern for them even now as the challenge in Loreto's voice echoed off the surrounding walls.

She crouched so low and close that the soft fabric of her slacks brushed against Loreto's bare calf. She eased back into the same position as Loreto, facing her, and then, tilting her head back, stared at the endless blue sky for a few seconds. With her point made and the silly little challenge answered, she rolled her head slowly to the side, intending to ask if they'd both made their points yet. But as her eyes met the water, the words evaporated.

There, reflected in the floor right next to her, was the most stunning infinity mirror image of the immaculate courtyard and elegant building. The stories, sky, roof, arches, balconies, all rose in the reverse order of the upper world, and closest of all shone the smugly satisfied face of Loreto, gazing back up at her. Her hair, her eyes, her shoulders, her arms, her torso, she looked every bit the part of statue or sculpture brought to life and set atop a marble pedestal to be admired amid the beauty of these alluring surroundings.

She looked slowly from reflected Loreto to the real flesh and blood version, then back again. "Stunning."

"The Moors didn't just know how to paint an image with tile or mold one out of plaster. They also used the basic elements we take for granted and turned them into art. Art upon art upon art."

She didn't disagree with the sentiment, but the water hadn't been at all what Simone was admiring when she'd made her comment.

"Look at this one," a woman said in a thick British accent, followed by the sound of a camera shutter clicking rapidly.

Loreto blinked at Simone, then down at her watch. "Eight thirty."

How long had she sat there staring at Simone, hypnotized by the subtle tells of her building desire, from her expanding pupils to the slight increase in the rise and fall of her chest? Apparently, the answer to that question was too long.

Simone raised her eyebrows. "And does eight thirty mean something special to the Spanish?"

Loreto hopped to her feet, making no move to help Simone do the same. "Not the Spanish, the tourists, in that it's the end of our early entry window. This place will be flooded with people within fifteen minutes."

Simone got to her feet. "In other words, if this were a fairy tale, the clock just struck midnight."

"I wouldn't quite go that far. The spell La Alhambra casts on her visitors lasts a lifetime, but we should probably move along to the big ticket selfie station of our tour," she advised with a quick nod to the Brits. "Before all the other souvenir seekers arrive."

"Lead the way."

She smiled at the expression. She could think of a few places she might have rather led Simone than the Court of Lions, but after last night's momentary mix-up, she wasn't about to let her mind wander off course again, no matter what diversions Simone's body suggested it might be open to.

"You think they'd get tired of the whole impressive courtyard business here," Simone said as they rounded another corner into yet another courtyard, "but then there's this."

Loreto tried not to show how inordinately pleased she was that Simone seemed to appreciate the palace. Some people didn't, and their disinterest had never bothered her. If a person couldn't see what was right in front of them, it wasn't any reflection on her. And yet Loreto had woken up early and cranky at the prospect of having to endure a tour of one of the world's most magnificent buildings with an entitled, judgmental American. Not that she didn't still believe each of those descriptors fit the woman beside her at any given moment, but at least they didn't seem to apply in this moment. And Loreto never counted on anything but the present moment.

"This one is called the Court of the Lions," Loreto offered.

"Let me guess, the big fountain surrounded by sculpted lions had some influence on that moniker?"

"Actually, that's a total coincidence."

"Really?"

"No." Loreto grinned.

Simone shook her head.

"If you can figure it all out on your own, what would you keep paying me for?"

"That's an excellent question," Simone said, giving a little grin of her own. "You better redeem yourself quickly. What's the trick to this one? Do I need to stand on my head to see the face of God in the fountain?"

"Sadly, no optical illusions here," Loreto said, "but there's a pretty gruesome story, or perhaps a legend, to contrast with these pristine white walls and marble."

"I don't frighten easily."

"I didn't think so, but don't say I didn't warn you." With a conspiratorial jerk of her head, she sidestepped into a room just off the courtyard. "This room is called the Hall of the Abencerrajes."

Simone stared up, her eyes once again wide as she took in the massive, eight-point star in the ceiling, surrounded by beautifully painted stalactites of hanging plaster spiraling several levels into a high tower. "Well that's certainly impressive, but I'd call it more beautiful than gruesome."

"That's because you're looking up instead of down."

She immediately adjusted her line of sight to the floor, where a gurgling fountain in a low, circular basin sent a stream of water trickling into a small channel that ran out toward the Lion Fountain behind them.

"Sorry, you're going to have to sell me hard. That's the least impressive thing I've seen here today."

"Right. No one chooses to focus there. Everyone cranes their necks back to see what's above them, which is probably how the first of the Abencerrajes lost his head."

Simone glanced at the ceiling once more, but this time she didn't arch her head all the way back so much as just lift her eyes. "Is head-losing a thing around here?"

Loreto laughed. "It was if you got caught sneaking into the bedroom of one of the royal ladies."

"Yeah, okay. I see a picture forming."

"Legend has it the Abencerrajes were a famous and wealthy family in Granada, but they got so powerful they began a rivalry with the sultan living in La Alhambra at the time."

"Uh-oh."

"Right? When does that end well? But it gets better, because little Moorish Romeo and Juliet enter the act, stage right, when one of the Abencerrajes' sons falls in love with a pretty young member of the sultan's royal house." Loreto was cheesing up the drama now, as Simone's eyes sparkled with interest and amusement. "And this young man, I mean, I don't know how old he was, but his recklessness and stupidity suggest teenager, and so does his fitness level, because Junior scales the walls of La Alhambra."

"Impressive."

"You know what they say. Lust gives you wings."

"I'm not sure that's what they say."

"Either way, he'd have done better to have an invisibility cloak, because he's spotted."

"Of course he is."

"But the sultan, being a reasonable man, doesn't cut off his *albondigas* right there. He sends him home and says something along the lines of, 'Boys will be boys. Let's set aside our differences and get our families together to chat. Maybe we can work something out.'"

"And they believe him?"

"Apparently so, because the whole cadre of Abencerrajes men, legend told, about thirty of them, show up for a dinner party, likely thinking they are about to make a deal that will consolidate their power for generations to come."

"Dummies."

"Greed and lust make for a deadly combination." Loreto shrugged. "And they learn this lesson a little too late, because as the sultan herds them all into this room, possibly under the guise of showing them that magnificent ceiling people are enthralled with to this day, soldiers attack and chop off every single Abencerrajes head in the place."

Simone wrinkled her nose. "Gross."

"Indeed. They say the blood covered the marble and streamed out to the lions, making the whole fountain run red. In fact"—Loreto paused for emphasis—"they say if you look closely enough in the water channels running through this very floor, you can still see the red stains from their blood today."

"No." Simone shook her head, but she did steal a glance down at the water running from the fountain.

"I'm not taking sides, but there are a few rust-colored streaks in the marble there."

"They're probably just variations in the stone."

"Could be," Loreto admitted evenly, then grinned. "Could also be the blood of the beheaded."

Simone's blue eyes sparked with that hint of challenge Loreto couldn't decide if she liked or loathed, and she walked across the room to a man standing behind a security rope. "Excuse me, *hablas inglés?*"

He nodded.

"Good. Do you know if the marble in the floors has naturally red highlights or if that could legitimately be a stain of some sort?"

His smile turned conspiratorial. "The color does appear in a few places around the palace, but then again, blood has been spilled in a few places around the palace as well."

"*Gracias.*" She pursed her lips and turned back to Loreto, who folded her arms across her chest, her smug expression tempered only by the realization of what Simone had just done.

"Where did you learn to do that?"

"Interrogate employees?" Simone asked dryly. "On-the-job training."

"No, I got that, but where did you learn the Spanish phrase to ask locals if they spoke English?"

She waved her hand dismissively. "I heard you use it with the saleswoman back in Málaga yesterday."

Loreto nodded slowly, giving herself the time to process the information.

"What, did I say it wrong?"

"Not at all. I just didn't think you'd put any effort into doing something you're paying me for."

"Then you're surprised?"

Loreto shook her head. "Not really. I guess picking up a few Spanish phrases along the way helps give you a sense of control, and nothing you do to maintain control would surprise me."

Simone eyed her for a moment before one corner of her pink lips gave a slight upward tick. "Good."

Then she turned and wandered off down the next corridor, leaving Loreto to catch up to her this time.

She trailed her from a comfortable distance. The more time they spent here, the more comfortable she grew. She still had the eyes of a woman seeing something for the first time, but her awe had turned to acceptance. She understood the magic around here, the captivating essence it provided, and she flowed along with the current now, soaking up her surroundings and exuding its more alluring qualities back into the world. Beauty, power, poise, elegance, a royal air. Watching her, Loreto understood fully how La Alhambra had held strong for centuries against Catholic kings, only to fall at the hands of a woman.

Had the locals watched Queen Isabella ride in? Had they marveled at her fair skin and light hair among the Moorish emirs. Did she seem out of place to them, or did her eyes tell them all they needed to know about the destiny that lay within her?

Loreto hung back as they reached the balcony that had once been home to the great American author Washington Irving. Would he have had the words to describe this woman who'd come to conquer the region that held his heart captive for so long? Surely, he would have noticed the way her eyes took in the glory around her, awe and appreciation in her gaze, but also something more calculating. In a single sweep of her view, she could both examine and appraise, then catalog it accordingly. And she made no effort to hide her final verdict. When something caught her eye, her expression clearly showcased her interest.

It hadn't escaped Loreto's notice that she fell into that category several times this morning. She wished she hated that fact as much as she hated Simone's colonizing gaze, but there was something alluring about being viewed in the same vein as a fine piece of art. She was drawn to Simone's unrepentant desire much more than she'd been drawn to her money, though she supposed the two sprang from similar sources. Lust, like cold, hard cash could function as an equalizer. It could grant power or withhold it. It might actually be the only true power Loreto could wield when it came to a woman like Simone. Thankfully, it was also one of the only types of power she ever let herself depend on.

"Really?"

Loreto stopped in her tracks as she realized Simone had just asked her a direct question. "Is there really any historical evidence for the legend about the beheadings?"

"Sadly, there's virtually no historical evidence for anything that took place here before 1492."

"Why?"

"When Granada fell, Isabella and Ferdinand set about erasing any indication that the Moors had ever been in Spain. They incinerated every book and archive associated with this place."

"Dear God, why?"

"Isabella arrived."

"Isabella and Ferdinand?"

"Yes, but don't let the equal billing fool you. Her marriage, like everything else in her life, served a primary ambition to rule all of Spain."

"She only married for power?"

Loreto shrugged. "I can't say what happened in the bedroom, but I know what happened in Spain. She was the heir to the region of Castile and he to Aragon. When they combined their royal houses and holdings, they owned the vast majority. I mean seriously, like ninety percent of what we now think of as Spain, and for the first time in human history, it was under the control of the same monarchs."

"They would've been emperors by the standards of the day."

"Exactly. Everything from the mountains in the north down to the sea in the south, all hers to rule and wield, if not for Granada."

"Ah, the old unstoppable-force-immovable-object argument."

"Well, the force won. Driven by ambition, religious zeal, an abject hatred for all Granada represented, she crushed the region and placed herself on the throne in this very building. To

Isabella's mind, this was hers, it had always been hers, and it always would be," Loreto explained. "She was brutal and absolute in her rule."

"I've heard the Inquisition was no joke."

"Understatement of history, but in some ways, her rewriting of history has been the more horrible crime, because the cultural erasure she oversaw largely succeeded. The stories of the Moors, of their genius, their innovation, their intelligence has been largely lost. Their rule in Spain saw to the translation of the works of Plato and Socrates that had been lost in every other part of Europe. Their navigational advancements laid the groundwork for trans-global expeditions, and their introduction of Arabic numbers made advanced mathematics accessible to everyday tradesmen. Yet can you tell me the name of a single Moorish caliph, sultan, or emir?"

Simone shook her head.

"But when I said the name 'Isabella,' you knew exactly who I meant." Loreto shrugged, trying to pretend that didn't bother her. "Winners write the history books." Internally she added, *white, rich, Christian winners*.

Simone frowned, but for once she didn't argue. Perhaps she needed some time to ponder, but more likely, she didn't feel the need to comment on what she likely saw as a natural order. Financial might made right in her world, too.

At the sound of more tourists entering the room behind them, they moved wordlessly forward into the last part of the palace.

This area was darker, cooler, and decorated in wood inlaid with streaks of lighter accents to lace the same geometric patterns that the plaster had held in other rooms, but it had a more solemn and stately feel than the grandiose courtyards.

"I take it we're nearing the end of the tour?" Simone asked.

"Just one more story before we go," Loreto said, trying to inject a bit of lightness into her voice. She couldn't change the past, and even if she could, she wouldn't have wasted those powers on Fifteenth Century Spain. Instead, she chose to relay plots of plays long past performed and let her modern audiences draw their own comparisons. Some of them did, though she honestly didn't expect Simone to do so. Still she forged on, secure in who she was and what she knew about this place and the people who time allowed to pass through.

"The year is 1492," Loreto said, stepping up behind Simone as she examined an ornate alcove. "A man stands before the king and queen. They're new sovereigns of the region they've spent years destroying. Their armies have marched for hundreds of miles, leveling cities, burning mosques and temples, slaughtering anyone who stands in their way, all to sit on the thrones they now occupy. Before they're done, they'll expel over three hundred thousand of the dark-skinned Muslims from the south of a newly unified Spain. For the first time, their empire is free of the people who built the very palace they rule from."

She was not quite whispering in Simone's ear, but she stood near enough to feel heat radiating off her bare arms. "The queen speaks first, because in a world where women always come second to their husbands, Isabella always makes it clear she's the exception."

The corner of Simone's mouth curled up, and Loreto knew she'd hit her mark.

"She looks down on the man groveling before her. He needs money. She has plenty to throw around, but she asks, no, *demands*, an answer to the question of what he'll bring her in return."

"He starts to speak of trade, of spices from India, silks from China, gunpowder to supply an army. She's bored with him, and she makes sure he knows it. She has all the spices of Morocco just across the straits. She's sitting in a palace at the heart of a silk-producing empire, and she needs no more army, as she has just crushed her last remaining threat. She tells him to piss off."

Simone turned to stare at her. "She didn't."

"She most certainly did," Loreto said smugly. "She denied him his request and sent him away."

Color rose in Simone's cheeks as what she thought she knew about her own origins butted up against the disorienting worldview La Alhambra forced her to try to reconcile. Loreto let her sit in that discomfort for a few seconds before she continued. "The legend here says she banished him to the stables to live with the animals for forty days for even daring to speak to her with such familiarity. It's only when he leaves the palace, thrown out like the long lines of Jews and Muslims being driven out of the country, that she calls him back and gives him three ships."

"She changed her mind," Simone said softly.

"As powerful women are allowed to do." Loreto smiled ruefully.

"But why?" Simone asked. "She'd already made her decision. If your story is to be believed, she made it in grand public fashion."

"I don't think we'll ever have the answer for sure, but I suspect when a woman owns everything she's always known she wanted, the only place left to turn is the unknown."

Simone shivered. It was just a shake, a momentary buzz, not enough to be noticed by someone standing at even a polite distance, but Loreto was no longer standing at a distance, and Simone seemed suddenly acutely aware of her proximity.

Stepping back, she looked away, from the floor to the ceiling and then to the door, before breathing a sigh of what sounded very much like relief. "Very interesting. You've given me plenty to think about for the rest of the day."

"Oh yeah?" Loreto asked casually as she strolled along behind Simone, who walked with more speed and purpose, if only toward the exit. "Like what?"

"Like, well, I think . . ." She sighed as they emerged from the building into a wide plaza lined with high edges and sunken pools. Simone turned slowly, her gaze traveling from where they were, over the mountains and down into the cascading whitewashed homes below, then back up at the vast palace they'd just left. "You said they destroyed everything—homes, schools, libraries, temples."

Loreto leaned against a low wall preventing her from falling off into the valley. "Isabella and Ferdinand? Yes."

"But not this place," Simone mused. "They wrecked anything that reminded them any other culture had ever challenged their authority, and yet the Alhambra still stands in all its Moorish glory. Why not level it?"

The depth of the question caught her off guard. She'd never had another tourist ask anything quite so esoteric of her. She took a moment to stare out over the immense complex before turning back to the modern conqueror before her. "I guess everyone has their boundaries. Andalusia just happened to be where Isabella found something she wanted more than total control."

Chapter Five

They drove through the heat of the afternoon again. First west, then north. Mountains gave way to more olive vineyards, then small, whitewashed towns began to appear by the sides of the road, but Simone barely glanced at them. After the morning's tour of the palace, they'd spent another couple of hours wandering around the gardens. They were every bit as beautiful as she'd expected from a culture that had built the Alhambra, filled with color and punctuated with ingenious uses of water, but at some point, her mind had simply become oversaturated.

Even hours after returning to the hotel, she couldn't shake the sense of being unsettled. She didn't know how else to explain it. She just felt off. She'd returned to the ideas that had upset her on the first day in the lobby when she'd met Ren, only on a deeper level. She once again suspected that nothing in this country worked the way it should. Or maybe it didn't work the way she thought it should. And yet she couldn't argue the fact that they did still work. The Alhambra had been a stunning testament to how well beautiful, powerful, enduring masterpieces could thrive here, and yet it also flew in direct opposition to so many things she'd known to be true since childhood.

Staring out the window for a second, she internally recited the old schoolyard rhyme, "In fourteen hundred and ninety-two, Columbus sailed the ocean blue." At what age had she learned the start of that poem, the start of that story, the start of history as she'd been taught? Later, of course, she'd learned more about civilizations like Greece and Rome and the British Empire, but never had she learned about the Moorish rule of Spain. How odd to only now learn the stories to which Columbus was merely a footnote in the momentous events of 1492.

It wasn't that what she'd learned was wrong, so much as it was shallow, incomplete, and centered on telling a different story than the ones she'd always put stock in.

Something about the idea of different stories tripped a trigger in the back of her mind, some inkling of a missing piece.

Pulling out her phone, she googled Juanes Cánovas again. Hundreds of results came pouring in, the vast majority of them in Spanish. Multiple listings for his books on various retail sites, his own website, his publisher's website, myriad interviews, and what appeared to be some fan sites. She'd already been through most of these, of course. She'd even gone so far as to copy and paste several of them into Google translators to get the basic gist. She'd seen several company memos with English language synopses of his books. She had no reason to question his talent, and the marketing department had done detailed write-ups of his crossover potential, sales projections, and possible movie treatments. The only things she hadn't read were the books themselves.

She got stuck once again on this particular stumbling block. She'd been sent to purchase an entire company, to get her hands on a set of books she couldn't even read. But she couldn't read them because they hadn't been translated, and they wouldn't be translated until she bought the company that published them. The frustration rose in her again. Who the hell wouldn't want to have their books translated for consumption of the world at large?

She stared at the results for a long time, looking for another way around this. The job should have been open and closed, and yet it wasn't, or she wouldn't be here. The longer she spent in Spain, the more her doubt began to creep in. What if it didn't add up because it didn't have to? What if there was nothing she could do to make this deal or this country work the way she needed?

She shook her head. She couldn't go there. It wasn't helpful, and it wasn't realistic. There was always a solution, always another angle, always something no one else had thought of or tried. She'd made a career out of being the person to figure these things out. Nothing in her experience suggested she couldn't do the same here. She just needed to solve for the missing variable.

She scrolled back to the top of her search results and went to the sales listings for several of Juanes Cánovas's books, then she pressed the orange button that meant the same thing in any language. Within seconds, the files appeared in her Kindle library, and a few minutes later, Loreto pulled up to a parking spot, killed the engine, and said, "Welcome to Cordoba."

Simone looked up, shocked to find herself in the middle of what appeared to be a small and ancient city. The street she'd parked on was narrow by American standards, but not nearly as small as all the other offshoots around them. In fact, she suspected Loreto had parked the car not out of convenience, but necessity, because it didn't look as though even their compact Peugeot would fit anywhere else.

"How did I miss our arrival into a place like this?" she mused aloud.

Loreto chuckled. "You were in your own world. I tried to point out a few things on the way in, but if you responded at all, it was more of a little hum."

"Work mode," Simone said. "I've been told I can get a little trancey and aloof when I've got business on the brain."

"I figured," Loreto said without much judgment. "The hotel for tonight is only about a block away, and I've been told they have good Wi-Fi even out by the pool."

Simone shook her head. "No thanks. I mean to the pool. The Wi-Fi sounds heavenly."

"I think you got that a little backwards." Loreto hauled both of their carry-on bags from the trunk and started up a cobblestone street. "Generally, people say 'no thanks' to the implements of productivity and that the pool sounds heavenly."

Simone snorted. "Well, lucky for you, my complete love affair with productivity means you get to spend the rest of the day lounging by the pool while I go back to work."

"Work? I thought that's what we've been doing."

"Right, the tour was lovely, and you gave me an alternative perspective to consider, but now I need a couple hours to buckle down and really do my job tonight."

Loreto reached for a gray door in a whitewashed stucco wall, but when her fingers closed around the handle, she didn't pull. She paused, lowering her head, her shoulders rose and fell on a soft exhale.

"What's the matter?" Simone asked.

Loreto looked up, her shallow smile expressing equal parts disappointment and exasperation.

"Nothing, *Rubia*. I'll have some room service sent up for you tonight."

"Now that's a fantastic idea," Simone said, quick to stave off her own unexpected flash of disappointment as she realized that meant they wouldn't be sharing tapas on a terrace tonight. The subtle prick of sentimentality only reaffirmed she'd gotten a little too far from the business element of this trip.

Loreto pushed through the door and stepped into another beautifully rehabbed building. The terra-cotta floors below and exposed wooden beams above had all been polished and shellacked to a gleaming finish, while clerks and bellhops bustled about in crisp, white uniforms. Loreto spoke to the necessary employees to get them checked in. She'd clearly made another good choice in lodging, a property luxurious enough to meet Simone's high standards and rustic enough to still showcase a distinctly Spanish character, blending two styles Simone didn't think could coexist two days ago. She seemed good at working in those spaces between worlds that weren't quite opposites. Classic and contemporary, opulent and comfortable, productive and playful.

As they made their way up a winding staircase and along a balcony lined with blue tiles, she looked down longingly at the pool inset in the courtyard below.

She shook her head. Perhaps Loreto's easygoing blend of work and leisure had started to rub off on her, which was all the more reason to get some distance.

When they reached the doors to their respective rooms, she reached into the pockets of her slacks and pulled out a check she'd written earlier and extended it to Loreto. "Go ahead and take the rest of the night off."

Loreto stared at the check in her hand for a couple of seconds as if trying to process the offer.

Simone grew a little uncomfortable and had even started to wonder if something about the offer had gotten lost in translation, until Loreto took it from her. Without looking at the number, she folded it in two and tucked it into her pocket.

"Have a good evening," Simone said.

"I will," Loreto called as she entered her room. Leaning back into the hallway, she added, "Simone, just remember what you learned this morning."

"Which part?"

"Powerful women are allowed to change their minds." Then she closed the door behind her.

Simone stood there for a moment trying to convince herself Loreto had only been referencing her plans for the evening, but she couldn't help wishing she could close off the disquiet of that parting comment.

"I assume you have another field trip planned for us this morning?" Simone said as they climbed a set of stairs inside the hotel. She was too chatty for Loreto's mood, but they had work to do, so Loreto forced herself to respond.

"You know what they say happens when you assume?"

Simone rolled her eyes. "You're an American, right?"

"No."

Simone frowned. "You don't really have much of an accent."

"Everyone has an accent. You don't hear mine because it's so similar to yours that you've normalized it."

Simone's steps faltered, and she fell a few stairs behind. "I suppose that's true. Nobody thinks of themselves as having an accent."

"Wrong again. You don't think of yourself as having an accent because yours is associated with the seat of power. People who run your business sound like you, the people running your schools sound like you, people in your movies sound like you. You never have to think about your accent, but trust me, people outside that circle are very aware of their accents."

Loreto could practically hear the wheels turning as Simone's brain was forced to consider a perspective other than her own. In Loreto's experience, Americans had two responses in these situations. The first involved a disproportionate urge to argue. The second was to apologize. Simone chose neither, apparently deciding to sit with the information for a while, probably trying to figure out if she could use it to her advantage before she determined how much credence to give the idea.

"I expected us to head out right after breakfast," she said, redirecting them back to her original point. She wanted to know what they were doing today.

Loreto could've told her. It wouldn't hurt anything. It wasn't even an unreasonable request, and yet instead of giving in, Loreto had continually chosen to withhold the itinerary. If pressed hard enough, she could always say she wanted to build anticipation or set the stage for a big reveal, but she wasn't delusional. She could also admit she enjoyed Simone's frustration at not being in complete control.

"What time were you up this morning?" Loreto asked in another transparent dodge.

"A little after five."

"You know if you keep getting up so early, you're never going to be awake for a genuine Spanish dinner." She reached the top of the stairs and waited for Simone to catch up.

"The tapas you had sent up last night sufficed."

"Don't you wonder what you're missing?"

"Not particularly."

"Let's see if we can fix that." Loreto pushed open a door and let her eyes adjust to the morning sunlight flooding a rooftop patio. Flipping down her sunglasses, she turned to see if her point registered at all on Simone's expression.

She had to blink a few times and squint before raising her hand up to her hairline and shading her eyes. Then her jaw slackened and her pursed lips softened. Loreto wondered fleetingly what it would feel like to kiss her. Would her mouth be hard like it looked when she wasn't getting her way, or would those lips yield for her the way they did when something surprised her?

Shaking off the question and all its dangerous implications, she walked right up to the low white wall dividing her from the full expanse of ancient Cordoba.

"Did you eat up here last night?" Simone asked, coming to stand beside her.

"Yes," Loreto said. Pointing to the west, she added, "The sun set in that direction, but that wasn't the best view."

"No?"

"When it drops low on the horizon, it basks all the white buildings in a warm, golden-orange glow and sparkles across the Guadalquivir in flashes of yellow and white. It looks like a line of jewels snaking across a magnificent Andalusian crown."

Simone's eyes scanned the scene below. "The river?"

"Yes, Guadalquivir. Try it."

She repeated the word, frowned, and tried again, loosening up enough to match her inflection. Loreto wondered if she was remembering their earlier quips about accents.

"Every other place in the world, mosques face Mecca, but here, they face the river."

"Mosques?" Simone turned to Loreto as she pointed toward a behemoth structure in the middle of the city. High support beams lifted a domed roof into the sky to tower over all the surrounding houses and buildings, and on top, an ornate spire and steeple rose even taller than the rest.

"Doesn't look like any mosque I've ever seen," Simone observed. "Though, admittedly, I've only seen a handful."

Loreto respected her a bit more for admitting the last part. "It's also a cathedral."

Simone raised her eyebrows. "And I suppose if I'd chosen to dine up here with you last night, I would've heard the story behind that little curiosity."

Loreto shrugged. She didn't want to be annoyed that Simone had chosen to hole up in her room with all this splendor at her doorstep, and she damn sure didn't want to feel anything about having missed her company, so she simply said, "You'll catch up."

"I take it that's our field trip for this morning."

She nodded.

"Did you get us early entry tickets?"

"No." Loreto pushed off the sidewall and headed back to the stairs. "We're scheduled for a ten o'clock slot."

Simone glanced down at the silver watch adorning her slender wrist. "That's two hours from now."

She didn't feel any inclination to respond to such a needless statement of the obvious.

"Are you going to offer up any suggestions as to how to productively fill our time for the next two hours?"

"Well," Loreto shrugged, not loving Simone's tone, "there's a pool."

She rolled her eyes, and Loreto bit the inside of her cheek to keep from smiling.

"I'm sure you've got some spreadsheets or emails you could go type on. You business types do that, right?"

"Type on emails?"

"Yeah."

Simone shook her head. "I suppose we do, but I don't know why we couldn't get an earlier timeslot to start our main event of the day."

"Because it doesn't open until ten," Loreto said flatly.

"Why not?"

She couldn't hide a chuckle. "Priests are lazy? Maybe the nuns can't get past their hangovers from the night before until mid-morning, or perhaps, I don't know, maybe they insist on holding mass for their parishioners before they do their little song and dance for rich American tourists who've come to mock their solemnity."

Simone took a step back, her cheeks flushing pink and her baby blues blinking as if Loreto had just transfigured in front of her and she couldn't believe what she'd just seen. Finally, she said, "Did you just quote Shakespeare?"

Loreto leaned back against the wall again. Seriously, that's what she took away from the conversation? She shook her head. Of course it was, because it was the only part inconsistent with her worldview. Yesterday, she'd learned Loreto hadn't gone to college and tucked her into a box labeled uneducated. Typical. "You're not the only one who can read."

"No." Simone shook her head. "I didn't mean to imply . . . I just found the quote . . ."

"Out of place," Loreto said, then sighed. "It probably was for you, but Spain works the way Spain works. That's what you said you wanted to learn about, and vague as those instructions may be, I'm trying to deliver. However, I can't simultaneously teach you about this place and make it bend to your will. You can have breakfast at seven, but you cannot go into UNESCO World Heritage sites until they open. You can have tapas in your room at six every night, but you cannot eat dinner on the terrace until ten. You can make me bend to your will, but when you do, you're going to miss out on the experiences you claim to be seeking. Choose whichever way you want, but you can't have both."

Simone's jaw tightened until a little muscle twitched, but to her credit, she didn't snap back. Instead, she rolled her head to one side and then the other before responding. "Okay. You've made your point."

"I have?"

"We've got two hours to kill. I want to be productive, but I'm fresh out of spreadsheets to—how did you put it?—'type on.'" One corner of her mouth twitched up in the way Loreto hated to love. "You're the expert in this area. How would you choose to spend that time?"

Loreto thought about the answer, but before she could respond, Simone cut back in. "Please don't say the pool."

Now it was Loreto's turn to grit her teeth. That hadn't been what she was going to suggest, but knowing that's what Simone still expected from her did inspire a quick fantasy of shoving her off the balcony into the cold water two stories below. Still, if Simone could show restraint, so could she. "Actually, we're staying in the historic Jewish quarter. We could stroll through the area for a while and end up on the other side of the mosque right around ten."

"Just stroll around aimlessly for nearly two hours and do—" Simone seemed to catch herself, then bit her lip and started again. "Okay, sure. A Jewish quarter on our way to a mosque-cathedral. Sounds like there's probably something, I don't know, educational? Interesting? Complicated?"

Loreto smiled genuinely for the first time all morning. "D. All of the above. Let's go."

"Why do I get the sense this whole Jewish quarter trip was a not-so-elaborate excuse for you to get more churros?" Simone asked, only partly kidding.

"That's ridiculous," Loreto said seriously. "I don't need an excuse to get churros."

Simone supposed that was probably true, but it didn't help that their supposedly educational, interesting, complicated stroll through the Jewish quarter had thus far consisted of a beeline for the nearest *churreria*.

"You want some?" Loreto pushed the plate across the table toward her without waiting for an answer.

"I already had breakfast back at the hotel."

"So did I, and you didn't actually answer my question. I asked if you wanted some."

"Now you care about direct answers to questions," Simone said dryly. "I didn't think that was really your MO."

Loreto laughed in that maddening way that said she wasn't

going to bite on whatever hook she'd had thrown at her and pulled the churros back to her side of the table. "Your body, your choice."

"For someone who's not an American, you sure do use a lot of American idioms."

Loreto shrugged and dipped her churros in barely liquified chocolate so rich and creamy Simone suffered a pinprick of regret at taking a negative stand on second breakfast. Then, as Loreto shoved half the churro into her mouth, Simone realized she'd once again dodged giving an actual answer to the question of her origin. Was that purposeful, or just another annoying instance where she seemed to take pleasure in withholding information?

Before she had a chance to really ponder the implications of either option, Loreto finished chewing and gestured to the whitewashed building closing in tightly around their patio table. "This is the Jewish quarter."

"Enlightening."

Loreto shrugged. "It's one of the oldest Jewish neighborhoods in Europe. Actually, Spain has several of them. Its heyday ran from the late ninth century until the fifteenth century, the same in Sevilla. Toledo's lasted a little longer."

Loreto met and held her gaze. It was something she did just rarely enough for the impact of her deep-brown eyes to still catch Simone off guard. She felt as though she were waiting for something. Something she wasn't sure she had, much less wanted to offer.

"Notice anything about those dates?" Loreto prodded gently.

As she reviewed them again, a connection floated to the surface of her mind. "They overlap with the Moorish rule of Spain. Wait, the Muslims and the Jews coexisted?"

"And when the Christians took over, they ran them both out at the point of the same sword."

"Isn't that the opposite of how world religions tend to function now?" she asked. "I mean, I'm not overly religious, but I thought the Christians and the Jews generally worked together more often than Muslims and Jews."

"There you go. The first complex lesson of the Jewish quarter is that alliances are fleeting and always shifting. The changes may seem too slow and subtle for us to see them in our own moments of history, but studying Spain proves nothing is fixed."

Simone nodded, once again struck by the level of Loreto's insight and the way what she knew about the world unnerved what Simone knew. Then again, unnerved was becoming a perpetual state in this country, and with this woman.

She glanced around the narrow, sloping, stone streets and noticed again virtually no one was out and about. They'd even had to knock on the locked door to the *churreria*, despite signs clearly indicating they should be open. And now it was past 9:00, but all the shops within their small circle of view remained shuttered.

"They'll open," Loreto said around half a mouthful of churro.

"When?"

"When they're ready."

"And we're just supposed to intuit when that will be?"

Loreto shrugged. "Or you could wait."

"Wait," she repeated, hearing the ire in her voice.

"That's the crux of it all, isn't it?" Loreto asked. "You can't stand being made to wait."

"On the contrary," Simone said, forcing herself to sit back in her chair and loosen her jaw. "I do nothing but wait."

Loreto raised an eyebrow. "I thought you worked, and created opportunities, and studied, and prowled, and pounced."

"I do those things, too," Simone admitted. "But I'm always waiting. Always biding my time. Always biting my tongue. Always pacing until it's my turn to take the lead."

"And when will that be?" Loreto asked, sounding genuinely interested.

Simone closed her eyes, tilted back her head, and breathed slowly. "Soon."

"After you close this deal here in Spain?"

"Possibly. It depends on how important this acquisition turns out to be."

"And does it kill you not to know?"

"Yes, but not as much as it burns to feel like I'm wasting my time."

"And that's what this whole trip feels like, does it?" Loreto asked without judgment.

"At times. I gave up my first real vacation in years to be here. I was supposed to be sitting on a beach, or shopping in Milan, or dining at five-star restaurants, or—"

"Alone?" Loreto cut in.

"If I wanted to be," Simone said quickly and wondered if she'd tipped her hand. She hadn't traveled with anyone else in a long time, and she hadn't had anyone she'd wanted to travel with in longer than that. "I'd looked forward to a week of doing whatever I wanted, whenever I wanted, with whomever I wanted."

Loreto smiled. "You could still make those things happen."

She sighed. She knew she could. She also knew she couldn't. "I don't generally mix business with pleasure."

Loreto didn't argue. Instead, she rose and arched her back. A sliver of her flat stomach showed between her low-riding cargo shorts and the black polo Simone had purchased for her. Simone's temperature rose slightly. Loreto lowered her eyes and caught her staring. Her smile grew slowly before she flipped down her sunglasses and said, "That's a shame."

Simone's temperature shot up another few degrees. The low timbre of Loreto's voice and the comment dripped with sensuality, but she didn't have a chance to linger in the moment as her guide sauntered off around a corner, leaving her to catch up once again.

"Do you like this?" Loreto held up a scarf when Simone joined her in the doorway of a store selling silk. "It's a fine price."

"It's a fine silk." Simone ran the blue and white scarf through her fingers.

"Of course," Loreto said. "It wouldn't be a fine price for a poor-quality silk."

Simone smiled slightly, suggesting her mood had lightened somewhat. Loreto didn't know what to make of the back and forth. Simone had obviously spent years training herself not to overreact, even when she clearly held an almost constant seething just below the surface.

Loreto had had plenty of occasion to take the tight-laced tourist type and break their restraint, but she sensed something different in Simone, something stronger, something darker, something that, when snapped, may never fit fully back together again. Perhaps that's why she hadn't pushed into her full, seductive press yet. She wasn't sure she wanted to be in the vicinity when Simone cracked, much less be the one to cause it.

And still, she did enjoy pushing this woman's buttons. She enjoyed the way her cheeks colored when she got flustered. She liked the way curly little tendrils of her hair fell down around her temples when she stayed out in the heat too long. She liked the way her jaw twitched when she had to concede a point to Loreto. Then again, she also enjoyed the playful little half-smile she tried to suppress but simply couldn't. But she also hated that she cared at all about this woman's moods, hated that she gave so much thought to how she affected them. Perhaps Simone wasn't the only one responsible for their up and down trajectory.

"I'll take it." Simone pinched the scarf between her fingers and pulled slowly so the length of it slid across Loreto's palm. "Actually, I'll take two of them."

"Two?" Loreto asked. "Of the same one?"

"Yes." Simone breezed past her, entering into the store without further explanation. She stopped in front of a rack holding silk shells and undershirts. She held up one in red before putting it back and picking up another in deep, emerald green.

Loreto watched, trying not to imagine how luscious her bare shoulder would look against the smooth, rich fabric.

"I'll take this one as well." She casually held it and the scarves out to Loreto. "And a set of those sheets along the back wall, in the midnight blue, king size."

"I take it you'd like me to handle the transaction?"

Simone nodded. "I'll join you in a moment."

She took that as her cue not to follow and instead set about procuring the desired items, once again marveling at her mixed emotions surrounding Simone's commanding demeanor. Or maybe emotion wasn't the most accurate term. Did lust and loathing count as emotions? Moods? Inclinations?

She didn't have the answer, despite having plenty of time to ponder, as Simone disappeared.

"Women," the middle-aged clerk said in Spanish, as if offering a total explanation.

Loreto set about having Simone's purchases tallied, bagged, and addressed to be sent back to their hotel before noon. She'd just about finished when Simone reappeared holding a skimpy piece of black silk and lace Loreto didn't recognize at first. It was too big for a napkin, way too small for a tablecloth, too unevenly cut for a towel, and being silk, it probably wasn't something to wipe her hands on.

"I'd like this added to my order." Simone handed it over by the straps.

Straps. Loreto's mind made the connection. The thin sliver of silk dangling from her index finger was a piece of lingerie, that would presumably, at some point, hang from Simone's alabaster shoulders.

She did not blush. She did not comment. She didn't even hold it up for a more complete inspection. But she did imagine what it might look like if worn properly, and her imagination left little doubt that Simone would wear it exceedingly well. Her mouth went dry and her brain a little woozy as she battled mental images that set her teeth on edge.

She had the wherewithal to wonder whether the purchase was meant to inspire such a physical reaction. Maybe Simone wanted to remind her of what she couldn't have. Or maybe she hadn't given a second thought to Loreto and her maddening libido.

She didn't know which idea stung less.

"Should we start making our way down to the main event?" Simone asked as they stepped into a now-sunny lane. They'd been inside the store for only fifteen minutes, but the sun peeked over the roofs to their right, or their left. They seemed to keep doubling back on themselves around tight corners or crooks in the narrow road that would have barely qualified as an alley in New York. Simone was totally turned around, and the way the light spun her sense of time into overdrive didn't help her disorientation.

"We'll get there," Loreto said in a tone completely devoid of urgency.

The silk store had been a nice little diversion, or maybe part of the lessons. Apparently silk had been produced in Andalucía for centuries, though it hardly seemed to create a thriving economy at present. The only economy in the area now appeared to be primarily tourist based, and she'd just substantially contributed to it. Though try as she might to justify the purchase through some cultural lens, nothing they'd done or discussed today fell solidly under the heading of work.

And yet, she hadn't exactly been on vacation, either. She hadn't spent any time by the pool. She hadn't eaten a single dinner since she'd been here. She hadn't even had any of the churros Loreto seemed fond of. And while she had purchased some silk products, if she clung to her rules about not mixing business with pleasure, she didn't suppose she'd have an occasion to wear her favorite of those items anytime soon.

The thought ratcheted up her frustration another level. She was getting nowhere on any front. Back home she worked hard, she played hard. She could excel at either, but she couldn't thrive in this liminal space. She had no frame of reference for the pace and duality that seemed so pervasively annoying here.

She glanced at her watch to see it approaching 10:00. She would have felt better about the semblance of a schedule, except their tour started in five minutes and they still hadn't checked in. And she hated to be late.

"Is the mosque nearby?" she asked after another minute or two of walking. Or strolling. Or ambling. Or whatever word described the way Loreto moved without any sense of urgency through streets that had all started to look alike. Or maybe they *were* the same streets and they were walking in circles. She didn't know

105

how she'd tell. The buildings they passed were all white with yellow or blue trim, and all the storefronts showcased the same racks of postcards and decorative hand fans.

"You see all the kitsch they're selling?" Loreto asked, as if reading her mind. "That's how you know you're getting close to a major tourist attraction."

She nodded. The comment was so logical, she wondered why she hadn't made the connection. At least now if she got lost, she'd follow the shops until she came to a major hub, then fall on the mercy of an English speaker, who also seemed more prevalent the closer she got to international tour stops. Not that she intended to get lost. Loreto, for all her faults, had more than proved herself capable as a guide and navigator, but Simone hated being dependent on anyone.

"There." Loreto pointed up at a towering wall with a more reddish-orange hue.

Simone glanced at her watch again. One minute to tour time. Not technically late, but too close for her comfort level.

"Now we just need to walk around the outer walls to the other side and enter through the courtyard."

"The other side? How big is this place?"

"Big." Loreto didn't sound concerned. "I mean the inside alone is the size of a couple football fields. Then you add on the courtyards and the outer walls. Oh, and there's the minaret over there, though I suppose if you're a Christian, it's a bell tower, but—"

"Loreto?" Simone cut her off, no longer trying to hide the tension in her voice. "We're late."

"We're fine." Loreto waved her off and pointed to a spire rising up above the rest of the walls. "Originally there weren't any bells. The Muslim *muezzin* would climb a winding set of stairs to the top and call the city to prayer five times a day."

Simone wasn't really listening. "I don't really like to be late."

"I told you, we're fine." Loreto dismissed her again. "As I was saying, the *muezzin* had access to the highest point in the city, which dictated the person holding the position be blind."

"And I told you," Simone asserted more fully, "I'm not comfortable blowing off commitments and schedules. You told me we'd start our tour at ten, and I prefer you maintain a professional adherence to what few plans you make when in my employ."

Loreto whirled around. "And I'd prefer you give me the professional courtesy of letting me do the job you've actually employed me to do."

"The tour started—"

"When I decided it did."

"You said at ten."

"Which is exactly when we arrived at the outer walls and I began to speak about the scope of the building, followed by pointing out the most distinctive feature of the mosque visible from the outside and trying to explain its various uses under different owners."

"But—"

"But you keep shooting off your mouth about what's not happening instead of paying attention to what's right in front of you, you stuck . . ." Loreto's voice trailed off as she apparently realized she'd lost her cool and, in doing so, stepped outside of the professional arena.

Perhaps Simone's tightly clenched jaw and the heat rising in her cheeks had helped foster Loreto's awareness, because she was currently fighting hard to bite back the two words she most wanted to say in that moment. It took physical restraint not to utter the phrase that would send Loreto and her insubordinate attitude packing.

You're fired.

She'd said it a fair number of times on her rise up the career ladder. Most of the time, she hadn't relished the task. Occasionally, she'd taken pleasure in uttering the words, but she'd never done so on a whim.

"I'm sorry." The words left Loreto's lips far more quickly and seemingly effortlessly than they'd ever left Simone's, and that fact took some of the steam out of her boiling anger.

"I guess I could've let you know the official tour started the minute we saw the walls around La Mezquita. I thought I was making myself clear when I tried to tell my story about the minaret," Loreto continued.

Simone gritted her teeth. Had she been clear? Had Simone even given her the chance? She shook her head slowly.

"No?" Loreto asked. "Shall I start over?"

Simone shook her head again, swallowing a knot of anger. She didn't quite know who the emotion was directed at anymore. At Loreto, for certain, for her maddening sense of informality and her insubordinate tone, and the flash of temper that seemed so discordant with her general nonchalance. But also at herself, which bothered her more. She hated being wrong. She hated missing cues. She hated having to second-guess. She hated having to control herself when she didn't have control of a situation. "Continue."

Loreto eyed her for a moment, her gaze suspicious and curious all at once. "Okay, so the, um, *muezzin* who would climb the tower, he'd have to be blind."

Simone struggled to focus on the words over the blood still pounding in her ears. "Why?"

"Because, well, normally I make the students guess why, but I get the feeling you're not really up for guessing games at the moment, so let's just look at how tall the minaret is and say the ladies of Granada would often bathe in their courtyards or rooftop terraces."

"Seriously?" Simone asked, the absurdity of the solution overcoming some of her frustration. "They blinded people so they wouldn't be Peeping Toms at prayer time?"

Loreto smiled. "I think they probably found them already blind, but now that you mention it, I've never researched that process."

Simone glanced up at the tower high overhead, noticing for the first time the large bells nestled under the pyramid cap. "I think the bells might be a better option."

Loreto shrugged. "I guess it depends on what you're into."

Loreto was still mildly shaken half an hour into the tour. She'd recovered her professional stride well enough by the time they'd finished touring the courtyard. Dates of construction and conquest weren't ever hard for her to recall, and her spiels about the mosque's elaborate infinity forests of marble and basalt columns didn't challenge her anymore. She'd given the speech enough times to recite the figures in her sleep. No, nothing about this rote delivery of very basic tourist trivia should've bothered her.

And yet, her heart still beat with an abnormal speed, and her breath still felt too shallow, and her fingers still twitched and tingled every time she met Simone's electric eyes inadvertently. She didn't know what had come over her and why it hadn't passed by now.

"Why didn't the Christians build their own church?"

"Why create a masterpiece of your own when you can appropriate someone else's?" Loreto asked rhetorically, then hearing the slight edge in her voice, she forced a smile. "I think the best word is 'domination.' They'd just pillaged one of the last crowns in Andalucía. They wanted to show they could do whatever they wanted with it."

"Well, you have to admit," Simone said, standing in the doorway where the mosque's low ceilings ended and the gothic cathedral arches shot high into a cavernous space above them, "the Christians were no architectural slouches, either."

She nodded reluctantly, though once again she didn't understand that emotion. She had no personal ties to either religion or style of building. And Simone wasn't wrong. As much as she preferred the algebraic elegance of Moorish arches, she had no reason not to acknowledge the marvels of the soaring Christian ceilings.

"They took something powerful and important and made it their own," Simone continued.

"Sure, if you're a fan of blasphemy and gouging your half of history out of someone else's accomplishments," Loreto said with as much casualness as she could manage. "You can see where Columbus took his cues from, though."

109

Simone turned from the doorway to look back at her. "How so?"

Loreto fought the urge to flip her sunglasses down and instead stared up at the sculpted image of St. Peter with his keys overhead. "You know, barge into someone else's civilization, vandalize the hell out of it, and then claim it was always meant to be yours from the beginning."

Simone snorted softly.

"You think I'm wrong?"

"Not at all. I was just trying to figure out how all the high school students and teachers like your militant little outbursts in the middle of their art and architecture tours."

"I . . . well, I guess I don't give them the same tour."

"Hmm," Simone hummed as she stepped fully through the doorway into the church. "Probably for the best."

Of course it was. Loreto knew better than to bring politics into her work. Hell, she didn't even bring politics into her life. She hadn't so much as breathed a contentious opinion to any of her clients in years. They were just that, opinions. She didn't care if Simone, or anyone else, shared them. She certainly didn't expend any energy trying to change anyone's mind.

But it did annoy her how much Simone moved with such self-assuredness, the way she viewed everything through such a cold lens, the way she managed to wave away the destruction of an entire civilization and yet completely blow her top at the thought of being two minutes late.

Loreto squeezed her fist so tightly several of her knuckles popped. Damn it, there she was, doing it again, letting Simone get under her skin. Why did she let Simone get her so riled up? So what if she didn't understand? So what if she didn't respect her? Those things were true of seventy percent of the tourists she worked with on a daily basis. Not one of them had ever made her lose her cool.

"You were saying about Columbus?" Simone asked, her voice so close and so cool the hair on Loreto's neck stood up.

"Uh, I forget."

110

"Something about this place and the way it inspired the voyage to the Americas?"

She shook her head, more in an effort to scramble her previous thoughts than to indicate disagreement. "It's not a direct correlation so much as a pervasive mindset. It's the idea that if you're stronger, you can take what you want and make it what you want it to be without considering what or who happened to be there first."

"Right, but in this case, the Muslims weren't even here first. You said the mosque was built on the site of a Visigoth church," Simone said, running the tips of her fingers along the smoothly polished wood of a church pew.

"And the Visigoth church had likely been built on some sort of pagan ground," Loreto admitted, trailing slowly behind her, "but the Moors are believed to have paid for land, and they allowed Jews and Christians to live among them, even at the height of their empire. It's that coexistence that allowed cities like Granada and Cordoba and Málaga to thrive."

"So what? I'm not sure what you're advocating for."

"I'm not advocating for anything," Loreto said quickly, maybe too quickly. "I'm just relaying what happened here."

"You don't sound neutral. You seem to side with the Moors coming in and taking Spain because they made the place better in your opinion, but you get worked up about the Christians doing the same thing."

"It's not the same thing." Loreto fought to keep her voice low in the hushed sanctuary. "The Moors took over, yes, and they did so with force if needed, but they welcomed immigrants, dissenters, different ideas, and cultures."

"And then they used them all to the advantage of their rule, which they maintained for almost eight centuries. It sounds like you're calling for a kinder, gentler Columbusing."

"No," she snapped, "that guy can fu—"

Simone's eyebrows shot up, and several people turned to stare as Loreto barely bit back the profanity. It didn't matter, none of the surprise on their faces could match the shock she felt at her own outburst.

111

"No," she said, with a pathetic attempt at approximating calm. "I wouldn't advocate for any brand of Columbusing. None."

Simone's smile flickered, then faded. "I'm not sure you should go quite that far. If not for Columbus, neither one of us would be here right now."

Loreto stopped short as the fire burned from her cheeks all the way up to her brain. She couldn't form a complete thought, much less give it coherent voice, so instead, she stood rooted to the stone floor, a rage she hadn't felt in years boiling up inside her chest.

Simone took several more steps into the choir stalls before seeming to realize Loreto wasn't following her anymore. Turning slowly, her eyes skimmed over Loreto from head to toe, then back up again. This time Loreto didn't shrink from the scrutiny.

"Is there a problem?"

"Do you have any concept of the privilege you have to be steeped in to make a statement like that?"

"Excuse me?"

"You. Not 'we.' *You* wouldn't be here without Columbus, or whatever impossibly blond ancestor sailed over to subjugate mine."

"Subjugate?" Simone's eyes narrowed. "Where are you from?"

"Nowhere." Loreto turned and started to walk back toward the door. "It doesn't matter."

"Which is it?" Simone pushed. "'Nowhere,' or 'it doesn't matter?'"

"Both, but that's beside the point. You're not paying for my past. You don't have any right to assume where I've come from or where I'd be without you or your people."

"I don't see how this tour became about our pasts or *my people*."

"And that's why you're not going to ink the publishing deal," Loreto snapped.

"What?"

"You don't get it. Maybe you can't get it."

"Get what?"

"The world doesn't revolve around you and your platinum card. We don't all think like you. We don't all view the world through your blue eyes. We don't all owe our ancestry to guys named Chris or Eric or John."

"I understand that."

"You don't," Loreto shot back, then she sighed at the futility of it all. "You can't."

"I can do whatever I damn well please."

Loreto laughed at the sickening truth of that blunt statement. "You doubt me?"

Loreto shook her head and turned to go. "No, *Rubia*. You're absolutely right."

"Then why are you walking away from me?"

Loreto shrugged and kept strolling toward the exit. "Tour's finished. Stay as long as you like. I'll meet you out front when you're done."

She didn't look back, not at the sound of Simone's footsteps, or her sigh of frustration, or the silence that eventually fell behind her. She didn't even draw a full breath until she stepped back into the sun-filled courtyard.

Making a beeline for the scattered shade of a small orange tree, she dropped to the ground below, leaning her back against the solid trunk and drawing one knee to her chest. She stared at the mulch under her foot, the Rorschach pattern of light the leaves cast around her, the back of her own eyelids. She poured every bit of focus she had left into examining any detail she could to keep herself from homing in on the one question she didn't want to answer.

Why had she let Simone drag her back there?

Chapter Six

Simone stayed in the dim confines of the mosque for several minutes after Loreto left. She wished she were trying to use the cool air to soothe her anger, but despite her frustration with Loreto's outburst, annoyance never flared that far. Instead, the feelings plaguing her now felt entirely more elusive. She couldn't shake the sense that she'd been close to something, something Loreto instinctively knew, something she felt sure would cost Simone her business deal. She didn't take that kind of knowledge lightly, yet she hadn't been able to push for more in the moment when it seemed to matter most. She'd let Loreto walk away.

Simone placed a palm flat against a nearby marble column. One in a forest of hundreds, they stretched out in every direction, and still she couldn't see them all from where she stood. The church in the middle of the mosque, beautiful and blasphemous, rose up defiantly to tower over them all. There was something in that contrast she couldn't comprehend, or maybe she simply made sense of it in a way vastly different than Loreto did. The difference shouldn't have been surprising. Art and beauty, and even history, all lay in the eye of the beholder, but the fire flashing in Loreto's normally dark eyes had spoken to something more than mere artistic interpretation. She generally wouldn't care if someone else's opinion differed from her own, but it wasn't just Loreto's wide, angry eyes that stirred her. She had a job to do, a job that seemed increasingly dependent on the woman who'd just stormed out on her.

She didn't make a habit of running after women, but she also didn't get to where she was in life without chasing a few unorthodox opportunities. When her pride butted up against her drive, she'd always chosen the latter. Setting her jaw and stealing her reserve, she stepped out into the sunlight.

Scanning the now-busy courtyard, it took her a few seconds to notice Loreto sitting on the ground. Something about the sight of her slouched shoulders and crooked knee held tight to her chest made her look smaller and younger. Simone's heart tightened in a way completely different from the tension in her jaw, and for a second, she questioned whether the entirety of her motivation to reconnect stemmed from a desire to seal a business deal. She shook away the silly thought. Loreto was an attractive but maddening means to an end.

Still, that little flash of affection had the power to make her job a little easier, or more enjoyable, and she clung to it as she approached her guide.

"I'm done with the mosque, or cathedral," she declared as she drew close, seeming to startle Loreto out of a daydream.

Loreto blinked up at her a few times, then slowly got to her feet without saying anything.

"What else is on the agenda for today?"

Loreto glanced up at the sun now shining high overhead, then back at Simone. "If you're ready to go, we should probably get on the road."

Simone shook her head. "I know I said you could set the schedule, but . . ."

"You retained veto power over me," Loreto finished.

"Right." Veto and power were two of the exact words she'd used a few days ago, and Loreto recounted them without any apparent judgment, but somehow the terms sounded more oppressive than balanced now, and a power imbalance seemed to play into their argument. "I didn't mean to overrule your judgement in this case, so much as defer to it."

Loreto raised her eyebrows.

"Yeah, I thought that might get your attention," Simone said wryly. "I only thought, perhaps, we should break up the schedule a little bit so it's more, well, Spanish."

"I'm listening."

"Perhaps we should try eating a later lunch, then take in the tradition of the siesta."

"You want to take a nap?"

"No," she answered quickly, then caught herself. "I only meant that if I intended to join you for dinner at nine o'clock—"

"Ten o'clock," Loreto interjected.

"Fine, ten o'clock," she said, with minimal wariness, "then perhaps we should spend this afternoon resting instead of traveling."

Loreto shrugged. Not quite the response she'd expected for such a concession.

"I just get the sense that there's more here for me to learn today, and perhaps if we stay a little longer, do some more exploring, maybe try to spend this evening the way you suggested I spend last night . . ."

"It's a long way until dinner," Loreto said.

Simone blew out a frustrated breath. Why did Loreto have to disagree with her even when she was trying to be agreeable? "So you don't think we should stay?"

"I wouldn't go that far."

"How far would you go?"

Loreto's eyes turned infinitely dark as she seemed to ponder the question. As the silence stretched between them, Simone started to fear she'd once again stepped across another invisible line. She was about to retract the question entirely and tell Loreto to forget she'd said anything, when she offered an unexpected answer.

"Sangria."

"The drink?"

"Yes," Loreto said. "You asked how far I'd go in reference to our afternoon plans?"

Still unable to make sense of the non-sequitur, she asked, "And you'd go as far as sangria?"

"Yes," Loreto said emphatically, as if that offered some sort of resolution.

Simone stared at her, waiting to see if this was some sort of joke, but when Loreto didn't crack a smile, she began to suspect it might instead be a test. Not wanting to fail or shrink from a challenge, she bit back every other instinct for control and said, "Lead the way."

"This is quite good." Simone sipped from the large glass of ruby liquid in her hand.

"Don't sound so surprised," Loreto said drolly.

Simone rolled her eyes. "I didn't expect turpentine or anything, but this is more fruit than alcohol."

"Practically juice," Loreto said, the wariness she'd felt over the last hour slowly being undercut by amusement.

"Technically, all wine is grape juice," Simone said, holding her glass up to the light streaming through the window next to their table, "but this has actual fruit in it."

"I suppose that's better than fake fruit."

Simone shook her head and pursed her lips, but instead of offering some sharp retort, she merely took another healthy sip of the sangria before saying, "It's refreshing."

"Maybe too refreshing." Loreto tipped her glass slightly toward Simone, then took a swig without taking her eyes off the woman across from her. She didn't know what had come over Simone back in the mosque. After the way Loreto had blown her top, she'd merely wanted to escape. Then she'd spent her first moments in the courtyard trying not to examine why Simone pushed her buttons in ways no one had in years. But as time went on, she'd started to consider that she might have the same effect on her employer. She'd seen the color rise in Simone's cheeks and the spark of indignation in her eyes. She suspected few people had the nerve or stupidity to talk to Simone so frankly, and few of them ever got the chance to do so more than once.

She'd fully expected to be fired the moment Simone had stepped into the courtyard. Part of her had even welcomed the ax, but it had never dropped. Instead, for the second time in as

117

many hours, Simone displayed a considerable amount of restraint in her response. Both times, Loreto had clearly lit her fuse and then waited in certainty of the impending explosion, but both times, she'd underestimated Simone's ability to maintain composure. Something about that kind of control scared her, and she had tread carefully on their walk back through the oldest part of town to their hotel bar.

"I can hardly taste the alcohol."

"Which makes it dangerous," Loreto explained. "It's meant for sipping instead of guzzling."

"I'm not guzzling," Simone said, then added, "I'm trying, okay?"

The flash of earnestness lowered Loreto's defenses another notch. It wasn't that she hadn't seen other little hints of something genuine in Simone, but it had been a while, and she still had no idea what had sparked this most recent bout. As much as Loreto wanted to believe some of what she'd said about Simone's insular worldview had gotten through to her, she doubted it had. More likely, the points she'd made about her impending business deal had struck a chord. Still, whatever string she'd tugged had had some mood-altering effects, and perhaps instead of overthinking, she could just be grateful, or at least take advantage of Simone's agreeability while she had it.

"You're right. I've got you day-drinking." Loreto cracked a little grin. "I think that constitutes a breakthrough."

"Are you saying all I need to do is get sloshed at noon and I'll unlock the key to Spanish culture?"

"Not at all. And you have to stop associating laid-back with lazy. You have to stop associating taking breaks with doing nothing. You have to stop thinking of different schedules as being the same as no schedule."

"I understand what you're saying," Simone said, almost apologetically. "And I want to buy into what you're talking about with the different-is-good pitch, but I can't buy something I don't see, and I don't see anything in your busy schedule of churros and sangria that suggests some profound level of productivity."

"Spain's GDP is thirteenth in the world," Loreto said flatly, "almost dead even with Russia. I don't hear anyone calling the Russians slackers. Why should the Spanish get slapped with that label just because they aren't working themselves into an early grave? In fact, Spaniards have one of the highest life expectancies in the world."

"Wait, back up. Spain has the same domestic output as Russia?"

"Roughly, and they do it without freezing their asses off or dying young."

"What's the primary export?"

Loreto shook her head.

"You don't know?" Simone asked, a bit of her incredulity creeping back into her tone. You've memorized the numbers on international rankings of gross domestic products, but you don't know what those products are?"

"I do know, but—"

"Then what are they?"

"A lot of cars and auto parts. Also, Spain is one of the world's frontrunners in renewable energy technologies, but the main issue is the way they manage to compete globally without succumbing to the rat race. We beat them without joining them."

Simone pulled out her phone and began to tap the screen rapidly. "Does Spain export the power itself, or the tech used to harness it?"

"Both actually, but—"

"What type of renewables?"

"Wind mostly, but also solar, but—"

"And I assume the production of turbines and panels falls under a manufacturing boon?"

"Simone." Loreto raised her voice enough to break through the barrage of questions. "You're missing it!"

"No, I'm getting this," she said without looking up from her phone. "The focus on renewables is—"

"Wrong." Loreto cut back in. "It's the wrong angle. You went down the wrong wormhole. You're doing it again."

"Doing what?"

119

"Missing the point. Forcing your own worldview on a set of statistics you completely misread. You're assuming everyone thinks like you when they don't."

Simone pursed her lips, and Loreto worried she'd once again overstepped the bounds of her employ, but she hadn't gotten fired yet, so she decided to push on.

"The production numbers aren't anything impressive when you look at them on their own. Honestly, they're similar to France and Italy, but what sets Spain apart is how they arrive at those figures."

"Which is why I asked about the specific exports," Simone said exasperatedly.

"And I'm trying to tell you you're confusing the 'what' with the 'how,'" Loreto shot back, her own frustration matching Simone's now. "The key to their economic rankings is only seen when you compare it to things like general life expectancy, worker satisfaction, mental health, and standard of living."

Simone sat back and set down the phone. "Go on."

"Spain doesn't sacrifice quality of life for financial gain, not on a national level, and not generally on a personal level. So many countries that have happy populations have low output, while countries with relatively high output end up with poor health and satisfaction ratings. We manage to fall into the top twenty or higher in almost every category. We're running the table."

Simone seemed to think for a moment. Reaching for her glass and taking a slower sip of sangria, she nodded. "Okay, how?"

"Balance," Loreto answered.

"Balance?" Simone scoffed. "All that entire economic spiel you just dropped like it's hot, and your one-word conclusion is 'balance?'"

Loreto laughed. "Sorry, it's not rocket science. If you value work and life equally, if you find ways to combine the two with something you feel good about, then mix in passion and productivity in equal measures, you end up both happy and successful."

Simone sat forward again. "Who are you?"

"What?"

"I'm serious. You don't make sense."

Loreto's laugh felt a little more strangled now. "I think you're going off track again."

"No," Simone said. "Your original point is well taken, and one I'll have to give a good deal of consideration over the next few days, but in the meantime, I want to know where you studied."

"I haven't," she said defiantly.

"No," Simone said quickly. "You just gave me a mini-thesis on GDP and world happiness rankings. What was your former life? Economist? Sociologist?"

Loreto laughed again. "I think you need to lay off the sangria."

"You're deflecting again. Don't think I don't notice."

"I read a lot. Okay?"

Simone eyed her skeptically. "Of course you do."

"Yeah, I don't expect you to believe me, and I don't care. You asked, I answered."

"It's not that I don't believe you. It's just that you answered in the vaguest way imaginable, which does nothing to explain where you come from or why someone with your skills and knowledge is content to bum around in shorts and sandals picking up odd jobs for under-the-table payments. It also doesn't account for your glaring national pronoun problem."

Loreto gritted her teeth against her urge to run. Any other time, she would've been out the door by now, but the last item of Simone's list caught her off guard. "Pronoun problem?"

"Sometimes when you refer to Spaniards, you use they/them pronouns, and sometimes, you use we/us. You even switch them up within the same comments. And your little rant earlier about your people and my people didn't seem to include Spain or America, and you weren't aligning yourself with Columbus, either. It's not like you're only transient in the physical sense, but at some deeper level of identity, too."

Loreto rose from the table and took one last drink, hoping Simone didn't see the slight tremor in her hand as she set the glass back on the table between them. "It's time for the siesta."

Simone stared at her as if waiting for more, and Loreto held her eyes for as long as she dared before turning to go. She made it the four steps to the door and pulled it open, feeling a dry blast of scalding, midday sun, before Simone called out. "Wait."

She stopped, hand still on the handle, but didn't turn around.

"Please," Simone said, something softer in her voice Loreto hadn't heard there before. "I didn't mean to pry. I honestly wanted to know what's made you who you are."

She closed her eyes and tilted her chin toward the burning sky. She could withstand temper and privilege, anger and entitlement, power and prowess, but the miniscule hint of pleading in Simone's voice took a sizable chink out of her armor. To turn around now would expose both of them to a firestorm she suspected neither of them would recover from.

Maybe it was noble, or maybe it was cowardly, but instead of looking back, she said, "Go take a nap, Simone. Trust me. This kind of heat is nothing to mess with."

Simone tried to sleep. She tried to hear the low rumbling in Loreto's voice as she warned against the dangers of the heat, though she wasn't sure if she'd been speaking of the temperature or the slow simmering between them all day. After Loreto had left, Simone had gone back to her room. She'd kicked off her shoes and lain down on the king-size bed. She'd closed her eyes and felt the cool air from the vent overhead wash over her body. She'd waited to drift off, for relaxation to take hold, for relief that didn't come.

No matter how still she forced herself to lie or how long she forced herself to try to sleep, she was still forcing herself, which seemed counterintuitive to napping. She didn't miss the irony that she couldn't do something that should take zero effort. She'd seen plenty of colleagues doze off without even meaning to, and in the worst possible moments or positions, like sitting up in a board meeting. She excelled at everything she'd ever set her mind to. Why couldn't she take a nap on sheets of Egyptian cotton in lush surroundings in the heat of the day when an entire region drifted off into dreams?

She hadn't thought of napping as a skill, much less one that took practice. Then again, maybe napping was just one of the many things she'd underestimated on this trip so far. Loreto's image came immediately to her mind, so sharp and clear she flashed her eyes open as if expecting to find her standing in the doorway, silhouetted against the sun the way she'd last seen her.

"Damn it," she muttered, realizing she wasn't just being silly, she'd also interrupted her nap, and now she'd have to start over again.

She closed her eyes once more, but this time, instead of seeing the back of her own lids, she saw Loreto again. The memory placed her in the doorway between mosque and cathedral. Her dark, expressive eyes flicked from one space to the other, while her feet remained planted squarely on the line dividing the two. Simone watched her, teetering on the threshold, as if unwilling to go forward and unable to go back. The thought surprised her. She hadn't quite thought of it that way in the moment. In retrospect, it occurred to her that Loreto might literally be trapped between two cultures.

She stood and walked to the window. Drawing back the sheer, linen drapes and unlatching the wooden shutters, she pulled them apart and let her eyes adjust to the influx of light. Below her, the city of Cordoba spread out, squat and whitewashed, the roofs little terra-cotta hats in a crowd surging toward the river. She didn't have the full view of the cathedral Loreto had shown her from the roof that morning, but she could certainly see the outer walls of the mosque rising above the surrounding buildings, and she could just make out the shadows cast by the much taller structure rising from the center. She'd viewed them both with the same detached lens of a tourist, the way someone might look at a picture drawn by someone else's child, two buildings built on the same spot she held no connection with, two cultures she'd never before given any thought to, two religions that had no effect on her own value system.

What did Loreto see in them that sparked such a dramatically different reaction?

She wandered back to bed and sat down, propping herself against some pillows and the elaborately carved headboard. Tilting her head, she stared at the exposed wooden beams that seemed common in this part of Spain. Exposed. That's how Loreto had looked when she'd lost her temper at the mosque, and again when she'd dodged the questions about her past. There was a mystery there. She knew it. What she didn't know was why it should matter to her.

Loreto was an employee. An insightful employee, a useful employee, sometimes an insubordinate employee, but no matter what modifier you put on the title, she wasn't someone Simone should care about outside the purview of what she could do to further her business connections. She'd had hundreds of employees over her career, some she valued or knew or liked better than others, but none of them sparked her curiosity the way Loreto had in such a short time.

Loreto didn't flaunt her credentials. She didn't talk herself up, and yet she didn't cower, either, or allow herself to be undercut. She talked like someone with both nothing to lose and nothing to gain. Her fearlessness gave her a flippant sort of competency and added to her ability to hold her own in an argument.

The corners of Simone's mouth twitched up. She wouldn't admit it even if tortured, but Loreto had more than held her own in their arguments today. She'd landed quite a few winning points. Simone generally hated to be wrong. She hated to lose anything. She hated misreading people. By all accounts, she should have hated being around Loreto, and yet, as she finally relaxed enough to drift off to sleep, she was dimly aware the opposite was true.

Loreto was sitting on her balcony with her feet kicked up on the wrought iron railing and a book in her lap when a knock sounded at her door.

Surprised out of a haze that consisted of half reading, half day-dreaming, she glanced at the clock. Nine o'clock. Too late for housekeeping, too early for room service, not that she'd ordered anything. The only other obvious choice was Simone, but that didn't do anything to lessen Loreto's surprise at seeing her there.

Tonight, she wore a white dress. Whiter than snow, whiter than the skin on her shoulders, broken only by the thin spaghetti straps holding the flowing cotton over the places it needed to cover, and little else. For a moment, Loreto's mind couldn't process anything other than how Simone's body managed to make even the simplest fabrics seem luxurious. And sexy. Actually, the dress wasn't sexy so much as what lay under it, or outside it, like long legs under a jagged cut skirt, and bare toes painted in a bold blue below the white straps of barely there sandals, and she was totally staring at her boss's legs.

Snapping her eyes up to meet Simone's, a jolt of electricity shot through her. God, what had she come for? Hadn't Loreto done enough to push her away today?

Clearly not, because Simone nodded toward the bedroom. "May I?"

Loreto stepped back to let her in.

"I know I'm early for our dinner date," Simone said breezily, "but I had a hard time easing into the siesta. Shocking, right?"

Loreto laughed softly, the little bit of self-deprecation easing some of the tension she felt.

"I actually didn't doze off until about the time most of the country was waking up, and then I slept for three hours."

"When you finally do something, you do it all the way," Loreto said dryly.

"Apparently, and maybe I did need a bit of a break. I haven't exactly slept well since arriving here."

"The jet lag struggle is real."

"Maybe," Simone admitted, "or perhaps the stress of my impending meeting has weighed on me more than I realized, along with other things over the past few days."

Loreto took "other things" to include her and the tension between them, but she heard no accusation in the explanation.

"Either way, I guess I needed the rest more than my body

125

wanted to admit, and now that I'm feeling endlessly more relaxed and focused and energetic, I'm also forced to admit, perhaps, the siesta isn't a terrible idea when circumstances allow."

"And you sort of hate that, right?"

"Admitting I'm wrong? More than you can possibly imagine."

"I'm sure it will get easier with practice."

"Then it's not likely to get easier, because it doesn't happen often," Simone said, "which brings me to my next point. I cannot wait until ten for dinner. I'm famished."

Loreto laughed. "You slept through tapas. That hardly counts as working the official Spanish meal plan. But I'll give you full points for effort, and because of that, I think we can compromise on dinnertime. I'm sure if we head down to the hotel terrace, someone will serve us something to eat."

"I've never liked compromise until this moment," Simone said with a smile, and another knot of tension slipped from Loreto's shoulders.

This little visit was completely unexpected, but then again, so were so many things about Simone. Every time she braced herself for the worst, this woman responded with her best. Not only did she not fire her today, she'd taken her advice, she'd made an effort, she'd changed her tone, she'd admitted her mistakes even while acknowledging none of those things came easy to her. Perhaps it was time for Loreto to stop assuming the worst and make a little effort of her own.

"If you give me a minute, I'll change into something a little nicer and we can go downstairs together, or if you want, you can go to the bar and get a drink before I meet you."

"I suppose I can wait a few minutes," Simone said, then injecting a little teasing into her tone added, "unless you're one of those women who takes forty-five minutes to change clothes."

"You never know, I could be."

Simone laughed. "You've surprised me a time or two, but I'll take my chances on this one."

Loreto grabbed some clothes out of the closet and headed for the bathroom. "Okay, you can time me."

She didn't really expect Simone to start a stopwatch, but she wouldn't put it past her, either. They seemed to share a competitive streak that came out in odd ways. Loreto chose not to examine why that might be as she shed her shorts and polo and dabbed on a bit of cologne. Thankfully, she'd showered after tapas. When she hadn't heard from Simone by five, she assumed she was being stood up for the evening, or maybe fired. Part of her had relished the prospect of another night off, right up until the moment she'd seen Simone in that dress.

She pulled on the khakis Simone had bought her and then added the light-blue oxford she'd tried on with them in the store. She had a flash memory of Simone's eyes raking over her in that moment, appraising, appreciating, almost possessive. She shook off the shiver of anticipation that ran up the length of her spine and fastened the long line of buttons up her chest. Simone's blatant attraction felt like a distant memory now. She hadn't seen any desire in her eyes for over twenty-four hours, and while that wasn't a long time under normal circumstances, Simone seemed to do everything at an accelerated pace. Twenty-four hours in regular time could carry a week's worth of mood swings and realizations in Simone time. They hardly felt like the same people they'd been back in Málaga.

Which didn't mean she didn't still find Simone every bit as attractive as she'd found her the first time she'd seen her, all buttoned up and aloof by the pool. She smiled at the mirror and rolled up her sleeves while indulging the memory. Even in those first few seconds of watching her pin her long hair into a bun, she'd sensed Simone had an unusual grip on her self-control, and she'd had an instant urge to wreck it. If she'd only known then what she knew now about the extent of that control, she might have walked away from the challenge right then. Unsure what that meant for her in this moment, she added the thought to the growing pile of things she didn't want to think too hard about. Running her fingers quickly through her dark hair, she exited the bathroom and called out, "Done. What's the stopwatch say?"

Simone turned from her spot on the balcony, her body backlit in a soft orange glow from the setting sun, the jagged hem of her skirt swirling around her mid thighs, her eyes sparkling with mirth as she held up the book Loreto had been reading.

"Hamilton? By Chernow, not Miranda?"

Loreto shrugged. "I liked the music from the play."

"Have you seen it?" Simone asked.

She shook her head. "Some students who came through got me hooked on the cast recording, though, and I got curious."

"I liked the play quite a bit when I saw it in New York a few years ago, but I never got the urge to tackle this beast." Simone lifted the book in one arm, as if doing a biceps curl. "Not exactly light reading."

Loreto didn't know what to make of the comment. Was Simone surprised? Impressed? Could one be impressed by something they didn't find at least somewhat surprising? It was hard not to be a little offended by the idea that her ability to take on weighty works of literature would still surprise Simone, but she wanted to stop assuming the worst, so she merely said, "It's well written."

Simone pursed her lips and stared at the back cover for a second before saying, "Maybe I'll have to give it a try after I finish this job. Shall we go to dinner?"

Loreto nodded, thinking the exchange ended pleasantly enough. Uncomplicated. Easy even. Maybe she'd been overthinking things. Then as they reached the door, Simone stopped.

"Oh. I nearly forgot." She opened her small, white purse. "Here's your check for today. Since we have a no-business-over-food policy, I thought we could spend the rest of the night off the clock."

Loreto accepted the check and dropped it on the bedside table without looking at the numbers. She didn't have to. She could still feel the outline of them scrawled across her skin long after the ink had faded.

"Sure. No problem," she said, with forced casualness, but as they headed out, she knew without a doubt she would absolutely overthink it.

Chapter Seven

"Phenomenal." Simone sat back from the table to prevent herself from reaching across and grabbing Loreto's food as well. It wasn't that she was still hungry. She wasn't. She'd once again let Loreto order for her, and each time she did so, it got easier, because she was yet to be disappointed. Tonight's entrée consisted of local pork pounded thin and sautéed quickly in a mango glaze, which gave it crisp sides and a tender center, and it was served atop a pineapple compote and paired with Iberian rice steamed in a broth of fragrant Moroccan spices. Loreto had chosen appetizers of shrimp drowning in garlic butter and a side of warm bread rolled in toasted sesame seeds and served with fresh, local olive oil. By the time she finished, she didn't have an ounce of space left in her stomach, and still she had to physically restrain herself stealing a bite of Loreto's filet of grilled tuna on a bed of ripe tomatoes drizzled in balsamic.

"You want a bite of mine, don't you?" Loreto asked, apparently reading the predatory gleam in her eyes.

"I do!" she admitted, hanging her head, but not managing to feel much shame.

"Go ahead." Loreto laughed.

"No, it's yours."

"Aren't you the woman who defended Columbus this morning?"

Simone groaned. "Now I'm definitely not going to take any."

"I'm teasing," Loreto said, her voice still light with amusement. "And I insist. If you don't take some, I won't have any room for flan, and flan is *mi favorito*."

Simone groaned again at the thought of more food but couldn't refrain from spearing a piece of the fish and a sliced tomato, then jamming them both into her mouth.

She let the flavors meld for as long as she could stand before swallowing and throwing her head back. "Why didn't you tell me sooner that ten o'clock dinner was worth waiting up for?"

Loreto laughed, a delightfully throaty sound. "I think I did, or at least strongly implied it. You have trust issues, remember?"

"No more implying," she said. "You tell me straight up there will be food of this level anywhere, anytime, and I'll deal with the trust issues."

"Lesson learned." Loreto sipped from her tall glass of sangria.

The sun had dipped below the horizon by the time they'd arrived on the terrace, leaving everything basked in the remnants of a warm, orange glow that slowly faded, first to violet, then to deep blue. Still the heat lingered. Simone guessed the ambient temperature hovered in the mid-eighties, but her internal thermometer felt much higher than the standard ninety-eight degrees. She took another sip from her second glass of rich, red wine. Though not chilled, it felt cool by comparison.

"So now would be the time to mention eleven o'clock dessert is worth waiting up for, too?"

Simone sighed. "I don't doubt you, but I'm stuffed."

"That's where the whole staying up part comes in. We don't have to order the last course right now. We merely have to sit here until we get hungry again."

"I may never be hungry again."

"Famous words, but you'll have to trust me. Wait an hour, and you won't be able to resist the flan."

Simone didn't disagree with the main point, but as she looked around the terrace, about ninety percent of the tables were occupied, with several people having just arrived. Crazy as it might seem, she couldn't deny the dinner rush seemed to be picking up steam at nearly 10:30. "I'm not sure we'll be able to hold down the table."

Loreto shook her head. "We will."

"Surely the waiter will hate us."

"Not at all," Loreto said calmly, "nor will he bother us. He won't bring the check or likely even speak to us until I give him a nod. Dinner is an all-evening event, and while he'll certainly earn a tip, he's most likely a full-time, salaried employee making the same living wage no matter how many seatings he cranks through each night."

Simone couldn't resist looking over at their waiter, a tall, thin, middle-aged man with a receding hairline and a quick laugh. "He gets paid a salary to stand around all night not interrupting us?"

Loreto nodded. "Could you eat at a nice restaurant without a waiter?"

"I don't suppose I could call it a nice restaurant if I had to go to the kitchen and get my food myself."

"Then there's no nice restaurants without waiters, and clearly from our clean plates, we value nice restaurants. Ergo, we need waiters to provide us something we value. It only follows that when someone provides a service we value, they're paid for it. Any work society deems worth doing is worth treating with dignity."

"Doesn't it make your food astronomically expensive?"

"No," Loreto said flatly.

Simone stared at her, waiting for elaboration, but none came, and she had to admit that even while she expected another economics conversation, she'd seen the prices on the menu. They were considerably lower than what she paid in New York. Something didn't add up, which sent her business sense into high alert. She wondered again about the elusive piece in her currently incomplete business puzzle. In a land where everyone made a living wage, would that change the dynamics of what people were willing to accept for their work?

"Simone," Loreto said in a low voice, the warning in her tone matched by an intimacy that did much more to shake her out of her thoughts.

"Yes?"

"I can see you making spreadsheets in your head. I thought we were taking tonight off."

She smiled tightly and took another sip of her wine before saying, "But I like spreadsheets."

Loreto laughed. "What else do you like?"

The question caught her off guard, and it must have shown on her face.

"You made a point of saying we're off the clock tonight for a reason, right? Why talk about the same things we talk about when we're on the clock? I already know Business Simone. What does Off-the-Clock Simone think about?"

"Spreadsheets," she answered quickly, then smiled. "Just kidding. I'm not actually a total workaholic. Or maybe I am, but I'm not killing myself in some corporate prison."

"What do you do to break away? I know you like nice things, fashion, food, travel. You have a work-hard, play-hard mentality. When you do something, you want it to be the best, no matter what sphere of your life it falls into."

"Yes," Simone said, inordinately pleased Loreto had taken even cursory notice of her interests, much less used them to make such an accurate assessment of the philosophy behind them.

"What else?" she asked. "What do you do that helps you break the business mold?"

She polished off the last of her wine, then relaxed into her seat a little further. "No one's asked me that in a long time."

"And you've forgotten the answer?" Loreto teased gently.

"No. I like books. I love stories. Good fiction is one of very few things that can make me forget about work for a while, no matter how consuming work happens to be."

"But you work in publishing, right? Isn't reading kind of work for you?"

"Sometimes, but that's part of my genius." She grinned. "Just like your waiter gets paid a living wage for providing something we enjoy, I found a way to do the same, only it's not just other people who get to enjoy the books I work on acquiring. I get to enjoy them first."

"I thought you didn't mix business with pleasure?"

Simone's cheeks flushed even warmer than the weather and the wine warranted. "Touché."

"I find it funny that, somewhere along the way, little-girl Simone was reading alone in her room one day and thought, 'Gee, I just love stories about ponies so much I want to be a publishing mogul when I grow up.'"

She rolled her eyes but smiled. "While I enjoy that image as well, I actually didn't want to go into publishing until college."

"Then what did little, blond, pigtails-wearing Simone want to be when she grew up?"

"Don't think I don't notice how you keep elaborating on your visions of me as a girl, but aside from the fact that I didn't read books about ponies or wear my hair in pigtails, by the time I turned six, I very earnestly wanted to be a writer."

"What happened there?"

"Apparently, I was quite good for a six-year-old novelist, but that's where I peaked."

"No," Loreto said dramatically.

"It's true. I tried for fourteen years of my life. I went to all the workshops and read all the how-to books and practiced. You can't even imagine how much I practiced, but I kept telling the same, rote stories over and over again. By the time I was in college, even I didn't want to read my writing anymore. I had no talent, no prospects, and absolutely no real hope of anything approaching job or financial security."

Loreto's smile turned pensive, and she raised one hand slightly to signal the waiter. "I think we're going to need more wine."

"I'm actually at my limit for a night."

"Yes, but your nights are usually over at this point. Extra hours call for extra allowances."

She suspected Loreto's real reason for plying her with alcohol had less to do with the time and more to do with the topic, but she didn't argue as the waiter refilled her glass. "Anyway, the writing wasn't working out, and you can imagine how well I take not being good at something."

"Yes, I'm sure you were a true joy to be around."

"You don't have to agree so quickly," Simone shot back, then grinned, "but I'll admit to being absolutely insufferable through my first few years of undergrad."

"What happened?"

"Women's Studies."

Loreto arched an eyebrow high over the rim of the sangria glass she'd just lifted to her lips.

"The academic discipline, not the hobby," Simone clarified. Grinning, she added, "Though I partook in both."

"I bet you did."

"At the same time I was trying to write the type of engaging, original stories I wanted to read, I was also learning how many women never get their stories told at all. So many smart, talented women with such essential voices going unheard. I wanted to be able to tell all their stories so desperately, and since I didn't know how to give them voice myself, I figured the next best thing would be to advocate for their voices within the existing system."

"So you infiltrated the fortress of mainstream publishing with the goal of staging a coup?"

"Something like that," Simone said, not hating the analogy, but also understanding it hadn't quite gone that way. "Turns out things were more complicated than I realized."

"How so?"

"Well for one, publishing is a multibillion-dollar industry."

"Hence the whole financial security you lacked on the writing end."

"Yes, I made money. The publishers made money. Sometimes the authors made money."

"Sometimes?"

"Sometimes they don't, but if enough of them don't, the entire system crumbles."

"Doesn't sound so secure after all."

"It can be if we only publish books we know will sell, and trust me, we've done all the market research. We virtually always know what will sell. The only problem is—"

"Let me guess," Loreto cut in. "The books you went into business with the hopes of elevating aren't the books you can guarantee will sell."

"Bingo," Simone said, pointing so emphatically with her wineglass that a few drops spilled over the rim and onto her hand. She lifted it back to her lips and drank the little bit she'd spilled, then a little more. "You have to find twenty-five books generic enough and comfortable enough to sell across the lowest common denominators, and then mass-market the crap out of every single one of them repeatedly in order to be able to supplement the one great book that doesn't fit the mold."

"That's a pretty uneven ratio, and a whole lot of compromise."

"It is," she admitted, some of the tension trying to return to her shoulders. Thankfully, the wine in her system had other ideas, and instead of internalizing the usual weight of responsibility, it rejected the stress, leaving no other choice but to vent it. "But that's life, right? Endless compromise."

"Is it?" Loreto asked, her voice a little higher.

"It's my life," Simone said with a terse smile. "I'm like the living embodiment of that compromise."

"I thought you hated compromise."

"I do, but the only other option is outright failure, so I've spent nearly twenty years marketing myself as a product palatable enough to people in power to get where I am."

"Yes, I remember now. The keys to the kingdom are nearly within your reach."

"And when I have them, when I have the power, I get to call the shots."

"I see," Loreto said. "You get to tell the stories."

"Exactly. I've put in all the work, and now I'm finally going to reap the reward. And that's the way life goes. You put in the time, you do the work, you prove yourself worthy, you get control of the system. Basic, core values, right?"

The corner of Loreto's mouth twitched, but this time, not upward. Her whole expression had grown tight and her eyes dark. Once again, Simone found herself almost frightened by what she couldn't see there, but before she had time to process that fear, Loreto looked away, finding the waiter once more. "I think it's time for dessert."

The sweetness of the flan managed to be both immense and insufficient at once. Perfectly textured and drizzled in the most delectable caramel syrup, everything about the dish should have washed the bitter taste out Loreto's mouth, and yet it didn't.

She knew she shouldn't begrudge Simone her success. She'd undoubtedly worked hard, and she'd paid her own price. She couldn't fault her for working within a system that allowed her that privilege. Loreto was self-aware enough to realize she might have done the same, had she been afforded the chance. She tried not to get angry or resentful of anyone who played the hand they'd been dealt. But that last, little, unwitting twist of the knife about basic core values had caused the old heat to burn through her once more.

"You were right again." Simone practically moaned around another mouthful of flan. "This might be the best dessert I've ever eaten."

Loreto managed a slight smile. She didn't want to be mad at the woman across from her, not because of what it said about Simone, but because of what that anger would say about herself. "Another trust issue bites the dust?"

"All of them," Simone said, then seemed to catch herself. "Okay, maybe not all, but all the trust issues surrounding food are gone. Please show me all the things I've been missing."

Loreto gave silent thanks for the dim light as all the blood in her brain flushed across her cheeks on its way to points farther south. Then she smiled, relieved to find her libido capable of subduing emotions her sweet tooth couldn't. "That might be a long list."

"Then start tonight."

"That could be arranged," she said coyly and watched the realization spread across Simone's face. However, instead of embarrassment, the surprise faded into something almost akin to smugness.

"That sounds like a proposition."

"Only if you want it to be, and only in the ways you want it to be," Loreto said. "I was going to suggest we start with churros tomorrow morning."

"Were you?"

"Initially," she admitted, "seeing as how you've been adamant about not mixing business with pleasure."

"Hmm." The sound made Loreto's nerve endings buzz in anticipation. "It would be unorthodox, but then again, I'm very good at my job."

"A fact you've also mentioned." Loreto took another bite of flan and held its sweet cream on her tongue long enough to keep the bitterness at bay. "You've clearly gotten where you have by making a few of your own rules."

"Indeed," Simone said. "I didn't backstab, or sneak around, or sleep my way to the top."

Loreto nodded, acknowledging the accusations that would likely be lobbed at any woman with both ambition and a sex drive.

"But I've gotten to the point in my career where I have to justify my actions to very few people."

Loreto couldn't resist saying, "I've only got to justify them to myself."

Instead of taking offense, Simone tipped her glass toward her in acknowledgment. The subtle move bolstered Loreto's confidence.

"I've become adept at taking what I want no matter how much work it takes."

"Back to the work-hard, play-hard mentality."

Simone pursed her lips and drummed her fingers on the table, and Loreto leaned forward, folding her arms and resting them on the table. "Be honest. You resent it a little bit, don't you?"

"What?"

"Always having to wait. Always having to plan. Always having to work twice as hard as the men. Always having to ask nicely."

"Every single day," Simone said. "Every minute of this job, part of me is quietly seething. Groveling before some mom-and-pop publisher is beneath me, but I've swallowed more bile in my lifetime than you can even imagine."

Loreto doubted that, but she didn't interrupt.

"I've spent forty years of my life saying 'please' and biding my time. I won't stop now, not when I'm so close to getting what I want, what I've worked for. Those are just the things we all have to do to survive."

"I don't," Loreto said, her smile slow and superior, letting the short, simple entirety of the statement hang heavy in the thick air between them.

As the truth of the comment and all the implications that came with it hit Simone, a little muscle in her jaw twitched, and something stormy flashed in her eyes. Resentment? Envy? Desire? Simone's pursed lips parted slightly, and in that second, Loreto knew she could have her. Or at least she could have part of her. She could never have her wealth, her privilege, or her heart, but right now, she could snap her restraint and claim her body. All the heat and temper and need welled up in her so quickly, she nearly choked on it. All the day's talk about bootstraps, and work, and Christopher-fucking-Columbus blurred together into a dull hum, drowned out by the steady drumbeat of desire pulsing through her. This time she didn't have to fight it, because while she'd never have what Simone had, she could have Simone. Tonight. And that seemed like much more than a consolation prize.

Simone poured all of her frustration out onto Loreto again, but this time it didn't vent itself in sharp words. Still, the exchange was no less heated than the ones leading up to it. In fact, the heat spread like a fire through her the moment they'd pushed open the door to Loreto's room. Grabbing her by the collar, Simone yanked her close and took control of her mouth. The kiss managed to be quenching without being cooling. Red wine and Loreto's tongue stoked the fire, hot, hotter than the air, hotter than her resentment, too hot to stand even the thin barriers between their skin.

She fumbled with the buttons on Loreto's shirt, managing to pop open two of them before losing her patience and yanking it up over head, breaking the kiss enough to stare at Loreto's chest. Her breasts were small and firm, her stomach smooth, and the most deliciously surprising feminine curve of her waist flared out again at her hips. Fuck patience. There'd be no more of that tonight.

Simone pounced again, and their mouths collided. She raked her fingernails down Loreto's chest, over the plane of her abs, and straight into the waistband of her khakis. Flattening her palm against burning skin, she slipped inside the elastic of her boxer shorts and through the curls beneath until she found the wetness she sought.

Loreto's hips bucked up under her hand, and a surge of power shot though her. She had this maddeningly defiant woman literally in the palm of her hand. She could make her move, make her moan, make her bend to her will. She hadn't realized how much she wanted that until this moment. But as the full weight of understanding bore down on her, her knees almost buckled.

"Easy there," Loreto mumbled against her mouth as she wrapped an arm around her waist and pinned them more tightly to one another, increasing the press of Simone's fingers against her need.

"No," Simone said emphatically. "Not easy. Hard."

Loreto's fist tightened at the small of her back, clutching the cotton of her dress and dragging it up. The hem skimmed along the back of her thighs and up over her ass, the coverage it had provided quickly replaced by Loreto's other hand. She kneaded and played as they ground against each other, the friction that had plagued them now pleasurably physical as khaki and silk slowly gave way to skin upon skin.

They didn't ever break apart fully, but they managed to grope, and tear, and shimmy out of their remaining clothes until Simone stood naked, the length of her reveling in the flush of Loreto's skin against hers. Their chests rose and fell, pushing breasts into breasts, and their hands wandered over newly exposed areas. Simone pushed a leg between Loreto's, the smooth, wet heat of her inner thighs sending fire flickering up through her again.

She didn't think she could get any hotter without combusting, then she felt Loreto's hands tugging at the back of her hair. She wasn't gentle as she pulled the pin holding her bun in place and shook out the strands until they brushed across her shoulders. Gentle wouldn't get the job done tonight. Not the way she needed.

With that thought, she moved both hands to Loreto's breasts, palming them only long enough to appreciate their firm weight before flattening her hands and shoving Loreto back onto the bed. Simone didn't even wait for her to readjust or find a pillow. Comfort became an afterthought at the sight of Loreto's prone body ready and waiting.

For her part, Loreto didn't seem to mind the position at all as Simone crawled on top of her. With a low growl, she placed both hands on Simone's waist and roughly urged her higher until she could capture a taut nipple in her mouth. Teasing with teeth and tongue, Loreto drew a moan from Simone's throat, the likes of which she hadn't exuded in ages. Low and primal, her whole body rumbled at the experience of having her desires fulfilled without having to ask.

Switching to the other breast, Loreto sucked a little harder, her mouth possessive and demanding, and her hand urged Simone to straddle her fully. Settling her knees on either side of Loreto's waist, she eased herself down until the evidence of Simone's arousal pressed low against the flat plane between her hips. It was Loreto's turn to moan. The vibrations against her nipples sent another jolt of heat racing through her senses, until sweat pricked across the back of her neck. She ground down on Loreto, pressing them deeper into the lush comforter and mat-

140

tress. She would have driven them all the way to the floor if it meant she could pin herself tighter to the hard abs flexing beneath her. She rocked and ground while Loreto drove her senses into overdrive. She closed her eyes against the white haze tinting her vision.

Still she wanted more. She wanted everything, and she refused to wait. Not tonight. Not with this magnificent body beneath her. Not with release clawing its way toward reality.

Sitting up abruptly and pulling her torso free, she perched across Loreto's hips and smiled down at her.

Loreto's body thrust up lightly, rolling and rocking in a slow steady rhythm even under the full weight of her. She moved beautifully, and Simone wanted to feel that motion consume her.

As if reading her mind, her body, Loreto grabbed Simone, cupping her ass and pulling her forward. She drew her knees up and eased Simone back onto them, a move that both tilted her hips forward and provided balance.

Staring straight into Simone's eyes, Loreto brought one hand forward and between her legs. This time she didn't play. Working her fingers over Simone's hypersensitive clit, she lingered mere seconds before pushing lower, feeling intuitively for the place Simone most wanted her to find.

Her eyes stayed fixed on Simone's, hovering, ready, willing, and from her confident gaze, very much able.

"Yes," Simone affirmed, intoxicated with anticipation.

"Ride me." Loreto growled.

It was one command Simone had no problem obeying.

Simone slid down, relishing the sense of control as she felt Loreto slip inside her. Undulating her hips, Simone was aware of every ridge, every muscle, every pleasure point as she tightened around her. Closing her eyes, she picked up the rhythm Loreto's hips continued to rock underneath her.

"Yes." She practically breathed the word on every exhale, even the tension felt like release. She was no saint or prude, and despite stereotypes of highly successful businesswomen being ice queens, she'd never forgone sex for the sake of her job, but

141

Simone couldn't remember the last encounter with anyone, in any area of her life, in which she got exactly what she wanted.

Loreto gave her that. Loreto had known. She'd seen. She'd understood. And most importantly, she'd acted.

"God, that's hot," she said aloud.

"So fucking hot," Loreto echoed, staring up at her in awe, lust filling her endlessly deep eyes now. With a small adjustment to her palm, she pressed the heel of her hand firmly to Simone's clit.

The added pressure sent every sensation into overdrive, and Simone cried out, an unintelligible call of elation, satisfaction, relief, and even victory as the orgasm ripped through her. There was no more waiting, no more working, no more wishing, and no more wanting. She rode that moment as long and as hard as she could, relishing every flash and fire flickering through her body. Her muscles ached from holding on so tightly, and her eyes squeezed shut against the return to reality. Loreto, for her part, never let up and never let her down, holding steady both in her rhythm and in the pressure she provided to all the right places until Simone could withstand no more and pitched forward in a heap on top of her.

They lay there for several minutes without speaking, the mismatched thumps of two rapidly beating hearts and slowly settling breath the only sounds in the room. Simone kept her eyes closed, her head rising and falling against Loreto's chest with each successive inhale and exhale. She enjoyed the scent of her, musky, hot, rich, like still-smoldering incense, but it didn't quite inspire relaxation. Instead, a new set of sensations and emotions stirred in her. She lay still long enough to try to sort them all out. There was the sense of being sated, a hint of smugness, and a few aches in her abs. Gratitude also made an appearance, which was a bit surprising, though it probably shouldn't have been, and there was lust. Maybe that last one wasn't new. She'd felt more than a twinge of desire, even in the first moment she'd seen Loreto upright in all her irreverent glory, but the level that desire reached tonight made her initial reaction seem as pale as her own skin against Loreto's beautiful bronze.

Perhaps most disconcertingly, all the emotions swirling in her now seemed to grow stronger the longer she lay there. Normally during a build-up-and-release cycle, everything both physically and emotionally flowed in an orderly and linear pattern for her. She was nothing if not efficient, even when losing control, but as with so many other things, Loreto injected a little chaos into the routine.

She turned her head slightly and placed a kiss in the valley between Loreto's breasts. Then she kissed a little farther over, and again another inch to the side and lower, until she'd kissed a tantalizing circle around the spot they both knew she was headed for. Loreto lifted her back off the bed slightly as if urging her closer, but Simone only smiled and glanced up.

"What?" Loreto asked, her voice thick and her eyelids heavy.

"I think I mentioned earlier how much I hate being forced to say 'please,'" Simone said.

"Yep." Loreto sounded more confused than annoyed.

Simone lowered her head until her lips nearly brushed Loreto's skin. "I have no such problem with 'thank you.'"

Taking one taut nipple between her mouth, she sucked hard for just long enough to elicit a gasp from Loreto, before kissing and sucking a trail down her torso. She ran her tongue in a hot, wet line over deliciously smooth skin, only stopping once as she crossed a small ridge. Glancing down, she noticed a thin, raised line of white scar tissue about three inches long and angled down from Loreto's right toward her midsection, like an arrow pointing the way.

Simone heeded the direction and kept moving south, her body easing Loreto's legs farther apart as she went. Propping herself on her elbows, she made sure to restrain her own urges just enough to feel Loreto's thighs tremble on either side of her, before running her tongue along her need.

Loreto let out a thoroughly satisfying mix between an exhale and a moan at the contact, and Simone felt a rush of power at the revelation of how much she'd wanted that. How much she'd wanted her. She wasn't blind. She'd seen the hunger in those dark eyes over the last few days, but she'd never been fully certain it was directed at her. Or maybe she'd known part of it was always on her, but she never understood its fullness. She still didn't, but as the muscles in Loreto's legs and ass constricted, pushing her up more fully toward Simone's mouth, she felt confident in her ability to meet at least her baser needs.

She lavished all the attention Loreto deserved, first with her tongue, then her lips, then her fingers. She thrilled to find that this woman, who responded to so many questions with so few words, had no problem providing answers with her body. When she liked something, she made it known through myriad physical cues, the clench of a muscle, the rise of her hips, the light thread of her skillful fingers through the loose strands of Simone's hair. Loreto never pushed, and if her mouth were free, Simone would have smiled at that realization. Wasn't that the point that had sparked this in the first place? Loreto didn't push because she didn't have to. Not only had she not needed to ask nicely, she hadn't needed to ask at all. The thought Simone had found maddening earlier seemed much more enticing now that she'd experienced having her own unspoken needs filled.

"*Dios*," Loreto muttered as Simone intensified her efforts. "*Madre de Dios.*"

She didn't have to speak Spanish to understand Loreto was close. She wanted to take her there, she wanted it with the same burning desire she'd had to chase her own release. She wanted to be part of this unwritten contract, the kind Loreto lived by, where things were granted without being requested, even if she could live that way for only one night, especially if she could live that way for only one night. And again, all she had to do was want, and Loreto provided for her by hurling them both over the edge. Shaking, writhing, sweating, she clutched one hand lightly to the back of Simone's head and twisted the sheets into a knot with the other. Simone's heart pounded with each of Loreto's panted breaths as the high of her own satisfaction buzzed through her again like an aftershock.

144

She was so enthralled with the experience, she would have continued long after Loreto's body went slack, if not for the hands urging her back up.

"For the love of God, woman," Loreto rasped. "Let me catch my breath. You're a machine."

Simone crawled up and eased down beside her.

Loreto rolled onto her side and smiled. "A beautiful, sexy, talented, tenacious machine."

"Does any of that surprise you?"

Loreto shook her head. "Not at all."

Simone rested her head on the pillow. "I guess I'll have to keep trying."

Loreto wrapped an arm around Simone's waist and tugged their bodies flush against each other again. Then rolling Simone onto her back, Loreto kissed her deeply for several minutes before pulling back just enough to whisper, "Did I mention I recover quickly?"

Simone smiled coyly. "Does that mean we can go again?"

"*Sí, se puede*," Loreto said, before biting down on her shoulder. Laughing softly, she confirmed, "Yes, we can."

Chapter Eight

The sun had already cleared the surrounding buildings by the time Loreto opened her eyes. From the slant of its rays well above her second-story window, she felt certain she'd missed early breakfast, and from the coolness of the sheets around her, she'd obviously missed Simone's departure as well.

The realization that Simone had left sometime in the night or very early morning didn't surprise her. It didn't displease her, either. Mornings after were always a bit awkward even under the most clear-cut circumstances, and this morning's circumstances were anything but. She rolled over to face the other direction and found evidence of how not clear-cut this whole thing was in the form of a neatly folded slip of paper on her bedside table. Simone's check was right where she had left it before dinner last night, and Loreto stifled the urge to just leave it there.

The urge was stupid and prideful to say the least. Aside from the fact that some housekeeper would no doubt get quite the shock when she found it, no one else could actually use it if she walked away. She wondered how many people would even feel comfortable using it if they understood what had transpired after that payment had been made.

She reminded herself she was technically off the clock last night. The payment had been for the day's work, not what came later, though given Simone's previous stories about tracking potential clients or acquisitions to a gym or a wine bar in her off time with the purpose of sealing future deals did make Loreto's stomach tighten a bit. Then again, she had nothing to offer Simone long term. She was of no value to her beyond the next few days. And it wasn't even as if Simone wasn't already getting everything she wanted out of their business relationship. She certainly didn't have to woo Loreto, another fact that could easily be evidenced by the check on the table beside her.

Loreto stared at the paper a few minutes more before snatching it up and hopping off the bed. She quickly tucked it away, both in her suitcase and in the recesses of her mind. Work was work, and they'd finished before dinner. Simone didn't become her boss again until they met up this morning. End of story.

But that thought led to another. Why hadn't Simone contacted her yet? Ms. Up-With-The-Dawn had to be awake by now. Glancing at her phone, she confirmed it was nearly 10:00, and she had no new messages. She tried to tell herself that didn't have to signify a problem. Maybe Simone had allowed Loreto to sleep in as part of a new attempt to honor a more traditional Spanish schedule. She also entertained the possibility that what they'd done with and to each other had worn Simone out, which caused another smile, because at no point last night had she gotten the sense that Simone had to exert herself fully. Even when that woman lost control, she still managed to stay in command of the situation.

She gave herself the luxury of reveling in those memories for another few minutes while she pulled on her old cargo shorts and one of the polos Simone had chosen for her, then shot off a text. "I'm up and moving whenever you are."

The phone buzzed back almost immediately. "Almost ready for breakfast. Meet you downstairs."

Almost ready for breakfast? Loreto read the text three times. Simone hadn't eaten yet? She wasn't somewhere tapping her foot impatiently checking her watch in anticipation of some appropriate time to pounce? This was the closest she'd come to surprising Loreto, but as she headed down the stairs, she promised herself she wouldn't admit to that unless tortured.

✺ ✺ ✺

"So," Simone said as she watched Loreto cut a tomato in half and scrape it across the top of a thick piece of toasted bread. "Today we go to Seville?"

"We call the city 'Sevilla.'" She pronounced the word "say-vee-yah" while drizzling a thin stream of olive oil over her tomato toast. "Using the English version will mark you as an outsider."

"Good to know." Simone took another bite of her utterly uncomplicated yogurt. "Anything else?"

"It's going to be hot," Loreto said.

"Like yesterday?" Simone asked.

Loreto glanced up, her eyes dark, and the corners of her mouth quirked up. "In some ways."

It was the first allusion to what had happened between them last night. No, that was too passive. It hadn't just happened between them. It was something they'd chosen, something they'd made happen, something they'd grabbed with both fists and held onto for hours. In short, it had been glorious. Every time she shifted in her seat, the ache in her thighs sent a flash of erotic memories through her mind, which was less than glorious, because she really needed to get back to work. Whatever that meant for her now.

"Do we have any tours scheduled?"

Loreto took a bite of her toast and shook her head before she swallowed. "No. Since you're embracing the schedule of Spanish life so well, I thought maybe now we could work on pace a bit."

Simone arched an eyebrow.

"Don't worry," Loreto said, her voice full of humor. "The main things I want to highlight in Sevilla don't require formal tours, and they're both better experienced in the evening. You won't miss out on anything by waiting until sunset."

"Why do I suspect this might be an elaborate yarn you've spun to justify an afternoon by the pool?"

"Now that's an interesting idea, especially since I didn't even mention the pool, but I'm glad you brought it up. I think you're

148

right. We would be wise to rest up and fortify our reserves for later in the day."

"I'm not sure that's actually what I suggested."

"Must've been your subconscious."

"Loreto," Simone said, as if her name were a warning, but she didn't quite manage to strike the playfulness from her tone. "We can't do this."

"Have breakfast? Plan our day? Continue working together after last night?"

She'd already opened her mouth to respond to the first two options when the last item on the list made her breath catch.

"It's okay, we can talk about last night," Loreto said casually. Then she shrugged. "Or not."

Simone blinked a few times at the bluntness of the statement, but after the surprise began to wear off, so did some of the tension she hadn't let herself acknowledge, despite her utterly unorthodox morning. How could she explain to her that last night had come as a thrilling surprise and that something in her had shifted during the night without overstating what that meant for them going forward. She didn't want to undercut how much she appreciated Loreto's skill and attention, but she also didn't want to give her the wrong idea about their relationship now. She decided to start with a basic statement of fact. "I slept until nine-thirty this morning. I can't remember the last time I slept past eight. Even on a weekend."

Loreto's smile grew smug. "Someone wear you out last night?"

She rolled her eyes. "Someone with a high opinion of themselves. And while I now have a better understanding of where that confidence might stem from, I wouldn't say you wore me out, so much as helped me relax. I suspect I've been a little high-strung lately."

"I suspect you're a little high-strung all the time," Loreto said, her throwaway tone taking all the sting out of those little observations.

"Perhaps, by your standards," Simone admitted, "but your points about balance yesterday did not go unheard. Last night provided that for me in the form of a much-needed release, both in the physical and the emotional sense."

"Aww, who knew you were such a romantic."

"You're quite a charmer yourself," Simone said, unable to keep Loreto's irreverence from infiltrating her own tone before trying to inject a little more seriousness into the conversation. "I'm glad we're both in a position to be adults about this. Business relationship aside, I don't feel any guilt about what we did."

"Nor do I."

"Last night was fine."

"Fine?" Loreto asked with seriousness in her voice and mischief dancing in her eyes.

Another shot of memories flashed through her mind again so fast and vivid Simone put her hand on the table to steady herself so she didn't fall back into them completely: Loreto above her, Loreto beneath her, Loreto with that same expression as when she pushed inside her. "Better than fine."

"So much better than fine," Loreto agreed.

"So much," Simone echoed, feeling the heat rising in her cheeks.

"But?" Loreto asked, pulling her back to the moment. Answering her own question, she said, "You still have a job to do. Which means, so do I. I mean, I assume we're having the let's-get-back-to-work talk and not the I-can't-work-with-you-anymore talk."

"Yes," Simone said gratefully. "The former, please. I know I've already stressed how much this job means for me."

"Yes, no need to rehash. I fully understand work comes first. We had a good time in our spare time, but no strings have been tied, no foundations laid, and no expectations have been set for a repeat performance."

"Really? You didn't come down here this morning expecting things to be different?" What she really meant to ask was if she'd expected her to be different, because if she were being totally honest, Simone didn't exactly feel the way she had the morning before, and she suspected the extra sleep didn't deserve all the credit.

"I don't see why they should. Nothing about our circumstances has changed," Loreto said and popped the last bite of bread into her mouth.

Simone exhaled a sigh of relief. "That's tremendously refreshing."

"Isn't it? Regardless of what we did last night, or how good we were at it, I don't need anything more from you today than I needed yesterday."

Simone nodded, overwhelmingly pleased with the pronouncement, though a part of her remembered the tension between them at various points the day before with minor trepidation. Still, the completely sensible separation of sex and business didn't come easily, and it seemed she'd once again been gifted with uncommonly good fortune in finding someone like Loreto to accompany her on this trip.

"I assume we're ready to go?"

Simone rose, feeling lighter and steadier than she had in ages with both her mind and her body sated, at least for the time being. "Yes, I think we are."

They pushed through the doors to the opulent lobby.

"For crying out loud, you weren't kidding about the heat. Just a two-minute walk across the parking lot and I'm thinking of pressing my face to the cool tile steps. Or maybe I should hug one of the marble columns." Simone gestured toward the pillars under the ornate Moorish archways leading off in every direction.

Loreto couldn't blame her, but she knew of better ways to beat the heat. "Why not let me get us checked in, and then we'll see what we can do."

"You weren't kidding about this hotel, either."

"Lush, right?" Loreto asked as she approached the front desk.

"Even by my standards, you keep winning with lodging selections," Simone admitted without the least bit of grudging in her voice. Loreto felt a twinge of pleasure at the easy compliment. Those seemed to come easier today, out of both of them. She'd like to consider their improved attitudes a reward for their frank conversation this morning or a by-product of the respect with which they handled the complexities last night had left them with, but she'd be an idiot if she didn't realize great sex also went a long way toward improving a person's mood.

Once they'd cleared the air and it had become clear neither one of them felt weird or possessive, the two-hour drive from Cordoba to Sevilla had been downright enjoyable. They hadn't suddenly become Chatty Cathys, but they'd made easy conversation about the scenery or shared relaxed silences while Simone checked email or did research, occasionally questioning her about things like local infrastructure or taxes. Loreto still suspected she was sniffing around the wrong trails at times, but she felt less inclined to say so today. She'd spoken her piece yesterday, and whatever Simone did with the info she'd been given didn't make any difference to her.

She collected their keys and led them both up a wide stairway lined with elaborately detailed tile mosaics.

"They don't ever waste a space here, do they?" Simone asked, running her fingers along the image of two cherubs lounging in a grassy field.

"Why would they? You have to have stairways. They might as well be beautiful."

Simone didn't respond, but she pressed her lips together in the thin line Loreto had come to recognize as her thinking expression. She never responded until she knew her own mind, and she must have still been undecided, because she still hadn't commented by the time they reached their rooms.

Handing Simone her key, she waited for her to open the door and watched with another pique of pleasure as those scrutinizing blue eyes surveyed her accommodations. Every touch, from the lush rugs to the large, upholstered headboard over the thick king mattress to the heavy drapes in maroon with gold sashes, screamed luxury.

"This invoice is going to set my boss's secretary's teeth on edge, isn't it?" Simone finally asked.

Loreto laughed. "It may."

"Good," Simone said, stepping inside. "It's what they get for sending me on this errand."

The edge in her voice made it clear she still felt the task she'd been sent to do was beneath her. Loreto, too, had begun to wonder about the wisdom of sending a business shark of Simone's caliber after a mom-and-pop company, but she wasn't being paid to think about publishing hierarchies, so instead, she whispered, "Go check the balcony."

Simone didn't question or even hesitate, another subtle shift from the day before. She crossed the room and pulled back the thick curtains. Her smile began to spread even before she swung open the French doors leading to a small ledge encased in a deep-green, metal railing.

"I see what you did there," Simone said, staring out over the azure waters of the hotel pool sunken into a secluded courtyard.

"Yeah?" Loreto said. "And?"

"The activities you planned for later, they're outside?"

"Outdoors, involve walking, and offer very little shade," Loreto confirmed, trying to keep the amusement from her voice.

Simone glanced up quickly, then wincing in the direction of the high afternoon sun, she turned quickly back toward the pool, her expression softening.

"And did I mention sunset isn't until about nine, so dusk extends until almost ten?"

Simone blew out a resigned breath. "You didn't, but I've noticed how the daylight hours seem to stretch into the night."

"I could explain to you now, or . . ." She pointed to one of the long, cushioned lounge chairs under a flowing white cabana near the edge of the water. "We could meet down there at three and sip some sangria while we discuss that topic and any others you have on your mind, research-wise of course."

Simone turned to face her, suddenly close on the small balcony, close enough to see the different shades of blue in her eyes, close enough to see the pink in her cheeks, close enough to see the little bit of white at the spot where she bit her lip.

The heat was back, and not just because they stood outside.

Thankfully, Loreto didn't seem to be the only one feeling it. Simone leaned closer for a fleeting second before stepping back and turning to face the pool once more.

"Three o'clock?" she asked.

The question pinged through her brain for a few extra seconds as her synapses seemed a bit overloaded. "Yes, right. Three o'clock. At the pool. For sangria and work."

"Work." Simone gave a half smile. "Sure, why not go with that?"

Chapter Nine

The heat hadn't significantly waned over the last two hours, but the sun had dipped a little lower, which allowed the clusters of palm trees to throw some much-needed shade around the pool. Simone fought the urge to hop from one spot to another like a kid playing shade-hopscotch. She couldn't remember the last time she hopped. Or played a game. Or played hooky, because that was, in effect, what she was doing. Despite Loreto's attempt to convince her they could lounge beside the pool and discuss Spanish philosophy, she doubted the conversation would go too deep. Surprisingly, she wasn't upset by the prospect.

She honestly hadn't been upset at all today, and in a sad commentary on her life of late, she couldn't remember the last time that happened, either. Perhaps the heat had broken her will to stay hot-tempered. Two kinds of hot was too much to handle. Then again, she'd handled the heat of last night well enough. The thought made her smile, but before she could get overwhelmed by the visual memories, a small splash of water sprinkled across her feet.

"*Hola, Rubia,*" Loreto called from the water.

"*Hola,*" she responded before realizing she'd responded both in Spanish and to a name other than her own. "Why do you call me that?"

"*Rubia?*" Loreto asked, then ducked under the water and swam a few strokes closer, before surfacing again with a wide smile on her face. "Let's call it a term of endearment."

155

Simone found the answer less than convincing. "What's it mean?"

"It's the feminine form of blonde."

"You're literally addressing me by my hair color?"

Loreto laughed. "Technically, but it's less formal, like I'm saying 'Hiya, Blondie.'"

"Sure, that's much better," she said dryly.

Loreto ignored the tone as she continued to tease. "I knew you'd like it. Really speaks to your defining qualities."

Simone shook her head and bit her lip as she set her canvas beach bag next to one of the lounges under a cabana. It was too hot to get angry over little things, she reminded herself, and surprisingly, it worked. What had come over her? The ability to go from content to annoyed in an instant had always been one of her so-called defining qualities. She turned around, intending to say so, but the words evaporated on her lips as Loreto pushed herself up out of the water and onto the edge of the pool.

Simone's throat went dry at the sight of that enthralling torso, soaking wet and completely uncovered. Water ran in rivulets down from her collar bones, over the high, firm breasts, and down across her smooth abs all the way to the waistband of her tight, black boy-shorts. In other words, exactly the same path her tongue had traveled the night before. The edges of her vision tinged red with a lust so swift and powerful she briefly entertained fantasies of a repeat performance right here.

"You getting in?" Loreto asked, shaking out her dark hair and reaching for a nearby towel. "The water's amazing, cool without being cold."

Simone couldn't even imagine cold right now, but as Loreto draped the towel across her neck, allowing the excess to hang down across her chest, she did at least manage to think, though maybe not at the high level she considered normal, because she managed only to say, "So, you're topless."

Loreto grinned. "Why yes, yes I am. The question is, why aren't you?"

"Honestly, it hadn't occurred to me."

"And now that it has?"

She shook her head. The thought almost frightened her. She'd never been so unexpectedly overtaken by attraction in her life. Her brain had ceased to function properly, and she was still fully clothed.

"Suit yourself." Loreto shrugged and strolled into the open cabana where Simone had set her things. "The water really is bliss, though."

She really could have used a cold shower, but the pool would have to do. She shed her gauzy skirt wrap and her semi-sheer cover up. "Actually, I think I will get in for a bit."

"You're wearing sunscreen, though, right?" Loreto called from behind her. "This sun has the power to fry skin like yours in half an hour."

"Skin like mine?"

Loreto peaked her head out of the cabana and froze, her dark eyes running a slow path over Simone's bikini-clad body. Simone wondered if her brain boiled the same way her own had, but Loreto seemed to recover more quickly. "You know, fair, soft, and, um . . . *rubia*."

It was Simone's turn to smile slowly as the power balance between them shifted again. "I do, in fact, have some sunscreen. Would you mind putting some on my back?"

"I'd be happy to," Loreto answered quickly, before adding a slightly more chill, "not a problem."

"It's in the bag." Simone lay down on the other lounge chair and rolled onto her stomach. Anticipation tingled across her skin as Loreto sat beside her. She was flirting with danger, but she bit her lip to keep from smiling at the thought. She had to wear sunscreen, skin care was important, and Loreto's assessment of what the sun would do to her if unprotected hadn't been an overstatement. Still, the idea of Loreto's strong hands on her again added a considerable bonus to the health ritual.

When she heard Loreto rub her hands together, she buried her face in her folded arms for fear her lack of control might show. Who had she become? She'd done so well in reasserting

157

some business parameters this morning. Then again, this morning they'd both been fully dressed. Still, she wasn't a teenager jonesing for a little glimpse of skin. She was a strong, powerful woman who made subordinates tremble before her, but after one night with Loreto's hands on her, she'd become the one doing the shaking. The thought should have horrified her, and it did, for all of five seconds, until Loreto touched her back.

She sucked a sharp breath through her clenched teeth.

Loreto chuckled. "Cold?"

"Little bit," she lied. The cool lotion actually did little to soothe the heat radiating off her now. Once again, there was nothing but heat, in the air, in Loreto's fingers, in herself. Loreto, for her part, didn't seem interested in taking the most economical path. Instead, she massaged and kneaded tight muscles, starting at her shoulders and working her way slowly down across her back, dipping low and then sliding back up along her sides. Each time, she inched closer to Simone's bikini bottoms, only to pull off at the last minute, like some game of sunscreen-chicken. Simone fought a war within herself, her brain screaming at her to stop now while she still could, but her body begged her to shimmy out of the little swimsuit and let Loreto finish the job properly.

Stuck in the middle of two options, she remained still and silent as Loreto finally reached the thin barrier between them, and skipping over it completely, she moved on to the back of her lower legs. She might have sighed in disappointment, but the emotion was short-lived, as Loreto's talented hands quickly started a march upward. Giving her legs the same elaborate treatment as she'd given Simone's back, she pushed and smoothed the sunscreen upward over tight calves to tender thighs. The higher she got, the harder Simone found it to breathe, until finally she wasn't breathing at all when Loreto's palms slid right up to the curve of her ass. Then suddenly, they were gone and all the pent-up air in Simone's lungs slipped past her lips in a silent scream of frustration.

"I think you're covered," Loreto said without so much as a hitch in her voice.

Simone didn't agree. She felt anything but covered. She felt open and vulnerable in ways she both hated and craved. Grinding her teeth together, she pushed up to sitting and waited for the spinning in her head to subside before saying, "Thank you."

"You're a little tense," Loreto said casually. "I think you might need a massage."

"I thought I just got one."

Loreto laughed. "If you thought that was a massage, you've never had a real one before. I know a place in Málaga. Maybe I'll make an appointment."

Simone shook her head and forced herself to think a few days in the future. When had she stopped doing that? "I suspect I'll be pretty busy prepping in Málaga."

"Don't worry," Loreto said with a wink. "I'll make it super cultural."

Simone hung her head. She should have put her foot down. She should have said no. She shouldn't let this business trip devolve one step closer to vacation. She should reassert herself right now and demand they get back to work. And that's exactly what she intended to do, as soon as she took a few minutes to cool off in the pool.

Loreto dropped onto a heavily padded lounge chair and silently congratulated herself on her epic restraint. Kicking her legs out to their full length, she stretched her arms up above her, trying to loosen the knots that had formed in her muscles while she'd massaged them out of Simone's. She interlocked her fingers and tucked them neatly behind her head so she didn't run the risk of brushing up against any of her sensitive skin. And all of it was sensitive right now as she sat watching Simone descend the steps into the pool in that tiny bikini of hers.

The swimsuit was three little strips of navy-blue cloth tied together by glorified shoestrings knotted in tempting bows. Seriously, what was the point other than to tempt the shit out of people like Loreto who got close enough to give them the tiniest of tugs?

But she hadn't.

She could have. She could have pulled the cords holding the cabana curtains open and then pulled that little bikini onto the floor. Simone would have let her. Hell, her body had practically begged her to, but Loreto had resisted. She hadn't turned away from temptation like that since, well, not in all the years she'd lived in Spain. She probably wouldn't have done so now except to prove she could. Which one of them she was trying to prove it to, she wasn't quite sure.

She watched while a feeling akin to hunger built in the pit of her stomach. Simone moved in the water the way she moved through the world, deliberate, confident, and at her own pace. She knew what she was doing, and she did it with pointed efficiency. Why didn't Loreto find the trait as annoying as she had before? Simply because she'd seen the benefits of it in bed last night? It was one thing to watch Simone thread strands of silk through her fingers, tugging, pulling, taking. It was another thing entirely for Loreto to feel those fingers sink into her hair with the same, direct possessiveness.

Simone made a graceful flip-turn underwater, because of course she did, and then surfaced again, cutting through the water like the shark she was. Loreto had never forgotten that fact, not even in the throes of passion, but with each passing day, the fact felt less important. Which, of course, was what made women like Simone so dangerous. They made you forget things you knew.

Simone reached the steps and glided to a stop before submerging herself once more, then she rose from the pool with her head tilted up so the water ran through her hair, pushing the strands out of her face and down her back. The scene was constructed like something out of a damn movie.

Loreto clutched her interlocking fingers so tightly to the back of her head she pulled out a few strands of hair, but she forced her voice to stay neutral. "Refreshing?"

Simone sighed contentedly. "Ridiculously. You were right again. Being anywhere but by the pool this afternoon would be absurd."

"Passing out from heatstroke isn't good for business," Loreto said. "You're merely doing what's best for the company by staying upright and functional."

"Functional, yes," Simone said, as she adjusted her lounge chair to a gentler incline, "maybe not quite upright, though."

"I'm sure there's a confidentiality clause implied in our unwritten contract, so I won't tell if you don't," Loreto said as Simone sprawled out beside her, every inch of her magnificent body languid and glistening.

"I'm still working," Simone insisted, pulling an iPad from her beach bag. It's not my fault that part of my job involves reading, and reading happens to be a task well-suited to the poolside."

"Uh-oh," Loreto teased, "careful now. Some might accuse you of mixing business with pleasure."

Simone pursed her lips, like she so often did when trying to hold back a criticism or sharp retort, but this time, Loreto suspected she might be trying to contain a smile. "Yes, maybe we should go back to discussing your confidentiality clause."

"Not to worry. I would never tell your bosses that their golden child spent the day reading by the pool on their dime," Loreto said, then without as much humor, she added, "and they wouldn't believe me if I did."

The corner of Simone's mouth twitched up in that little half-smile thing she did, but she didn't argue, which was something else she did a lot. The combination only confirmed the truth of the statement. No one would ever take her word over Simone's. The thought made a little flame of frustration flicker in her chest once more, but when she glanced at Simone's long, lithe body, the fire grew, though the frustration feeding it now stemmed from a different spot.

She turned away and stared up at the sheer cabana cover above them. Nothing about this woman could be easy. No, actually, everything had been easier when she hadn't liked Simone as a person. The attraction had existed between them, but only on a physical, raw, and animalistic level. It had been easier to compartmentalize when she'd tucked Simone into some neat boxes labeled rich, entitled, controlling, American.

Loreto didn't kid herself. Simone still fit into those boxes, but she'd also begun to fit into some other ones, too. The more time they spent together, the more Loreto saw her as smart and driven and intense and responsive. That's when Simone had started to get under her skin. Somewhere along the way, Loreto had started looking for the little signs Simone was listening. She got her own knowledge affirmed enough that she started trying to convince Simone of things. She started caring if she understood. She started caring what she thought, which made her angry.

The anger had simmered in her. The resentment of caring about Simone's opinion when she knew Simone wouldn't even remember her six months from now had built in her until it, once or twice, had boiled over. She'd come too close to revealing something stupid.

Then last night, things had changed. Simone had come to her. She'd taken a conciliatory stance. She'd opened up. She'd shared part of her dreams, and part of her desires. Then she'd shared her need. Loreto understood those things, too. She relished in the level playing field. Sex was currency as much as money, maybe more so. Last night, she'd had something Simone wanted.

She stole a glance at Simone's body, so open and tempting beside her. It had been no hardship to fill its demands. She'd been able to meet those needs while doing something she enjoyed. Not a bad way to settle a balance. Except this morning, that's exactly how she felt.

Balanced.

While they shared an amicable breakfast, she didn't feel like she'd won some victory over Simone, nor did she carry any sense of indebtedness. So much of the tension that had plagued them from their first moments together had faded. She supposed a night of great sex went a long way to smoothing over rough edges, and the sex had been undeniably satisfying, but with their newfound peace, she didn't quite know where that left her in the desire department. She and Simone were no longer adversaries, neither were they friends.

Loreto watched her openly now. Simone had fallen into her

own world, or at least into her task. Her eyes were intently focused, first on her iPad, then on her phone as she seemed to move back and forth between the two, occasionally tapping on one screen or the other. It didn't quite look like the leisure reading Loreto had pictured when they had joked about Simone taking an afternoon off. She frowned, pursed her lips, flipped back and forth between devices, then frowned some more. Though clearly frustrated, she didn't sigh or flop around on the chair. She remained steadily and intently engaged, as if in some battle of wills, and while Loreto didn't know what Simone had put herself up against, she wouldn't have bet against her.

The thought disturbed her and came with the sudden urge to put some distance between them. Simone never even looked up as Loreto rose, left the cabana, and padded across the hot concrete to the pool. Easing off the side wall, she sank up to her waist. The water, while cool against her skin, did little to soothe the embers threatening to reignite within her. She kicked her feet off the bottom and reveled in the sensation of weightlessness, but as she leveled out to float effortlessly on her back, she had an unimpeded view of Simone once more. She didn't even know this woman, not really. Why did she care if she grew frustrated or agitated with her work? She'd never spent any serious amount of time trying to alter someone else's mood. And yet, when Simone scowled outright, Loreto felt torn between the foreign desire to go to her and the familiar desire to swim away.

Something drew her to Simone's intensity, to the way she immersed herself in experiences, the way her stubborn brow creased and her blue eyes burned. At the same time, she missed seeing her relaxed, open, amused. There had been such pleasure in seeing the other side of that business façade last night, and again this morning. How could Loreto feel drawn to both sides? She couldn't simultaneously want a woman to be relaxed and intense. Or perhaps she could want such a mix, but she couldn't have them both at once.

Therein lay the problem. She and Simone had always existed on opposite ends of that spectrum. Loreto embodied relaxation, and Simone personified intensity, or at least they had until the last day or so. Yesterday, Simone had brought out something frighteningly intense in her. Today, she'd fostered something relaxed in Simone. The thought would have been nice if they had been able to coexist in the middle, but she feared they had merely passed by each other on the way to opposite poles.

Simone scowled. It actually took her a moment to realize Simone hadn't intuited her musing and had instead grown displeased with something in front of her.

Loreto instinctively moved to intercept her displeasure and cut it off. Without allowing herself even a second to overthink, she flipped over and swam to the edge of the pool, hauled her body out of the water, and returned to the cabana. Grabbing a towel, she barely managed to swipe it across her legs before noticing the images on Simone's dual screens. One appeared open to the early stages of a novel and the other an internet translator.

"Are you trying to read a book in Spanish?"

"Trying is the operative phrase," Simone said without looking at her.

Loreto eased down onto the edge of the lounge chair without even asking. She ran her eyes across the text, the meaning of the words fluid and unencumbered in her mind. She couldn't even imagine the contrast between her own, easy understanding and the frustration Simone clearly felt.

She gave into the need to state the obvious. "You don't speak Spanish."

"Why didn't that occur to me?" Simone shot back, her voice tight but her skin soft as she eased over enough to welcome Loreto onto the lounge chair more fully.

"If only you had some easier way, like, I don't know, if you could employ a personal translator with an affinity for reading."

Simone nudged Loreto's shoulder with her own. "If only I'd thought ahead to do such a thing."

Loreto dropped her voice. "Why didn't you ask me?"

Simone shrugged, her arm rubbing slightly against Loreto's. "I don't know."

Loreto tried not to take the nonanswer personally. She should have gotten up and walked away. She should have jumped back into the pool. She should have sunk beneath the surface until she couldn't hear or see Simone anymore.

Instead, she picked up the tablet, eased back into a more comfortable position with her entire left side flush against Simone, and began to read aloud. "My first lover filled our shared air with the fragrance of oranges and olives hanging heavy, but unripe."

She had no idea how long Loreto had been reading. Minutes? Years? Simone hadn't intended to let her keep going. She'd only wanted a sample, but as the rich prose rolled over her, she sank ever deeper into the words, into the story, into Loreto's voice.

"You speak of fate as a linear path or some fixed point upon some lifeline, but destiny is an ever-shifting storm of sand. It swirls and blows. Destiny is as effervescent as light and as pervasive as the fragrance of olive oil on the *levanter* that carves Andalusian hillsides." Loreto stopped reading and stared down at Simone, who'd allowed her head to loll so far to the side it nearly grazed her shoulder.

"Is that the end of the chapter?" Simone asked, wishing fervently for the answer to be no.

Loreto blinked a few times, as if waking from a dream and not quite understanding which had been real, the dreaming or the waking. "Almost, I just, I wondered if you knew about the *levanter*."

"It's a wind from the sea, right?"

Loreto nodded. "The Mediterranean, yes. Where did you learn the word?"

"I've never heard it before until this moment," Simone admitted, "but I just knew, something to do with the context clues in the passage, or maybe the way he writes. He's made such beautiful sense of everything, it seems impossible not to know what he means."

"This is Juanes Cánovas?" Loreto asked, speaking in the same hushed tone one might adopt while touring a church or mosque.

She nodded, her cheek brushing lightly against Loreto's arm.

"He's the one you've come for." It wasn't a question, and Simone felt no pressure to respond, though she hoped Loreto wouldn't wait for more explanation. She didn't want to think about it right now. She didn't want to go back to that world yet. She didn't want to examine that thought, either. She wanted to stay here in this cabana, with Loreto's dripping body firm and warm against her own and her voice rich and smooth in her ear.

"And that's where *la levant* found us." Loreto continued with the passage. "Exposed to our own elemental natures and nestled in a nook she'd carved centuries ago in anticipation of our coupling. Drenched in liquid heat and held aloft by earth, oil, like ichor, pressed between the planes of our bodies until she absorbed fully into my skin."

Loreto set the tablet down, signaling the end of the daydream, and a surge of regret welled up in Simone. Why hadn't she listened sooner? Why hadn't she looked at the olive groves Loreto had pointed out on their first drive? She'd had her chance to soak that scent into her own senses, to feel it against her skin. If she'd rolled down the windows, would she have felt the *levanter* stirring her the way the story had?

"Have you felt that wind? The one that carries destiny across the sea?" she finally asked.

Loreto nodded. Simone didn't see her so much as she felt the movement. The subtle shift shook a drop of water from where it rested on Loreto's chest. Simone saw it tumble down the hollow between her breasts and come to rest again on her stomach. She had the urge to lift her body over Loreto's and settle more fully against her, skin to skin, until she'd absorbed everything between them. God, who was she becoming? Had that damn book seriously melted her into a puddle of lust and sentimentality, or had some uniquely Spanish combination of heat and Loreto done that?

"It blows from the east," Loreto murmured.

"Do you believe it brings change?"

"Yes," she said softly, then after a silent moment, she said, "they say it's what carried the Moors to Spain. There might be more legend than fact there, but I know for certain it churns the Strait of Gibraltar. I sailed through it once. I'd been meant for Italy, but the wind ripped through the channel, caught swells that made the North Atlantic look like a farm pond. It pushed me back to Spain. When we docked at Málaga, I just knew this was as far east as I could go. I'm sure it sounds silly to you, but the *levanter* carved the Rock of Gibraltar. I felt no shame in letting it wear me down as well."

Without conscious thought, Simone turned more fully onto her side and rested her head on Loreto's chest. "It doesn't sound silly."

"No?"

"I want to go there."

"Where?"

"To the Rock of Gibraltar."

Loreto's muscles tightened underneath her, but if she hadn't just shifted into her current position, she wouldn't have noticed the change, because her voice betrayed nothing out of the ordinary. "Why?"

The bluntness of the question and the reaction of her body gave Simone enough pause to stir candidness in her. "I'm beginning to suspect I've missed some opportunities."

She'd meant on the trip, but as Simone allowed the statement to hang suspended around them, she had another creeping suspicion those missed opportunities might have stretched to other areas and times in her life as well. She didn't care for the thought, and in order to keep it from lingering, she asserted herself again with a bit more force. "I'd like to see the Rock of Gibraltar. I feel strongly about this."

She tilted her chin up so she could see Loreto's dark eyes again before adding, "It's not an order. I just want to, or, I don't know, I feel like I should."

Loreto looked away.

"You think I've lost my mind, don't you?" Simone sat up, breaking the contact between them. "I probably have. I honestly don't know why this matters. It probably doesn't. Maybe the heat's gotten to me."

"No," Loreto said softly. She forced a smile that barely grazed her cheeks. "It's not the heat, or maybe it is, but the heat, it's Spain, too, as much as the wind, or the water, or the dirt, or the people. Gibraltar, it's, well, it's complicated."

"Complicated?"

Loreto's smile grew. "Yes, so it makes perfect sense that you'd want to go there."

Simone didn't fully get the joke, but she knew it had been directed at her, and she grinned anyway. "Fine. I'm complicated. I've been called worse. I am looking forward to going to Gibraltar, though."

Loreto nodded and pushed up off the chair. She didn't share Simone's enthusiasm for their side trip. That much was clear. But she said, "It's beautiful down there. I don't think you'll regret it."

Simone looked up at her, standing there in all her glory, muscles taut and her bronzed skin glistening with drops of water from the pool. As her eyes traveled up strong thighs, over the thin cover of her tight swim shorts, across her firm abs and high breasts, Simone had a sudden and overwhelming urge to pull her back down onto the chair. The impulse was raw and rough, and she might have been powerless to resist if she hadn't continued her path upward to include Loreto's beautiful face and those deep, unreadable eyes.

There was a warning there, one she'd blown past last night. If she did so again, she wasn't at all certain she'd have the strength to stop. She wet her lips with her tongue as the heat within her crackled to the surface again. The prospect of losing control felt distant and almost academic in the face of such formidable physical temptation. Her resolve perched precariously on the knife's edge of restraint and abandon when Loreto made the decision for her.

"We should go," she said, breaking the spell, though she made no actual move to leave.

"We should," Simone agreed and found the strength to stand, but the move put them dangerously close again. She'd only have to tilt her head an inch to cover Loreto's mouth with her own. In this moment, in this heat, in this little linen paradise, the kiss would be so easy.

Then it wouldn't, a fact she should have been the one to draw attention to.

Instead, Loreto again stepped back. "We have work to do."

She nodded. "That's what we're here for."

Loreto smiled. "No, that's what we're going out for."

Chapter Ten

"The weather's actually pretty mild in the—" Loreto stopped talking as she realized Simone was no longer walking beside her. She turned back to see her frozen in the middle of a long, wide pedestrian boulevard. "What?"

"Shut. Up," Simone said as her arms fell to her side with a little flop, her eyes wide and her gaze focused past Loreto at the full expanse of the Plaza de España.

"That isn't exactly the reaction I'm used to," Loreto said, though she didn't find this one unpleasant, especially out of someone as reserved as Simone.

"Seriously, though." Simone gestured ahead to the impressive building in their path with its semicircle arc, ornate towers, and half-moon courtyard. "Does every place have to be more impressive than the last?"

Loreto laughed and walked over to stand beside her. She'd been here many times, usually with a large group of camera-wielding tourists. Normally, this was the point where she had to take seventy-five photos on fifty different cameras. She'd spent so much time telling people to squeeze in or scoot over, she couldn't remember the last time she'd just stood and taken it all in.

"I mean, really. It's a bit much for *every* city in Spain to just have some gloriously beautiful, ancient treasure hidden in the middle of their streets and parks," Simone continued. "You people are like magnificence-hoarders."

170

Loreto felt the stretch of pride against her rib cage. This was the most effusive praise Simone had heaped on her, or not her so much as the things she had to share about Spain, though sometimes those things did feel like a part of her.

"What's the story behind this one?" Simone asked with a droll sort of humor as she started walking again. "Home of some Moorish concubines who overthrew the Prince of Tides? Columbus's personal shoe-storage venue? The first resting place of the Holy Grail?"

"Municipal buildings," Loreto answered.

Simone threw her some side-eye.

"No joke. The rooms behind the arched promenade are mostly filled with regional government offices."

"But what was it originally? What kingdom did the sultan or caliph or queen who sat in the throne room rule over?"

Loreto laughed and stopped to let a horse-drawn carriage pass in front of them before they continued toward a large, circular fountain in the stone courtyard. "No rulers, no thrones, no great history lesson here. The park we just came through, and this plaza, were both built for the nineteen twenty-nine World's Fair."

"It's less than a hundred years old?"

"Yes, practically Johnny-Come-Lately on the whole historical spectrum of Spain."

"But it looks downright ancient with the detailed tile work and pointy spires shooting up into the air."

"The spires represent the four ancient kingdoms of Spain, and the tile alcoves each showcase scenes depicting the various provinces. The style was part of regionalism and Moorish revival of the time."

"She says with all the architectural background of someone who claims no formal education."

Loreto shook her head. "It's all on the Wikipedia page. I can read."

Simone sighed. "Indeed, you can."

She had a flashback to them ensconced on the shared lounge under the shade of the cabana, Simone's body hot and soft against her own as she read about heat and vigor and making love in a grove of olive trees. Simone had melted into her then every bit as much as she had the night before. The thought sent the images in her mind tumbling, back to her bed as she slipped inside.

And she tripped.

She hadn't been watching where she was walking and a raised stone caught the tip of her toe, sending her stumbling a few steps toward the fountain.

"You okay?" Simone asked, a hint of amusement in her voice.

"Yeah." Loreto nodded to the large basin of water only a couple feet away now. "Could've been worse."

Simone nodded. "I think we've had enough swimming for today. You were saying? Or rather reciting the Wikipedia entry?"

"No, I'm done, just trying to tell you this isn't an old building so much as a relatively newer building meant to look like an old one."

Simone still looked suspicious as they skirted around the fountain and onto a footbridge. "I want to believe you. And I do, but there's a moat. We're literally crossing a moat."

"We are," Loreto said, recovering from her mental lapse and reveling in the lightness, both in Simone's voice and spreading through her own chest. She'd been so worried when she woke up this morning that things would be different between them today, but she hadn't even considered the possibility that they'd be different in such wonderful ways. Simone had become almost a different person, but Loreto couldn't deny a shift in herself as well. Simone's little comments of disbelief or challenge felt more humorous now, her studiousness more attractive than annoying, her regal air more grounded in confidence than entitlement. Maybe Simone hadn't been the only one who needed to relax a little.

"I know we're in the middle of a major modern city," Simone said. "I remember you sprinting across four lanes of traffic to get here."

Loreto laughed. "The light was still yellow when I entered the crosswalk."

"But in here," Simone continued, without comment on Loreto's weak defense, "I don't know. It just feels like we've gone back in time, or landed on some other planet."

"You're not alone," Loreto said as they climbed a series of steps up to the wide, covered promenade that ran along the entire front of the building in a gentle arc. "They have filmed several movies here, including *Star Wars: Episode Two*, so while we are still in Sevilla, technically you're also on the planet of Naboo."

"Ah, treading in the footsteps of Natalie Portman. Nice."

Loreto felt a silly little jolt of happiness at the fact that a woman as polished as Simone knew her *Star Wars* movies. As attracted as she was to her electric eyes and sharp tongue, she also enjoyed the little cracks in her completely together façade.

They strolled leisurely along the promenade, looking out over the moat and courtyard, the entire vista bathed in an orange glow cast by the setting sun. Simone's eyes wandered over the steps and arches and tile work, skipping from one to another like a child at a carnival. Loreto enjoyed watching her take everything in, her eyes narrowing as something caught her attention, her lips pursing as she inspected something closer, her smile slow as interest turned to appreciation. Loreto wondered briefly if the gaze she'd previously read as calculating had merely been a keen interest, or maybe something in Simone's approach had changed.

"There are rowboats in the moat," Simone said, the excitement in her voice pulling Loreto out of her musing. "With people in them."

Loreto chuckled and leaned up against the stone railing nearest the end of the plaza. "Numpty Cove."

"What?"

"'Numpty' is a British word like doofus. I refer to that part of the moat as 'Numpty Cove' because it's where the dullest tourists go to crash into each other."

"They aren't so bad." Simone stared out at them. "I mean, except for that guy."

Loreto followed her line of sight to a young man standing up in the middle of his boat and trying to use the paddle by jamming the oar into the bottom of the moat and pushing off. "It's a rowboat, not a gondola, dude. Sit down."

Simone shook her head, then focused on another couple. "Whoops, those two are going in a circle."

"They are facing in opposite directions but paddling the same way," Loreto said. "Probably a metaphor for their relationship."

Simone snorted softly, then gasped, "Oh no, the guy at the dock is going in the drink."

Loreto saw him a second later. A tall, overweight gentleman with a beet-red face flailed his arms, one foot on the bench seat of his boat and the other on the loading platform as the two surfaces drifted farther from each other. He teetered and wobbled, but at the last second, the two teenagers working the dock station hit the deck and pulled the boat back in. The man dove toward dry land with a heavy thud they could hear all the way from their balcony above it all.

"Whew," Simone said with relief. "That was close."

Loreto shook her head and relaxed so her entire back rested up against one of the support columns. "Would've served him right."

Simone eyed Loreto suspiciously.

"What?"

"Just seems unlike you to turn up your nose at the whimsy of rowboats."

Loreto nodded toward the chaos below. "Are you kidding? That's not whimsy. It's nearly a hundred degrees outside, and they are sweating and cursing and knocking into each other. And they all pay by the half hour for the privilege of working their asses off."

"Not all of them," Simone said, watching a boat a little farther down the moat. "I'd be that boat. I'm not a numpty. I could steer through them all to open water. I bet I could make it all the way to the other end of the plaza in my half hour."

Loreto shook her head. Maybe Simone hadn't changed so much after all.

"You doubt me?"

"Not at all. You'd probably win the all-time Plaza de España boating record, but why?"

Simone stared out over the scene, pondering the question. "Just to prove I can?"

"That's the victory of a cat on a hot tin roof, right?" Loreto asked.

Simone turned back to her, one eyebrow arched. "The just-staying-on?"

"Not for me. I won't play a game I can't win, or a game without a prize at the end. I refuse to live for some meaningless fight."

"What if it has meaning for them?" Simone shot back.

"What could be worth turning such a lovely night into a sweaty slog? Are they judged on speed or distance? Does their God of productivity simply demand they turn everything into a race?"

"What should they be judged on then, if all the traditional metrics are beneath you? Is all of life one aimless day after another without goals or reflection? What gives anything any meaning? Meaning requires judgment calls of some sort. There has to be a difference between doing well and not, or else why do anything?"

"Simone," Loreto said, hearing the old, familiar fire rise in her voice again and wanting to cut it off at the pass, but also wanting to win this argument.

"No, I'm serious." Simone brought her decibel level down another notch and met Loreto's eyes earnestly. "Please, I want to know what you think they should be judged on if not their productivity or their effort."

"What about artistry? Or generosity? What about learning? Or originality?" Loreto offered. She tried to keep her voice neutral, but she couldn't quite hide the quaver there as she said, "What about passion?"

Simone's chest rose and fell lightly, her lips tight, her eyes sharp. She looked every bit like a woman about to do battle. Loreto waited, equally ready to defend what she felt certain would fall under attack. She'd had this fight before. She'd had it so many times she could recite both sides in her sleep, and sometimes she did. She had the next round of volleys ready to fire as soon as Simone so much as opened her mouth. Instead, she simply turned back to the boats and with a slight smile said, "Gondola-dude survived."

Loreto turned to see the man still standing in the middle of his rowboat, which was now parallel parked next to the dock, but by the time she turned back to ask what lesson she was supposed to take from that observation, Simone was already walking down the steps and into the sun-soaked courtyard.

What about passion? The question echoed through her brain hours later. It had become a refrain, first whispered in her ear, then sung to the strum of a Spanish guitar, and now tapped out to the rapid beat of a flamenco dancer's feet against a wooden stage. *What about passion?*

There was certainly plenty of passion on display in front of them tonight. Simone didn't have to understand the language to feel a haunting chill up her spine as a man's call wailed, unamplified, through the cavernous room. The dancer responded by tapping her heels faster, castanets raised in one hand and her flowing skirt clutched in the other. The frenetic pace of her feet dizzied Simone's brain as she wondered how long either of them could go on, and yet she didn't want them to stop. The sensation of aching for release and dreading the end carried a heavily sexual undercurrent, or maybe she was merely projecting her own feelings onto the show.

Loreto, as if sensing her discomfort, glanced across the candle-lit table at her, dark eyes reflecting the single flame between them. With a slight smile, she nodded toward the sangria on the table between them.

Taking the hint, Simone lifted her glass, the thick red liquid filling her senses with hints of fruit and alcohol, but another sharp chord from the guitar suspended her in the moment, the drink centimeters from her lips, eyes riveted on the woman now as she spun, her feet a blur of motion, fingers clicking with blinding

176

dexterity. With one final crescendo of voice, instrument, and dance, they soared, then snapped. One instant everything, the next nothing, as they simply stopped.

Simone felt like she'd been doing one hundred miles an hour down a dark highway only to hit some invisible wall. All her senses slammed out of her body, leaving her empty and bereft.

Then the applause exploded around her, and she fought back an unexpected sob as sound and light and scent slowly returned to her world.

What about passion?

The performers took their bows, and Simone began to breathe more evenly again. Closing her eyes, she sipped her sangria, reveling in the cool, rich texture on her tongue. She tipped the glass higher and took several full gulps before lowering it back to the table.

"You like?" Loreto asked over the din of conversations starting up around them.

Simone wasn't sure if the question referenced the show, the drink, or the gluttonous dinner they'd consumed during the course of the performance, but it hardly mattered as the answer to all options remained the same. "Yes."

One corner of Loreto's mouth curled as she lowered her eyes, dark lashes brushing against bronze skin. "I enjoy hearing you say that word."

Simone's breath gave a little hitch in her throat. "Yes?"

"Yes," Loreto repeated. Her tone, just a little lower than earlier, sent a little shiver up Simone's neck.

"Hmm," she mused, "now that you mention it, I've developed an affinity for the way you say it as well."

Loreto's smile grew only enough to cover both corners of her mouth.

"I'm also a fan of the little half smile you get when you think you've won a point or think you've gotten away with something, even if you haven't."

"What makes you think I haven't gotten away with something?"

"Because you've yet to get anything I haven't meant to give."

177

"I wouldn't ever take something you didn't want to give," Loreto said with sudden gravity, "but convincing you that you want to give something to me constitutes a sort of win in itself."

Simone refused to take the bait by asking for an example of what she'd been convinced she wanted to give, partially because she needed some time to figure out if she had, in fact, bent to Loreto's will, and partially because she wasn't sure if she could prevent herself from escalating that trend. At the moment, she very much wanted Loreto in ways she suspected Loreto would approve of.

Instead of admitting that, though, she leaned forward, arms resting on the table, and gave Loreto just enough of an angle to think she was about to get a line of sight right down the front of her dress. She waited for those dark eyes to dip lower before saying, "Then right now, what I want most of all, is for you to . . . go get us another pitcher of sangria."

The soft exhale of Loreto's breath fluttered across the skin of Simone's arm, giving her a little jolt. She appreciated knowing she wasn't the only one experiencing the thrill of anticipation.

Sitting back, she asked, "Did you convince me of that as well?"

Loreto shook her head and pushed back from the table. Snatching up the empty pitcher between them, she said, "I'll never tell."

She was a good sport, Simone mused as she watched her walk away. Or rather watched her ass as she walked away. It really was a great ass. She had another memory flash of feeling those perfect muscles tighten underneath her last night. Maybe she should call her back and tell her to forget the sangria in favor of another round of after-dinner entertainment back at the hotel.

No.

Full stop. How had she let her mind go so far down that path again?

She didn't know what had come over her tonight, or this afternoon, or this morning even, because those little lapses had happened a lot. She'd felt like a stranger in her own body since last night.

Last night. She sighed. Last night had been the real lapse, but she couldn't bring herself to regret anything. They'd promised it wouldn't happen again. The ease of their agreement had given her so much hope, but now she worried everything had been too easy. Maybe a little anguish might have been good for them. Maybe they needed to feel the discomfort of a burn in order to keep them from dancing right back to the flame, because that's exactly what they'd been doing all day, dancing ever closer to something they promised they wouldn't do tonight.

Simone watched Loreto approach the bar. She looked so natural, so confident, so sexy. Even if she hadn't known what she knew about her skill, she would have been drawn to her from across the room. No, if not for what she knew about Loreto, she wouldn't be in this room. She'd be back at the hotel, working, or more likely, already asleep.

She watched the bartender chatting with Loreto as she filled the pitcher once more. What had Simone been thinking, flirting with her so openly? As close as she'd come by the poolside, after the damn sentimentality of that book and the raw sexuality of Loreto's body, why had she thought a late night of drinking and dance sounded like a great idea?

Sure, the flamenco undoubtedly qualified as a cultural experience. Aside from its beauty and the talent it took to perform, she'd spent enough time in Spain to recognize the dance and music she'd seen here tonight captured a type of energy and essence unique to this place. But wasn't that just another part of the same problem? Spain refused to allow her to think straight. There was something intangible to it all. Then again, she'd come to suspect those sorts of unspoken qualities factored very much into the job she'd been sent here to do. Still, try as she might, she couldn't convince herself she'd really been working at any point since dinner last night.

She glanced back over at Loreto, who still stood talking to the pretty young bartender, even though the pitcher had to be full by now. The twinge of something unpleasant in the pit of her stomach brought Simone back to her previous thought.

All of these feelings and her lack of defense against them had started over dinner last night. The sex had been the culmination of her lapses, but everything had really gone off the rails when she'd sat across from Loreto and opened up about her love of books and her frustration at not being able to pour the stories she wanted into the world. She'd exposed herself too much. She'd opened up and revealed too much about her ... what? Her goals? No, she'd never hidden those. Her drive? No. Her passion.

"*Perdoname, Señorita?*"

Simone blinked up, not only unable to process the Spanish, but also the presence of another human being so close. For a moment, only she and Loreto had existed, but as she tilted her head back, she could make out a less familiar set of dark eyes. The woman's smile wasn't as subdued as Loreto's, and her dress, long and thin at the bust before flaring out over her slender hips, offered yet another striking contrast. The question was why, when faced with a beautiful woman, did Simone immediately compare her to Loreto?

She must have stared an inordinate amount of time, because the woman asked, "*Español* or English?"

"English," Simone managed, then asked, "you're the dancer from the show, right?"

"And you are the woman whose eyes I felt on me the whole time."

Simone flushed. "I'm sure every eye in the room was on you during that performance."

The woman's smile spread. "And yet yours were the only ones I felt at my core."

Bold. And flattering. Two things Simone appreciated in a woman. And yet she wasn't naive enough to ignore the fact that she also appreciated the distraction from her thoughts. Glancing over once again toward the bar where Loreto now leaned casually against the oak barrier separating her from the woman who clearly held all of her attention, she decided to respond to the dancer's assertion in kind.

"My tour guide seems to have lost her way back to the table for a bit. Why don't you join me?"

Loreto watched Valentina take her seat. Simone laughed at something she said and then leaned closer in the enticing way that showed off her chest and made a person feel as if they were being let in on a secret. Loreto gritted her teeth and turned back to the bar. Just because she understood Simone's moves to be calculated and practiced didn't mean she didn't still find them appealing.

"Uh-oh," Paula said in Spanish as she set the pitcher back between them. "Which one bothers you?"

Loreto shook her head but didn't insult her by playing dumb.

"Come on," Paula nudged. "It's not like you to brood over a woman."

"I'm not brooding," Loreto said, then wondered if that were completely true. "Or maybe I am, but not for the reasons you think."

"I think you're bothered that two women who normally fawn over you are now fawning over each other."

"First of all, no. Second, Simone has never fawned over me. Third, no."

"You already said no."

"The second no was a different one. Valentina and I . . ." She waved her hand, not even having the time or the energy to give voice to how not an issue that was.

"So, it's the American who doesn't fawn over you," Paula said matter-of-factly. "Not used to that, are you?"

Loreto snorted softly. "I never knew you had such a high opinion of me."

"Yes, you did," Paula said.

Loreto nodded. She had, actually. The fact that she was brushing it off now didn't sit right with her, either. Simone seemed dead set on proving she could go home with Valentina. Why shouldn't Loreto embrace the same with Paula? None of those facts were in dispute. None of them needed to flaunt them, unless, of course, sleeping with other women was just a ploy to cover up the fact that neither of them really wanted to.

Loreto strongly suspected the latter was true. And therein lay the real problem. She and Simone had had great sex. They'd had great conversation. They'd had a great afternoon, and they'd come to a great agreement that they should leave it there. No strings. They'd agreed. No expectations. Only they had set an expectation, that they'd both move on. And now here they were with prime opportunities to move on, and Simone was clearly trying to prove she intended to do so. The way Loreto saw it, she had two choices. She could play along with her little charade or call her bluff.

She sighed.

"What?" Paula asked.

"I hate charades."

"So don't play them."

Loreto grabbed the pitcher and shook her head. "I don't intend to."

She wove her way back through the crowded room, having to thread carefully between tables and chairs crammed entirely too close together for the subterranean venue. The rough walls had been painted white, but no amount of bright colors could disguise a glorified wine cellar, and she got the feeling it was about to feel a lot more claustrophobic.

"*Hola, Rubia,*"

"My name's Simone," she said, without looking up.

"Glad you didn't get lonely while I was away." She plopped the pitcher of sangria down between the two women sitting at her table. "*Bienvenido*, Valentina."

"Loreto," Valentina said warmly, but she made no move to vacate her seat. "I thought I saw you here during the show."

"Yes, I had to bring Simone here to see the best Sevilla has to offer."

Valentina turned back to Simone. "This one likes to flatter."

"Does she now?" Simone asked.

"Always so smooth with all the compliments."

182

"Hmm." Simone made a little noise in the back of her throat.

"I should've known she'd be here with the most beautiful woman in the room."

"Are you referring to the bartender?" Simone asked coolly as she poured herself another sangria.

Valentina laughed, then looked from Simone to Loreto. "A little snap to this one, Reto."

"Not snap, bite," Loreto said. "What good is a growl if you haven't got the teeth to back it up, right, *Rubia*?"

"Actually, my name isn't 'Blondie,' it's 'Simone.'"

Valentina chuckled, and a muscle in Simone's jaw twitched. "I admire your spark, Simone. You and Loreto are well matched. I am a performer, and I always recognize my cue to exit the stage."

"We're not well matched," Simone said, a little too quickly, her voice just a smidge too high. "You're very welcome to join me."

Valentina started to rise anyway, but Loreto clasped a hand on her shoulder. "No, please stay. We're all consenting adults. Simone and I have a business agreement and a personal understanding."

Valentina shot Loreto a knowing look. "I understand."

Loreto laughed. The comment couldn't have been more perfect, and neither could Simone's pursed lips as she did the math. Her eyes darkened as any doubts about Loreto and Valentina's relationship vanished. Loreto, sensing her work was nearly done, added, "I'm happy to go back to the bar and let the two of you get better acquainted."

Simone's smile twitched, and her hands tightened only enough to put a minor wrinkle in the black tablecloth. Neither move constituted a major tell, but they were enough to assure Loreto that wasn't at all what Simone wanted.

Still, Simone didn't break easily. She managed to keep her voice completely even as she said, "If you wish. We're both off the clock now. You're free to go."

Now it was Loreto's turn to grind her teeth. Of course Simone would grant her permission to leave work, even though she hadn't requested it or even felt like she'd need it until that moment. The power play was blatant and cheap, and a flash of anger crackled like lightning through her chest, but she tightened her mental grip. Simone was clearly acting out, which meant she was scared or flustered, which in turn meant Loreto had gotten under her skin.

Still, understanding why someone had made a shitty comment and letting them get away with it were two different things. "Does rattling those purse strings make you feel better about yourself? Give you that false sense of control you need so much?"

Valentina hopped up, her dress swishing around Loreto as she positioned herself for a quick exit. "Actually, I do think I'm going to go see what Paula's up to. I didn't mean to step into whatever this is."

She didn't wait for either of them to argue, but Loreto didn't expect they would have. The only argument brewing now was between the two of them. She retook her seat and poured her glass full of sangria. Then sitting back, she calmly asked, "Do you want to talk about what just happened or not?"

"You just—" Simone started, then stopped.

"I what?"

"I don't know, what's the lesbian equivalent of a cock block?"

Loreto nearly shot sangria out of her nose as she tried to stifle a laugh.

"Is that humorous to you?"

"On so many levels," Loreto admitted, "but you seem very serious right now, seething even, so I feel like maybe I shouldn't laugh."

Simone shook her head. "It doesn't matter."

"Your mouth says so, but your eyes don't agree. That's happened a lot today. I feel like maybe we've had a misunderstanding. If you want to start with this whole lesbian cock-blocking thing, we can, because it's very easy to clear up. I'd happily call Valentina back over and provide you both with stellar references if you'd like."

"Because you've slept with us both," Simone stated flatly.

"Yes," Loreto said matter-of-factly.

184

"And the bartender?"

"Not . . . no."

Simone scoffed. "You were about to say 'not yet.'"

"Does that bother you?"

"Don't flatter yourself."

"I wouldn't dare," Loreto said with genuine seriousness. "I'm sorry if I gave you the wrong impression last night, or with Valentina. I enjoy the company of passionate women, but I don't consider them notches in some bedpost. And even if I did, I don't doubt you do as well in that department as I do."

"Don't flatter me, either," Simone shot back. "I'm plenty confident in my prospects. I don't need your patronizing affirmations."

"I'm not patronizing. I only meant that you have nothing to prove to me, and I'm not trying to prove anything to you. There's nothing to feel jealous or insecure about, but if—"

"I am *not* jealous of that woman, or the bartender, or you for that matter," Simone cut in.

"No?"

Simone pushed back from the table. "No."

"Because jealousy would be too straightforward for you? Because jealousy would be easy enough to control? You'd only have to say you wanted me in your bed tonight, and I'd be there, but admitting that would be too much like asking, and we both know how you feel about that."

Simone remained stone-faced, but her knuckles had gone white where she still held her glass of sangria.

"So you watch me talk to someone else, and instead of letting yourself want me, you only let yourself feel annoyed."

Simone shrugged one shoulder. "You do annoy me."

Loreto laughed. "And that's what turned your annoyance to anger. You're mad I have the power to annoy you. That's why you faked an interest in Valentina. That's why you made your shitty aside about giving me permission to talk to someone else. That's why you're all hot under the collar now. You care about me enough to be bothered when I look at another woman." Loreto laughed as she saw the truth of her statement flash like a strobe

185

light through Simone's eyes. "That's it, isn't it? You're annoyed that you're annoyed."

"Do I need to be here for this armchair psychology session?" Simone asked, standing up, "or can I leave you to your delusion while I run to the restroom?"

"Come on now, sit down," Loreto said, calmly reaching for her hand, but Simone swatted her away and stormed off.

Loreto took another long swig from her sangria. That hadn't gone as well as she'd hoped. She'd sort of expected Simone's cool, analytical side to allow them to have an adult conversation about their feelings, but she'd underestimated her resolve. Now they were going to have to have it out.

She stood and followed Simone across the room, catching up to her just as she pushed open the door to the single-stall bathroom.

"What the hell?" Simone snapped as Loreto shut the door behind them and flipped the dead bolt. She was too close, the space too confined. She was close enough for Simone to smell the sweet red wine on her breath and see the subtle way her pupils dilated as they landed on Simone's heaving chest.

She had to stop this. She had to get away. It wasn't that she didn't trust Loreto. She did, but she didn't trust herself around her. Loreto had been right, or at least partially right, in her assertions about her anger. She wasn't mad at Valentina or the bartender or even Loreto, and she could have admitted that if Loreto had also been right about the underlying emotion behind her annoyance. She got annoyed a lot. Annoyed was a feeling she had plenty of experience dealing with. What she felt for Loreto now, so close, so strong, so hot, felt much more like obsession.

"*Qué pasa, Rubia?*" Loreto asked softly, causing Simone to flinch.

"Will you stop calling me that?" Simone turned and pretended to check her makeup in the mirror.

"No."

"Why?"

Loreto pressed up lightly against her back, causing Simone to meet the dark eyes reflected in the mirror. "Because I love the way it drives you crazy."

They stared at each other in the mirror for several heavy seconds before Loreto opened her mouth again, but her next comment was smothered by Simone's mouth pressing hungrily against her own.

The force of their collision threw them two stumbled steps across the room until Loreto backed into the bathroom wall, but she returned the kiss fiercely.

She grabbed two handfuls of Simone's ass and lifted her onto the edge of the sink as their tongues wrestled for control of the other's mouth.

Animal instinct took hold, seemingly of them both. Simone lost her sense of place and time. Her hands were under Loreto's shirt. She raked over smooth flesh and slipped her fingertips along the base of Loreto's bra. She loved the sensation of softness yielding within the tight confines. As she pushed the obstruction up and out of the way, without taking the time to remove it fully, her fingertips zeroed in on Simone's nipples, hard and waiting to be lavished with attention. As she rolled one between her fingers, Loreto's head rolled back, exposing her neck for Simone to nip and suck. Reveling in her abandon, she ran her tongue from Loreto's proud collarbone to her earlobe and bit down lightly, while simultaneously cupping both her breasts.

Loreto wasn't one to remain passive long, though, and in a desire to assert herself, she placed both hands on Simone's knees and pushed them apart. The possessiveness in the move made Simone squirm on the edge of the sink, which caused her skirt to ride up her legs. Loreto glanced down at the exposed skin of her thighs and made a noise somewhere between a groan and growl. Loreto pushed her delicious hips between Simone's splayed legs and rocked forward.

Simone freed one hand and, snagging a belt loop on Loreto's khakis, pinned their bodies tight enough to grind into her. They rocked like that, panting, kissing, clutching, until the friction nearly sent Simone over the edge, but before she had a chance to orgasm like two teenagers making out in their parent's basement, Loreto pulled back.

"No." Simone gasped and clutched at the front of Loreto's shirt. "I'm not done with you."

Twisting the thin cotton in her fist, she jerked them back together, but as their mouths met again, it became apparent Loreto had used their time apart to position one hand between Simone's legs. She roughly pushed aside the thin strip of lace left between them, and Simone's breath caught as cool air hit the wet heat of her need. Loreto wasted no time covering her again and pressed one finger, then two inside her all the way until her palm cupped Simone fully.

Then she stilled and, leaning closely enough to Simone's ear that her hot breath ran down the curve of her neck, whispered, "Move against me."

It wasn't a request, but Simone's natural tendency toward defiance had left her the minute she'd seen those dark eyes in the mirror behind her. She wouldn't deny what she wanted simply because Loreto wanted it, too.

Rocking her hips forward on the edge of the sink, she wrapped her legs around Loreto's waist, holding their bodies together as they ground against each other. The friction between them was excruciatingly beautiful as every muscle and sinew screamed toward climax. She had no inclination to slow down or stop. She had no inclination toward thinking or even breathing at the moment. Her entire brain and body craved only Loreto, deeper, harder, faster, until, like the dance they'd witnessed earlier, they soared, peaked, and then crashed to a halt.

Chapter Eleven

Loreto eased Simone down off the sink, but given the way her legs wobbled, she should have left her up there a bit longer.

"I can't feel any of my extremities," Simone admitted as she braced herself against Loreto's shoulders. "My feet aren't working."

"It's okay. My brain isn't working."

"Obviously," Simone said, but the hint of humor had returned to her voice.

"Are we going to chalk this little escapade up to misfiring synapses, then?" Loreto asked, not at all sure what she wanted the answer to be.

"That would be nice, but thanks to your little tirade out there, I think we're past the point where we can lie to ourselves or each other. We're all—how did you put it?—consenting adults." Her eyes went wide. "You consented to that, right?"

"Yes, I mean, I would've said so, but your tongue was in my mouth. I sort of hoped the part where I lifted you onto the sink and pushed your legs apart made my wishes known."

Simone gave her a wry smile and turned back to check her makeup in the mirror. "Glad I read that correctly."

"It's not what I came in here intending to do," Loreto said truthfully.

"Me neither." Simone straightened her hair. "But I think we might need to acknowledge that anytime we're alone together, there's a distinct possibility we might end up in this position."

"Or any number of pleasurable positions."

Simone reached up and smoothed a strand of Loreto's hair, then kissed her on the mouth. "That, too, because as much as I'd like to say we've gotten whatever that was out of our systems, I'm a realist."

"I don't know if I'm a realist or an optimist, but I am human, and as long as I've got a pulse, what just happened here will rev it up."

Simone nodded and unlatched the lock. As the door swung open, they found a short line had formed. Simone smiled politely at everyone waiting, and without even a hint of visible embarrassment, she strode back out into the restaurant, seemingly unfazed, both by what they'd done and the fact that several people around them clearly knew it.

Following in her wake, Loreto couldn't help being a little in awe of her. Not many women could have body-quaking sex in a bathroom and then stroll back out into a crowded venue with grace and poise and a complete lack of fucks for anyone who might judge her. She found the quality impressive and attractive, and she intended to say so as soon as they settled up the bill. But as they climbed the stairs back to street level, she barely had time to inhale her first breath of fresh, night air before Simone's phone rang.

They both startled at the sound, a rude reminder the world existed in places and with people outside what had occurred between them tonight.

Simone checked the screen and her brow creased immediately.

"A problem?" Loreto asked.

"My boss."

She couldn't tell from her tone if that was a yes or no to her question, so she stated the obvious. "It's midnight."

"Not in New York," Simone said. She lifted the phone to her ear and turned her back to Loreto. "Hello, Mr. Alston."

Loreto could hear a man's voice on the other end of the line, but she couldn't make out his words, only Simone's answers.

"Yes, sir. Not at all, I'm still wide awake and . . . working."

Loreto didn't know whether to laugh or grimace at that assertion, probably because she didn't know if it was an alibi or the truth.

Loreto leaned casually against the building and watched
Simone pace up and down the sidewalk in front of her.

"Yes, very solid progress, I think. I actually spent the afternoon
reading one of the books, or rather having it translated aloud for
me." Simone shot a little half smile at Loreto. "Yes, I thought it
worthwhile as well."

Loreto grinned and stared up at the night sky. *Worthwhile.*
That was one way to put it.

"No, total agreement. We have to land him."

Loreto could hear the man on the other end of the phone say
something then laugh loudly.

Simone winced. "I think my assessment of the work would've
gone a little deeper."

Loreto arched an eyebrow, and Simone stopped to look at her,
blue eyes serious as they ran up and down her body.

"No, I don't disagree with the idea, but I wouldn't have used
the term," she cleared her throat, "'sex on a stick,' to describe such
a nuanced work."

Loreto did a poor job of hiding her amusement at Simone's
discomfort.

"Right, sexuality is not a bad thing. You've met me, Henry. I'm
no prude. I just don't think that's the best angle to pursue in these
negotiations."

She stopped pacing for a long minute, her brow furrowed, her
lips pursed, and Loreto wondered what this Henry guy was saying
on the other end. She shouldn't care. She didn't have any business
in Simone's business, and she shouldn't have any opinion on the
way Simone's entire demeanor had changed from the time they'd
left the restaurant to now, but they were supposed to be off the
clock. Simone had said so herself. But this little intrusion offered
a major reminder that Simone was never off the clock. Her entire
time here in Spain was her job. Hell, Simone herself was her job.
The longer she stayed on the phone listening to whatever directive
she was accepting, the lower Loreto's heart sank.

"I agree," Simone said again, whether or not she meant it. "Once we hook them, the marketing department has to have *carte blanche*, but in the meantime, you sent me here to figure out the hang-up and seal the deal. Give me the freedom to craft the narrative necessary to reel them in. All our opinions are useless until we get them into the system."

Loreto blew out a soft breath. There it was, the blanket statement some poor mom-and-pop publishers would never get to hear. They'd be told only what they needed to be told to get them to accept a big, fat check. Then once they signed on the dotted line, everything they'd worked their whole lives to build would belong to a multinational corporation that would make it part of some system designed to market books, ideas, even people, in exactly the ways they hadn't wanted to be seen.

"Really?" Simone said, her voice taking on an almost breathless quality. "No, I mean I'd suspected, but I didn't know for sure. Well, I guess congratulations are in order."

The boss laughed loudly.

"No. I understand. I wouldn't presume . . . I appreciate the heads up, and this opportunity. Thank you."

Then she hung up.

Loreto blinked at what seemed like an abrupt shift and end to the rather one-sided conversation.

Simone seemed no less surprised, but judging by the faraway look in her eyes, the emotion went deeper for her.

"Everything okay?" Loreto asked.

Simone nodded, then focused in on her as if maybe her presence didn't quite compute.

"Want me to hail a cab?"

Simone seemed to ponder the question longer than warranted before saying, "Are we close enough to walk?"

"About a mile. I don't mind if you don't."

She shook her head. "Let's."

Loreto started them off in the right direction, turning toward the river at the end of the block. They walked in silence until they reached a wide, well-lit path dipping low and close to the banks of the Guadalquivir. Soft street lamps reflected off the shimmering dark of the river, and the city sounds were muted by the gentle lap of water against the stone walls holding it in.

After they'd walked in silence for several more minutes, Loreto asked, "Do you want to talk about it?"

"No," Simone said with knee-jerk quickness. Then she sighed. "Maybe."

"It's up to you."

"Thank you for that," Simone said. "Despite what happened back at the flamenco club, you're pretty good about not pushing."

"I get the sense we've both been pushed enough tonight," Loreto admitted.

"My boss just let it slip, though I suspect he did so intentionally, that he plans to retire at the end of the next fiscal year."

"And he asked you to take over for him?"

Simone laughed. "No. He'd never say such a thing. He just wanted to make sure I knew it was coming as I prepared for my meeting back in Málaga."

"Sort of like a carrot-and-stick thing?"

"Sure, with the biggest carrot of my career." Simone shook her head. "He didn't say my promotion hung on this deal, but when you do the math, it's not hard to infer this might be my last shot at a major acquisition before the board of directors begins discussions about his replacement."

"So basically what you're saying is shit just got real."

"It's always been real," Simone said flatly. "Every day of my life for the last fifteen years it's been real."

"What then?"

"The end is in sight. I mean, I knew it was coming, I knew we were close, but now I have a date, and a finite number of chances, and that number is one."

Even Loreto got a little chill at the thought, and the hair on her arms stood on end. Not that she cared about Simone's promotion *per se*, but she could sense the gravity of the moment the same way she could sense the gravity settling between them once more.

"Well, that's great."

193

Simone didn't respond as she looked out over the water.

"It's great, right?" Loreto asked. "'Cause you're going to close the deal."

"I am," Simone said, the confidence of the statement undercut by the weariness in her voice.

"And you're happy about that?"

"I'm happy about signing Juanes Cánovas to a much bigger contract. I'm thrilled to share his work with the larger world, and I'm proud to be a part of making sure thousands more readers get to hear what I heard this afternoon."

"Though not in such a soothing, sultry voice, right?"

Simone's smile curled back to life for a second. "Right."

"But it is a book you can feel good about releasing." Loreto tried to tread carefully. She expected landmines lurking below the surface of this conversation.

"It's exactly the type of book I got into this business to publish. It's actually a rare find for the company in that it ticks all of their boxes and all of mine at the same time." The excitement began to creep back into her voice. "The plot arc is smart, the point of view is unique, the themes are powerful on so many personal levels, and yet, still universal enough to have a wide appeal. Plus, the narrative offers such stunning visuals, and after being in the places he describes so flawlessly, I see unending potential for film adaptations."

"Sounds like all systems are go."

"And I've got a decent angle forming for the pitch. The details are fuzzy but something about the world needing Spain right now. We need their heat, their openness, their sense of history and generosity. Spain has so much to teach the world in these times of transition and turmoil, and with this book and the others they've published, more people will want to visit this area," Simone said, the fire igniting for real now. The pitch didn't sound at all fuzzy, either. "These works, when put in the right hands, could provide the spark for a renewed global exchange of Spanish sensibility and hospitality. Instead of making the publisher more like us, they could help make us more like Spain."

"Wow," Loreto said. It's all she had. Even after hearing what she'd heard on the phone call just a few minutes ago, she had a hard time disbelieving a word of what Simone had said. Everything about that sales pitch hit the right notes, right tone, right message, right woman at the helm, and she very much suspected the woman doing the delivery was every bit as persuasive as what was being delivered. Even before she'd learned to respect Simone as a woman, Loreto had always respected her authority, her competence, her drive to get a job done. Now that she'd developed just enough insight into what might appeal to a Spanish psyche, she should have been unstoppable. And she might have been if she didn't seem so down. "I get that I don't know you very well in the grand scheme of things."

Simone grinned. "No, just well enough to tell me what I'm thinking and feeling and should be doing with my body less than an hour ago."

"Touché." Loreto did her best to ignore the memories trying to surge up in her. "I should have said I don't know you well in the business sense. I mean, you've got this job. It's important to you. You're doing well, and you just got good news."

"Correct."

Loreto stared at her as if waiting for her to fill in the invisible blanks.

"You forgot one small thing you also know about me."

"What's that?"

"My feelings on compromise."

"You hate it!" Loreto said with the gusto of someone winning a game show, then a little more softly added, "oh, that's where that conversation ended up, isn't it? You get the book, you get the promotion, someone else gets to market the whole package in a way you hate."

"Bingo," Simone said, keeping with the game show theme. "We have a winner. And while we're being open and honest with ourselves, this is not a new conflict you're witnessing here. Normally, I swallow the jagged pills alone, but I always have to do it, and it never gets easier."

"Thank you," Loreto whispered.

"You're welcome. But what for?"

"I love that you accepted my thanks before knowing what I gave it for." She smiled. "Thank you for being honest, being open instead of dodging."

"Ah, for being weak."

"For being human."

Simone pursed her lips.

"You care, Simone. You're good at what you do. The work matters to you, which is why you have to make tough choices, and the fact that those trade-offs still bother you after so many years of making them should tell you a lot about who you are as a person."

"It doesn't," Simone said flatly. "It doesn't tell me anything new anyway, because I always make the same choice. I find the most well-written, smartest, important book the American public can handle, and then I hand it over to people who will dumb it down and polish it up and slap a picture of hard abs or tight asses on the cover and try to trick the broadest swath of readers into consuming something that might actually be good for them, though by that time it's been so processed you can't quite tell."

"Then don't," Loreto said simply.

"That seems like such an obvious choice, doesn't it?" Simone said. "Just stop giving good books to people who don't appreciate them. But guess what? Then none of those people ever get to read a good book. Middle America goes their whole lives without ever having a single experience that makes them think outside the box. They go their whole lives without peeking into another part of the world or another person's worldview. And minorities and women and people outside the USA never get their voices heard by the masses at all."

"So you get tiny crumbs from the pie or you get no pie at all," Loreto said, an old bitterness coating her tongue. "Sounds just like the American dream."

"Yeah, we're living it."

"*You're* living it," Loreto corrected.

"Compromise is the name of the game. I'll make the deal, because even a dumbed-down version of the book you read to me today is better than ninety-nine percent of the stuff hitting the Amazon bestseller charts, and it deserves to be read by a global audience."

"Doing so also gives your career a nice little boost."

"It does. This is what I got into the business to do. This job, right here, right now—it's the reality of what I've always wanted. I may not always like the rules, but the stakes are too high to quit now, so I'm playing the game to win."

Loreto didn't argue as they edged away from the river and back up to their hotel. She'd heard similar comments from Simone in the past. She knew they signaled the end of the debate, both between them, and, more importantly, within Simone. But she'd heard them enough to recognize that when Simone said them this time, she didn't say them with nearly as much conviction as she had a few day ago.

"How long will it take to get to Gibraltar?" Simone asked.

"A little under three hours," Loreto said, steering them out of the city in their little blue car. "We can have lunch on the rock if you want."

Simone glanced at her watch. It was nearly ten, which she supposed constituted an early start in this part of the world. "Spanish lunch, I take it?"

"English lunch, technically."

Simone raised her eyebrows.

"Gibraltar is a British overseas territory, so every time you cross the southern tip of the peninsula, you step into the empire."

"You're joking."

"I am not. The line of *concepción* is an international border." Loreto's voice grew tight as she passed a group of tour busses moving more slowly up a small hill. "We'll stop on the Spanish side, go through customs on foot, then walk across an active runway and hail a local cab."

"An active runway? Now I'm sure you're joking."

Loreto shook her head. "If only."

Simone eyed her suspiciously for a few seconds, but the hard set of Loreto's jaw and the dead focus of those dark eyes on the road told Simone that's all she'd get for now.

The minimal description was surprisingly sufficient. They drove in along a thin peninsula, sunlight glinting off azure water, as a large, sharp peak rose proud and verdant in their path.

"It's quite a shock after all the brown and orange and heat of the plains," Simone remarked. Loreto said nothing as she navigated through increasingly narrow streets before pulling to a stop in what appeared to be the last available space nearest a flurry of activity ahead.

"You have your passport?" Loreto asked as they exited the car.

"Within arm's reach at all times." Simone patted the small cross-body bag she'd slung over her shoulder.

"Good for you," Loreto said flatly.

"Excuse me?"

"Nothing. Let's go." Before Simone had time to process her surly mood, much less react to it, Loreto strode off through a line of cars creeping slowly toward a checkpoint of some sort and up to a pedestrian line moving at a much faster clip.

"It's just like the airport," Simone mused aloud, taking in all the signs in both English and Spanish, "only outdoors."

"You'll go inside the little building, but only for a hot second. It's the loosest border check you'll ever face."

"Why?"

"Because it shouldn't even be here," Loreto snapped. Lowering her voice, she said, "We're going from one European Union country to another. It's only because the English think that—you know what? Never mind."

"What? I want to know," Simone said, Loreto's tension taking hold of her now.

"It's not important." Loreto eased out of line. "I'll meet you just on the other side."

"Wait, what?"

"You're an American citizen. You go through this line. I'll go in a different way and meet you at the exit."

"You're my translator. Surely they'll make an exception."

Loreto snorted. "Of course you'd think that, holy shit."

"What's that supposed to mean?"

"It means no one makes exceptions for people like me, and they *all* speak English for people like you. You're going into the bloody United Kingdom for fuck's sake." She seemed to catch herself. Pushing her hands roughly through her hair, she said, "Sorry. I didn't mean that."

"I think you did," Simone said seriously. "Clearly something's upset you and—"

"It's nothing new," Loreto cut in. "And it doesn't affect you. I'll see you on the other side." She walked away without waiting for Simone to comment.

As she watched her walk through a crowd and around a corner, Simone fought the urge to go after her. She needed to stay in line. Loose security or not, this was still an international border, and the guards up ahead still had the power to deny her entry if she drew too much attention to herself. She'd need to answer questions about her travel plans, which she didn't know. She'd need to provide information about lodging that she didn't have. She might need to tell them who she was traveling with and where the hell she'd gone. Loreto should have been here. She should have helped. It's what she paid her to do. The line moved quickly as she entered the low, narrow building and saw groups of people beside her filtering into lines for other nationalities, but she didn't see Loreto in any of them.

She watched carefully as people streamed through at a steady clip. Still, the tightness in her chest spread first to her shoulders, then her neck, then her jaw. By the time she flashed her passport at the bored guard, who barely managed to look at it before waving her through, it became clear she wasn't at all uncomfortable with the process. She was uncomfortable without Loreto.

Something wasn't right, and not just with her fulfilling the terms of her employment. She didn't like not knowing where she was. She didn't like not knowing what had upset her. And much like the night before, she didn't like the fact that anything

199

Loreto did, thought, or felt had the power to throw her this far off-kilter.

She stepped through another door into the bright sunlight and prayed it would burn away the vivid images blurring her mind. As much as her body would enjoy a replay of parts of last night, she didn't want to relive the fight that had led to them. Why was she letting Loreto get to her like this?

More importantly, where was Loreto? She watched the only two exits she could see for longer than she felt comfortable, long enough to worry, long enough to start wondering how long was long enough to be reasonable and what she should do if they passed that point without finding each other again. Surely, there had to be a problem. No one else had taken anywhere near this long to clear customs. And yet—she shielded her eyes against the sun—yes, there came Loreto, strolling casually up with a group of men in black slacks and white shirts coming in from the other direction.

The joy that exploded though Simone's chest overrode her annoyance at having to wait, and the worrying she'd done during that time took a back seat to relief, at least for the moment.

"Everything okay?" Loreto asked as she approached.

Simone nodded, not sure that was the case, but she didn't want to comment on a situation she didn't fully understand. "You?"

Loreto shrugged and turned to a middle-aged man with close-cut salt and pepper hair. "Simone, meet Berto, our taxi driver and tour guide to the top of the rock."

He extended his hand. "Nice to meet you, Miss."

"Likewise," she said, before turning back to Loreto. "I thought you were my tour guide."

"You need a special permit to take people up the rock, and I don't have one," Loreto said. "Add it to the long list of things I don't have and move on."

Even poor Berto seemed a little taken aback by the comment as he stared first at his shoes and then at the sky. Simone wouldn't play that game. She stared straight into Loreto's eyes, searching for any sort of answer or even a clue as to what had gone so terribly wrong between last night and now. She found only the vague hint of unspecified challenge.

"Miss, I'm well certified, and I've got a little picnic lunch for you to eat by the cannons, after you see the Pillars of Hercules and the monkeys, of course."

"Monkeys?" Simone asked, then backing up, repeated, "The pillars of what?"

"Hercules, Miss," Berto said as if that made more sense. "They're our first stop."

"I'd only expected to go up to the Rock of Gibraltar and, well, feel." She glanced at Loreto, who was scowling off in the general direction from which they'd come. Something cold in her gaze made their plans, made in the heat of yesterday, feel flat and silly. What had she been thinking coming all the way out here simply to feel some wind? What did it matter where the weather blew in from or toward? Straightening her shoulders, she said, "I hadn't expected to see any other sights or visit a zoo."

"Seems like I've got a lot of explaining to do." Berto laughed then hitched a thumb toward a nearby taxi. "Shall I start the tour?"

Simone nodded. "I suppose you might as well."

Loreto sat in the front passenger's seat as they wound their way through a tightly packed town and past coastal high-rises.

"So, you see, Miss," Berto continued his lesson, "the Barbary macaque monkeys are sort of like our good luck charms. Our government feeds them and gives them medical treatment."

"All because of some superstition about the British leaving if the monkeys die out?"

He smiled broadly. "That's what we tell the tourists, but honestly, they are a great gimmick to get people to the top of the rock, and if we didn't feed them up there, they've been known to come down into town and try to swipe food off the restaurant patios. I even saw one walk into a bar once."

"A monkey walked into a bar," Simone said, then shook her

head. "I'd be certain you were setting me up for some punchline if I hadn't already seen what I've seen today. I'm still getting over the fact that we all had to wait for the plane to land before we could drive across the runway."

"If you think it's funny in a taxi, you should try doing it on foot."

"We might on the way back," Loreto said.

Both Berto and Simone turned to look at her, and she realized it was the first thing she'd said since getting into the car. How long had she been sulking? Five, ten minutes? She knew she wasn't being fair, but nothing about this morning had been fair. Hell, the world wasn't fair, and they still found a way to keep going, so she couldn't manage to summon much sympathy for Simone's discomfort at the moment.

"I can drop you wherever you'd like," Berto said, then quickly added, "on this side of the border."

"And you can't cross back into Spain?"

The driver shot Loreto a not-so-circumspect look.

"He can," Loreto said, "but there's a bunch of stupid rules in place we'd rather not deal with."

"Like which rules?"

"All of them are stupid," Loreto snapped. "The whole damn border is stupid. It's all so fake and useless, as if the people who live in this square mile are fundamentally different than the people born in some hovel two miles from here? Why? Because they speak a different language? Because their skin is a different color? Because their parents had Latino last names instead of Anglo ones, that somehow makes people less worthy?"

"Hey, it's okay." Simone's sickly patronizing voice served only to ratchet up Loreto's temper another three levels.

"It's not okay. It's white people trying to hoard what's theirs by drawing lines and stringing up fences. It's inhumane. People don't belong in boxes, and no person should be owned by anyone else or anything else, but those inalienable rights have never applied to all of us equally, have they?"

"No, they haven't," Simone said quickly, which once again

made Loreto angry. She didn't need Simone to agree with her. She hadn't asked that question for affirmation from someone who couldn't possibly understand the magnitude of what she'd said or what she felt.

"I hear ya, mate," Berto said. "My dad was English, my mum Spanish. I got family on both sides of the line. I'm happy to be a dual citizen, and I support Gibraltar staying a territory, but there's no need for the barbed wire."

Loreto clenched her teeth so tightly her jaw hurt, and sweat prickled the back of her neck. She had to stop. She couldn't go back to swinging wildly. She'd come too far, literally and figuratively. She was safe. No one in the car dared challenge her. This wasn't her fight. She didn't even care what anyone thought.

Maybe the last two statements were lies, but she'd told them to herself often enough that she could sleep at night, or at least she could before she'd had to face the border.

"Okay, we're almost to our first stop." Berto sounded relieved to make the assertion.

"The Pillars of Hercules mark the mythological door to the Mediterranean. The Greeks believed the rock was one of the two posts you had to pass between to sail into or out of the sea, and it was guarded by a big, bad, heartbreaking demigod with a temper." Berto laughed as if he found the idea amusing. "But even if you don't believe in demigods, this spot will offer your first great view."

"I'll take it from here," Loreto said as the car came to a stop in a small, circular drive.

"Take your time," Berto said kindly, then after Simone hopped out, he grinned and added, "She's paying me by the hour."

The little aside was almost enough to start draining the anger boiling Loreto's brain. The view didn't hurt that process, either. As she followed Simone right up to some small, reproduction Greek pillars, she took in the panorama. There was blue nearly as far as the eye could see. Cerulean water met a robin's egg sky in two directions, and in the opposite points lay two hazy promontories of sepia.

Loreto pointed toward the west and said, "That's the Spanish mainland. And over there," she indicated the southerly land mass, only slightly farther off, "is Africa."

"Uh-huh," Simone said, "and?"

"The water in the middle is the Strait of Gibraltar, which connects the Mediterranean Sea with the Atlantic Ocean."

"And?"

Loreto shrugged. "And you could take a picture. It's a thing people do when they see a new continent for the first time, or maybe you've seen Africa before. I don't know. Or we could go back to the car."

"Or you could tell me where the hell your little outburst back there came from."

The defiance she'd only barely gotten control of slammed against the inside of her chest again. "I don't know what you mean."

"That's not cute," Simone said.

"I'm sorry. I didn't know 'cute' was in my job description."

"If you don't want to tell me, then don't tell me, but don't lie and pretend you haven't been twitchy all morning. Something's bothering you."

"I'm fine."

"Sure you are. I've only been with you every waking minute for six days, and the only thing I've seen you get animated over is food, history, and sex."

Loreto shrugged. She didn't hate that summary.

"But this is the second time you've gone off about white people taking or hoarding something. It's not the first time Ms. I'm-So-Cool-I-Don't-Care-About-Anyone-Or-Anything went off about politics and conveniently lumped me in with some 'them' you obviously see as the enemy, which I find odd since you clearly didn't feel that way last night."

Loreto's face burned from a mix of anger and embarrassment, and those emotions were entirely too muddled for her to sort out which parts of Simone's comments had caused each of them.

"If you don't want to talk about whatever's going on, that's

fine," Simone continued. "We don't have that kind of relationship, but we also don't have the kind of relationship where you
get to bite my head off without doing the courtesy of telling me
why, and if you do it again, I'm going to call you on it again."

"Fine," Loreto said flatly. What else could she say? Even in her
frustration, she knew Simone wasn't being unreasonable, but
even that frustrated her. She'd much preferred it when their roles
had been reversed.

"Fine?"

"I don't want to talk about it, so I'll keep my mouth shut."

Simone pursed her lips as if she didn't love the answer but
didn't see a way to argue, seeing as she'd laid the ground rules.
"Fine. Now, shall we continue this tour or not?"

"We might as well," Loreto said. "Next up, monkeys."

Simone shook her head. "I did not expect monkeys."

"Who does?" Loreto asked. Forcing herself to reign her temper back in, she added, "Come on. Maybe they'll be cute enough
to make up for what I'm lacking today."

Simone rolled her eyes, but her voice held a hint of teasing as
she said, "Then they better be damned adorable."

"So?" Loreto asked as they got out of the car at their next stop
near the top of the rock and gestured to the multitude of Barbary
macaques lounging around, eating fresh fruit or scurrying from
tourist to tourist, hoping to get something a little more enticing.
"Are they damned adorable?"

Simone smiled in spite of the tension still radiating between
them. "Actually, yes. I'd say the term fits." She still hadn't fully
forgiven Loreto for her comments or her refusal to explain them.
The whole thing felt a little hypocritical, given how a similar
argument had ended the night before, but she wouldn't play that
card. Doing so would imply they owed each other something,
when they'd both been adamant no strings had been tied. They
had a business relationship, they had an affinity for each other
that, at times, approximated friendship, and they had serious sex-

ual chemistry, but none of those things entitled her to Loreto's thoughts or emotions. That shouldn't bother her, and she wouldn't let the fact that it did wreck her mood, especially with a distraction like actual monkeys running around at her feet. "I can't believe they just frolic out in the open."

"Right?" Berto laughed, not even unbuckling his seatbelt despite a large Barbary macaque hopping onto the hood of his cab and climbing up to his windshield, as if wanting a closer look. "As far as tourist attractions go, these guys aren't terrible, but mind your wallets and phones, 'cause they have sticky fingers."

Simone chuckled.

"He's not kidding," Loreto said dryly.

"Of course he's not," Simone said airily. "The way the day has gone, it makes perfect sense that the local monkeys would steal my phone and rack up outrageous international charges by calling all their friends in Asia."

"Probably want to FaceTime with all their cousins and take a bunch of selfies to post on social media," Berto added from his front seat.

Loreto snorted but didn't join in the whimsical scenario. Instead, she strode a few feet up the road to the bottom of some stone stairs. "I'm going to the top. You can come along if you want a better view."

It wasn't exactly an invitation, so much as an opening, but the promise of a view seemed neutral enough to ease both of their egos, so she nodded and followed along, leaving Berto to hold his own with the monkey, who'd now climbed onto his roof.

Simone climbed the steps a few feet behind Loreto, steadfastly refusing to check out her ass on the way. She didn't want to be as attracted to her as she was, and the fact that Loreto was, once again, in her worn cargo shorts and plain gray T-shirt helped in that area. Simone didn't know what had sparked the transition, or reversion rather, but that seemed to be par for the course today. Still, even the grungier look didn't do anything to cover the way her muscular calves flexed as she climbed. Suddenly, the heat in Simone's cheeks had nothing to do with the weather or her exertion, and once again, she fought down a mix of arousal and embarrassment for being aroused when she wanted to remain aloof.

"So, is it everything you came here looking for?" Loreto asked as they reached the top and had three hundred sixty degree views for miles.

Simone paused to take everything in. She couldn't deny the vista was probably the most stunning she'd ever seen. She stood at the place where worlds and cultures met. The elements, wind, rock, water, all swirled and collided. Every one of her senses was engaged, right down to the subtle taste of sea salt on her lips. She got the overwhelming sense that she should feel something, which wasn't quite the same thing as actually feeling something.

She shook her head.

Loreto frowned slightly, leaned against a low, stone wall, and stared out, not over the vast expanses of water, but back toward the airfield at the border. Her jaw tightened and her forehead creased. Simone knew better than to ask again, and as she watched the emotions play across those normally noncommittal features, she felt emotions stirring in her that the dramatic landscape failed to inspire. For the second time in as many minutes, she was faced with emotions she didn't want to feel, and a lack of ability to banish them, and for the second day in a row, she was left wondering who she was becoming in this place, with this woman. She didn't appreciate the questions. She didn't appreciate the uncertainty. She certainly didn't appreciate her business trip turning into some morose introspection session. She needed to cut this trend off right now and reassert the original parameters of their travels. She opened her mouth to do just that, but something fluffy moved across her arm, and all that came out was a startled little yelp.

Loreto jumped, and Simone jerked away. The only being who didn't seem bothered was the little gray monkey who sat on the wall next to her.

"You scared the shit out of me." Simone scolded him gently, her breath rapid and shallow. "You shouldn't sneak up on people when they're lost in thought."

Loreto raised a questioning eyebrow, but Simone wouldn't offer any more explanation. Petty or not, she had no intention of opening up when Loreto wouldn't.

She turned back to the monkey. "Sorry, I don't have any snacks for you."

The monkey blinked his big, black eyes a couple times, then made a chattering noise.

"He likes you," Loreto said flatly.

"At least someone does."

Loreto didn't bite, but the monkey chattered his assent and reached out both of his skinny little arms.

"No food," Simone said a little louder and held up her empty hands.

The monkey jumped back along the wall a few inches.

"Hey now," Loreto said, "no sudden moves. They aren't pets."

"I wasn't going to hit him."

"He doesn't know that. You might be a trapper for all he knows, or you might be one of the vets who have to cage him in order to give him his shots. Nobody likes to be restrained."

Simone turned back to the monkey. "I'm not going to restrain you. Be free, little friend."

The monkey seemed to approve of the message, but instead of heeding her advice, he inched closer once again, this time his chattering more insistent as he stood on his back legs. She turned back to Loreto. "What does he want?"

She shrugged. "I know you probably see me as a little animalistic, but I don't speak ape."

Simone let her arms fall to her side as she stared fully at Loreto now. "Really? What does that little dig even mean? I see you as animalistic? Is that some reference to last night, because if you're not okay with what happened—"

Something jumped on her back.

She yelped.

She spun.

Two tiny hands gripped her shoulder tightly as equally small feet pressed into her back.

She let out a squeal.

It all happened at once, or at least in rapid succession. Somewhere in the back of her mind, she knew the monkey had hopped onto her, and yet the idea of a monkey hopping onto her was so crazy her brain refused to process this information. She turned quickly to the other side, trying to see the furry little hitchhiker with her own eyes, which she obviously couldn't. Still, she tried again.

"Freeze," Loreto commanded firmly.

She did, a fact that probably would have bothered her more if there weren't a primate crawling onto her head.

"Hold very still," Loreto continued calmly.

"Will he bite?" she asked in a whisper.

"If you try to grab him, he will absolutely bite you."

"I don't want to hurt him," she said sincerely, even as her voice shook.

"He doesn't know that."

"Well, tell him."

Loreto sighed. "You can't tell him. You have to show him."

"Fine." She sighed as she grew more accustomed to the foreign sensation of an animal on her shoulder with its hands in her hair. "Tell me how to show him I only want my personal space."

"Hold very still."

"You already said that. I'm currently holding my most petrified pose."

The corner of Loreto's mouth curled up. "Now look straight ahead. Focus on me."

"Doing that, too," Simone sang out as the monkey began to rake his miniature fingers through her hair right on the top of her head. She kept her head completely motionless, but she did call up to him, "Hey, buddy, you're not going to find any bugs in there. I washed it this morning."

Loreto fished in her pockets. "I know I've got something in here somewhere."

"Something to feed him?"

"No." She pulled her phone from her cargo shorts.

"Will he be interested enough in your phone to climb off me?" she asked hopefully as she adjusted to the warmth and weight of him on her shoulder and neck.

"Doubt it," Loreto said, lifting it up and tapping the screen.

"Then what's the plan?"

Loreto laughed. "To take as many pictures of you in this position as possible before he gets bored and wanders away."

"Son of a bitch." Simone's face burned as she realized that not only was she the butt of this joke, but also there would be photographic proof to live on long after the moment had passed. *If* the moment passed, because the worst part about Loreto snapping photos was that it meant she wasn't actually trying to help her.

"Come on. He's not hurting you." Loreto took a few more shots from a side angle.

"No." She pouted. "He's kind of like a big cat with opposable thumbs, but I wouldn't want to wear a cat on my head, either. His fur is tickling my neck."

"I think he likes your hair clip," Loreto said, just as the monkey gave it a little tug.

"Ouch." Simone winced. "He can have it, but he can't have the hair underneath it. Come on, Loreto, it's not funny anymore. Get him off me."

"Wait, maybe I should shoot some video first."

"Don't."

"Oh, was that an order?"

"Yes," she said through gritted teeth. "I've been a good sport long enough. I don't like being made a fool of."

"I know. That's what makes this so hilarious."

Before she could respond, the monkey grabbed as big a handful of hair as his palms would allow and yanked it roughly forward, right into Simone's face.

"All right, enough of that," she snapped and reached up to brush the blond strands away from her eyes. In a flash and a growl, a tiny mouth clamped around her index finger as two sharp points punctured her skin.

She let out a high yelp of pain, and the monkey flew off her back. She turned in time to see him scurrying away, then stared down at her finger in horror.

"Simone?" Loreto asked, all the teasing gone from her voice.

She looked up, her eyes wide, her voice eerily calm as she held out the finger with two drops of blood for Loreto to see. "He bit me."

Loreto's complexion paled.

"I didn't want to hurt him," she said, almost to herself.

"I know," Loreto murmured, stepping closer.

"I only wanted to move my hair out of my eyes."

"I know." Loreto took Simone's hand and lay it gently across her palm to inspect the wounds.

"It hurt." She continued to state the obvious. She didn't know how to stop.

"I know," Loreto said, using the hem of her gray shirt to press against the cuts.

Try as she might to break down what had happened, she couldn't make any of the pieces fit together in any way that made sense for her world. "A monkey bit me."

"It's going to be okay, though. Look, it's already stopped bleeding." She lifted the shirt off Simone's finger to prove her point. "You can't even see the cuts."

"No," Simone said.

"Can you still feel them?"

She nodded.

"Does it hurt bad?"

She shook her head. "It scared me more than anything."

Loreto wrapped her into a hug and, pulling her close, kissed the top of her head. "Scared me, too."

"Really?" Simone asked, genuinely.

"Yes."

"I'd have thought you'd find it funny," Simone said, with more sadness than accusation.

"I'm sorry." Loreto held her tighter. "I don't want anything to hurt you."

211

Simone didn't even try to resist the urge to snuggle closer to the rhythmic sound of Loreto's heart beating in her chest. It was much steadier and more soothing than her own racing pulse. "I don't want anything to hurt you, either."

They stood there in each other's arms as the words and their deeper implications stirred around them on a gentle breeze, but the longer they held on, the more the wind picked up. Trees rustled nearby, and little paws scraped across the pavement as monkeys scurried for cover. Simone's hair wafted off her shoulder and whipped around, encasing them both in a blur of blond.

Loreto eased back just enough to smile at Simone. "There."

"What?"

"You got what you came for," Loreto said with a smile. "The *levant* is blowing for us."

Simone closed her eyes and surrendered to the sensations of salt air rushing over her skin. Standing there at the top of the Rock of Gibraltar, a thousand feet above a turbulent sea with the wind whipping around them, she felt more anchored than she had in years. There, in Loreto's strong embrace, the world could rock and sway beneath her, but she felt no need to budge or bend. She would have thought those circumstances would make her feel small or weak or insignificant. How surprising it was to find the opposite was true.

"So?" Loreto whispered, close to her ear. "Do you sense any change in you?"

Simone opened her eyes and stared into Loreto's for as long as she dared before nodding. It was all she could do to offer such a small affirmation. To say more would require an explanation, and she wasn't yet ready to admit that, while she did feel a change occurring inside herself, she suspected it didn't stem from the wind so much as from the woman sheltering her from it.

Chapter Twelve

Loreto wrapped a Band-Aid around Simone's finger and kissed the tip of it, without stopping to consider the intimacy of the move. Her cheeks flushed warm at the realization of what she'd done, but when she glanced up to check Simone's reaction, she only saw a little quirk of a smile. She returned the expression, grateful not to have to examine anything else too deeply right now. She'd done enough of that today to fill a year's quota of self-reflection.

"I really am sorry about the bite, Miss." Berto glanced back at the two of them in his rearview mirror as he steered the taxi back on the main road around the base of the rock. "I should've gone up top with you."

"Nonsense," Simone said, sounding infinitely less bothered than she had been half an hour earlier. "I'd been warned not to reach for the monkey, and I didn't really, but he thought I did. Apparently, these things happen?"

"They do," Berto said with a shrug.

Simone shook her head, disbelief written all over her face. "Well, okay then. These things happen here, and I've been assured there's no danger of disease from the bite."

"None, not from a little thing like that. They're all vaccinated."

Loreto had already cleaned the invisible puncture site with rubbing alcohol from Berto's first aid kit and slathered it in antibiotic ointment, but she didn't feel the need to reiterate either

213

of those points. Simone knew she was okay. She wasn't freaking out so much as trying to make sense of the fact that a publishing executive from Manhattan had indeed been bitten by a wild animal and survived with little more than a good story to tell someday. Honestly, the whole encounter could've been worse, on so many levels. Loreto could hardly fault Simone for being amused. Even she'd been affected in unexpected ways.

She'd simmered all morning, her anger always just inches from exploding, even in the moments when she hadn't allowed it to boil over. And yet, everything inside her turned to ice the moment she saw the monkey's mouth close around Simone's hand, saw the shock of pain flash across her beautiful face. In that moment, Loreto would've given anything to take away the hurt and fear. Her remorse was so powerful and immediate that she might have buckled under the weight of it if Simone hadn't melted into her arms. Still, the thought of her own crass, cavalier attitude moments earlier made her stomach turn. How had she let her own insecurities and long-dormant rage blind her to the danger or to the woman who, once again, held her captivated? The warring emotions and the way they'd consumed her brought with them fresh terror, but Simone's stomach growled loudly, pulling her out of the memory before she allowed them to shake her core again.

"Excuse me," Simone said, placing a hand flat across her midsection.

"Not at all," Berto said. "I have a lunch for you two, but we forgot it in all the excitement on the rock. What about a boat picnic to make up for things?"

"A boat?" Simone asked at the same time Loreto said, "Yes."

Simone looked at her warily. "He said 'boat,' right?"

"My brother has a boat, Miss. A sailboat. He guides tours sometimes," Berto explained, then made eye contact with Loreto via the mirror again. "I mentioned it to Loreto before you came through customs."

"Oh?" Simone asked absentmindedly. "I didn't know you beat me through customs."

Loreto's stomach knotted again, but she forced herself to keep her voice even. "Berto's brother could sail us back from this side of the rock. It would give you a beautiful vantage point and save us the traffic and congestion back at the border."

"But the wind and the choppy seas." Simone looked a little green at the idea, but Loreto didn't think she could bear to repeat their entry into Gibraltar this morning. She knew she wasn't strong enough, so she was going to have to ask Simone to be, and while that opened a wound deep inside her gut, she wouldn't be able to heal it with venom or anger. So in a moment of both fear and courage, she looked into the blue eyes she'd avoided too often and said, "If you want to go back through customs at the airfield, you can, but I'd like for us to stay together this time, and to do that, I need you to trust me enough to do it this way."

"But why?" Simone asked, then quickly shook her head. "Never mind. I'm sorry. Okay."

Loreto smiled at the three answers and the way Simone had worked through them in such a beautifully rapid succession. "Thank you."

Everything happened with merciful speed from there. Berto made arrangements via cell phone, and by the time they arrived at the dock, they were greeted by a similarly graying man with an even more weatherworn face. Tomas, as he was introduced, wasted no time bringing them aboard his little sailing sloop and accepting the picnic basket from his brother. The two men stood talking in hushed tones on the dock for several minutes, and Loreto sensed Simone's nervousness growing, but she forced a smile as Berto called a cheerful goodbye. Tomas slipped ropes from the dock, and off they sailed into the blue Bay of Gibraltar.

Loreto tapped her feet nervously under her bench seat as they edged farther from shore. The great rock loomed green and gray above them, like the mythological giant people had once believed it to be.

"It's hard to believe we were up there less than an hour ago," Simone mused. "It seems like so much has changed since then, but I don't know that anything really has."

215

Loreto nodded, understanding the sentiment.

"Go ahead and eat," Tomas said. "The day's half done, and Berto tells me you've had a real pisser of one."

Simone smiled. "That's one way to put it."

"He's right," Loreto said, despite the steady tension at her core. "We should eat."

Simone grimaced as the bow rose and fell over a little swell and the sail fluttered above them. "I'm not sure I can."

"Come on. I don't feel great either, but let's try together." She forced her hands to steady and not fumble with the clasp on the little basket Berto had lent them. Opening it, she lifted out a small loaf of fresh bread, a wedge of white cheese, two oranges, and a small pack of sugar-roasted almonds. "Not a bad spread, right?"

Simone's stomach rumbled again, and she smiled. It was a sweet smile, a mix of chagrin and pleasure. Loreto's heart rate picked up for the first positive reason she'd had all day. The rest of her body warmed to the idea as well. The tension slipped from her shoulders, and she again leaned into even the slightest warmth exuding from Simone's expression. Two days ago, she would've considered herself pathetic, but a lot had changed in two days.

"We're past *La Línea* now," Tomas called up to them from his position at the tiller.

"The border," Loreto offered for Simone.

"So we're back in Spain?"

"Technically," Loreto said, tearing a hunk of bread from the loaf between them and popping it in her mouth without really tasting it.

"Technically?"

She swallowed the bread in hopes it would push down the bitterness trying to resurface. "There's always a chance some border guard could be patrolling the shore."

"Not much of a chance, mate," Tomas called cheerfully. "We're going to swing wide and come into the harbor from the north, which will give you the prettiest views of the rock and smooth sailing right into the dock."

Loreto nodded slowly at the explanation. Everything sounded copacetic. She and Simone were together and safe, and she didn't want to examine too closely why those things mattered so much to her right now. Staring back up at the rock once more, she couldn't help but ponder the change that had come over them both up there.

As if to accentuate her point, Simone touched her hand softly. "Thanks for today."

She shook her head. "Today was a disaster."

Simone laughed. "It really was, but you're still here. I'm still here. I know a lot of people see me as uptight and demanding and a control freak, and maybe I am."

"Maybe?" Loreto nudged her playfully.

"Okay, I totally am, but I'm also a hard worker, and I'm dedicated, and I do what needs to be done even when I don't love it. I know things aren't always going to be perfect or go the way I think they should, but I also know I have what it takes to rebound and try again. I respect people who can do the same."

Loreto took another bite of bread and cheese to give herself time to ponder that before she responded. Was that really how Simone saw her? As someone who did what needed to be done? As someone who got knocked down and got back up again? She didn't hate that vision of herself. And she didn't hate that Simone respected her for those traits. In that moment, in international waters, in the sunshine, in the glow of Simone's heartfelt praise, Loreto couldn't bring herself to hate anything.

Simone didn't question. She simply accepted Loreto's hand as they disembarked at a lonely dock down the coast from where they'd parked their car earlier. Loreto's smile was tired but genuine as she gave her hand a little squeeze before turning back to Tomas. The two of them talked in hushed tones, and Loreto slipped him what Simone assumed to be a tip, because she'd already paid for the ride up front. She would have questioned that, she would have questioned so many things actually, but

217

something in Loreto's eyes silently pleaded with her not to. The only thing left to question was why she felt compelled to heed an unspoken request.

She walked a few steps down the dock to give them and her a little space. The sun had dipped well into the afternoon section of the sky, but the breeze off the water offered a refreshing break they hadn't had farther inland. Right now, she appreciated any chance to cool down. Her life, her brain, her body had been nothing but heat for days. She'd felt heat from the weather, the heat of anger, the heat of lust, and now the heat of something she couldn't quite name, but it flared with every unexpectedly tender touch from Loreto.

"We're about a mile from the car," Loreto said from behind her. "We could walk, or I could call a cab."

"Let's walk," Simone said quickly. "I need to reacclimate to flat ground."

Loreto didn't respond, at least not verbally. Instead, they fell into easy step beside each other as they strode along a wide sidewalk at the water's edge. They weren't wandering, nor were they rushing, they were just taking an unhurried but direct path back to where they'd been earlier. Simone found the idea soothing, mostly.

She liked being back on equal footing. She liked them both being more even-tempered. She liked knowing where they stood and the general direction in which they were headed. But as they arrived back at the car and drove north off the peninsula, she didn't like the quiet distance reemerging between them.

"We're staying in Málaga tonight?" Simone asked, even though she already knew the answer.

"Yes, right by Calle Larios," Loreto said. "I remember how much you liked the area."

"I did, though it seems like ages ago. Has it really only been five days since we left?"

"About that long," Loreto agreed, but her eyes were still fixed on the highway ahead.

"I'm sure it'll jog my memory when we arrive."

They lapsed into silence again, and Simone had to fight the urge to fill it with inane chatter—another change. Normally, after a long or taxing day, she wanted nothing more than quiet time alone with her thoughts. Now, though, she wanted . . . what? Talk? No. To have Loreto talk to her? Maybe. Or perhaps what she really wanted was for Loreto to reach across the space between them and take her hand.

She sighed and shifted in her seat. What the hell? That was not her. She did not need anyone to hold her hand, and even if she did, she would have made the first move. She could do so now if she needed comfort, but she didn't. It was only a moment of feeling unsettled. She wasn't quite herself right now.

God, she was getting sick of thinking that. What if this was who she was, or at least who she was becoming. She shook her head at the idea.

"You okay?" Loreto asked softly.

"Of course," she shot back quickly, then realized she'd practically curled herself into a ball with her back to Loreto. Is that what she had to do to control herself around Loreto? How childish.

She straightened up and faced forward. "It's been a long day after a long night."

"Sorry," Loreto muttered.

"Me, too." She shook her head again. "Actually, I'm not. I don't regret anything we've done together, but we've been running a lot, and processing a lot and—"

"It's a lot," Loreto offered, the corners of her mouth curling up in the disarming way Simone found irresistible.

She relaxed more fully into the seat, her head resting against the cushion and tilting to the side to take in Loreto's full profile. Lord, she was stunning, from her strong jaw to her bronze complexion to the way her dark hair fell over darker eyes. For a second, she lost herself completely in admiration of her, but when she pulled herself together, it was only enough to admit, "I don't know what's going on with me."

"I know the feeling," Loreto said, without a hint of judgment. "It's exhausting."

"Thank you."

"For what?"

"I don't know, for understanding."

"Understanding something and knowing what to do about it are very different things," Loreto said wistfully. "Any suggestions on that front?"

Simone shook her head. "I've sort of been following your lead. You're the one who's supposed to know all the things about this Spanish mind-set I seem to keep slipping into."

Loreto chuckled lightly. "I'm not sure we can blame Spain for everything."

"Why not? It's so convenient. Plus, then it's Spain's problem, not ours."

"You've never struck me as someone who's eager to settle for convenient, or for leaving the solutions to someone else."

"No, I don't leave the control to anyone else, but I'm perfectly comfortable putting the onus of finding solutions on them. That's why I hired you."

Loreto laughed outright this time, and the sound sparked a little more energy in Simone. "Really, what's the answer, O tour guide extraordinaire? Surely, even in the perfection of Andalucía, people get overworked or overwrought. There must be some sort of Spanish magic for curing body and soul, or some special Moorish remedy for existential exhaustion."

"Actually," Loreto's eyes brightened with a spark of something resembling mischief, "I might know a place."

"Why do I get the feeling I'm going to like this?"

"I don't know, but how do you feel about splurging on something a little lavish."

Simone moaned contentedly. "Now you're speaking my language."

The sun was setting over the Port of Málaga, but they turned their backs to the last neon slivers streaking the sapphire sky and ambled up Calle Larios toward the Plaza de la Constitución. Peo-

220

ple bustled in and out of stores. Restaurant patios overflowed with young tourists and locals who worked in the historic core. Music wafted down from side alleys, and a canopy of twinkling lights flickered overhead. Loreto watched Simone take it all in. Her expression had changed drastically from their last walk down this street, her features more relaxed, her gaze less calculating. She scanned her surroundings with more passive amusement, rather than an open desire to consume. And, she stayed close, close enough for Loreto to smell her perfume or brush the back of her fingers against the bare skin of Simone's arm.

"It's a lot busier than when we were here before," Simone mused.

"It'll only get more so as the night moves on. Most of the restaurants won't be in full swing for another hour, and the bars several hours after that."

"I may not have mentioned enough how much I appreciate your insight in getting us out of the city."

Loreto let the simple compliment wash over her as she indicated a turn away from the busiest part of the street. "I know it wasn't what you wanted initially, but you trusted me to do my job. A lot of people in your position wouldn't have."

"That's a nice response. Most people would've simply taken that opportunity to say, 'I told you so.'"

"I think we've firmly established neither one of us is much like most people."

"Indeed," Simone said, her voice a little lower.

They turned down a side street so narrow the small balconies overhead nearly obscured the darkening night sky. A thrill of anticipation ran over her skin at the thought of what was coming, but she felt Simone's pace falter beside her. She didn't know what treasure hid down this alley or inside the dimly lit doorway up ahead. To her, this looked only like a wrong turn, a dead-end, and a potentially dangerous one at that. The significance of that wasn't lost on her, so she whispered, "Trust me, again."

Simone accepted the request without comment, any questions

221

remaining in her eyes alone. How many times had she simply put her faith in Loreto recently? Another thing Loreto hadn't given her enough credit for. Was it a change in Simone or in herself that had facilitated this new awareness as, little by little, she'd learned to see Simone as so much more than the uptight ice queen at their first meeting?

Loreto stepped into an open doorway hung with Arabian silks and illuminated only with the flickering lights of scented candles. With a quick glance to register the wonder on Simone's face, she stepped up to claim the reservation she'd made earlier.

"*Señora Molina*," the young attendant said with a broad smile, "*bienvenidos a Hammam Al Ándalus*."

Loreto motioned for Simone to follow them into a short hallway tiled in stone and paneled in oak, then down a staircase and into a foyer. They stopped while the attendant issued a series of instructions, which Loreto translated to Simone. "The door ahead is to the changing room. There are lockers for our clothes, and robes have been provided for us. When we're comfortable, we can proceed into the next chamber, and she will meet us there."

Simone nodded, seriously, but as they pushed into the dressing room and allowed the door to close behind them, Simone whirled on her and said, "Okay, where are we?"

Loreto laughed and opened one of the lockers. "Hammam Al Ándalus."

"Right, I speak enough Spanish to gather that, but what does it mean?"

"*Hammam* is a style of Arabic bath. I could give you all the details, but that would ruin the surprise. Why not get changed and see for yourself?"

Simone ran her palm over the robe waiting for her and sighed. "Normally, I wouldn't appreciate the wait-and-see-for-yourself approach, but I like the direction this seems to be going. I'd just like to go on record now as saying I fully expect there to be some sort of heaven on the other side of that door. You better not be setting me up for mud wrestling or something."

222

Loreto laughed. "There's no mud, I promise."
Simone arched an eyebrow. "And the wrestling?"
"That's entirely up to you."

Chapter Thirteen

Simone slipped into her bikini and steadfastly refused to look at Loreto as she changed into her swim shorts. She had seen her body before, and she could picture her naked anytime she wanted, which was often, but she didn't trust herself not to surrender to that delicious distraction right now. She told herself she was simply excited to see what lay on the other side of the locker room, but deep down, she also still feared the reactions Loreto had stirred in her on top of the rock.

"Ready?" Loreto asked.

"Absolutely."

Loreto held the door open for Simone, who stepped out into another candlelit corridor, where their host waited patiently. She spoke in hushed, soothing tones to Loreto, who translated in the same vein. "She says we're now to begin our journey through a series of complementing and contrasting Arab baths. Inside we will find several pools, cold, warm, and hot. The traditional order is warm, then hot, then cold, but depending on your needs for serenity or invigoration, we're encouraged to choose our own path and pace."

Simone sighed dreamily, then smiled at the woman, "*Gracias.*"

"*De nada,*" she whispered, then, gesturing for them to continue, she backed into the shadows.

Loreto motioned for Simone to go ahead. Taking a deep breath of humid air, she padded slowly down the slate floor until the hallway opened up to a small room. Fountains flowed into stone basins only slightly larger than a standard bathtub.

"Those are the cold baths," Loreto whispered, close behind her.

"I could've used those a couple times this week," Simone said, "but I'm not sure I want to start there tonight."

"Agreed, on both counts. Let's keep going."

Simone took the suggestion willingly, excitedly, as she stepped through the room and deeper into a hazy dream-world of steam and incense. Passing through the next doorway, the entire space opened up into a high cavern. Walls receded, and the ceilings soared two stories higher before reaching a grand dome laced with carvings of stars and moons that offered little windows into the actual night sky. Balconies hung with silks and gleaming candelabras surrounded the second floor. Stunning tiled archways descended from them in aqua and midnight. In the center of it all stretched a large pool, its still surface as smooth as glass.

"This is the warm pool," Loreto said, her voice low and smooth in the thick silence.

"Yes." It was the only word Simone could muster. With a slight smile, she remembered how much Loreto liked to hear it.

Slipping out of their robes, they eased into the water to a soundtrack of moans and groans. Almost immediately, the tension that had gripped Simone's muscles all day began to ebb and drain.

"Heaven," Simone murmured, easing her way into the middle of the pool and lowering her body all the way up to her shoulders.

Loreto grunted her agreement as she took a seat on the low bench along the outer wall and slouched back until her head rested on the pool's edge. Simone turned to take her in, so relaxed and languid, her neck long, arced, and exposed. Below that, only her collar bones and the top of her firm breasts remained above water, but it was enough to send a jolt of pure arousal through Simone's unguarded body.

"You like it?" Loreto asked, her eyes still closed.

"Yes," Simone said again, the word coming easier with each utterance.

"This is only the beginning."

"Hmm?" The question was no more than a hum, and all the possible implications of that phrase swam through her increasingly foggy brain.

"There's more," Loreto promised. "Just you wait."

Simone didn't question, though for very different reasons than before. This time, she didn't want to know. She wanted to trust. She wanted to be surprised. She wanted to flow like the water she'd submerged herself into. Pushing her feet lightly off the floor, she floated effortlessly to the surface, her body suspended as she spun in a slow circle and stared up at the stars above.

She didn't know how long she'd rested atop the water. Maybe she'd dozed off in the warm ripples around her, or perhaps she'd only succeeded in achieving a liminal sort of consciousness. But even as she felt Loreto stir the surface close to her, her body urged her brain not to engage. She stayed nearly limp as skin brushed her side and fingers threaded tenderly through her hair to cup the back of her head.

"It's time," Loreto whispered.

She blinked her eyes open to that beautiful body, so taut and tan. She wanted to press against it. She wanted to go back to dreaming of all the things they'd done and could do. She wanted to ask what it could possibly be time to do, when everything worth doing was already being done right here, right now.

Instead, she slowly lowered her feet and, sighing, rose up out of the water.

She asked no questions as Loreto steadied her with a strong hand and urged her out of the pool. Only then did Simone notice their host had returned and stood waiting for them at the base of a wooden stairway. They followed her up to another level, the one with the silk-laden balconies. Small alcoves housed burning incense, and ornate basins brimmed with fragrant oils.

Loreto bent her head to inhale each scent, and Simone mimicked her motions. Each breath carried a new and exotic aroma of jasmine, rose, orange blossoms, and more her palate couldn't discern. Loreto indicated one to the host and turned to Simone.

"Which do you prefer?"

Simone pointed to the orange blossom that carried memories of Sevilla. Then they were led into a stone-encased room. Shower-heads lined the walls, and lattice nearly covered the Moorish-styled windows. Their hostess handed them their robes and silently left the room. She needed no translations or instructions to strip down and rinse off before donning her robe, though it did require some restraint to watch Loreto do the same. Still, something awaited them ahead, the unspoken anticipation drawing her forward amid potential distraction. They were taken to yet another room, this one lined with a long row of heavily cushioned massage tables.

Simone practically whimpered as she took it all in, then she turned to Loreto, eyes wide with gratitude she couldn't bring herself to articulate.

Loreto's slow smile, infused with not only pleasure, but also a need to please, said she'd received the message.

Two masseurs beckoned them forward and helped them discreetly disrobe before lying face down on their respective tables. Then strong hands were on her. If the pool below had been heaven, this was nirvana. As capable fingers worked to wring any residual tension from her overworked muscles, Simone melted, mind and body, in a puddle of sated needs.

How did a place like this exist in such lush perfection? How had Loreto found its secrets down a dark alley? How had she known to bring her here, at the exact moment she'd be able to surrender so completely to its utter extravagance? She would have undoubtedly enjoyed this experience a week ago, but there's no way she would have been capable of submitting her senses so fully then. She had to be broken, she had to be molded, she had to have her reserves exhausted to the point of utter depletion before she'd allow the hollow shell to be refilled.

She smiled into the mattress beneath her. When had she become so melodramatic? She felt as if she were living in that Juanes Cánovas novel Loreto had read to her. She couldn't bring herself to even think about selling it, not when she wanted to exist in this world, this moment, eternally.

She smiled at the hyperbole she felt inspired to once more. How could she not think in superlatives? The only thing that could have possibly improved on this perfection would be for the masseurs to disappear and have his talented hands replaced by Loreto's more knowing touch.

The thought made her sink deeper into the lush mattress and deeper into the fantasies she'd held at bay since those moments spent in Loreto's embrace at the top of the world. She didn't need her full mental capacities to admit that something had shifted between them in that moment. Maybe her unguarded state allowed her to see more clearly what she'd tried to deny for days. Whatever had developed between them, through the fighting and growing, the lust and frustration, the respect and admiration, it wasn't a lapse or an escape. It was truth and a perpetual state of being. Here in this moment, she knew with certainty she'd eventually have to deal with all the implications of that relaxation, but the reckoning would not come tonight.

Slowly, her emotional cognizance gave way to a physical awareness as the hands across her back slowed, stilled, then lifted. She didn't move. She didn't want to disturb the peace radiating through her body. She didn't remember the last time she'd felt so relaxed. Not in the last decade, that much was certain. The thought should probably upset her, but nothing could do that right now.

She heard whispered voices and a subtle brush of air as someone walked past her. Then the silent stillness returned and lingered for several more minutes before a rustle of sheets told her Loreto had stirred.

Reluctantly, lazily, Simone pushed herself into a sitting position, and blinking away the clouds in her vision, she scanned the room to find it empty and the door open. Her eyes slowly found Loreto, sitting upright and nude, except for a sheet thrown haphazardly across her waist and upper thighs.

"Where . . ." Her voice sounded so gravelly, she had to swallow and start again. "Where did our guide go?"

Loreto's smile was slow and smug. "I'm your guide."

"You are," Simone said, "and you've more than earned the title and a sizeable bonus today, but I meant the woman who keeps taking us from one marvelous place to another."

"That's my job now, too," Loreto said, hopping off the table and making no attempt to shield her glorious ass as she retrieved their robes. It almost felt silly to watch her put her robe back on after everything Simone had already seen, and wanted to continue seeing, but any thoughts of silliness left her mind as Loreto stepped much deeper into her personal space than a robe delivery required.

"We're their last customers for the night, so I took the liberty of arranging our exclusive use of the facility for a few hours."

"Exclusive use?" Simone hoped those words meant what she thought they meant, but given Loreto's close proximity, she didn't trust her verbal processing skills at the moment.

Loreto's smile turned sly. "The hostess will be waiting upstairs to lock up, but until then, she's assured me we have the place entirely to ourselves. No interruptions."

Simone reached down and grabbed the terry cloth tie around Loreto's robe, then yanked her so close she nestled between her knees. Snaking a hand up Loreto's lapel and around the back of her head, Simone pulled her down so she could whisper in her ear. "You . . . are . . . perfect."

With a slight turn of their heads, she claimed Loreto's mouth with her own.

If the extravagance of the evening had made Loreto dizzy from the onset, she didn't know what to call the whirling blur of sensations now, because the kiss had certainly taken everything to the next level. It took every bit of restraint Loreto had not to push Simone back onto the table and ravish her right there, but she leaned into the urge only a second before pulling back.

Taking Simone's hand, she urged her onto her feet before saying, "Come on."

Simone whimpered softly, and Loreto had to fight the urge to give her what they both wanted, but she silently promised herself she'd hear that noise again before the night ended. "Come on, there's one more place I want to show you."

They showered off the excess oil, but Loreto's skin still felt soft and slick as she slipped back into her robe. She turned to see Simone tying the string on her bikini.

"You don't need that."

"No?" She pulled the strings into a loose knot. "Then come take it off me."

Loreto crossed the room in two purposeful strides. With an arm around Simone's waist, she turned her so she had easy access to the knot. She skimmed the back of her fingers down the nape of Simone's neck, reveling in the sexual tension, while simultaneously remembering what it felt like to hold her gently in her arms. A wave of new emotions crested in her—or maybe they weren't new, but it was new for her to acknowledge them. She wanted Simone in ways that went beyond the raw attraction they'd shared from the beginning, or even the competition for dominance that had plagued them for days. She wanted to hold her, to know her, to make Simone feel everything she felt inside herself.

Leaning close enough to fill her lungs with the scent of her bathed in incense and orange blossoms, Loreto whispered a response to them both. "Not yet."

Taking her hand, Loreto led them back along the balcony and down the stairs, but instead of heading toward the warm pool, she turned under a large, Moorish arch and into a smaller cavern with a low, rounded roof and a hexagonal pool that shimmered with tendrils of steam.

"What fresh Shangri-La is this?" Simone turned slowly, her gaze sweeping the circular room as she surveyed the intricate tile patterns lining the thick columns.

"This is the hot bath."

"Yeah, it is," Simone said, her eyes falling on a dimly lit doorway opened to reveal a smaller room, big enough only to house a long, low, marble pedestal.

"It's a cooling table," Loreto offered. "It's going to feel amazing against your bare skin after you get overheated."

"What makes you think I'll get overheated?"

Loreto met her eyes for as long as she dared before winking and heading toward the pool. "Don't lose faith in me now."

She eased into the water via the stairs, her body relishing the heat on her already languid muscles. She felt like she was melting into the water as much as moving through it.

"Oh, yes," Simone groaned, stepping in gingerly behind her. "Please and thank you."

"You're welcome," Loreto said, lowering herself fully and holding still long enough to acclimate herself to the temperature, which hovered somewhere just above a well-heated hot tub. She hadn't thought she could possibly relax any more than she had on the massage table, but she settled into one of the corners of the pool and spread her arms out along the outside. She nodded for Simone to join her, and then held her breath slightly as she realized what she'd done. For the second time that day, she'd invited a strong, self-assured woman into her embrace, only this time, Simone wasn't hurt or scared. Would she still welcome Loreto's tenderness now that she didn't need it?

Mercifully, Simone didn't make her wait long before sliding over to nestle herself into the crook of her arm, resting her back against Loreto's side. Rolling her head onto Loreto's shoulder, she asked, "How long can we stay in here before we liquefy and float away?"

"I don't know, but let's try to find out."

"Deal." A moment later, Simone said, "Five days ago, nothing would've scared me more than the thought of melting and floating away."

"And now?"

"Less so. At least, in this moment."

"What terrifies you in this moment?"

Simone shrugged. "Nothing."

Loreto's heart swelled with pride at having helped to provide a few worry-free moments. She didn't delude herself into thinking they could last for long, but no matter what happened later, she would always know she'd done something for Simone that few others had been able to do.

She lifted her hand and ran her fingers down Simone's arm from the water up to her shoulder, then back again. Her skin was soft and smooth. She wanted to take her time kissing as much of it as she could. She wanted to look her in the eyes as she slipped inside. She wanted to hold her after their passion had slipped into sleep. She wanted to see her in the early morning light. She wanted to know her at every time of day, in every mood and every situation. She knew Simone wasn't likely to accept overtures of a deeper nature, but she also knew that wouldn't stop her from wanting to offer them.

The thought scared her. Apparently, she didn't have Simone's ability to grow weightless and worry-free, no matter how soothing the water or how low the light. She'd always seen clearly how this would end. The worlds between them were too large to even contemplate, much less conquer, and even if they weren't, she'd known from the first kiss that their time together was finite. Still, she hadn't quite expected the ticking time clock to matter so much.

She wrapped her arm around Simone's chest, pulling her close, and kissed the top of her head, then her temple, then, breathing in her steamy citrus scent, she kissed her neck.

The physical sensations grounded her more than her mental musing did, and her body came awake once more. Her lips reached the corner of Simone's mouth, and she turned toward her, seeking more. The kiss was slower but no less passionate than the ones before. Where the others incinerated in an instant, this one caused the heat to spread, consuming steadily as it branched out in tendrils. Seeking more, Loreto lowered her other hand to Simone's waist and easily lifted her. In the warmth of the water and the strength of her desire, it took little effort to reposition Simone on her lap, her long legs stretched out along the bench beside them.

Simone melded against her, kissing her in a slow, languid rhythm. She took her time, sucking at Loreto's lower lip, tracing her tongue into the corners of her smile. She parted her lips and invited Loreto in, not escalating the pace or the pressure, but opening herself to whatever path they took. And sweet heaven, what a path. Loreto had such extravagant access to Simone's body. With one hand, she reached up and tugged the tie on Simone's bikini, and with the other, she pulled the suit off. Then, with both hands free and a beautiful expanse of skin before her, Loreto set about touching as much of it as she could, as leisurely as she could.

Reveling in the time they'd never allowed themselves before, she stroked and massaged and traced Simone's spine, her side, her stomach, before easing up to cup her breasts. She memorized the weight of them in her palms, the taut skin, the way Simone shifted against her lap as she tested and teased. All the while, they continued to kiss, as if the only air in the room had to be sipped from the other's lips.

She didn't know how long she spent exploring Simone's upper body before she gradually drifted downward. Tugging the two little strings at each of Simone's hips, she finally beat the barrier that had taunted her the day before, but any sense of victory was tempered by wonder at the body now fully revealed, shimmering and submerged in the clear water. Had she ever taken the time to fully see it, to soak it in and imprint it on her memory? How many opportunities had she missed? She didn't want to make the same mistake again. She didn't want to view this woman through a filter any longer.

"Come on," she whispered, standing up slowly and holding Simone upright long enough to let her adjust to the shift.

Simone whimpered at the withdrawal, but her alabaster skin flushed pink from the combination of several kinds of heat, reminding Loreto of her earlier promise. They crossed the pool, fingers interlaced, and climbed the steps on the other side before Loreto pulled her close and joined their mouths together once more.

Picking up where they'd left off, she pressed as much of her skin as she could to Simone's as she slowly walked her back to the marble slab behind them. Cradling Simone fully in her arms, she gently lowered them both down.

Simone gasped as the cold stone grazed her skin, and Loreto felt goose bumps prick both their flesh, but the initial shock quickly gave way to heightened receptors. Every place their hot bodies collided with each other, the heat between them continued to scorch, and in every place they didn't, coolness began to soothe. It might have been a metaphor or a larger life lesson, but she couldn't process anything outside Simone's body cradled in her arms.

"No one's ever put me on a pedestal before." Simone nipped at her ear.

"You deserve it," Loreto said, easing back to look down at her. "You're a work of art."

She couldn't be sure, but she thought she saw Simone's blue eyes shimmer before she pulled Loreto's head back down to continue the kiss. With that, they were off again, dancing back into territory she'd covered before, but this time allowing herself the luxury of exploring fully.

Simone reached up and stroked Loreto's face, cupping her jaw in her hand and massaging her fingers into the back of her neck, increasing her pressure as Loreto's hands did some massaging of their own. She caressed, gradually lower, in a meandering path that encompassed breasts, stomach, thighs, the curve of her waist, but not necessarily in that order, and never just once. She couldn't bring herself to focus on any one piece of perfection for too long with so many to choose from. Until Simone let her legs fall apart and pushed her hips off the pedestal in an unspoken request no one could misunderstand.

Loreto obliged immediately, dizzy with arousal and a sense of honor as Simone once again opened herself up for her. As Loreto dipped her fingers into wetness that didn't stem from the water or the steam around them, she marveled at how movements so similar to ones she'd made each of the last few nights could feel so different.

She set about slow-circling the center of Simone's need, not teasing or toying so much as easing and appreciating. Simone, for her part, accepted the pace, moving her hips in time to the rhythm Loreto set, without pushing back or attempting to escalate. The passion of their previous encounters had only grown, but gone was the race, the game, the competition, leaving space for appreciation, and even awe, as their slick bodies melded together.

Breaths grew short, then sharp, between them. Simone broke their kiss with a gasp but kept Loreto's head bowed close by tightening her fingers in the hair at the base of her neck.

"Yes," she moaned.

"Yes," Loreto echoed in her ear and picked up both her speed and pressure.

"You feel so good." Simone panted. Then her eyes opened, bright and blue and vulnerable in ways they'd never made her seem before. "You *are* so good."

Loreto's stomach clenched with so much more than lust, and she fought the urge to look away from the piercing gaze. It wasn't that she was no longer afraid of what Simone would see in her. She was simply more afraid to miss a moment of this connection between them. So she stood firm, holding Simone close, eyes locked as they built toward climax. Loreto watched the tension play across her features as she neared release, watched her eyes gleam, then cloud, as dark pupils expanded and azure turned to sapphire before her eyelids grew heavy and closed.

As her body tensed, every muscle contracting in the grip of pleasure, Simone's eyes flashed open, brilliant, clear, and so intensely focused, Loreto forgot to breathe as the shakes and shivers running through Simone's body reverberated through her own.

Slowly, muscles went slack, heartbeats decelerated, and breaths grew deeper, but neither one of them moved. They stayed there, tightly connected, both physically and visually, long past the time when the aftershocks subsided. The realization of what they'd done settled somewhere deep in Loreto's core.

Despite all her attempts to anchor them with a return to the physical sexuality that had offered balance time and time again, tonight she hadn't been able to lose herself in lust. She hadn't been able to blur her emotions with sex. They hadn't even had sex. They'd made love.

Simone lay on the marble pedestal trying desperately to use the cool stone as some sort of physical anchor. She wanted to stay firmly tethered to the external, but as everything moved more slowly and the blood returned to her brain, she had both the time and ability to think. She didn't want to think. She wanted only to feel. Then again, she'd done plenty of that, only she hadn't felt the things she'd expected, or she had, but she'd also felt the unexpected. Things she'd never felt before and certainly didn't want to put a name on.

Loreto kissed her forehead, softly, then her temple, then her cheek as she gently lowered them into a more relaxed position, Simone using Loreto's arm as a pillow against the hard stone.

Simone was taken aback by the tenderness of it all. She'd had plenty of sex with plenty of women over the years, but she couldn't remember a single time any one of them had taken the time or the effort to put their own body between her and such a slight discomfort. The thought touched her in ways even Loreto's skill hadn't, and she snuggled in closer, inclining her head to Loreto's chest.

"Thank you," she murmured against warm, smooth skin.

"Thank you," Loreto said, her voice thick and low.

She should say something more, something to convey the gravity of the moment, or to temper it. Instead, she pulled Loreto's other arm more tightly around her waist so that magnificent body angled more fully across her own. But as they settled in, a little flash of white caught Simone's attention.

Squinting, she looked closer to inspect a thin, raised scar a little wider and a little longer than the one she'd noticed the other night.

This time the urge to ask was stronger than passing curiosity. She wanted to know what had dared to mar such perfect skin. She wanted to know if the wound had hurt Loreto. She wanted to know what or who had offered her comfort. She wanted to know Loreto.

The desire scared her, and yet so did the prospect of not having it fulfilled.

Lifting a finger shakily, she ran it down the length of the scar and back up again. "What happened here?"

Loreto didn't look at where Simone pointed. "A cut. A long time ago."

"From what?"

She sighed as if tired, but her heartbeat gave her away. Simone could feel it beating all the way through Loreto's chest and into her own.

"You don't have to tell me if you don't want. I don't want to upset you."

Loreto shook her head. "It's nothing. I slipped . . . while climbing a fence . . . the barbed wire cut me."

"Barbed wire," Simone repeated, trying not to form a mental image of what that might have looked like. "I hope whatever lay on the other side of the fence was worth it."

She felt Loreto's smile against her forehead. "It was."

Then she waited, silently, patiently for an explanation that didn't come.

A week ago, that wouldn't have bothered her. Yesterday, she wouldn't have admitted that bothered her. Today, she'd progressed past both of those stages, but she still didn't know what to do about it.

Closing her eyes once more, she forced herself to sit in the not knowing, to let the uncertainty wash over her. Despite what had transpired between them over the last few days, she wasn't impulsive. She listened to the facts. She paid attention to her intuition. She trusted herself to know what she needed in any given situation, if only she gave herself enough time and the right opportunities to figure out what that entailed. Why had she fought those instincts where Loreto was concerned? What had she been so afraid of?

It had seemed so important at the time, but here, now, in her arms, safe and sated in such a perfect place, she couldn't seem to remember what it was. Perhaps it was clarity, or maybe oblivion, but suddenly the answer seemed so obvious she had no choice but to give it voice.

"Stay with me tonight." Then, without the slightest twinge of displeasure, she added, "Please?"

Chapter Fourteen

"Oh my . . . something," Simone moaned as she bit into the chocolate-drenched churro. She snapped her fingers at Loreto. "Come on. Give me a word, or some sort of Spanish exclamation to describe this heaven in my mouth."

"*Madre de Dios?*" Loreto asked with a laugh.

"Yes. *Madre de Dios.* Mother of God and all things holy, thank you for this bread and oil and molten bars of real chocolate, amen."

"You didn't really grow up religious, did you?" Loreto asked.

Simone shrugged. "My grandma went to church. They didn't have churros there."

Loreto shook her head slowly but found it hard to see blasphemy in anything so beautifully joyous.

"Wait, are you religious?" Simone asked, her eyebrows high under the blond hair she wore down this morning. It was about the fifth personal question that had seemed to pop into her head and right out of her mouth since they'd woken up together this morning, each one delving a little deeper than the previous. So far, Loreto had provided true but short answers. Have you always been a big reader? Yes. What was your first job? Babysitting. What age did you come out? Sixteen. Do you plan to stay in Spain indefinitely? I don't make a lot of plans. Now she had to consider her relationship to God. It was a lot, really, and if anyone else had asked, she would have found a way to get away. Hell, if Simone had asked even yesterday, she may have bolted, but yesterday she hadn't awoken with Simone in her arms. She hadn't snuggled closer to feel her warmth or breathed deeply to memorize the scent of her.

"I grew up Catholic," Loreto finally said. It would've likely been enough, but for some reason, she added, "I don't really go to Mass anymore because of my schedule and other hobbies, but I don't know, things got complicated."

Simone smirked. "Was it those 'other hobbies' that complicated things for you?"

Loreto got the gist, and part of her wanted to explain it wasn't her sexual orientation or escapades that got in the way of her faith, but she figured it was easier to let Simone make her assumptions. "Something like that."

Simone didn't seem to find anything off about the nonanswer as she took another bite of her churro. "Seriously, why didn't you force one of these on me when we were here a week ago?"

Loreto shook her head. "Can you even imagine? You'd nearly fired me for simply walking you down a street you didn't like the night before."

"I did not," Simone said, then smiled. "Maybe I did. It's all fuzzy now. I hardly even feel like the same person I was when we sat here then."

Loreto didn't argue that point as she watched Simone look around the little cobblestone courtyard. It was as if she were seeing the palm trees and balconies for the first time. Maybe she was. Even if she wasn't exactly a different person now, she'd certainly removed the blinders of privilege and productivity she'd worn then. The real question was whether she'd put them back when she remembered that her big meeting was only twenty-four hours away. Loreto found herself both bracing for that moment and trying to make the most of whatever time they had left.

Right now, the latter impulse was winning. It was hard to stay guarded when Simone insisted on being so beautifully open and happy.

"Seriously, these are rapturous." Simone continued to extol the virtues of the churros.

"I know. I tried to tell you so many times."

"Because you ate them so many times." Simone shook her head. "Right in front of me. What else have I missed? Wait a second, how do you manage to keep a body like yours when you keep eating things like these? I mean, seriously, I've seen all the areas. Where do the calories go?"

And there it was, another blatantly appreciative comment. Simone had been more liberal with those this morning as well, and Loreto found them a lot less unsettling than the personal asides. "I actually got a pretty good workout last night."

Simone's complexion took on a little bit of pink, but instead of looking away, she held Loreto's eyes and said, "Indeed you did. Have I thanked you properly for that?"

"Several times," Loreto said, "both last night and this morning."

"Good." Simone sat back and dipped her churro into the chocolate once more. "I'd hate to feel indebted."

"We're even."

"Except, we're not, really," Simone said, frowning for the first time that day. "I'm loath to even mention this now, because I am so enjoying living this Spanish life you've shown me."

"But you have to get back to work," Loreto finished for her.

Simone blinked a few times, then tilted her head to the side as if trying to see the comment from a different angle. "Actually, that thought hadn't occurred to me yet, which is probably a problem, seeing as how I will be in the biggest meeting of my career exactly twenty hours from now, and I mean, if my boss could see me now . . ."

"He can't," Loreto reminded her quickly, "and he couldn't see us last night, either."

"Thank God, but no, I wasn't actually thinking about the meeting tomorrow."

"Because you have your sales pitch ready to go?"

Simone shook her head. "No. I mean yes, I basically do, but I honestly haven't even thought about it since yesterday on top of the rock."

"Before or after you got bit?"

"Now that you mention it," Simone said playfully, "perhaps it was the exact moment. Maybe there are some things a monkey bite really puts into perspective for you."

"We should put that in the brochures."

Simone sighed and smiled. "You're incorrigible."

"And you like that about me."

"I do," she admitted, her gaze softening as she held Loreto's.

This time she didn't even reach for her sunglasses. Ever since she'd held Simone's eye contact in that moment of vulnerability, she'd had little trouble doing so in other situations as well. It didn't hurt that they were openly flirting now instead of bickering. "You were saying?"

"Something about you being incorrigible, or how attractive I find that trait?"

"Before that," Loreto prompted. "Something about work, but not that you've got to get back to it, because we have so many better ways we could spend today."

"So very many," Simone agreed, but then her eyes focused. "Actually, I do remember now, though I'd rather go back to doing those other things, so can you promise me we'll get back to those discussions, or actions?"

"You have my very enthusiastic word that my mind, and probably hands, will begin to wander almost immediately."

Simone pursed her lips, then with a deep breath said, "I have to pay you."

"Huh?" Loreto asked, unable to process the abrupt change from flirting to business.

"The going rate, or at least the one we agreed on. I haven't given you a check since our last night in Cordoba, which is sort of where we . . ."

"Started sleeping together," Loreto said, pushing her plate of churros away from her as her stomach dropped.

"Or not sleeping, as the case may be," Simone said, as if trying to interject some of their former levity into the new topic.

"Right, there was no sleeping in Cordoba."

"Or Sevilla," Simone added, "and then last night, there was sleeping, but also so much more."

Loreto nodded numbly.

"And I don't want to cheapen that so-much-more part by just handing you a check this morning, because you know that's not what this was about." Simone stared at her for several more seconds before saying, "You do know that, right?"

"Of course," Loreto managed. "Neither one of us needs to pay or charge for those experiences."

Simone grimaced, and Loreto suspected her comment fell short of the assurance she'd hope for, so she tried again. "It's fine. I don't care. I get it."

"Good. Because as much as I don't want to go anywhere near putting a price tag on what we've shared the last few days, I also don't want to negate your very real knowledge and expertise, both of which I would be lost without. Plus, I know I can be demanding to work for at times."

Loreto snorted, and Simone rolled her eyes.

"It's fine. I've never denied that. I'm just trying to say here that, well, I appreciate everything you've done for me as a tour guide over the last few days, and I wouldn't want to discredit any of that because our relationship deepened over that same time period."

Their relationship had deepened. It wasn't bad, as far as euphemisms went. It managed to admit to something more than sex, yet it stopped short of any real declaration or definition. Which, of course, made sense. How would you define what they were to each other now? They weren't quite friends. Lovers didn't seem to go quite far enough. Simone would be gone in two days, so Loreto wasn't naive enough to use a more lasting term.

Simone wasn't her girlfriend. She was her boss, which, of course, was why they were having this conversation. Whatever else had happened between them, their foundation was still transactional. Funny how she'd managed to let that fact slip her mind when it was in this very city only a few days ago that she'd wanted to milk those transactions for everything she could. At the time, she'd planned on new clothes, fancy dinners, fine wine, and luxury accommodations. She'd be lying to herself if she said she hadn't considered that sex might be on the table as well, but it hadn't occurred to her then how awkward that would make this conversation.

"Reto?"

The name pulled her back into the moment. "Sorry, what?"

"I asked if you understood what I was trying to say."

"Yes," she said, then as Simone waited for her to elaborate, she asked, "Did you call me "Reto?""

"Yes, I guess I did. I think I heard other people call you that sometime? I assumed it was just an abbreviation of your name."

She nodded at the explanation but was still uneasy with the way the word had rolled so easily off Simone's tongue. "It is."

"Then why do I get the sense I just made an already awkward conversation even more so?"

"No, you didn't. It's just a nickname for people who know me. Sort of a little play on words."

Simone smiled. "Sort of like you calling me *Rubia*?"

Loreto shifted in her seat, not sure if that was the opposite of what she meant, or maybe it was an accurate comparison. She'd never meant *Rubia* as a compliment so much as a marker of their difference. It had been condescending at first, though over time she'd found the term more endearing. She supposed the same could be said in the case of her name, though that wouldn't uncomplicate her reaction. "'Reto' means 'challenge' in Spanish."

"Oh," Simone said, her brow furrowing. "I suppose that's not terribly unfitting. You do have a way of pushing buttons, or limits, or, well . . . me."

That summed it up pretty well, but it didn't make her feel better. Instead, she felt worse by the minute.

"It would probably take a certain amount of familiarity with someone to call you 'challenge' and have it feel affectionate."

Her heart ached so painfully, she had to fight the urge to push her hand to her chest.

"I suppose I'm not quite in the category of someone who could pull it off."

Loreto opened her mouth and then closed it. There was nothing she could say, no way to explain that Simone actually could fall into that category. It hadn't felt foreign coming out of her mouth. She'd probably earned the right to use the name. All those things terrified her, because none of them should be true. She shouldn't have let any of them become true. Even if she could somehow make Simone understand, she wasn't sure she wanted to.

She desperately needed to extract herself from this situation before she got in any deeper. Instead, she blurted out, "My mom used to call me that, before she died."

Simone's eyes clouded over. "I'm sorry. I didn't know."

"It was a long time ago," Loreto said, as if that meant anything.

"Still, I shouldn't have used a word I didn't understand."

"It's just a word."

Simone's smile was sad. "Words matter, at least in my world. I hope you know I'd never intentionally hurt you."

"Yeah." Loreto waved her off, despite her increasing difficulty breathing. *Intentionally.* That's what she'd said, and Loreto gave her the benefit of the doubt, but not doing something on purpose and not doing it at all were two very different things.

"I've made a mess of a glorious morning, haven't I?"

"No." Loreto pushed back from the table.

"It's okay to admit it. Relaxation has never been my forté," Simone said, resignation back in her voice. "I should've never brought any of this up."

"It's fine. Really, I'm fine." Loreto tried to sound a little more convincing. It really wasn't Simone's fault her insides felt like they'd been wrung out like a wet dish towel. Loreto hadn't told her anything about her life, about her upbringing, about her past. And why would she? Weren't they just having a conversation about payment for services rendered? A person didn't just follow that up with the intimate details of their life story.

"Are you sure?" Simone asked, reaching across the table as if she intended to take her hand, but Loreto forced a smile and rose from her chair.

"Absolutely," she said, despite the fact that her lungs still felt unbearably constricted. "Why don't we go back to Calle Larios? The shops should be open now."

Simone eyed her almost mournfully before folding her napkin and laying it on the table. "Okay, I just wish . . . I mean . ." She sighed. "Sure."

Loreto swallowed a mix of relief and disappointment at the fact that Simone didn't push for more. She didn't know what she would've done if she had, and mercifully, now she'd never have to know, because she had no intention of letting herself get anywhere close to feeling this way again. And in order to make sure she slammed that door once and for all, she pulled the conversation back to where it needed to be. "And then you can pay up the money you owe me in one check instead of multiple invoices. There's no need to make this any messier than it has to be."

"What do you think about this one?" Simone asked, holding up a little red dress that would have been short even on a smaller woman.

"It's nice," Loreto said, barely looking over her shoulder as the rest of her body faced the large picture window looking out on Calle Larios.

"Nice?" Simone asked.

"Uh-huh."

"Then why don't you go try it on?"

"Sure," Loreto said, "go ahead."

Simone shook her head but decided not to repeat the joke. It wasn't funny if you had to explain it, and she suspected that no amount of emphasis on reiterated pronouns would make Loreto laugh right now. The best she'd gotten out of her over the last hour was a couple half-hearted smiles and the occasional polite compliment.

Despite Loreto's assurance that she was fine, she'd been distant since their conversation at breakfast. Simone wished she could read her mind. She wanted to know what had upset her. She wanted to know many things, but some topics seemed painfully off limits, and she didn't want to accidently trip into any of them like she had by saying 'Reto.

Challenge indeed. Loreto continued to offer those on plenty of levels. She'd been nothing but challenging in every moment they'd ever spent together, though the nature of those challenges had varied greatly from day to day. The challenge of this moment seemed to be the shocking realization that Simone missed her. She couldn't remember the last time she'd missed another person, much less when they were in the same room.

She was still trying to make sense of how that was possible as they stepped back onto the street.

"Do you need to have anything printed up for the meeting tomorrow?" Loreto asked. "If so, I probably need to translate it today."

She pursed her lips. Of course, the contract offer had already been made in Spanish and all of the official paperwork had been translated and vetted by their business department, but she hadn't considered what other written items she might bring with her. Why the hell hadn't she thought about that? Probably because she wouldn't bring any. She generally relied on her presentation and persuasion skills in these situations, but she also generally made these sorts of pitches in English, to English speakers. Maybe, with the language barrier and the active translator, it would be better to have her key presentation points bulleted in Spanish. Now her mind was spinning, and Loreto had stopped walking to turn and stare at her.

"I don't know," she finally admitted.

Loreto raised her eyebrows.

"What, did I finally surprise you?" Simone asked, a defensive edge to her voice she hadn't heard in a couple days.

"No." Loreto shrugged. "I guess not. You've probably done this sort of thing a hundred times. I guess someone with your experience pretty much has the whole routine down to a science by now."

That wasn't untrue, and to have Loreto state her qualifications so bluntly made her feel better.

"I would just be freaking out less than twenty hours before the biggest meeting of my career."

That did not make her feel better.

"I guess you've known roughly what needs to happen for a couple days, so what, the rest of it is all filler?"

"Pretty much," Simone lied. Nothing about a great pitch should be filler. Every single word should have meaning, power, and purpose. She just didn't want to think about any of those things right now. Not this morning, not in this place, not with this woman who'd made her think about so many other wonderful things. And why should Loreto be the one to keep bringing it up?

Simone didn't really need reminders that she should be cramming and rehearsing, not shopping and not neglecting the most important responsibility of her life to date in an attempt to win back the undivided attention of a woman who was, at best, her tour guide, and, at most, a vacation fling.

An image of Loreto holding her in her arms flashed through her mind, accompanied by the echoes of that low, sultry voice whispering, "You're a work of art." Her stomach roiled. She couldn't do that. She might not fully understand all her feelings for Loreto, but she refused to boil her down to her basest components of work and sex. She was so much more than those things combined, so much more than Simone could put a label on, and she was running out of time to figure out what that meant. Twenty hours until the meeting meant that Loreto had only about twenty-one hours left in her employ. What would they be to one another then?

She stared at Loreto as if seeing her for the first time. Today, she wore her trademark shorts, but she'd paired them with a sleek, black polo Simone had purchased for her on this very street. Despite the clear day, she'd yet to flip down her sunglasses, and her deep, pensive eyes were reflected back in the glass of a storefront window showcasing luxury watches.

"Can I buy you one?" Simone asked, without thinking.

248

"What?" Loreto turned to stare at her as if she'd spoken a different language.

"You don't have a watch. Could I buy one for you?"

Loreto smiled, but it didn't crease the corners of her eyes. "Are you worried I'll be tardy for something?"

"No, I didn't mean to imply you'd be late."

"Why not? Seems a reasonable thing to worry about given the disconnect between your sense of time and mine."

Simone frowned. She hadn't thought of that since Sevilla. Another item to add to the growing list of things that had either slipped her mind or ceased to matter in the way they once had. She tried again. "I meant as a gift, to thank you for all your help."

"You pay me for that."

"Right, then for the stuff I don't pay you for."

"I don't think I'd be comfortable accepting a gift in return for rendering those services."

Simone's cheeks burned. "I didn't mean it that way, either."

"What did you mean then?" Loreto asked seriously.

"That I want to buy you a present, because, well, I want to."

Loreto's expression softened and her pupils widened, but she still shook her head. "Save your money."

"I have plenty of money."

"And I have plenty of stuff," Loreto snapped. "I have plenty of everything. I don't want anything else, and I don't share your affinity for buying things, like clothes or jewelry or authors."

Simone swallowed the sting of the comment. Did Loreto think of her as frivolous or materialistic? The tone felt so different from the one she'd used with her last night, or on the boat back from Gibraltar, or even on the top of the rock. Then again, it wasn't inconsistent with their earlier encounters. Maybe yesterday had just been some sort of weird, emotional time-out.

"Okay," she finally said. "I guess we can head back to the hotel then."

"Sounds good," Loreto said quickly and reversed course back down Calle Larios. "Let's get back to work."

"Work," Simone echoed, trying not to overthink the fact that

Loreto had, once again, been the one to return them to the subject. Maybe it was time for her to take the hint. "If the meeting is at nine-thirty tomorrow morning, what time should we leave the hotel?"

"Ten after nine."

"Really? It'll only take five minutes to drive there?"

"You said the office was by the Picasso Museum, right?"

"Yes."

"Then you can walk in ten minutes and still be there your required ten minutes early. No cars allowed on that street."

"Okay, then we'll do that, but could we leave at nine? I want to have time to gather myself, and maybe go over a few key points with you so you're ready to share them."

Loreto kept walking but turned to stare at her.

"What?"

"Me share them?"

"Translate them."

"I offered to do that today. Why wait until you're in the lobby of the office?"

"Not in the office. In the meeting."

Loreto's footsteps faltered. "I'm translating for you in the actual proposal?"

"Of course," Simone said, but the way Loreto's beautiful complexion paled told her Loreto didn't find the news obvious at all. "I'll need a translator."

"Most people can speak some English."

"Some English? You think I can parse together a proposal of this magnitude in broken English? And what kind of respect would that show for Spanish culture if I showed up and demanded they speak my language?"

"Fair point," Loreto said grudgingly. "That probably wouldn't go over well with people who are already afraid you're going to Americanize their prized author."

"Then you'll be there?" She hadn't meant it as a request, but the uncertainty in her voice made it sound like one.

Loreto shifted from one foot to the other as she seemed to

weigh her options. "Yeah, I guess. I mean, translation was part of the original contract, right? And I don't go around breaking contracts unless . . . no, I mean . . . yes, we made a deal, and you've lived up to your part, so I'll live up to mine."

Again, Simone suffered a little prick of something between hurt and embarrassment. Where did that new wound stem from? That Loreto had to think so hard about spending one more morning with her? That she seemed to agree only under duress? That her motivation came from fulfilling some heavy responsibility, or an unpleasant work requirement?

That's what it was though, right? To Loreto, at least, the meeting would likely be meaningless and boring. Or worse, she remembered her quip about buying authors like someone would buy a watch. Maybe she didn't want to be there at all. The fact shouldn't have bothered Simone, but it did, and not just because someone who didn't care about the job generally didn't do their best work. She knew Loreto wouldn't let her down in the meeting, but she realized with another little shock that she wanted her there for reasons that went beyond a professional obligation.

She wanted Loreto by her side for a major moment of her life and dreams. She wanted to draw on her calm, confident presence for comfort and support. She wanted to go into the meeting with someone in her corner, and she felt a rush of sadness at the realization that Loreto didn't feel the same way.

What the hell?

She picked up her pace, growing angrier at herself with each step. What stupid sentimentality. She was going to a business meeting, not prom. She didn't need support. She needed a translator. When had she started to see Loreto's worth resting more in the first category than the second?

They'd had great sex and a genuine connection, and over time she'd developed tremendous respect for Loreto's insights, but she didn't need her affirmations. She certainly didn't need someone to hold her hand during a business meeting. This morning had gotten totally out of hand and so had her priorities. She had to pull herself together. She had to reassert herself.

"Maybe we should rehearse the meeting today and then call it an early night," she suggested. "We should probably rest up for tomorrow morning, and I'm not sure either of us can be trusted to remember that if we're in the same room after a few glasses of sangria."

The corners of Loreto's mouth curled in the sly way they hadn't for hours. "We didn't have any sangria last night."

The tension in Simone's chest loosened dramatically. "Two nights in a row without sangria. They won't take away your Spanish visa, will they?"

Loreto's expression clouded over again immediately, and her tone turned grave as she said, "It's always a possibility for me."

The words, or the lifeless tone in which they were delivered, sent goose bumps crawling up Simone's arms. She wanted desperately to go back in time and swallow whatever comment had triggered the icy transition, but she didn't even understand what that was. Instead, she grasped frantically for anything to turn them back around.

"Well, then, how about after the meeting tomorrow, we change into something more comfortable and go out for a Spanish-style lunch. We can have multiple dishes and a pitcher of sangria each, either to celebrate my ascension to the throne or to commiserate my fall from grace, because either way, by this time tomorrow, the die will have been cast."

"You'll be celebrating," Loreto said so bluntly Simone didn't know how she felt about the assertion.

"Oh?"

"You'll seal the deal," Loreto said, her inflection unchanging. "By this time tomorrow, a couple of Spaniards will have a few extra zeros in their bank account and Juanes Cánovas will be the property of your million-dollar marketing department to do with what they please."

She nodded slowly. The words were right, and to hear Loreto state them like a foregone conclusion or an absolute truth should have felt like a compliment, but for some reason, or perhaps many reasons, she couldn't take any comfort in them.

※ ※ ※

"Ugh." Simone tossed her notes on the hotel room desk in front of Loreto. "This should be straightforward, and it is. It really is," Simone said, her voice rising in both pitch and volume.

"But?" Loreto fought not to get swept up in her tension.

"It all feels empty. Like the research is good, the contract is beyond generous, and I think my pitch keys into their main concerns about authenticity," Simone said, as if ticking off items from a grocery list. "I get where they are coming from now, and I think I can offer them a path to move forward that will assuage their concerns."

She couldn't argue. Everything Simone had said so far was persuasive, and, at least in the strictest sense, true. Her presentation, while lacking passion, managed to sound both thorough and genuine every time she'd run through it over the last two hours, which was a lot.

"Maybe that's the problem." Simone sat on the edge of the king-sized bed they'd shared the night before. "Maybe it's just done without any drama, and I'm merely freaking out because I have nothing left to freak out over."

"Yeah, that sounds like you."

Simone rolled her eyes and fell back so she lay flat on the bed with her feet dangling off. "I know I should be happier, and part of me is. At least freaking out is normal for me. I'd started to worry I'd turned into someone else over the last couple days."

Loreto's chest tightened at the apt description of her own concerns.

"I started to think I'd lost my desire to do any work. I mean, really, who could blame me, with all the temptations you've introduced me to this week, but I'm not usually distracted by the mere prospect of spending a day being lazy."

Loreto grimaced at the word "lazy," glad Simone was currently staring at the ceiling. Was that how Simone still thought of her? Lazy? She understood she was likely still a little sensitive about the conversation she'd dodged at breakfast, but really? All the

253

travel, all the planning, all the knowledge, all of the deep conversations, and the best word Simone could find for how Loreto spent her days was lazy?

Simone rolled onto her side. "Do you really think they'll sell the company?"

She shrugged. "You'd know better than I in that area."

"Normally, I'd agree, but something's always felt off about this deal. If they really wanted to sell, they should've done so by now, but if they didn't want to sell, then there's no reason to keep taking these meetings, and believe me, I'm not the first."

"But you want to be the last."

Simone pursed her lips, and Loreto wondered what knee-jerk reaction she'd just held at bay. "I want this to be the last meeting of this kind for me."

That made sense. Simone was ready to be done begging. She wanted to be the one other people begged. She didn't care about this acquisition any more than any other. She liked the book, but she knew she might not like it before the whole process was over. Yet she was still ready to sell the author, the company, and the people who'd worked their whole lives to build it a line of half-truths and flowery language about the world needing Spain. What she really meant was she needed a high-profile deal to secure her own promotion. And she'd asked Loreto to help her.

Why had Loreto agreed? Because of some agreement they'd made days ago? They'd both said they could end their business connection at the end of any day. Why not today? Why not pull the plug before she did something she couldn't take back?

A muscle in her jaw twitched, and she realized she'd been clenching her teeth. She sighed and resigned herself to the fact that she couldn't take anything back. She'd fallen in way too deep with Simone, and that's why she'd go with her tomorrow.

"What do you think about mentioning that we wouldn't just translate the book into English?" Simone asked, causing Loreto to startle at how close she was behind her. "It's likely to be shared in French and Mandarin and countless other languages."

Why hadn't she heard her approach when she felt her presence

254

so acutely? The heat of Simone's body warmed Loreto's back as she pressed close, leaning over her shoulder to look at the papers again. A hint of arousal flickered in her like the scent of orange blossoms filling her senses, and she struggled to answer the question she'd been asked.

"Maybe I need to add that to the portion on translation rights?"

"No," Loreto managed to croak. "It's a good point. Put it up front in the what-the-world-needs-now-is-Spain section, then carry it throughout. Don't specifically talk about Juanes's books in English. Talk about all their books out in all the world."

Simone tilted her head to the side, bringing their faces within inches of each other. "Normally specifics are good, but maybe here it's better to be more general."

"Yes. No one here feels threatened by the idea of the Chinese or the Italians taking over their culture.

"Fair or not, I suppose you're right."

"It's fair," Loreto said, a shot of defensiveness pushing into her arousal. "Anglicizing is a thing people talk about, 'Mandricizing' isn't."

"Hmm." Simone brushed against Loreto as she reached over her shoulder to scratch a note in the margin of her presentation. Then as she stood, she ran her hand up the length of Loreto's arm seductively. "You're very insightful."

"Thanks," Loreto mumbled.

"I mean it," she said earnestly. "You understand people. You're good with nuance. You see the big picture of history, but you also understand the little things that matter to individuals. You know when to push and how to comfort."

The compliment soothed the residual burn of defensiveness, and she tilted her head back so it rested against Simone's chest. It felt so good to have someone to lean on, someone behind her, someone who saw her the way she wished she could see herself.

Simone ran her fingers through Loreto's hair. "I think you're too valuable to give up."

Her heart pounded in her throat, but before she had time to

let the perfection of the statement sink all the way to her core, Simone added, "I think I should bring you back to New York and put you to work on my staff full-time."

The statement hit her like a kick to the chest, and the impact made her pull away from Simone as she fought to keep her voice as steady as possible. "I've never had any luck finding work in the States."

"Why?" Simone asked casually as Loreto rose.

"I lack your Ivy League appeal."

"Don't sell yourself short." Simone stepped toward her again. "You're much smarter than you let people see, Loreto. You could be so much more if you weren't so—"

"Lazy?" Loreto asked, backing up out of reach once more.

"I was going to say 'lackadaisical.'"

"Same thing."

"If you insist." Simone sighed. "I only meant that if you put in a little more effort, you could make yourself marketable. You're already well read and intelligent. Maybe if you gave up on the siesta and dinners at ten you could function earlier in the morning, and—"

"And what?" Loreto shot back, the anger burning so hot and sudden it tinged her vision red. "Pick a few more buckets of tomatoes, maybe bus a few more tables, then I could make something of myself?"

"That's not fair. I was just saying the only thing I can see standing in your way is your lack of motivation."

"My motivation?" Loreto laughed, the sound harsh and raw in her throat. "Is that upper class code for calling out another lazy spic?"

Simone looked like she'd been slapped. "I have never in my life used that term or anything close to it."

"But you've thought the people who clean your office should just learn to speak English or that the Mexicans who want to wash your windows should just get a real job." The floodgates had opened now. She'd hadn't felt rage like this for years. Honestly, she thought she'd lost her ability to feel wrath, but maybe she'd only buried it. She'd likely be horrified by that realization later, but now it floated through her mind on a wave of indignation.

"I don't know where this is coming from," Simone stuttered. "I simply said—"

"That the only obstacle I had to overcome was my laziness, not the color of my skin, or my accent, or an entire society that thinks I'm a socioeconomic pariah." Loreto was losing control, but it felt good. Control was overrated. Control was an illusion for people like her. Only women like Simone got to wield that tool, a fact that only served to fuel her fury. "I'm sure that thinking works in your world. You work hard and you can overcome anything."

"Yes," Simone said, though she didn't sound as sure as she had the other times she'd espoused those beliefs.

"How crazy of me not to have seen it until now. All this time, I'd thought doors were closed to me because my parents brought me across some invisible border before I was ever old enough to know any better. Or because I don't have a social security number, or a birth certificate from any country, much less the one I lived in. What a silly idea! Why couldn't I just see that the American dream was right there for the taking and I didn't grab it because I was too busy drinking all night and sleeping all day?"

Simone blinked and stared. Her lips parted, but they were not moving, much less emanating any sounds.

"What? Don't have anything to say?"

Simone shook her head slowly. "I don't . . . I didn't . . . I don't know what to say."

"You should probably go call your company lawyer and tell him you've been unwittingly employing an—" She screwed up her lips and spit out the words she'd had hurled at her too many times to count, "—illegal alien."

Simone sat back on the edge of the bed as a million thoughts flooded her mind, but try as she might, she couldn't manage to care about any concerns related to her own job in this moment. Loreto was angry and hurt and lashing out in pain. All Simone wanted right now was to offer solace, but she couldn't even take a step in her direction without sparking more anguish across her beautiful features. So she sat there replaying everything she'd said, everything she'd overlooked, all the questions she'd left unanswered. How many clues had she missed? How many careless comments had she made?

Finally, she whispered, "I'm so sorry. I didn't know."

"Didn't know what? Didn't know I was one of those illicit illegals your politicians rail against? Or didn't know that the American dream was just some big lie teachers tell brown kids to make them behave? And tell white kids so they don't feel guilty when you glide through all those open doors?"

She didn't respond. There was nothing good that could come from it, but Loreto must have sensed her thoughts, because she pushed on.

"You think because you worked hard, because you put yourself through college, because you started at the bottom and clawed your way up, you didn't have doors open to you that weren't open to other people?"

"I didn't say that."

"But be honest. You've wondered why someone like me didn't just try a little harder to do the things you've done. Work and reward, right? That's your motto. You've said there's always a way."

"I have, yes," Simone said, a flicker of fire sparking in her. "In some situations, the work is harder than others."

"Hard work." Loreto laughed bitterly. "Hard work. My mother died when she went into premature labor because she couldn't afford to take off during the strawberry harvest. Did you work that hard to get into college?"

Simone stared at her in horrified silence.

"And did you get your first job because you worked harder than all of the people who bussed your tables, or cleaned your hotel room, or sucked pesticides into their lungs while trying to keep your salads green, because that's what eventually killed my dad."

"I'm so sorry—"

"Don't." Loreto shook her head. "Don't try to apologize for my orphan status after you, just seconds ago, suggested that the only thing standing between my parents and a corner office was their lack of motivation."

The words hurt on so many levels, but none of them compared to the pain she felt thinking about the loss and trauma Loreto had faced.

"I'm sorry, and I'm sorry for being sorry, but I don't know what to say."

"Then don't say anything."

"But I want to help."

"There's nothing you can say that will fix my life."

"I didn't say fix. I honestly mean help. There has to be a way to—"

"To what? Produce a birth certificate for a kid who wasn't born in a hospital and who got carried across a river in the dead of night before I could even walk?"

"Well, no, but if you know you were born somewhere in Mexico, you could—"

"Go find some town I don't even know the name of and talk to people I've never met to try to get them to produce some forms that don't exist to prove I'm a citizen of a place I have no record or memory of ever being? Do you think this fictional official will take the secondhand word of my dead parents, who, incidentally, risked their lives to flee there? I have no way to prove Mexican citizenship. How does anyone in Mexico know I'm not an illegal immigrant to Mexico from Guatemala or Honduras?"

Simone's frustration level grew. "I suppose if you have no record of ever being in Mexico, you aren't likely to find resources to support a visa, but maybe on the American side I could—"

"Get me a social security number? A passport? Why stop there? How about full-blown American citizenship?"

"That has to be a possibility," Simone said weakly.

"Does it? I don't qualify for political asylum. I can't get a legitimate job without a work visa, and I can't get a work visa without paperwork that doesn't exist." Loreto's voice was level, almost bored, as she listed all the things she must have been through a thousand times, but beneath the surface something seething underlined her exasperation. "So unless you're proposing a marriage, which I don't want, there's no way for me to legally get into America, much less stay there."

Simone's stomach knotted as her mind kept trying to wander down different avenues, only to find each one blocked. Still, she couldn't believe there was no way. There was always a way, or at least there'd always been a way for her.

"My very existence is against the law in the country of my birth, the country where I grew up, and the country where I live."

Simone shook her head. She couldn't accept a world in which Loreto's very existence was an affront to every country on the planet. Loreto knew too much, she'd seen too much, had done too much, for no one to see her value. "Wait. You got into Spain. You left America at some point without any documents and you entered a different country."

"Here's the point where your neat little world gets extra uncomfortable, because I'm undocumented here, too. No matter how you look at it, you've employed an undocumented worker, or as your boss will probably see it, an illegal immigrant."

"Please stop saying that." Simone pinched the bridge of her nose.

"Why? You can't handle the truth, *Rubia?*"

"Because I don't care!" Simone shouted. "I don't care that I paid you, I don't care that I slept with you. I mean, I do care, but not about what documents you have and which ones you don't. I care about *you.*"

That was the first thing that seemed to slow Loreto's steamroller of an argument. She paused, mouth open, eyes wide, long enough for Simone to take a single breath and ask, "How did you get from America into Spain?"

"I got hired under the table to do dishes on a cruise ship." She shrugged but refused to meet Simone's eyes. "After seven days holed up below decks, retching my guts out in tubs full of the food rich people threw away, I wanted off badly enough to drag my body over a barbed-wire fence at the customs point."

Barbed wire. More pieces fell into place. "Your scars . . . the customs point . . . what was on the other side was—"

"A new life. A new chance. A choice I made for myself because I wanted to, not because I had to." She made a soft snorting sound. "When I felt the *levant* blow through my hair, I felt like my parents were pushing me. I finally, truly understood the choice they'd made. I would've climbed a thousand barbed wire fences to cross a thousand borders for a shot at something better than what I'd have if I went back."

A thousand borders, a thousand fences. That must have been what so much of Loreto's life had felt like. Simone's mind jolted to a stop again as it landed on another sticking point. Borders and fences. "How did you get into Gibraltar?"

She rolled her eyes. "Gibraltar isn't nearly as tricky as some of the places I got into or out of growing up. All that one cost me was a hundred euros and a sizable chunk of my pride."

"You could've told me."

"Could I?" Loreto asked sharply. "Could I have turned to you the morning after we'd fucked in a bathroom and told you I was an undocumented, double immigrant?"

"Yes," Simone said emphatically, mentally pushing away concerns about what her own response would have been that morning. "We could've made other plans."

"No!" Loreto snapped, all the anger back again. "I did my job. I'm *not* lazy. I did what you wanted."

"I didn't want you to break the law."

"Every moment of my life is breaking the law."

"I didn't want to put you in danger."

"Have you not heard a word I said?"

The sense of being trapped, confined, helpless pressed down on her so firmly, she shouted, "I could've helped!"

"I don't want your help."

"Because you're stubborn? Or prideful?"

261

"Because I don't want your life," Loreto practically spat. Clenching her fists and bringing her outward anger to one notch below boiling, she added, "I don't want to play games I can't win. I don't want to become a citizen of the country that worked my parents to death. I don't want to compromise my beliefs to get ahead. I don't want to sell my soul for decades for some compromise palatable enough to feed the dumb, tasteless masses."

The comment burned in a new way, not like the sharp sting of a slap, but a slow scald that spread across her skin and began to sink toward her core. Even with all the horrible experiences she'd had, even with all the terrible restraints and indignities and deadends, Loreto would rather live indefinitely in her precarious position than live the life Simone had spent hers trying to build. "I don't know what to say."

"Get it through your head. I don't need you to say anything. I'm building my own life by my own rules here. I have a job I enjoy. People value my contributions more than they care about where I was born. Lina and Ren are in the process of sponsoring me for a refugee visa, which is more than any businesswomen in America did."

Simone exhaled at the news. She didn't even care about the dig at American businesswomen. She just felt an overwhelming sense of relief that someone cared enough about Loreto to stand up for her, even if she felt a twinge of regret at not having the chance to do so herself. "I'm glad they're in a position to help you. If there's anything I can do to expedite the process—"

"Stop," Loreto commanded. "Don't do that. Don't act like some white, rich savior who can swoop in with your money or your reputation and make me a more palatable case. I don't need your pity or your platitudes. I don't need someone who can't find her own damn moral compass to assuage her guilt by tossing a few scraps my way."

"I'm not assuaging anything. I want to help."

"What you want isn't more important than what I want. You're not better than me. You're not smarter than me or stronger than me or superior to me. You just have more privilege."

"I agree. I've spent my whole life trying to use my privilege to lift up—"

"No, you haven't," Loreto cut her off again.

This time Simone's frustration at the situation tipped over to anger. "Stop interrupting me."

"No. I've listened to your bullshit all week."

Simone's face flushed. "My bullshit?"

Loreto shrugged. "You want to do this? Because I will lay it out."

"Enlighten me."

"Your work-hard-and-get-rewarded mind-set is bullshit. I think we've already established that you might've worked, but you didn't get where you are by working harder than the millions of people picking your food or sewing your fancy suits in sweat-shops. Your I-make-things-happen mind-set is bullshit because you're no more responsible for the doors you had open to you than I am for the ones I had slammed in my face."

"Okay." Simone held up her hands. "I understand why you're upset. The system is broken. I get that, which is why I'm working as hard as I am on this acquisition."

Loreto snatched Simone's notes off the desk. "This? This is your answer? Your great fight?"

"I'm trying to give voice to an author the world needs to hear."

"He doesn't need you to have a voice. He's already got one."

"I can give him a bigger platform."

"Only if he conforms." Loreto shook her head. "Do you want to know what feels so off about this presentation? Why it feels so empty?"

She didn't. She wanted this whole conversation to be over. She was having a hard time drawing a deep breath as Loreto circled her like a cat preparing to pounce.

"Your pitch feels wrong because what you're doing is wrong."

"You don't understand."

"Yes, I do. You said so yourself. I see people, I hear people, and you're coming in loud and clear." Loreto stepped nearer again, causing Simone's emotions to war between the desire to pull her

263

close and the equally strong impulse to push her away. "You're selling your soul for a sliver of some pie you don't even really want."

"I do," Simone said weakly.

"You don't. You can't even taste it anymore. You just keep swallowing the same lies you've told yourself for years about working inside the system, about changing the game. None of them are true."

Simone's last reserve of anger kicked in. "You don't understand a thing about what's true in my life."

"I understand that you're killing your soul under the illusion that if you play like the men in power long enough, you'll become one of them, only you'll be a kinder, more benevolent version of the guy who came before you."

"I will."

"Yeah, you'll get to sign all the important books and hand them over to the exact same people who are bastardizing them right now. You can sit in your corner office and watch them get carved up like cuts of meat. Is that the shift you want to see in the system? A few more good books to dumb down? A few more sharp minds to dull enough for Middle America to turn them into a movie? That's the change you wish to see in the world?"

"It's better than no change."

"It *is* no change, Simone," Loreto yelled. "There's no changing that system, the same way there's no changing the immigration system."

"So what?" she exploded back. "We give up? On those books, on those voices, on the people who haven't found a way to bum around Spain long enough that they've stopped caring?"

A muscle in Loreto's jaw twitched, and Simone suspected she'd hit a nerve. "How many siestas do I have to take before I stop caring? How many churros do I have to eat until nothing matters anymore, or until I just become good at pretending it doesn't, because that's what you're doing, right?"

Loreto shook her head.

"You're a hypocrite, talking about me deluding myself. Look in a mirror. If you really didn't care, you wouldn't have blown your top over some offhand comments in the mosque at Cordoba. And if you didn't care, you wouldn't have fallen apart when you had to cross the border at Gibraltar. And if you didn't care, you wouldn't be yelling about me wasting my time in a job you also claim not to care about."

Loreto backed toward the door once more. "I don't care what you think of me."

"Now who's dealing in bullshit? You're clearly just as upset as I am about so many things in the world, but you'd rather demean my efforts than lift a finger to try to effect change on your own."

Loreto stared at her for a long second, those dark eyes filled with animus. "You don't know what I've seen. You don't know what I know. I refuse to kill myself caring about things I can't change."

"So what does that include?" Simone shot back, "because from here it looks like the list of things you're refusing to care about includes everything."

"Not everything." Loreto swung open the door and turned to face Simone one more time. "But it does include you."

The slam of the door behind her shook several of the photos on the walls and rattled through Simone.

Chapter Fifteen

Loreto hadn't even checked into her usual hotel yet. She'd merely plopped herself down at the bar and kicked her small suitcase far enough under a table that it wouldn't trip other patrons. Not that there were any other patrons. Too late for tapas, too early for dinner. In other words, the time of day Simone was generally at her most annoying.

She scoffed at her own internal dig and took another swig of sangria. So much for sipping. She couldn't consume the wine and fruit fast enough. Then again, maybe the problem wasn't her pace but the drink itself, because she was halfway through her third and the tension hadn't even begun to slip from her shoulders. She needed something stronger if oblivion was the order of the evening, but damned if she'd let Simone drive her to drink something coarse like tequila or vodka. She'd seen enough sappy movies to know drinking like that meant you cared about someone enough to let them wreck you, and if there was one thing she'd made abundantly clear this afternoon, it was that she didn't care.

She lowered her forehead to the table, relishing the coolness of the wood against her flushed skin. There had been so much burning today. It seemed like every part of her body had been on fire at some point in the last twenty-four hours—her muscles, her throat, her cheeks, her lungs. Another reason not to switch to vodka. She needed something soothing, though she didn't know what that might be. She hadn't been the kind of person who needed to be soothed in years, and even back when she had cried out for such things, those cries had rarely been answered.

"'Reto?" a familiar voice asked.

She sat up, grateful for the distraction, for any distraction.

"*Dios mio*," Lina exclaimed. "*Que paso?*"

What happened? If she knew how to answer that question, she wouldn't be sitting here right now. "Nothing."

Lina rolled her eyes. "Stay there."

Loreto shrugged. She hadn't planned on going anywhere, except maybe to bed at some point, but she watched Lina stride purposefully over to a group of approximately thirty people waiting in the lobby. She suspected the front desk would be busy for a while, so she might as well follow Lina's order. It was easier than trying to think for herself at the moment. Even if the sangria wasn't kicking in, she wasn't clear-headed enough to rebel right now. Plus, she needed her job back, for so many reasons.

"*Hola, amiga,*" Ren said cheerfully, as she separated herself from the crowd a few minutes later. "May I join you?"

Loreto nodded to the empty chair across the table. "So she sent you over, huh?"

Ren smiled as she sat and slouched back. "I drew the short straw."

"No, you've been sent in to play good cop."

"I thought the bad cop came in first, then the good cop. Maybe I'm here to play bad cop."

They both grinned at the absurdity of the idea.

"You drinking?" Loreto asked, gesturing to the pitcher of sangria.

"Looks like you've only got enough left for one. Better save it for my wife."

"I can order more."

"I wouldn't if I were you."

Loreto nodded. If the first few hadn't done the job, there probably wasn't any use returning to that well.

267

"We missed you on the last run," Ren said, her voice light but sincere.

"Yeah, me too," Loreto said.

"Really?"

She thought about the question a little harder. Had she missed the tour? At times, she'd missed the ease of working with students who didn't push her. Maybe she'd missed the ease of neutral encounters. Or not. Even when she'd gotten her most frustrated at Simone, she'd never wished to be back with thirty high schoolers. She missed the ease of working with Ren and Lina today, though. Didn't she? Funny, she'd hadn't really thought of them until now. She hadn't had any great yearning to go back.

"You know, if you have to think about it that long . . ." Ren let the ending of the sentence dangle.

"No, it's not that. I was just replaying the events of the last week."

"And."

"Working for you is easier."

Ren laughed. "I bet so."

"Maybe we need to work you a little harder," Lina said, joining them.

"Everybody all checked in?" Ren asked.

"*Sí*," Lina confirmed, snagging a chair from another table and sitting down next to Ren. "Now spill."

Loreto shook her head and turned to Ren. "I told you she was the bad cop."

Ren burst out laughing. "Damn. Someday I'll get there."

"You will never get there."

"I might. She's worn off on me in other ways. Did you ever hear about the time she had to haul me out of a lesbian bar in Chueca?"

"No. Do tell."

Lina drummed her fingers on the table and sighed. "Ren, you know I love you, but this is why you will never play bad cop."

Ren looked from Lina to Loreto and back again. "Oh."

Lina smiled at her so sweetly it made Loreto's heart ache, another new feeling she didn't want to get used to.

Thankfully, Lina didn't give her the chance before turning to her and saying. "So, you slept with this woman, too?"

She nodded. She didn't see any reason to argue with a bluntly stated fact.

"Except this one didn't play along with the script you have in your head for how these encounters should go."

She shook her head.

"And now you've fallen in love with her."

"Whoa." Loreto nearly jumped out of her chair. "No. Not even a little bit. Not even whatever is smaller than a little bit. I am not in love with Simone."

"Wow." Ren's eyes went wide. "You totally are."

"No. No. Nope, and in Spanish, *no*," Loreto said emphatically. She would have said it again and again, but each time she said the word, her throat constricted a little tighter. "I don't care."

"Oh, Loreto." Lina reached across the table and placed a hand over hers. "Please tell me you didn't start that again."

"What?"

Now even Ren sighed. "The 'I don't care' business."

"It's not business. I honestly don't care."

They stared at her, both of them, with the same, awful look of pity in their eyes. The same look Simone had given her. It made her feel trapped, and stupid, and sad, and powerless.

"I don't care," she whispered, more to herself than to them. Lina squeezed her hand.

"I don't care," Loreto repeated, her voice thick. "I told her." Lina nodded.

"I told her I didn't care about her." She swallowed the bile trying to push up in her throat. "I told her the other stuff, too. And then I told her all the truth. I told her about my status, about my parents, about getting to Spain. I told her ... I told her she was full of shit, and ... and her dreams were bullshit."

"What did she say?" Lina asked calmly.

"She called me a hypocrite."

"Good," Ren whispered.

"And then I told her I didn't care about her."

Lina nodded but didn't say anything as Loreto sat there, stewing in her own anger and regret. The line hadn't even felt good when she'd delivered it. There had been no moment of satisfaction, no thrill of victory in landing the decisive blow, not even for a few seconds. She'd heard Simone's sharp intake of breath, had seen the pain flash across her stoic features. That's why she'd stormed out so quickly. No, scratch that, stormed out felt too controlled. She'd fled.

She'd run back to the place where it all started, sat at the same table, and spent the last few hours poring over every memory she'd made since then, but any way she'd tried to rearrange them, she'd ended up in that awful moment when she'd felt more seen, and scared, and vulnerable than she had in ages. Simone had uncovered her deepest insecurities, the ones she'd dedicated herself to banishing. She'd nearly drained a pitcher of sangria trying to figure out if she'd gotten so desperate because of the reminder of her own circumstances or because of the woman who'd finally understood them.

"I've seen you not care about a lot of women," Lina said softly. "This isn't what it looks like."

Loreto hung her head, not sure which of those statements embarrassed her more. How many women had she used, or let use her, in a vain attempt to prove she had something to offer, that she was valuable, desirable even, to try to level some playing field in a game she'd sworn she didn't want to play. She'd tried to do the same thing with Simone. She'd even thought she'd succeeded. She hadn't realized until too late that the game hadn't just shifted, it had ceased to be a game altogether.

"Is it really so hard to admit someone matters to you?"

Loreto shook her head, then forced her clenched jaw to open enough to speak. "No."

Lina smiled sweetly. "Try."

Loreto released a shaky breath. "You two, you matter to me. You, uh, took a chance on me. And, well, you keep giving me second chances, and I care about that."

Ren smiled encouragingly.

Lina nodded for her to continue.

"And you're helping me get a visa, which . . . maybe it will work out, and then I might feel like I'm supposed to be here. Or I would, actually, belong here, which has never happened before in my whole life, and I think I didn't let myself care about that because I never thought I could have it, but now that I might, I think I might have really cared all along."

Tears shimmered in Lina's eyes as she squeezed her hand. She waited for Loreto to go on.

"And I guess, maybe, I don't know, I might've developed some feelings for Simone, like beyond the initial annoyance. But, I can't have her, not for real, and . . ." She blew out another ragged exhale, then opened her mouth, but the words wouldn't come out.

"It's scary," Lina supplied.

She nodded. "So I lied. To her, and to me. And I hurt her feelings, which kind of hurt me more than I expected."

"Because you're connected," Ren said gently.

"But that's the thing," Loreto said, an old familiar certainty settling in her chest. "Feeling something and wanting something doesn't actually change anything. I'm still me. She's still her. She'll still be an American, and I'm nothing. She's still rich, and I have nothing. She's still powerful, and I'm . . . nothing. Women like her go slumming with people like me. They don't throw away their lives and dreams and worldviews."

Ren and Lina exchanged one of their all-knowing looks before they both said, "Some do."

She didn't need to hear that. She didn't want to hear that. Simone was not Lina or Ren. Simone was proud and stubborn and driven. "You don't know her."

"No," Ren admitted, "but you do. And you care about her. Loreto, she got to you. She got through all your walls and bravado, and she changed you. Don't underestimate a woman like that."

"I can't care enough for both of us. I can't change who I am. I can't take back what I said. I can't make her want to stay, and I can't go with her. I can't do anything."

"You can show up," Lina said, letting go of her hand. "For the first time in a long time, you can go to someone, stand there with your chin up, look them in the eye, and admit what you want, what you need, and tell her why it matters to you."

The thought made her stomach roil. "She'll leave."

"Maybe," Lina admitted, then sadly added, "probably, but if she does, that's on her. If you don't go, that's on you. And Loreto, for what it's worth, I think you're better than that."

Ren nodded resolutely and pushed back from the table. "We know you're better than that."

Lina took Ren's hand and rose to stand beside her wife. "Admitting you care is a good first step. Now find the courage to take the next one."

"Just don't try to find it there." Ren pointed to the pitcher on the table. "Trust me on this one."

With one final squeeze of her shoulder, they walked away.

Loreto didn't speak. She didn't move. She didn't share their optimism. She wasn't Ren and Lina. She didn't believe that caring about something could change it. She didn't get happy endings. And Lina's *just show up* felt a lot like the *just work hard* mentality Simone had espoused. Maybe those pie-in-the-sky ideals worked for some people, but not people like her. Or at least they never had in the past.

Then again, she'd never met anyone quite like Simone, either.

Simone sat on the small balcony of her hotel room overlooking the harbor. The sun had set hours ago, which in this part of the world likely meant she was nearing midnight. Still, the area below was bright and relatively busy. Cars and motorcycles sped past. A lighthouse flashed at regular intervals. Groups of pedestrians strolled along wide boulevards on their way to or from Calle Larios. In the distance, music played the fervent sound of a Spanish guitar.

Simone sat and stared. She'd done nothing else since Loreto slammed the door. She wished she could say that she'd been thinking, or reflecting, or processing through everything she'd heard and felt, but that would require some sort of cohesive effort, and she simply couldn't muster any. Everything felt disjointed and scattered. Random memories butted up against mismatched echoes, Loreto's words, Loreto's pain, her own hurt and embarrassment. It all swirled like leaves in a tornado. She couldn't reach out and grab any single piece to inspect more closely without the fear of being ripped apart, so she curled into a ball, knees held tightly to her chest, and prayed the storm would die down soon.

She'd been waiting for what felt like an eternity and might have gone on doing so all night if not for the ring of her cell phone causing her to jump.

Her limbs ached and her feet tingled as blood rushed back into her extremities, but a desperate need for distraction overrode the needle pricks of pain as she hobbled back toward the desk where she'd left her phone. She didn't dare hope Loreto might be calling. She wasn't even sure she wanted that. But even a wrong number, the voice of another human, would be welcome now.

"Simone!" Henry Alston's voice boomed as soon as she accepted the call. "I knew you'd still be up burning the midnight oil."

She shook her head. She should be, but she wouldn't correct his assumption.

"You ready for the big meeting tomorrow?"

She shook her head again, but said, "As much as anyone ever can be."

He laughed. "Modesty isn't your strong suit. What do you make of our prospects?"

"I haven't spoken to the owners, but I suspect if they have any real intention of selling, tomorrow's presentation will sway them."

"And if they don't have any real intention of selling?"

She knew what he wanted to hear. She should tell him she could handle that, too. She had before, and a week ago she wouldn't have doubted her ability to talk a king out of his crown, but today had shaken her to the core. For the first time in her adult life, she stopped to ponder the possibility that some things might really be impossible.

"This country, these people," she began carefully, "I mean, they're human, with the same hopes and dreams as any other human, but their values, their worldview. They're different. They might want the same things on a baser level, but the priorities and the way they're willing to arrange them are very different."

"Then arrange them in a way that works for everyone," Henry said flatly.

"Simple." Sarcasm dripped from her voice. The disturbing part was that's exactly what she'd thought of this job when she'd taken it. She'd even considered the task beneath her, and yet, nothing about the actual task had changed over the last few hours. Nothing about the world had, either, but everything *felt* drastically different than it had this morning. Did that mean the change had occurred in her?

"Are you okay?" Henry asked, nervousness creeping into his voice.

She didn't answer. She didn't know the answer.

"Because if you're not up to this job, you need to tell me now so I can replace you with someone who is."

There was the crux of his concern. Not her so much as her ability to seal the deal. She was replaceable. Her cheeks burned again with the sting of another verbal slap that felt entirely too close to the one Loreto had delivered earlier. Simone was not on the list of things Loreto cared about. She'd walked out with little more than a backward glance. Henry had all but offered to do the same. And she'd be damned if that didn't burn.

"Simone?"

"Yes, yes," she managed. "I think we've got a bad connection."

"Can you go somewhere else? Maybe more open?" he asked.

Their connection had nothing to do with a cell signal, but the question went deeper than he could know. Could she go somewhere more open? She rose and wandered back to the balcony.

"Oh, there, I can hear some street noise now, I think we're better."

She was definitely not better as she leaned against the railing and stared out at the lights of ships bobbing in the harbor.

"Anyway," he continued, "can you do the job or not?"

"I can do it as well as anyone on your team."

"That's why I sent you. I believe you've got what it takes, Simone, and not only for tomorrow. I see you sitting in my chair a year from now."

"Thank you," she said, though this pep talk didn't stir her the way they had in the past.

"I know you'll do great tomorrow. You're a shark, and these people have dropped blood in the water by agreeing to take this meeting. Go in for the kill."

She grimaced at the image. It didn't fit with her presentation of presenting a gift to the world. It didn't even fit with how she saw her role. Sadly, it fit with how Loreto seemed to see her. *You can sit in your corner office and watch them get carved up like cuts of meat.*

"You've got all the resources you need on the ground, right?"

"Actually, about that . . ."

Henry laughed. "Uh-oh, I feel a last-minute funding request coming on. Well played! Make me nervous, then ask to expand the budget. How much do you need?"

"Nothing," Simone said. "It's not immediate to the project, but I've found a prospect here, well, not a prospect, but a person. A guide and translator who's smart and insightful, and she has an innate ability to assess business situations with the human angle intact."

"Okay," he drew out the word, clearly uncertain as to where Simone was going. To be fair, she didn't exactly know where she was going, either.

"If I were to offer her a job on my team, could the company sponsor her visa?"

"Oh, well, I don't know, but I'm sure if she's as good as you say, she can apply for a visa of some sort on her own. I think those things are relatively easy with the EU now, right?"

"She's not an EU citizen." Simone tried to keep her voice steady. "She'd need a sponsor, and likely some legal aid, due to documentation issues."

"What kind of documentation issues?"

"She's undocumented."

Silence.

"Henry?"

"I'm sorry, you just caught me off guard there. Did you say undocumented? As in, like . . . well, honestly, I don't know the PC term."

"I mean totally undocumented, no birth certificate, no passport, no—"

"Yeah, I'm going to have to ask you to table this for now."

"Table it or drop it?"

She heard his desk chair squeak as he shifted in it. "Tomorrow's a big day, and we shouldn't worry about any other details until the ink has dried on that contract."

"Right, but hypothetically, could I hire someone with the understanding—"

"No," he said flatly, "that's above your pay grade."

"Is it above yours?" She closed her eyes and held her breath, not because of the insubordination tinging the question so much as the fear he'd say yes, the fear that even the person at the pinnacle of this tower she'd sacrificed so much to scale might be as powerless as she.

"I honestly don't know. It's not the sort of thing I've ever looked into. There's been some company memos, of course, a few bits in human resources trainings. I get the sense those sorts of projects take years, maybe decades of money and red tape, and even after all that, they fail as many times as they succeed. A sponsor guarantees nothing for the immigrant and assures the business a lot of trouble."

She couldn't argue. The helpless sense of dread and over-whelming frustration began to tighten around her throat again.

"Besides," he added quickly, "those kinds of people aren't generally worth the effort."

"Those kinds of people," Simone repeated, bitterness coating her tongue.

"You know what I mean. It's not their fault. They're not all bad, but usually uneducated, unrefined, transient. And that doesn't mean they don't have their place. I'm as liberal as the next guy, but what business can take on years of charity work for someone who probably won't ever rise above the mail room?"

Her face flamed and her stomach roiled as his words pinged through her brain—*charity, those people, mail room, red tape, trouble, transient*. Every word felt like a cut. She remembered the scars across Loreto's perfect skin. No wonder she'd been willing to endure barbed wire. What were a few more cuts amid a life-time of wounds? Had Simone added to them?

"Can we please just focus on what's really important here?" Henry asked.

"Yes," she managed softly.

"You're so close to everything you've wanted, Simone."

Powerful women can change their minds. The echoes of the Alhambra returned unbidden in the moment she least wanted them.

"We all have to choose our battles. Only fight the ones worth winning." Henry pushed, not understanding that every word inched her closer to a cliff.

"Yeah," she said, her heart pounding in her ears so loudly now she could barely hear herself speak, much less think.

"Good girl," he said, his tone laced with relief he had no right to feel. "Can I trust you to do what needs to be done tomorrow?"

Simone pursed her lips, closed her eyes, and swallowed all her frustration, anger, and fear. "Yes. Of course. I've been working my whole life for a chance like this."

Chapter Sixteen

Loreto sort of hoped there would be an elevator. She would've even been grateful for a flight of stairs, anything to give her just a few more minutes to compose herself. It wasn't like she hadn't had all night to try to figure out what she wanted to say, what she needed to do, but she would've preferred three more minutes. Instead, she was greeted immediately upon entering the lobby of Libertad Publishing.

The young receptionist smiled brightly until Loreto said she was there as a translator for Simone Webber. The solemn change in her expression and demeanor told Loreto everything she needed to know about how the staff felt about the prospect of their employer being bought out by someone who needed a translator. She remained professional as she rose and walked to a door across the room, but as she nodded for Loreto to follow, her tight smile held none of the warmth it originally had. It was clear her assessment of Loreto had changed from local to Judas by proximity to Simone, and she realized that's exactly what would happen if she facilitated this meeting. The thought made her stomach lurch, and she might have turned to go if the woman hadn't swung open the door to reveal Simone sitting at a small conference table.

As their eyes met, everyone else faded. God, she was beautiful as she rose from the table. She wore a navy pencil skirt and a form-fitting suitcoat, but she'd left the jacket open, revealing she'd failed to fasten the top few buttons on her white Oxford shirt. The choice showed off her throat and a hint of collarbone that brought her look down a level from slick to sexy, or maybe Loreto just found her sensual in any outfit.

"You're here," Simone said, after the receptionist closed the door. Her tone held a mix of surprise and awe that made Loreto's heart ache.

"I said I'd come."

"I know, but I thought . . . I worried, actually, that you wouldn't want to anymore."

"Want is complicated," Loreto said, "but I made a commitment, and I keep my word."

Simone's shoulders fell slightly, and her smile didn't light that electric spark in her stunning eyes. "I see."

The sadness in those two words softened Loreto's defenses, and she spoke before she thought. "Yesterday was . . . hard."

Simone sighed. "Yes."

"I got scared," Loreto admitted, the pain of saying the word pushing her forward instead of holding her back. "And hurt, and it'd been a long time since I'd felt that way. I didn't like being pulled back into a place I didn't want to go, so I lashed out."

"You had a right to. You have a right to be angry. The world has been terrible and unfair—"

"But you haven't."

Simone let a soft shot of a laugh escape. "Yes, I have. I told you so many stupid things. I went on and on about work ethic when you've had to work harder than anyone I know to get so much less."

Loreto smiled reluctantly. "Yeah, that was kind of shitty and wrong, but you didn't understand. I didn't give you the chance to. But even if you had, your life experiences have shaped you as much as mine have me. I can't control either of those two things."

"We've lived very different lives. I'm sorry."

"Don't be. You made some good points, too. Ones I hadn't let myself acknowledge."

Simone shook her head.

"It's true. You made me see that not being able to control something and not caring about it are two different things." She swallowed the last sticky bit of her pride before adding, "And I do care, Simone. I care about you."

Simone opened her mouth and took a single step toward her, but the door to the conference room opened again.

"*Buenos dias*," a man's voice said, and Simone's eyes left Loreto's. It was just a little flick, but it was enough to break the spell. When she turned back, she'd already covered the openness of her previous expression with a polite, apologetic smile.

"Please hold that thought because we're going to come back to it," she whispered, before leaning past her to greet the man and woman who'd come in behind her. "*Gracias, y buenos dias*, Señor Navarro, Señora Navarro," Simone said as she plastered a polite smile on her face.

She shook each of their hands, giving Loreto a chance to take a few slow, deep breaths. She wasn't nearly as adept at switching between the personal and the professional, and it stung a little bit that Simone had managed to do so quickly. Still, she shouldn't be surprised at Simone's ability to put work above everything else. She hadn't gotten where she had by letting emotions get in the way.

Loreto heard Simone say her name, and she turned to greet the couple, who appeared to be in their late sixties. While the woman was a few inches shorter and a few inches slimmer around the middle, they both had gray hair and wore glasses over deeply creased eyes. They had similar almond complexions and easy smiles as well. She wondered if they'd always looked alike or if their styles had merged over a lifetime of sharing space and dreams. The thought only amplified the wound she felt at Simone's withdrawal, but she managed to greet them both and introduce herself as a local translator as they settled around the small, rectangular table.

"Thank you for agreeing to meet with me today. I'm honored to be here," Simone said while facing the Navarros. Loreto translated, and they nodded serenely, like they'd heard all this before.

"I've read some of the books you've published, obviously with Loreto's help," Simone said, with a smile they didn't quite return, "and I've been deeply impressed with both the content and quality of the work."

She waited, both for Loreto to catch up and for the Navarros to respond. She got the first, but not the second, as the couple's expressions never changed.

"And clearly I'm not the only one who's been moved by these compelling stories." Simone forged on. "I was sent here to your beautiful country with a very generous offer from one of America's biggest and more resourceful publishing houses."

Loreto translated, trying to keep her voice even and her inflection as close to Simone's as possible, but her stomach tightened again as they approached the heart of the meeting.

Simone slid some papers across the table. "You were privy to this information before the meeting, but I feel obligated to point out the number at the top because it is, I think, generous."

Loreto couldn't read the number, but she could tell it was a long one, with more place values than she was accustomed to seeing. The Navarros didn't look impressed, though, and Loreto felt a little twinge of satisfaction that these two Spaniards couldn't be easily bought, even with so many zeros. Then she glanced at Simone and felt immediately guilty. She did care about this woman, and she did want her to succeed in business. Or rather, she wanted her to be happy. She wanted her to see a payoff for her years of work and want. And she wanted to be part of fulfilling Simone's dreams, even if only for these moments.

Finally, *Señora* Navarro spoke in Spanish. "We've seen the numbers, but we didn't bring you here to talk about money. We want to discuss values."

Loreto translated for Simone, who only nodded solemnly.

"Ultimately, we need to know our legacy will be protected, for us, and for all our authors and employees, not only now, but going forward."

Loreto gritted her teeth only a second before relaying the message to Simone. This was it. This was the moment she'd dreaded, the moment where Simone's dreams hung suspended on a single lie. Loreto didn't even blame her for saying it. She saw a bigger picture, a broader scenario where the end would undoubtedly justify the means. The literary world would gain a treasure, and she would gain the power to alter a system that had stymied her and hundreds, if not thousands, of others. Simone smiled, slowly and genuinely, like a woman secure in the choice she'd already made, and Loreto said a silent prayer that she'd feel the same sort of peace when it came time for her to echo the lie sitting on those beautiful lips.

"No," Simone said, emphatically.

Loreto stared at her, then at the Navarros, who clearly needed no translation.

They all sat there trying to process the single word hovering between them, until Simone offered a little more. "No one in New York cares about your legacy."

Loreto translated, her own confusion seeping into her voice, but Simone continued bluntly.

"You could certainly write caveats into the contract to keep authors in print or providing Spanish translations for future works. Those conditions would likely be honored for a while. But as to respecting a uniquely Spanish voice or tone or mind-set, they'll never be given a second thought."

Loreto repeated the words, but before she'd even finished, *Señor* Navarro had already pushed back from the table. The only thing stopping him from storming out was his wife's hand landing gently on his forearm as she asked, "Why come here today to say these things?"

Loreto translated, wanting very much to hear the answer as well.

"Because I want to buy your company," Simone said, a little tremor of uncertainty creeping in her voice.

Loreto had barely caught up before a red-faced *Señor* Navarro said he wouldn't sell to her.

Simone waited for Loreto to explain before raising her hands slightly and saying in her clearest voice, "I understand. I think you've made the right decision, but I'm not speaking for my company anymore, or any company."

Loreto translated the comment before turning back to Simone every bit as confused as the couple across the table.

"I resigned my employment this morning, or last night, maybe. It was kind of a blur. But the point is, *I* want to buy Libertad Press. Me, personally, on my own, which is why I've prepared a competing offer." She slid several new papers over to them. "It's not nearly as much money, but I'm desperately hoping the other terms might be more attractive on a personal level."

Loreto glanced at the contracts the Navarros were reading intently, but she couldn't bring herself to make sense of what Simone had said, much less translate any of it. Instead, she stared at the stranger beside her and said, "Wait, what?"

"I quit," Simone said bluntly. "I was terrified for about ten minutes, because I hadn't really thought it through, but my boss asked me if I could be trusted to do what needed to be done, and then I did."

"What?" Loreto asked again, a little louder to be heard over the rush of blood in her ears.

Simone sighed dramatically, but her smile only grew. "I don't want to be part of a system that keeps people like you down. I don't want to live in a country where you aren't welcome. I don't want to play a game we can't win. And you were right. Juanes Cánovas and the other authors here don't need a voice. It was stupid of me to ignore the fact that they've already told their own stories, and the Navarros have already shared them. What they need now is someone who knows how to amplify the work they've already done. I can do that. I have those skills, and I've had the passion my whole life. None of us need a high-rise in New York or a million-dollar marketing department. I could keep the company here if I had the team or people . . . or person beside me."

"But what about your dreams? You were so close to having everything you wanted. All the power, all the control. Why throw them away?"

Simone smiled. "Remember what you told me about Isabella and the Alhambra? Well, it turns out the same was true for me. Andalucía just happened to be where I found something I wanted more than total control."

Loreto's vision swam and her mind reeled. She could barely breathe for the unfamiliar press of hope filling her chest, but her brain rebelled. This couldn't be real. Things like this didn't happen to people like her. "What if these people don't sell to you?"

Simone laughed, a bubbly sound laced with a nervousness that suggested she might not be as confident as she seemed. "I don't have a plan for that, but I have faith, and hope, and the skills to make this work. And I have passion for this work again."

The uncertainty in her voice made Loreto's emotions even stronger. Simone was flying by the seat of her pants, for her.

"Oh, and I have love," Simone said. "I love these books, and I've fallen in love with this country. And you. I've fallen in love with you along the way. And this is Spain, so I'm hoping that's enough."

Loreto stared at her, disbelieving everything she'd heard and yet not disbelieving.

Simone's chest rose and fell with shallow breaths, and her eyes widened dramatically. "Oh God, Loreto, come on. Please tell me that's enough for us to figure this out. Please tell them, too."

They turned to the Navarros, who were both staring at them with the same wide-eyed expression.

"Quick," Simone urged. "Translate part of that, but maybe not all of it, just the good parts, or the business parts."

Señor Navarro raised his hand placatingly, then said, "That won't be necessary."

"Yes," his wife said kindly. "We've heard enough."

"You have?" Simone asked. Backing up, she added, "Did you just speak English?"

"Of course," *Señora* Navarro said, as if she found the question absurd. "We run a business in Málaga. Everyone speaks English here."

Simone turned to Loreto. "Everyone speaks English?"

Loreto finally grinned. "Pretty much. But eye on the prize, make your pitch."

Simone blinked and drew in a deep, flustered breath before saying, "I think I just did."

"You did," *Señor* Navarro said, "and I think my wife and I are on the same page. This is exactly the type of proposal we've dreamed of."

"Yes," *Señora* Navarro confirmed. "We'd like to run the offer by our lawyers, but assuming everything checks out, we'll sign this contract by the end of the week."

"Really?" Simone sounded more astounded than professional. "I didn't really think this would work."

The Navarros laughed, and Loreto put her hand on Simone's arm, just like *Señora* Navarro had to her husband. "I think she means thank you."

"Yes. Thank you."

"Thank you," the Navarros echoed, before rising from the table.

Simone and Loreto shook their hands, and they all promised to be in touch as soon as possible. Then, with a steady hand at Simone's elbow, Loreto led them out into the narrow, stone street and around the corner before slumping against a wall.

"What just happened?"

Simone rested her back beside her on the wall as they both stared straight ahead. "They spoke English!"

Loreto laughed. "I think the bigger issue is that you just bought a Spanish publishing house."

"Really?" Simone asked, her voice a little breathless. "I sort of hoped the bigger issue would be the fact that I'm in love with you."

"Oh," Loreto said, all the adrenaline that had only begun to fade rushing back again. "You really said that."

"I did."

"I didn't just imagine it amid all the other confusing stuff."

"You did not."

For once, Loreto didn't rush to react. How could she? Nothing in her life had prepared her for this moment, or for this woman. Simone had just thrown all her work and dreams away for a terribly risky investment, and she wasn't just talking about the publishing house. Simone had done that for her. She'd listened. She'd cared. She'd changed the entire course of her life because she loved her. What could Loreto possibly say to convey the depth of what she felt stirring inside her right now? All the hope, all the anguish, all the fear and joy and absurdity added up to something powerful and wonderful and terrifying.

"Love." Loreto opened her eyes and rolled over onto her shoulder, still bracing herself against the wall, but now staring at Simone. Then she began to laugh. Deep, throaty, shoulder- and stomach-shivering laughter that cracked her façade and shook it to the ground.

"What?" Simone asked.

"You finally did it," Loreto answered.

"Did what?"

"I told you, one day you'd surprise me, and you finally did."

"I surprised you by falling in love?" Simone asked, almost incredulous.

"No. I mean, yes, but more surprisingly, you surprised me by making me fall in love with you, too."

Chapter Seventeen

Simone had no idea how long they'd been kissing in the alleyway. Thankfully, none of the locals seemed to pay them any mind. Perhaps this sort of thing happened every day in their world, but to her, the entire situation still felt dizzyingly magical. Or maybe that was just the effect Loreto's lips and hands had on her. She got the sense that if she pushed a little, they'd both end up naked right here.

Thankfully, the thought was still unfamiliar enough to startle her. Pulling back just far enough to catch her breath, Simone stared into Loreto's eyes. "This is really happening, right?"

Loreto nodded and ran her tongue along swollen lips. "Totally happening. All of it."

"Okay," Simone said, then took a steadying breath. "What do we do now?"

"I have no idea," Loreto said.

"You're the guide."

"You're the boss."

Simone laughed. "I can only be the boss of so many things. I quit my job, emptied my bank account, and bought a publishing company. Also, I bared my soul. I think that's all the decisions I'm capable of making this morning."

"Okay." Loreto kissed her quickly once more. "Fair enough. We should probably celebrate, right?"

"I thought that's what we were doing." Her smile turned coy.

"Then we should move the celebration to some place horizontal."

"I like the way you think." She kissed her again, and for a heated moment, the possibility of going horizontal right there resurfaced, but their make out session was interrupted by the low growl of an empty stomach.

"Did that sound come from you or me?" Loreto asked between kisses.

"Probably me. I haven't eaten since churros yesterday."

Loreto paused and furrowed her brow. "I had some fruit last night."

"Healthy."

"It was soaked in wine, so technically I had sangria last night."

Simone laughed again, the joy rolling through her whole body. She could get used to that sensation. "Is it wrong that I'm glad you struggled last night? I mean, I hated upsetting you, but I can't stand the thought of going through that torment alone."

"You were not alone in being tormented," Loreto said. "I was a mess. Honestly, it stung a little bit to see you looking so good this morning. I went in hoping you'd be a little more haggard."

"You should've seen me at midnight after I hung up the phone with my boss, or my ex-boss. Though to be honest, I don't know which of us was more astonished, me or him."

"Me," Loreto said. "I win most astonished."

Simone shook her head, but her stomach growled again.

Loreto stepped back. "We need to eat before we take this conversation or this celebration any further. Let's find some simple and complex carbs to offer sustenance."

"You're talking about churros, aren't you?"

"Of course."

"Lead the way."

Loreto took her hand, intertwined their fingers as if they'd done so a hundred times, and led her through the narrow, winding streets that would now be her neighborhood. The realization made her head spin. She was moving to Spain. Her knees wobbled, just as Loreto pulled out a chair for her.

"You okay?"

She nodded.

"You've gone a little pale. Do you need food? Or, I don't know . . . a psychiatrist?"

She grinned. "Start with the food, then you can talk me down."

Loreto disappeared into a nearby restaurant, and Simone stared up at the palm fronds overhead. The sun was nearing its height, and the warmth of it caused her to strip off her suit jacket. Would she ever have to wear it again? Probably. There would still be meetings. There would still be formal events. There was still hard work ahead. She knew that for sure. What she didn't know was what her daily life would look like. She hadn't even begun to envision it yet by the time Loreto returned with a plate of hot churros and an oversized mug of molten chocolate.

For some reason, the sight of the purchase made Simone blurt, "I'm broke."

"What?" Loreto pulled a chair right up beside her before sitting down.

"I just spent my life's savings," Simone gushed, "and it still won't be enough to cover the bid. I'll sell my condo in New York, and my studio in Chicago."

"You have two houses?"

"I did," Simone admitted. "That's about to change. Everything's about to change."

"You'll probably have to cut down the shopping trips to Larios," Loreto said, not sounding bothered.

She nodded numbly. "I hope the clothes we bought last week will constitute our business attire for a while, but that's not even the start of it. I'll need a work visa, and an apartment, and a car."

"You don't need a car," Loreto offered.

"Okay, no car," Simone said. "Public transportation is good here?"

"So good."

"What about insurance?"

"We've got socialized medicine. You're set."

"I do love this country."

Loreto laughed. "It'll be okay."

"I don't speak Spanish." The panic surged in her again until her fingers began to shake. "Oh my God, Loreto. I just bought a Spanish publishing house, and I don't speak Spanish!"

"Hey." Loreto put a hand on her thigh and squeezed. "You'll learn."

"What am I going to do until then?"

"Hire a translator."

"The company is stable. It's turning a profit, but it'll take time to handle the transfer. I don't know if adding staff in the first few months is wise, but I don't see how I cannot hire a translator—"

"Hey," Loreto said again, "I know a good translator who works for churros, but she'd need the siesta off every day, because she's, how did you put it? A little lackadaisical."

Simone pursed her lips, but this time she was trying to hold back a smile. "I'm sorry. I can't hire you to be my translator. It's a serious business, and it's not a good idea."

"Oh." Loreto swallowed a bit of churro with a little more force than usual. "Right. I get it. You're new to Spain and the business, and I don't have a work visa, so I'm probably not the best qualified for a job like that."

Simone took her hand. "You're not qualified for that job. You're *over*qualified for it. Besides, it's not smart to double dip with your most valued team member."

"Double dip?"

"I can't waste your talent sitting in a side room typing up translations when I need you in the boardroom beside me."

Loreto raised her eyebrows but didn't speak.

"I need a partner, Loreto. In every sense of the word. I won't lie and say I didn't look into the visa process, for both of us, because we're both going to need them, but business owners are given priority over even skilled laborers. With the amount of money I just sank into the local economy, we should be able to pull some pretty big strings, but only if we're equals in this endeavor."

Loreto shook her head. "You just said it. You put down all the money. That's not equality, that's charity."

"Stop," Simone said sharply. "I know you came by that mindset the hard way, but you have to fight against it now. I need you much more than you need me, much more than you need money or a visa. I bought a publishing catalog full of books I cannot read. I'm packing up my entire life to move to a city where I've spent three days. I'm going to try to run a business in a country whose laws and culture I've only skimmed the surface of. I'm in way over my head."

Loreto stared at her, and Simone's heart hammered in her throat. What if that little speech hadn't worked? What if love and passion really weren't enough? What if Loreto's stubbornness actually outstripped her own? Or what if Loreto didn't actually want to go into publishing? This was Simone's dream.

The darkness began to close in once more until she whispered, "I meant what I said yesterday. You're too valuable to give up, in so many ways. I don't know what I'd do without you."

Loreto leaned so close her forehead touched lightly to Simone's temple. "This is going to take some getting used to."

"The idea of changing jobs?"

"No. The idea that someone needs me, that someone believes in me."

Simone's heart melted. "Well, that's a reality now. What can I do to make it easier on you?"

Loreto kissed her cheek. "Give me lots of time to practice I suppose."

"That can be arranged." Simone turned her head so their mouths connected in a deep, soulful kiss before saying, "We could even start exploring my needs right now."

"Oh? Is there something you need from me in this moment?"

"So many things, but let's start with a hotel room."

"Yours or mine?"

Simone grinned. "We can't afford mine anymore."

Loreto laughed. "Fair, but can we go get your suitcases at least?"

"Why?"

"Because I've been dying to see you in that skimpy little bit of silk you bought in Cordoba."

Simone blushed at the memory of choosing the lingerie. How she'd wanted, even then, to have Loreto slip it from her shoulders. "I only bought it to drive you crazy."

"Then come on." Loreto pushed back from the table. "Start driving."

Simone caught her hand and tried to pull her back, but with one tug, Loreto lifted her out of the chair and into her embrace. She kissed along Simone's neck until she reached her earlobe and whispered, "Are you really going to make me beg?"

Simone laughed, "I surrender. I promise to put on whatever you want, as long as you promise to rip it off me."

As her half-smile spread, Loreto's deep brown eyes swirled with mischief, mirth, lust, and something Simone now suspected was love. "*Rubia*, that's the best deal we've made all week."

She did not disagree.

Epilogue

"*Gracias.*" Loreto shook the hand of some executive whose name she had forgotten. She'd gotten better at paying attention to the men in suits who flew in from all over the country, and occasionally other parts of the world, just like she'd gotten better at staying focused and polite during long days in dress clothes, but it was nearing midnight, and she'd been on her feet for seven hours solid. Her eyes had begun to blur, and all the publishing people had started to look alike. Mercifully, this man was the last of them, and he finally turned to offer some platitudes to Simone.

"*Sí, por supuesto,*" Simone said, her cheeks pink and her blue eyes sparkling. Funny, every other face in the room had melded together, but Loreto still saw hers in vivid detail. "*Encantada de conocerto.*"

"Lo," Loreto whispered.

"*Conocerlo,*" Simone corrected quickly.

The businessman nodded appreciatively, then headed out. They stood side-by-side, mirrored smiles plastered on their faces until the door shut behind him, then with heavy exhales, they slumped against each other.

"You did well," Loreto praised, slipping her arms around Simone's waist and snuggling close, both for comfort and support, but what had started as sweet stirred something deeper in

293

her as her palm settled against the flat plane of Simone's stomach and her perfect ass pressed against her.

Simone shook her head, causing the scent of oranges to fill Loreto's senses. "Have I mentioned how much I love your new shampoo?"

"I used the wrong article."

"What?"

"I said 'te' when I meant 'lo.'"

"A minor slip," Loreto murmured, kissing the nape of her neck softly.

"But it was the last thing I said to a major bookstore rep. You never want to bumble the first impression, or the last one."

She briefly considered mentioning that Simone never wanted to bumble anything, but she didn't figure that would go over well, so instead she said, "You've only been taking Spanish lessons for four months."

"She's right," Ren said. "Cut yourself some slack."

Both of them jumped, then laughed.

"Are you still here?" Loreto joked.

"Both of us," Lina confirmed as she collected a few stray cups from a nearby table.

"We can clean up," Simone said. Stifling a yawn, she added, "You've already done too much."

"It's exciting," Ren said, accepting the cups from her wife and placing them in a recycling bin. "I'd never been to a publishing party before."

"I have," Simone admitted. "This one was tame by comparison, and we probably need to up our wine budget next time. But the food was better here. The food is always better here."

Loreto smiled. "Even though we had to serve it at ten o'clock?"

Simone yawned again. "I'm getting better on that front, too."

Lina tossed a few remaining paper plates in the trash and crossed the room. "You are, and on so many other fronts as well. Ren is right, you need to cut yourself some slack. You've been here less than half a year, and already it feels like you're a local."

"I wouldn't go that far," Simone said.

"The neighbors love you," Ren said.

"They love Loreto," Simone said, tossing her a grin. "That's why I keep her around."

"They love you, too," Ren said. "You fit here in Málaga. You're passionate and dedicated. Your Spanish is beyond passable. You've signed a new, local author and translated ten books from others. Now you're working on a movie deal."

"A *possible* movie deal," Simone corrected, turning back to Loreto. "Which reminds me, can you make sure I call Levy and Levy tomorrow, or maybe it's not too late tonight?"

"It's too late," the other three said in unison.

"No, if it's one a.m. here, it's only"—she ticked off the math on her fingers— "eight in New York. Mimi almost never leaves her office before then."

"Simone," Loreto pleaded in a soft, intimate tone.

She looked up at her, electric eyes flashing, and whatever Loreto had planned to say died on her lips. She'd yet to build any immunity to that gaze, and when it landed on her, the thrill of excitement coursed through her. Dropping her hands to her side, she merely shrugged and smiled back at the woman who'd come to encompass so much of her world. Then she turned to Ren and Lina. "It looks like we've got more work to do tonight, but thank you so much for helping with the party."

"But," Ren started, only to be cut off by Lina's hand on her arm.

"We understand," Lina said in her usual, knowing tone. "If anyone gets what it's like to build a business on a foundation of passion and sheer will, it's us."

Ren chuckled. "Yeah, I remember now. You two just take care of each other, okay?"

Loreto nodded. "That's the plan."

They shared hugs all around and said goodbyes laced with promises to have dinner next time Lina and Ren were back in town between tours.

"I'm so glad they were here tonight," Simone said, after they'd left.

"No kidding. I know we're trying not to take on new staff yet, but having friends who're willing to act as servers, greeters, and conversation starters made a huge difference. This place was packed."

"Indeed. We made good contacts." Simone hooked a finger in a belt loop of Loreto's slacks, pulling her close again. "And you were amazing."

"You think?"

Simone rocked her hips forward so they brushed against Loreto's. "I do. When I saw you talking to the reps for *Egales*, with your hair falling down across your forehead and your shirt sleeves rolled up like some sexy, rakish, publishing conquistador, I almost told everyone to get out so I could have my way with you."

Loreto laughed, but her heartbeat picked up speed with the hope that the playfulness of the comment didn't undercut its main focus. "Me as a conquistador? That's ironic, but shouldn't I be the one doing the ravaging?"

Simone pursed her lips, and Loreto fought the urge to kiss them. She didn't want to rush this part. Or any part with Simone.

"I think," Simone said coyly, "conquest requires some sort of pushback, and 'ravishing' implies a bit of resistance."

"Thankfully, you're adept at both."

She shook her head. "Not anymore."

"I know several printers, translators, and paperback distributors who'd argue otherwise."

"And none of them are here right now." Simone smiled ruefully. "It's just you and me, 'Reto."

Her heartbeat revved again, both at the name Simone had more than earned the right to use, and at the intimate way in which it had been delivered. Her fingers twitched with the impulse to push Simone's silk shell up and off the perfect body she craved, but still she waited, pressing for the cue she'd learned to seek. "And?"

Simone leaned close, so close her breath brushed warm against Loreto's skin as she whispered, "I surrender."

Acknowledgements

As I mentioned in my author notes, a large part of this book was inspired by the time my family and I spent in Spain in 2018. I have loved that country fiercely since a formative trip as a teenager, but this was the first time I'd been back as a full-fledged adult, with a family in tow. Part of me worried as we left England after the happiest six months of our lives together that I was headed for an inevitable disappointment. Is anything ever really as good as it seemed when you were seventeen? Had that trip only been a single, shining moment? What if my memories of the place and the lessons learned there said more about me and my own developmental needs than the country itself? However, as our plane banked low over the Costa Del Sol and my son's eyes filled with wonder, those fears began to ebb. By the time we stepped onto the palm tree-lined tarmac, with mountains in the distance, and I felt the air on my skin, excitement took over. As we strolled Larios and wandered the markets, woke to the sounds of cathedral bells and the smell of fresh churros, my worries seemed a more distant memory than even my teenage self. Our family spent the next few weeks eating candied hibiscus flowers while roving from one ancient treasure to the next. The places in this book became our playgrounds. We roamed vast gardens of La Alhambra, rowed boats in Numpty Cove, wound our way through the Jewish quarter in Cordoba, and played with monkeys atop the Rock of Gibraltar. And we ate, we danced, we ate some more, we jumped into pick-up futbol games, chased bubbles, wielded swords, and ate some more.

I think what I am trying to say in the rambling paragraph above is "thank you." Thank you to Spain, and its people for proving themselves to be every bit as open and wonderful and magical as my young self believed you to be. Thank you for showing my wife and son the legendary hospitality you are known for. Thank you for the inspiration and the education you continue to provide in our lives. Thank you for the contrast you offer to the lives and walls and priorities we as Americans are told we must pursue. I want to especially thank Carmen for welcoming us into her home, answering all our questions, and feeding both our bodies and our souls. I owe another great debt of gratitude to the Worldschoolers of Andalucía, especially Elin Morgan for welcoming us warmly into her wonderful circle. This wide and varied group provided a lot of insight to Spain immigration rules and how they differ widely from America's.

And on the subject of immigration, I want to thank every immigrant, no matter what their status, who spoke to me, who wrote about their own experience, or shared the experience of loved ones in person, on social media, and via email. I won't name names or even specific stories due to the precarious nature of so many wonderfully brave people, but I thank you for that bravery and trust. There is no way to capture all those experiences, as there is no single immigrant experience. They are as wide and varied as humanity itself. However, I hope many of you can see parts of your essence in Loreto's heart and strength and defiance and perseverance.

And while no story can be told without inspiration, I also need to acknowledge that no book of mine is ever published without a team of dedicated artists and professionals. Thank you first to my beta readers, Toni and Barb, who continue to be consistent voices of both reason and enthusiasm in my writing process. Thank you to Lynda Sandoval, my kick-ass editor, who understood not only this story, but also how important it was for me to get it right. Thank you to my friend and fellow Redbird, Jon Crawley, for putting your talent for details toward my copy edits. Thank you to Kelly Smith, who was not only my typesetter even in her retirement, but who also played an essential role in getting us to Europe in the first place. Thank you, Ann McMan, whom I continue to push, and who continues to answer every challenge with brilliant and evocative covers, hopefully without hating me. Thank you to every single proofreader (Cara, Diane, Ann, and Susan) who served as final stop-gap between typeset and typos getting to print. And thank you, last but not least, to Susan and Carolyn of Brisk Press, whose generosity to me seems to know no bounds. When I approached them and said, "I have another book I'd like to get out this summer, but it's kind of erotic and political. Would you be willing to look at it?" They replied by saying, "We trust you, we want to help, and the hotter the better." I adore you two!

To my friends, colleagues, and readers, your contributions are harder to quantify, but no less essential to life and work. Whether you are someone I regularly chat with about writing (Georgia, Mel, Anna, Jenn) or someone I may have heard from only once, or someone who simply left a review on a website, I hope you know how much you mean to me.

And to my family, you do more than support me. You make my life worth living. Sharing the place I love with the people I love means more to me than I can put into words. Thank you, Jackie, for making every day an adventure, and thank you, Susie, for traveling beside me, wherever my heart tells me to go. Come what may, I wouldn't want to do any of this without you.

And as always, I end with offering thanks to one from whom all these blessing flow. *Soli deo Gloria.*